The mall is under new management

"No touching," a voice commanded. "And put on your mask."

"Say what?" Jazmine barked. "If I want to hug a person, I'm hugging her."

"New rules." The voice came closer. Shay turned her head and saw a security guard, stun baton gripped in both hands across his chest like a shield.

Jazmine gave Shay a look like she would kill this man before she'd stop hugging people, but then she let go of Shay, replaced her mask, and shuffled off the gurney. "I'll check on you later," she said, squeezing Shay's shoulder, then walked away.

Shay nearly screamed for Jazmine to come back, but the security guard with his black stick shut her up. He looked both nervous and cocky, and Shay did not like that combination. Would he attack her? No, he was here to protect her. *Right?* Cold sweat broke out over her body. She was alone with this guy who looked ready to beat the crap out of anyone and everyone.

Shay did not trust these strangers. She did not feel safe.

OTHER BOOKS YOU MAY ENJOY

DAYNA LORENTZ

NO EASY

DISCARD

WAY OUT

speak
An Imprint of Penguin Group (USA)

SPEAK
Published by the Penguin Group
Penguin Group (USA) LLC
375 Hudson Street
New York, New York 10014

USA * Canada * UK * Ireland * Australia
New Zealand * India * South Africa * China

penguin.com
A Penguin Random House Company

First published in the United States of America by Dial Books,
an imprint of Penguin Group (USA), 2013
Published by Speak, an imprint of Penguin Group (USA) LLC, 2014

THE LIBRARY OF CONGRESS HAS CATALOGED THE DIAL EDITION AS FOLLOWS:

Lorentz, Dayna.
No easy way out: a No safety in numbers book/by Dayna Lorentz.
pages cm   Sequel to: No safety in numbers.
Summary: "Teens Marco, Shay, Ryan, and Lexi form new alliances in the quarantined
mall—as the bodies pile up, the disease mutates, the Senator's authority is questioned, and it becomes clear there's no one to trust"—Provided by publisher.
ISBN 978-0-8037-3874-4 (hardcover)
[1. Interpersonal relations—Fiction. 2. Survival—Fiction. 3. Quarantine—Fiction.
4. Biological warfare—Fiction. 5. Shopping malls—Fiction.] I. Title.
PZ7.L8814Nk 2013   [Fic]—dc23   2012032618

Speak ISBN 978-0-14-242524-4

Printed in the United States of America

3 5 7 9 10 8 6 4

For Jason

NO EASY WAY OUT

STONECLIFF SENTINEL

QUARANTINED

SHOPS AT STONECLIFF MALL
LOCKED DOWN BY NATIONAL GUARD

Yesterday evening, the National Guard ordered that the Shops at Stonecliff mall be quarantined until further notice. After a week of near radio silence from government officials on the situation within the mall, it was revealed yesterday in the early afternoon that a flu virus had been released into the air vents of the mall and that all people inside have been deemed exposed to the contagion. While the Centers for Disease Control have promised more specific information on the type of virus, they have yet to release any reports. They have also declined to provide information on the situation inside the mall or the conditions of the people quarantined except to say that the situation is secure, that a qualified individual has been appointed to manage the population in the mall, and that the people inside have been provided with all the resources they will require for the duration of the quarantine.

Sentinel sources, however, claim that the situation in the mall is anything but secure. One local resident has been using a high-powered telescopic lens to observe the mall and he reported seeing crowds rushing past the windows of the food court's atrium after the announcement yesterday. He also claimed that the government evacuated the facility in a hurry, suggesting some problem inside the mall, perhaps related to the movement of people.

There have also been reports of arrests of individuals outside the mall. Mary Havershaw of Ossining reported that her neighbors Barbara and John Kravis have been locked inside their home for the past twenty-four hours. "Barbara went to buy some new pillows at that mall last Saturday," Havershaw stated yesterday morning via telephone. "She got out before the quarantine, but now they want to lock her down too, like those other folks." *Sentinel* reporters confirmed that a patrol car is outside the home and the home phone number has been disconnected.

After the demonstration of two nights ago, police have cordoned off the streets around the mall, allowing only local traffic into the area. This is in addition to the thirty-foot-high fence erected around the parking lot of the mall, which has been reinforced by cement barriers and is patrolled by the National Guard. News helicopters have been banned from flying over the airspace within the fence's perimeter, though there were reports of a government helicopter on the roof of the mall earlier today.

If you have any family or friends inside the mall, the Federal Bureau of Investigation has set up a hotline through which you can receive information about your loved ones. The hotline number is 1-800-555-XXXX. The FBI has asked that you not try to approach the mall, as any trespass within the perimeter may result in your being arrested or detained for testing.

DAY

SEVEN

NOON

t was like reading the cast list for a twisted new reality show—*Mall Quarantine: Shop 'Til You Drop . . . Dead.*

DANIEL JANCOWISZ, *Age 24, Pace University*
EILEEN MYERS, *Age 36, pregnant, Dental Hygienist*
YOUSSEF HADDAD, *Age 16, asthma, Ossining HS*

Except this wasn't a show, it was reality. Some of these people really were dead.

That kind of thinking was too depressing, so Lexi Ross decided to not even focus on the names anymore. She just input the words. Her mother, Senator Dorothy "Dotty" Ross, the now official head honcho of the mall, had charged her with re-creating the population database her father had made for the government hazmat people. When they bolted from the building, they took all copies with them, which suggested that locking all the civilians in a mall with a killer flu was not the only secret they were keeping.

The monotony of the task—logging name after name into the program—was soothing, and a welcome break from the screaming chaos of yesterday's mall riot. So she sat like a good little girl typing away in the dank employee lounge in a corner of the Apple Store's stockroom.

KATHLEEN MASON, *Age 18, Tarrytown HS*
WILLIAM TSU, *Age 14, Rockland HS*

The only frustrating aspect of the task was that all the relevant information was handwritten on scrap paper. The Senator had given Lexi the lists of names created on the first night of their collective captivity—this was all the government had left behind. Scrawled next to some entries were chronic conditions, and employers or schools. Some names had a cryptic *V* marked beside them in the margin. More relevant information—like whether or not the person was still alive—was not to be found on the page.

As Lexi flipped a rumpled sheet over and began scanning her next entry, she was startled by her mother's voice over the mall's loudspeaker.

"Attention, residents of the Shops at Stonecliff. I apologize for the manner in which yesterday's announcement was made. It was not our intention to cause anyone to panic."

Understatement of the year. How coy of her mother to label a mall-wide riot a mere instance of "panic." Lexi had spent the previous evening pinned down by a gurney and the dying, then dead body that had occupied it, all buried under collapsed curtains and whatever else from the medical center the rioters had stomped down on top of them.

"Anyone who suffered any injuries as a result of last night's incident should report to the medical center located in the PaperClips on the first floor. Anyone with any medical training should also please report to the PaperClips to assist in helping those injured."

Lexi wondered if there was anything the medical personnel could do to cure her of the memory of being trapped under a body—alone—for hours, all that time convinced she'd left her father to be trampled to death by the crazed masses. She could still feel the cold, dead, clammy skin against her back.

She glanced over the top of her laptop to check on her father, and saw that he had fallen asleep on the lounge's crummy, fake leather couch. Turned out, he'd spent the night trapped under rubble, too. Only he had the additional disadvantage of having been shot by a looter with a nail gun and having his arm broken after being pushed down an escalator. Compared to that, trying to sleep without suffocating while being crushed by a corpse didn't seem so bad.

Lexi decided to let her father rest. Closing her computer, she relocated from the stockroom to the sales area of the Apple Store. At least from there, should the masses decide to riot for a third time, she'd see them coming.

Her mother droned on over the loudspeaker: ". . . if you begin to develop symptoms, including chills, a cough, or a runny nose, please report to the PaperClips for treatment.

"Security guards will be handing out medical masks and hand sanitizer. Please wear your mask and apply the sanitizer before touching any surface and before meals. Avoid touching your face. These small measures will help prevent the spread of the disease."

Too little too late. If only her mother had announced the flu as soon as she knew about it. If only the stupid government had hinted that they figured everyone inside the mall had a disease. Maybe people would have taken precautions. Maybe that saleslady Lexi had tried to save in the Abercrombie wouldn't have died.

"We have been given additional cots by the government and will set these up in three locations within the mall. Families, please report to the HomeMart for registration and assignment of beds. Women and girls, please report to the JCPenney; men and boys, please report to the Lord and Taylor. These locations will be your Home Stores."

Organization: This was the Senator's specialty. Lexi's mother had a label maker and by god, the woman knew how to use it. Only Lexi was not sure everyone in the mall would appreciate Dotty's penchant for pushing people around. For example, how would all those kids accustomed to nonstop hooking up in the Abercrombie, no parental units in sight, deal with single-sex dorms?

"If you are in need of a change of clothes, depots will be established on the first floor of each Home Store where you can trade in your clothes for a new set. You will no longer be able to purchase clothing. You will also not have a choice in what clothing you are given. We apologize in advance for any inconvenience this may cause."

Lexi nearly dropped her laptop from the burst of laughter that shook her. Just wear whatever they hand you? *Like* that *won't cause a riot?*

"We have been given sufficient quantities of food by the government for the duration of this quarantine, however long it lasts. Meals will be served in the first-floor common areas. If you have a life-threatening food allergy, please notify the security guard when you register at your Home Store. Other than life-threatening conditions, we cannot accommodate any dietary requests.

"If you have any comments or concerns, please bring them to the attention of one of the security guards. We will try to address every situation to the best of our ability. This is an unusual and trying situation, but we are all in this together. By working together and following a few simple rules, we can all make it through this with the least incident and suffering. Thank you for your patience and attention. God bless you all."

Lexi gave it a day, maybe less. No one would go for this. She flipped open her computer on one of the barren tables—the salespeople had cleared the decks of valuable merchandise to keep the looters at bay. Not like there was much use for laptops and iPhones anyway, what with no cell service or Internet to speak of. The screen blinked on and she got back to work.

BRITTANY FOX, *Age 20, SUNY-New Paltz*
ROBERT GAUDINO, *Age 52, pacemaker*
JOHN FITZGERALD, *Age 45, Lawyer*
ALANNA BROWN, *Age 17, West Nyack HS*

"Thought I'd find you here," Maddie said, entering the Apple Store.

Lexi glanced up from her laptop screen. She could cry seeing her friend walking around like one of the living; the last time she'd seen Maddie, she was pale as a vampire and lying under a puffer coat on the concrete floor of the Abercrombie stockroom.

"You know me so well," Lexi said, trying to sound as cool as possible.

"Well, you do have the Apple logo tattooed on your face." Maddie gave Lexi a one-finger shove on the forehead, then slumped onto a neighboring stool. "*Geraldine Simpson, age sixty-two, Prilosec*? What is this, a list of people we're *not* inviting to live with us?"

Lexi laughed despite her otherwise black mood. "I'm doing a job for my mother. It's a new list of everyone in the mall. The government took all the records when they abandoned us." She pointed to the stack of crinkled paper beside her.

"How do you know she's not dead?" Maddie said, slicing a finger across her neck.

"I guess we'll know once people check into their Home Stores," Lexi said. "Or don't, in which case I click the box marked 'deceased.'"

Maddie contemplated this as she flipped through the pages. "Thanks," she said finally, laying the papers aside. "Without you, I wouldn't be checking in anywhere today."

Lexi nodded, though did she really deserve to be thanked for what any decent human being would have done? *Decent human being* here obviously excluding Ginger Franklin, a coward who abandoned her friends to save her own bony butt. Lexi gritted her teeth and continued to type.

"What happened to you?" Maddie said, spinning on her seat. "I thought you'd come back after dropping your dad off in the med center."

Lexi wasn't sure what to say, so she went with the truth. "I got crushed under a gurney during the riot. I spent the night under a dead body."

"Sucks to be you," Maddie said.

"I spend the night under a dead body and *that's* your response?"

"Well, it does." Maddie shrugged and elbowed Lexi in the side. "At least it wasn't your first dead body."

"That makes it better how?"

"I don't know," Maddie said. "I'm trying to cheer you up."

It was more than anyone else had tried to do. "Thanks," she said, hoping that moved them on to something else topic-wise. She typed another entry into the system.

Maddie spun slowly on her stool. "We're all going to die, right?" she said after a few minutes.

"You just survived the flu," Lexi said. "If anyone's going to live, it's you."

"But that's why the government left," Maddie continued. "They're going to blow this place up with everyone in it or something. To keep the virus from getting out."

This horrible, hopeless option had not occurred to Lexi. She wondered if it had occurred to her mother. It had to have. "There's no way they'd do that," she said, more to herself than anyone else.

"Why not?" Maddie said. "There's like a couple thousand people in here." She waved a hand at the stack of rumpled papers. "What's that compared with the millions outside these doors?"

"My mother would never let that happen," Lexi said. "She's not the kind to go down with the ship."

"Why would they tell her about their plans?" Maddie said. "Us disease carriers are obviously far down on the need-to-know list, given how long it took them to share the news about the flu."

Lexi's heart rate was climbing. If her mother hadn't known about all the dead bodies in the Pancake Palace's freezer, what else didn't she know? What if Mom was as in the dark as the rest of them? What if she was just as screwed as everyone else? Lexi felt a wave of sympathy for her, and the sensation was strange to say the least.

"My mom is not out of the loop," Lexi said, as if saying the words made them true. "She knew about the flu days before they announced it. She told me."

"She told you?" Maddie said, eyes bugging. "And you thought that wasn't something of interest to the rest of us?"

Crap. "I couldn't tell," Lexi said. "My mom made me promise."

"Dude!" Maddie yelled. "There are some promises you just don't freaking keep!"

"Look, I'm sorry!" Lexi yelled back. Yelling felt better. "I didn't think you'd get it!"

"Well, I did!"

"It's not like if I'd told you, you wouldn't have gotten sick! We've all breathed the stuff in." *Plus,* Lexi thought, *you were kissing every guy with a pulse.*

Maddie grabbed her stool. "Everything's woozy," she said. Her face drained of blood.

Lexi took her arm and helped her to the floor. She propped Maddie against a shelf and brought her some water from the lounge in the back.

"You shouldn't be walking around if you're still feeling sick," Lexi said.

"I had been feeling better," Maddie mumbled.

"I wish you hadn't gotten sick. I'm sorry for not telling you."

"I'm sorry for yelling," Maddie said, lifting her head. "This whole thing just sucks."

"Let's make a pact," Lexi said. "No more secrets. I tell you everything, you tell me everything."

Maddie smirked. "Not really a fair deal, since you're the only one with secrets."

"You're the most popular person I know," Lexi said. "Who knows what you'll learn from the cool kids in the mall? You give me intel from the masses, I give you intel from my mom. Deal?" She held her hand out.

"Gossip for actual information?" Maddie took her hand. "You're getting a pretty raw deal."

Holding hands with Maddie, Lexi felt relief flood her body. She had a friend, someone to share secrets with. She wasn't alone. "I'm okay with that."

Maddie let go first. She gulped the water. "I guess we should check into our Home Store," she groaned.

Lexi stood and examined the stack of names she had yet to enter. It was at least another hour or two of work. *Screw it.* Her dad would put it in when he woke up. Or someone else could do it. It's not like data entry was brain surgery. Her mom could do it herself, for that matter.

"Let's go," Lexi said, closing her laptop.

"Can we please stop running for like one freaking minute so I can get the fire extinguisher foam off my face?" Ryan Murphy grabbed the nearest shirt and pulled.

Drew halted. "Shrimp," he said. "Your face is messed up."

Not like anyone looked good in the fluorescent gloom of the service hallway, but certainly Ryan had a decent excuse for whatever mess his face was. Just that morning he'd pulled a Lazarus and defeated the flu, then he'd free-fallen some thirty feet to rescue the ass who ruined their entire rooftop escape plan, only to be captured by security and then rescued in a cloud of fire-extinguisher foam. He swiped the wicking fabric of his climbing shirt over his skin and felt something smear around.

"That didn't help," Drew said.

"Can we stop at a bathroom or something?" Ryan rubbed his hands on his face and came away with crusty white crap.

"No one here cares what you look like," Marco said.

Ryan remembered Marco from their failed escape attempt through the parking level hatch. Something had changed in the guy over the last four days. He had a nasty edge to his voice. Ryan hated people with attitude. "I'm not worried about turning you on. This crap is burning my skin."

Mike pulled his T-shirt off, spat onto it, then came at Ryan. "Lemme get that," he said in a faux mommy voice.

Ryan smacked him away. "I'd rather let my face burn."

Mike snorted. "Your choice, Jumbo Shrimp." He threw the shirt at Ryan's head.

"Dude, this reeks," Ryan said, trying not to barf. All motion made him sick in the gut—like he needed shirt stink on top of that.

"Real men sweat," Mike said.

"While I appreciate the clever banter," Marco interrupted, "it's not helping us avoid the troop of security guards on our asses."

Mike stroked the gun in his waistband. "I could come up with a more permanent solution than running."

"We are not *killing* people," Ryan stated, like he had any control over Mike's use of his new toy, lifted from the police officer Ryan had tackled. He'd been as effective as a ninety-pound linebacker in stopping Mike from killing the dude in Shep's Sporting Goods. Of course, that guy had shot an arrow at them first.

"Unless you have some endless supply of ammo for that thing," Marco said, "that is not the answer to our problems."

"So what *is* the answer?" Drew snorted. "And it better involve food, because I'm starving."

Why were Mike and Drew listening to this guy? A week ago, they'd been trying to, no-joke, kill him. The change was freaky.

Marco closed his eyes like this was all such a waste of time. "Let's head to the third floor."

"Lead the way, Kemosabe," Mike said, sweeping his arm.

The guy had gotten a nickname? He wasn't even on the football team and he was getting a nickname? Ryan had only been out of the loop for like twenty minutes, but he was apparently years behind on information.

Despite what he'd just said, Marco Carvajal wasn't actually that concerned about security. They had woven through two stockrooms, shifting between service hallway systems, and moved up a floor already. Between that and the senator's new orders for reorganizing the mall, he doubted many guards were still in pursuit. Nevertheless, he liked to dangle that danger over The Three Douches' heads. Liked to remind them that without his help, they'd all be up a fraking creek.

He would have to have a word with them about "Kemosabe." Kemosabe was worse than "Taco."

They crept down the hallways toward the Grill'n'Shake, Marco's old place of employ. Things he did not miss: wiping tables and scraping food scraps as busboy to the ungrateful mall-walkers. Things he did miss: free fries and unlimited soda.

At the back door, he swiped his actual card key for old times' sake; he didn't want to wear out the mag strip on his shiny, new, stolen all-access pass. For a brief moment, he thought of Shay—how they'd taken the card key together, how their escape plan had fallen apart, but how their relationship had grown stronger—and he wanted to abandon these douches and check to make sure she was still okay in the med center. But he reminded himself that the whole reason he was with Mike, Drew, and Ryan was to ensure the safety of Shay and her sister, Preeti. Not to mention his own.

"Bathroom's in the back, food's this way," Marco said, holding open the service door.

"I think I know my way around the Grease'n'Suck," Ryan said, tromping toward the bathroom. Just as he was about to open the swinging door to the dining room, he froze. "There are people out there," he whispered.

Marco crept to the door and peered through the window. Regular people sat at the tables, some swilling stolen sodas, some with fistfuls of ice pressed to various appendages.

"There's a staff bathroom in the back." Marco said. He led the three into the kitchen.

People had raided what remained of the salad station.

"Where's the grub?" Drew asked, poking at the empty tubs.

"Relax," Marco said, approaching the monolithic metal door of the walk-in refrigerator. Everything worth eating was kept in the fridge, which, lucky for them, was still locked.

Marco pulled out the keys he'd inadvertently stolen from the manager on his last shift—two days ago. It wasn't like the man would miss them, given that he was dead. He wondered where his coworkers were now, Josh especially. Josh was a good guy. Marco hoped Josh was still alive.

It took several tries, but Marco finally identified the key to the fridge. The door swung open slowly, exhaling a cold mist.

"Hit the lights," Drew said, chops already wet with saliva.

Marco flicked the switch. The fluorescent lights

blinked, revealing a wealth of comestibles. Another door inside separated the freezer section, which contained more food, most of it unfortunately frozen solid.

The two douches thrust themselves inside and began pawing the merchandise.

"Dude, crackers," Mike said, throwing a gigantic bag of saltines at Drew, who grunted happily. The manager must have thrown all the food—from saltines to salt—in the fridge for safekeeping. The two douches didn't even bother to pull the things from the wrappers; they slit the bags open and poured the broken contents down their gullets.

Marco had certainly surrounded himself with some charming company. But beggars could not be choosers, and these two were the best this mall had to offer in terms of personal security services. He had traded his freedom and chosen to act as mall tour guide in exchange for Mike and Drew's formidable protection—an excellent deal, even if it meant having to watch Drew spit crumbs like a camel.

He needed to figure out how this whole security thing would work with Shay. Should they all hide out somewhere? Would Shay agree to living like this—stealing food from the Grill'n'Shake's fridge, sleeping in stockrooms? What if she was sick or really hurt? No, she needed something better than this. So he would have to run a dual operation—one to keep Shay safe, one to keep these idiots safe so they could keep him and Shay safe.

The fridge door swung away from his shoulder, startling Marco.

"Relax," Ryan said snidely, slipping past Marco into the fridge. He no longer had a fine layer of white all over him, though his face was splotchy—not splotchy like

Marco's face always was, but the handsome splotchy that guys like Ryan were blessed with. Even on a bad day, the douche was a billion times better looking than Marco.

"What's for breakfast?" Ryan said.

Mike chucked a bag of frozen chicken fingers at his head. "Gnaw on these."

Ryan caught it like he had bags of chicken launched at his head on a daily basis—which Marco guessed was essentially the definition of being a football player.

He definitely could not bring Shay here. Not with a handsome, coordinated jerk like Ryan around to mess up everything Marco had going with her.

The voices from the restaurant got louder; Marco thought he heard the kitchen door squeal. Not wanting to get involved in a firefight over frozen chicken, he checked that the inside release button for the handle was still working and closed them into the fridge. As he dug open a giant bag of baby carrots, Marco said a silent prayer that no one would test the lock.

Shaila Dixit was shaken awake by her bed, which was rattling its way out of the PaperClips. Her first instinct was to start patting the sides of the gurney looking for the brakes, but she quickly realized that, since there was no hill in the PaperClips, the gurney could not be rolling of its own volition.

"Just lie back and enjoy the ride," a voice behind her said.

"Where are you taking me?" The panic began to choke Shay. "Where's my sister?"

The gurney stopped and a round face with a mask over

its smiling mouth appeared at her side. "Dr. Chen said you had quite a scare," the face said. "I'm Jazmine, and I'm a nurse. I'm taking you to the new medical center."

"My sister?"

"Right behind you. You can relax, sweetheart."

Shay's head throbbed, so she sank back onto her pillow. If she hadn't felt like she'd hurl if she stood, she would have run. She did not trust this woman. She did not trust any of them. They had let her grandmother die. They said her sister, Preeti, was okay, but who knew if that was true. This place was horrible. Where was Marco?

Jazmine rolled her out into the hallway and then turned onto the main artery of the mall. Shay noticed half of the windows in the central skylight were covered over.

"What happened to the skylight?" Shay asked. Had the riot reached the ceiling?

"Some crazy people tried to bust out onto the roof," Jazmine said, her tone implying the inanity of the action.

Shay did not think this was stupid. In fact, she wished she'd thought of it. Ryan had taught her how to climb, after all. She wondered if it was he who'd made the attempt. That would mean he hadn't escaped through the garage. But had he made it out onto the roof?

"Did they escape?" Shay wanted the answer to be both yes and no.

"You think those government nut jobs in their plastic suits would let anyone out of here?"

That meant Ryan might still be in the mall. Shay closed her eyes and hoped it to be true. Didn't the universe owe her something good?

The gurney soon rolled to a stop under a fancy chandelier and a banner advertising a perfume. The room smelled sickly sweet. "The new med center is a department store?"

Jazmine fiddled with something on the underside of the gurney, then stood and brushed her palms on her jeans. "Harry's has been converted into this glamorous new hospital. Too many people showed up with riot injuries to try to keep making due in the PaperClips."

Shay lifted herself to her elbows and looked around. The makeup counters and racks of clothes still stood in their regular places.

"It's a work in progress," Jazmine said, following her gaze. "We moved you first, as you're non-critical."

"And my sister?" Shay asked.

"Flu cases will be moved last. We're trying to keep them separate."

"Can I see her?"

Jazmine, sensing perhaps from Shay's strident tone that the panic had returned, lifted her face mask and sat on the gurney beside Shay's hips. "I know you've been through a lot, honey," she said. "But you have got to trust somebody and it might as well be me."

"Why?" Shay asked, feeling peevish.

"You see anyone else around here?" Jazmine raised an eyebrow.

Shay allowed herself a smile.

"Your grandma was a special lady?" Jazmine cocked her head.

The question drove the smile away. "Don't you have to move the other people?"

"They won't miss me for another minute or so."

She stared at Shay like she was waiting for an answer,

like Shay was really going to talk about Nani to some complete stranger who probably was part of the team that let her die. No, that wasn't fair. That team, the ones in the hazmat suits, had fled, leaving only the contaminated, the damned.

Shay rubbed the edge of her sheet. "She was my best friend."

"That's a good grandma." Jazmine smiled as if waiting for more.

"She let me steal her henna."

"So that's what the mark on your cheek is." Jazmine stroked Shay's skin gently.

Shay flinched, surprised by the touch. The last time someone touched her, it was a zombie hand reaching out from the rubble of the old med center.

Jazmine, unfazed, smiled and held open her arms. "Can I at least give you a hug before I go?"

Tears pricked out along Shay's eyelids at the word. When was the last time someone offered her a simple hug, nothing else implied or wanted? Just a hug, just for her? *So long.*

Shay nodded her head and felt Jazmine's thick arms wrap around her, enveloping her in warmth. The tears dropped down her cheeks, darkening the fabric of Jazmine's shirt.

"No touching," a voice commanded. "And put on your mask."

"Say what?" Jazmine barked. "If I want to hug a person, I'm hugging her."

"New rules." The voice came closer. Shay turned her

head and saw a security guard, stun baton gripped in both hands across his chest like a shield.

Jazmine gave Shay a look like she would kill this man before she'd stop hugging people, but then she let go of Shay, replaced her mask, and shuffled off the gurney. "I'll check on you later," she said, squeezing Shay's shoulder, then walked away.

Shay nearly screamed for Jazmine to come back, but the security guard with his black stick shut her up. He looked both nervous and cocky, and Shay did not like that combination. Would he attack her? No, he was here to protect her. *Right?* Cold sweat broke out over her body. She was alone with this guy who looked ready to beat the crap out of anyone and everyone.

He turned and walked out of the store. Another gurney was rolled in by some woman, not Jazmine.

Shay did not trust these strangers. She did not feel safe. But she couldn't move off this gurney, not yet, so she fell back and stared at the chandelier until her eyes watered and the world became a bright blur.

T
W
O
P.M.

The first thing that struck Lexi was the scant number of people who had showed up to sign in at the JCPenney. It was basically her and Maddie and a pair of old ladies.

"Where is everyone?" Lexi asked, weirded out by the emptiness. There still had to be thousands of people in the mall. Where the hell were they?

"Dead?" Maddie offered. "Sick on their way to being dead?"

Lexi gave her a look, but saw that Maddie was not joking.

"Fine, they're not *all* dead," Maddie said, shrugging. "Maybe they're afraid of those thugs with the stun guns." She pointed to a group of four security guards, all leaning on a giant planter in the middle of the hallway, each displaying a two-foot-long nightstick-slash-electrocution rod.

The dudes looked less than friendly. Apparently, the

riot had made everyone, especially the cops, suspicious of their mall-mates.

This was not a good development. Lexi was not in one hundred percent agreement with her mother on anything, but the Senator's rules were the only option at the moment, and if the choice was between them and another riot, Lexi knew which side she was on.

"We should help," Lexi said. Maybe people didn't trust that the JCPenney Home Store thing was actually happening. The place certainly looked like it was still a JCPenney and not a home of any sort.

"Help what? The cops?" Maddie asked. "The old ladies?"

"My mom."

"Your mom is like the last person I'm in the mood to help." Maddie flipped her hair and glared at the cops.

"My mom is the one person trying to pull this place back together," Lexi said. "Come on."

Lexi didn't wait to see if Maddie followed. There used to be nylon barrier things, like the ones used in airports to organize crowds, near the checkout lines in the JCPenney. Lexi figured if she set them up outside, it might show people that her mother was serious about this plan and also control any crowds that hopefully showed up to register.

Just as she was about to cross the threshold, a guard yelled at her. "Hey kid, stop!"

"I'm just going in to get some barrier things," Lexi yelled back. "You need to do something to make this place look official."

The guy came strutting toward her. "The Senator said not to allow anyone in until they registered."

"The Senator's my *mom* and she told me to help her." It was sort of true.

The guard took a few moments to process Lexi's information. "Okay, but what's your name? I have to write down everyone's name."

It was like talking to a 16-bit NPC. "Alexandra Ross. As in the Senator Ross."

The guy wrote something on his hand. *That's professional . . .* "What barrier things?" he asked, sounding less like a jerk.

Lexi scanned the sales floor and saw one. "That," she said, pointing.

The guy nodded. "I like it," he said. He switched on his walkie-talkie and told whoever was on the other end of it to collect the tension barriers from the checkout lines and set them up for crowd control outside the Home Stores. "This whole thing is kind of a clusterf—I mean, confusing."

Lexi smirked. "Sounds like my mom's doing." She instantly regretted talking badly about her mom to this guy who was supposedly the Senator's underling.

He didn't seem to notice. "The chief told us to just write people's names down until we got some computer system, but so far there's just been these two old ladies and you. I'm not even sure where to tell people to go. The whole store is still, like, full of stuff."

The sales floor looked like it always did, though there were toppled racks and tables—evidence of the riot. Most of the store, however, had escaped harm.

"Are there people in here?"

"Security did a sweep," the guy said. "Most bolted into the service hallways. A team is searching them for stragglers."

"Are there bodies?" Lexi was not sure if she really wanted to hear the answer.

The guy stiffened. "I'm not allowed to say anything about bodies."

Okay, that's *not weird or anything.* Why the clamming up over bodies?

His walkie-talkie bleeped. *"Nice idea with the barriers,"* the voice barked. *"Get the registrants to begin clearing the sales floors for the cots."*

The security guy pulled the radio from his belt. "Roger," he said. "Where should we put stuff?"

"Stockrooms for now."

Lexi told the guard she had a friend outside who could help. As she exited, she saw that the four guards who'd been lounging on the planter were setting up the barriers in front of the store. The place looked a lot more official. People were bound to come out to register now.

Lexi hoped the guard would tell the Senator that this had all been her idea. She may have bailed on the data entry assignment, but security had totally needed her help with the Home Stores. She was being even more useful out here. *Now who's going to feel bad about throwing a radio at my head?*

Maddie was suspiciously willing to accept Lexi's invitation to clear the sales floor, and the reason for this became immediately apparent. For every rack she rolled into the stockroom, she removed an item from it and draped it over her neck. Lexi tried to ignore the shameless shoplift-ing, but then she caught Maddie actually changing into an entirely new outfit.

"We're supposed to be storing the stuff from the sales floor, not stealing it."

Maddie slapped a hand to her chest in mock offense. "Stealing! Why, I'd never." She pulled a hat onto her head. "I see this as just compensation for my labor." She glanced at herself in the mirror. "Is the hat too much? Yeah, I agree." She took it off and Frisbeed it into the depths of the stock area.

Lexi checked to see if anyone else was around. No, they were alone. So what if Maddie *was* taking clothes instead of waiting for the guards to give her a new outfit? That was okay. It was one outfit. No one would even know it was gone.

"You should get something," Maddie said, her face lighting up. "Something sexy instead of this depressing hoodie situation you seem to always have going on."

"No," Lexi said. "I mean, I like this hoodie. Picked it out from the Abercrombie myself."

"Girl, that thing had a dead body lying on it all night." Maddie grabbed Lexi's sleeve and pulled her arm free of it. "This hoodie must be trashed."

Maddie made a good point. Okay. One outfit for each of them. No one would know. It would be totally fine. And Lexi had just revolutionized the whole Home Store check-in process. She deserved an outfit. The Senator would totally agree.

Maddie pulled an expensive-looking sweater from a

pile and a pair of skinny jeans off a rack. "You're what, a size ten?"

Lexi had no idea. Sizes were not her thing. She usually bought men's jeans. They hid her curves better. "Sure?" she said.

Maddie tossed the pants at her. "You're a ten." She looked at Lexi like something should be happening. "Well? Go on. Before those old bags roll in another rack."

Lexi did as she was told. She dropped her jeans and stuffed herself into the pants Maddie had thrown at her. They were pretty much a nightmare, hugging every inch of skin like the things were glued on.

"*Ooh la la*, the girl has legs," Maddie cooed. The sweater beaned Lexi in the forehead. "Now the *pièce d'rèsistance*."

Obediently, Lexi dragged off her safe, comfortable T-shirt and tugged on the sweater. It felt like delicate fur. Judging from the wispy hairs, it was made of delicate fur. This too stuck to her skin, but in a nice way, like a hug. The only downside being that the thing revealed that Lexi had boobs like nobody's business.

Maddie looked pleased with her work. "Now see if the boys don't start eating each other for a piece of you."

"You have just described my worst nightmare."

Maddie raised an eyebrow. "You just haven't met the right boys."

"What are you two doing?" a male voice barked.

It was a security guard, another guy with a stun baton. He did not look pleased.

Maddie put on a sad face. "Don't yell at us, officer! We

were just moving this big heavy rack and it nearly fell on my friend and I was comforting her."

Lexi froze for a moment, then realized she should be in some sort of pain. "Yes," she said through gritted teeth. She grabbed her upper arm. "Very painful."

The guard gave them the once-over. "You change clothes?"

"No way," said Maddie. "That would be against the rules."

The guard nodded toward the table behind them. "Then why is your friend wearing *that* sweater?"

"She bought it, back before all hell broke loose."

"Yeah, right."

Maddie slapped a hand on her hip. "If she hadn't been trampled and lost her bag with the receipt in it, she could prove it, but I guess if you hadn't let this whole mall go to the crazies, she wouldn't have lost her bag, so it's just a nasty little cycle we find ourselves in."

Maddie was so totally out of line, Lexi had no idea what to do except shut up and try not to freak out. The guard shifted his hold on his stun stick. Maddie stared at him like she dared him to use it. Did she actually think the man wouldn't?

Then, miracle of miracles, the guard turned. "Just get back to clearing racks." He left them in the stockroom.

Maddie burst out laughing.

"What the hell?" Lexi cried.

"Come on, like that loser was going to really do anything?"

"He had a freaking Taser! You think after everything that's happened that he's afraid to use it?"

Maddie pretended to faint. "Oh, big scary man with a big scary Taser!" Then she shoved Lexi. "Grow a pair, dearest. Life's too short to give a crap about little things like electrocution."

As Maddie sashayed out of the stockroom, Lexi tried to comprehend the last few minutes. For all her bitching at and about her mom, she had never so much as jay-walked before meeting Maddie. And what had following Maddie gotten her? Mortified in front of a group of guys Lexi didn't even find remotely attractive, floor-burn from sliding down a bowling lane, and nearly infected with a deadly virus during a game of Dare or Dare. But without Maddie, she was alone.

"Wait up!" she yelped, and raced after Maddie's shadow.

The mall speaker was barely audible in the kitchen of the Grill'n'Shake. Marco, however, gleaned from what made it to his ears that the senator was serious about people checking in at the Home Stores. He heard "assumed dead" and "calculation of rations." Now was the time for him to make the call: *Do I stay or do I go?*

"We should try to check in," Ryan said, swallowing his defrosted chicken.

"Dude, we're outlaws," Drew mumbled through a mouthful of reconstituted fries.

"Forget outlaws," Mike said. "I am not like these other drones. I will not be a part of this goddamn experiment."

Marco was floored. "*Experiment?* Are you suggesting that our current situation is the result of a government test gone wrong?"

"You really think that some terrorist would bother to attack a freaking mall?" Mike pulled another thawed chicken strip from the bag. "This has government cover-up written all over it."

Riiiiiight . . .

"We're safer if we just try to fit in," Ryan chimed in.

If the three of them joined the plebes in the Home Stores, they would have no need for Marco's card key access services. This idea of Ryan's had to be shot down.

"No," stated Marco. "Bad idea. They put you in jail once, they will find another jail for you."

"We could use fake names," Ryan offered.

The kid would not give up. "They have a list of everyone in the mall from the first day. You think a couple of strangers appearing on the roster wouldn't attract attention?" Marco put on his most dismissive glare.

"So, what then?" Ryan winged the remainder of his chicken at the trash and glared back. "We live in the freaking freezer of the Grill'n'Shake?"

"We could find Reynolds, try his escape plan?" Drew said.

"The mall is surrounded," Marco said. "If they had helicopters scanning the roof, you think they don't have people watching the grounds?"

Mike stood. "You all are missing the point." He sat on the stainless-steel countertop. "This mall is a death trap. Our only goal is to survive until whatever the hell is going on ends. If we really are dealing with the flu, then the key is to keep ourselves isolated. We find a hole and stay in it."

Drew kicked a plastic bucket. "This sucks."

"It's better than being dead."

No one argued with Mike.

"Okay," Marco said. "So we find a suitable hole and put you in it."

"What about you?" Ryan asked, eyebrows knit in a scowl. "Aren't you hiding out with us?"

"I'm your eyes and ears," Marco said. "Someone's got to keep his head aboveground to watch for security and stay on top of the situation." This was working out better than he expected. The three would be entirely dependent on him for everything: food, water, intel. If any problem should arise for him and Shay, he could convince Mike to sneak out of his hidey-hole to resolve it based on whatever lie Marco thought would best motivate him, and the douche would never be the wiser. Better yet, Shay would never know that Ryan was even in the mall.

"I better go check in," Marco said, pushing himself up from where he'd been scrunched on the floor between two large, empty containers.

"Cut off for check-in's not for another half hour," Mike said, glancing over his hunched shoulder.

"I have to check on someone in the med ward." Marco brushed off his jeans. "I'll be back in an hour. Then we can move down to the hiding place I have in mind."

Mike nodded. "We'll gather supplies from the freezer."

The coast was clear outside the fridge. Marco crossed the kitchen, pushed through the service door, and started down the dim hallway.

"I thought you were alone in the mall," Ryan said.

Marco nearly jumped out of his skin. The kid was near silent in his climbing slippers. "I told you to wait here until I come back."

"I told Mike I'd collect supplies from the med ward in case any of us got sick again."

"Again?" Marco couldn't help the gooseflesh that prickled out on his arms at the idea that one of the douches was contagious.

"I had the flu," Ryan said, a touch of pride in his voice.

Marco took larger steps, tried to put a bit more real estate between him and the potentially infectious douche. "It's not a bad idea," Marco said.

"So who's in the med ward?" Ryan sped up to keep pace with Marco.

"My girlfriend," Marco said, wondering how hard to twist the knife and deciding the harder the better. "I think you know her. Shaila Dixit?" That took the jock down a few pegs. He stopped following for a moment, then jogged a few steps to catch up.

"Is she hurt?" Ryan asked.

Not the response Marco had expected, but he figured why not tell. "She passed out when she learned that her grandmother had died, at least that's what the doctor told me."

"I have to see her," Ryan said.

"You have to stay hidden." Marco kept walking. "People are looking for The Flying Kid."

Ryan grabbed Marco's arm. "I have to see her."

Marco glowered back at him, not sure if Ryan could see in the dim light the amount of pissed-off-ness he felt. Ryan didn't back down.

"It's your funeral," Marco said, and continued to walk.

Ryan stumbled slightly, trying to keep up—*aftereffects of the flu?* "So Shay's your girlfriend?" he asked, panting as if walking was too much for him.

Marco tried to sound casual. "It started when she asked me to help her—you were in jail, I believe—but then her sister and grandmother got sick, and now I'm kind of all she's got." He watched Ryan's face change. Watched the realization sink in.

"Does she know I was in jail?"

The douche looked like he was about to cry. Marco threw him a bone. "I didn't tell her."

Ryan nodded. "Thanks."

Like I did it for you . . .

The med ward was now in Harry's department store, according to the senator's last announcement. Marco maneuvered through the service halls and between the empty stores with ease. Ryan followed silent as a shadow. They only communicated when Marco stopped in front of a door marked HARRY'S, LEVEL 1, and then Marco merely held his finger to his lips and cracked the door open.

The space before them seemed empty. It looked like some back area—shelves of shoe boxes lined narrow corridors.

"We're clear," Marco said. Ryan nodded and they both slipped into the stockroom.

They followed a path between the stacks of shoes to a swinging door, which opened onto the main level. What had been the shoe department was now lined with cots and walled off from the rest of the showroom floor by a curtain wall. A young guy with his arm in a sling dozed in a corner; otherwise, the room was empty.

"Must have been where they treated the riot victims," Marco said, weaving toward the only space in the curtain wall.

"Why do you think that?" Ryan followed a step behind.

"No bodies."

"I had the flu," Ryan said. "I survived."

Marco glanced back at him. "You're lucky."

Beyond the curtain wall was a makeshift hallway. The entire sales floor had apparently been divided into "rooms" using curtains salvaged from the PaperClips.

"Which way?" Ryan asked.

"Does it matter?" Marco said, feeling defeated. He turned onto the hall leading away from the front of the store, hoping security was stationed there and nowhere else.

They'd checked five rooms when voices reached them from another part of the curtain complex: "An unauthorized entry was logged through a door off the service halls. We're looking for a fugitive."

Ryan grabbed Marco and dragged him into the nearest room. Through some wonderful twist of fate, the room contained Shay and her sister, both asleep on hospital beds.

Ryan's face fell. "Is she sick?" he whispered.

Marco walked to her side. "No," he said quietly, willing it to be true. "At least, she wasn't when I left her a few hours ago."

Ryan stood on the other side of her bed. "She asked

you to help her," he said, staring down at her face. "Help her do what?"

"Escape." Marco took her hand. If there was going to be some battle between them for her, he wanted to claim ground early on.

Ryan's arms dangled at his side. "Did she say anything about me?"

"She never mentioned you." Marco was being honest. Though of course he knew about them, had seen them all lovey-dovey outside the Grill'n'Shake. And he worried, or at least a very small part of him he was trying desperately to ignore worried, that if she opened her eyes right now and saw them both, she would choose Ryan.

Ryan was caught between kicking Marco's ass for touching his girlfriend and concern that the dweeb had actually, through some horrible cosmic joke, won her from him. "You obviously didn't help her escape," he said. "What did you do?"

Marco raised his head slowly. "I was there for her when she needed someone. While you were off skydiving from the rafters, I saved her from being crushed in the riot."

Ryan did not consider himself a particularly competitive person off the football field, but seeing Marco's grip on Shay's fingers filled him with a primal instinct. He had an inkling of the brain-space Mike lived in every day, a place where everyone was a threat or a target, where every move you made had better put you closer to your goal. Judging by Marco's hold on Shay's hand, Ryan sensed that there was little Marco wouldn't do to keep her. Ryan decided that he had better play it conservative; after all, his survival and that of Mike and Drew depended on the weasel.

"If she's not sick, then why is she hooked up to that machine?" Ryan asked, playing the safest card he could.

"I told you, she got crushed in the riot. I *saved* her."

Footsteps stopped outside the curtain wall; Ryan dropped to the floor and crawled under Shay's bed, sure they were looking for him. Yet when the guard stepped into the room, he said, "Marco Carvajal?"

Marco shifted his feet—that was all Ryan could see.

"Who's asking?" Marco said.

Why would security be looking for *him*?

"The senator." The guard stepped forward, but Marco went toward him without waiting to be dragged away.

Ryan was thankful that Marco did not alert the guard to his presence, and merely walked with the man out of the room.

He crawled back up to standing. Shay groaned softly. Was she having a bad dream? What horrible things had happened to her while he'd been running around like an idiot? He should have stayed with her. She needed him— not anymore, he guessed. Not now that she had Marco.

But Shay liked him. He was sure of it. Marco had to be a stand-in at best. Ryan would win her back. A part of him wanted to shake her awake right then and demand that she dump Marco and run away with him. They would hide out in some corner together. But he didn't let himself do it. Instead, Ryan leaned forward and pressed his lips to her forehead like a promise.

"I gave her a sedative, so no matter how long you kiss her, Sleeping Beauty is not waking up."

A large nurse stood in the "door" in the curtain wall.

"Sorry," Ryan mumbled, jerking himself to standing. "I'm a friend."

The woman folded her arms across her chest. "I would hope so."

"I'll go." Ryan was ready to bust through the curtain to get out of there if that's what it took.

The woman thankfully stepped aside. "Don't let me catch you in here again."

Ryan shuffled out, glancing behind him to see the woman disappear into Shay's room. He debated eavesdropping to make sure Shay was okay, but not wanting to tempt the nurse to violence, decided to exit while he still had the option. He grabbed a bottle of pills from a tray—what kind of pills, he had no idea, but he figured he'd better return to the Grease'n'Suck with something or risk having to explain his failed expedition to Mike. Ryan had a feeling Mike wouldn't have a lot of sympathy for his nearly getting nabbed while checking up on his would-be girlfriend. Especially when Ryan's whole goal was to steal her from the only person in this mall Mike seemed to trust.

The security officer led Marco up to the third floor, then toward the skating rink, which was closed, according to a piece of paper taped to the door. *Weird . . .*

This end of the third level was opposite the more exciting part, which offered movie theaters, a bowling alley, restaurants including the Grill 'n' Shake, a bookstore, the arcade, etc. The officer stopped in front of a nondescript metal door with a pane of glass in the wall next to it, behind which sat a bored-looking guard. Marco's guard nodded to him, the door buzzed, and the guy opened the door for Marco.

"After you," he said.

Marco walked through, eyes wide and ears open. This was like the most wonderful, unexpected recon opportunity ever. Every question he had about what the hell was going on in the mall, the answers were somewhere in this cluster of offices. He tried to absorb the information through osmosis.

One room held cots, another had piles of what looked like weapons and shields, in the next an older guy was futzing with computer wires between four cubicles, the one after that, three cots. Opposite the computer room was a dark closet with flashing screens showing the feeds from the mall's closed-circuit camera system. Then, at the end of the hall, the senator. She had a stack of paper on her desk. A heavyset man in a uniform sat on the other side of it.

"We've done all we can to convince people," she said, setting aside a sheet. "It may take a few days, but they'll see that this plan is going to work and get in line."

"You're the boss," the man said, sounding like he was not sold on the idea.

"I am not establishing a police state," the senator responded. "At least not as a first option."

The man got up and left.

The senator waved at Marco. "Come in," she said, pointing to the chair the heavyset man had abandoned. Marco sat. The senator folded her hands on her desk. "You know what's stuck in my mind?"

Marco did not like the smug look she was giving him.

He'd stared down enough authority figures at this point to know the palette of looks they displayed and what each one meant. You can only be in so many scuffles before you're just hauled in every time there's even a rumor of a fight. Not like Marco really had a choice in whether he got the crap beaten out of him.

Unsure of where the senator was hoping to lead him, he gave her a noncommittal shrug.

"How exactly did you get into the back of the Paper-Clips during the riots?"

This was not the question Marco was expecting. "I saw an open door and went through it." He tried to be as vague as possible.

The senator's eyebrows flicked up. "Interesting. Because it occurred to me that maybe you can answer not only this question, but the question of my missing security card key."

Marco swallowed. This was not the usual interrogation session with a guidance counselor; this was like staring down a shark. He sensed that one false move and she would tear his head from his body.

His brain spun into high gear. He couldn't afford to give up the card. It was the only bargaining chip he had in this place. Without it, he would lose Mike, lose any freedom he'd gained, forget being able to protect Shay. But they could search him and find the thing without his saying a word and where did that get him?

Better to play some hand than none at all. He slid his fingers into his pocket and felt around for his old card key. He pulled it out, leaving the universal card safely tucked away, and placed it on her desk.

"I only wanted to help Shay," he said, trying on his most pathetic voice.

"And those Spider-Men who tried to get out to the roof."

Motherfrakingcrap.

She pushed the card back toward him. "Don't hyperventilate just yet," she said. "I have a job for you."

Marco did not take the card back. What the hell did she mean by *job*?

The senator leaned back in her desk chair and stretched her hands behind her head. "I have a bit of a problem, Marco. There are around four thousand people in this mall and I only have a small private security force to control them. As we saw yesterday, when the people want to take over, they can.

"I am trying to pull this place together out of that chaos. But I can only do so much. People who don't want to jump on my bandwagon? Well, I don't have much of a way to get them on by force. So here's where you come in.

"I have a hunch, and you don't have to answer, but my hunch is that you know where my Spider-Men are. I don't want to waste my precious police resources hunting and trapping them, so I am offering you the job."

"You want me to hunt and trap the guys who tried to escape through the skylight?" He tried to play it as dumb as possible.

"No," she said, smiling. "I want you to keep tabs on them and keep me informed of any future problems they plan on causing."

"And I get to keep the card key?"

"You can keep the card key."

This deal was like a freaking dream come true. Not only was he not in trouble, he was being ordered to do exactly what he was planning on doing anyway. His arrangement with the douches was now blessed by the cops, and Mike and the others would never be the wiser.

"Okay," he said, taking back the card key.

The senator held out a hand. "Glad to have you on board."

Marco took it. "No problem."

"There better not be." She gripped his palm and stared hard into his eyes. "I am trusting you to be on my side in this. Do not cause me to regret that trust." She released Marco's hand.

"I won't," he said.

"Come back here tomorrow after dinner to check in," she said, then turned to a computer screen.

Marco assumed he was dismissed. The guard who had led him in was waiting outside the door. He shuffled Marco along the hall and let him out the front, depositing Marco back in the mall.

The hallway seemed brighter now. Maybe it was the late-afternoon sun coming through the windows of the food court, maybe it was the relative emptiness of this part of the mall. Marco took a deep breath, like he was sucking in the light, then trotted down the hall toward the escalators, his sneakers bouncing off the tiles like he was made of light himself.

F I V E

P.M.

Having worked in her sexy outfit for half a day, Lexi longed for the comfort of her old tee and hoodie. Her old baggy jeans. Every time she bent over, she felt like some part of her pants was going to split. The pink sweater itched—maybe she was developing a rash. And it seemed to suck in the heat, so she was sweating buckets. Lexi had never felt less sexy.

"Cot number seven million and two, done." Maddie flopped onto the flat bed, then winced. "I think I'd rather sleep on the floor."

Lexi found it bizarre how everyone was eager to help; even the whiny girls like Maddie who bitched and moaned still did their assigned job. It was like everyone felt bad about the whole riot thing, and couldn't we put that behind us and all pretend nothing happened?

After clearing all the clothing from the sales floors into the stockrooms, people asked what they could do next. The guards found new jobs for everyone, assumedly handed down from the Senator, who'd yet to appear in the flesh. Some were given the sucktastic job of cleaning the bathrooms, others the much less smelly job of collating travel-sized toiletries into Ziploc bags, and a few trusted old ladies were given the job of pulling suitable clothes for sleeping from the piles in the stockrooms. Lexi and Maddie were assigned to the largest team, charged with setting up the cots.

Lexi sat beside Maddie. "At least we're not cleaning the johns," Lexi said, swabbing her forehead with her sleeve. "I heard that half of them are clogged, with like—"

Maddie put a finger to Lexi's lips. "Stop. TMI."

Lexi shrugged. "You said you wanted *all* the gossip."

"Not the gross stuff," Maddie said. "Keep the gross stuff to yourself." She looked at Lexi like Lexi was the only gross thing in the place.

"Okay," Lexi mumbled. "No gross info. Check."

Maddie looked around the room at the other women and girls setting up the cots. There were people of every age, but most looked like they were in high school or college. Lexi held still, waited for Maddie to break the silence.

Instead, her mother's voice boomed through the space: "For those registered at the Home Stores, dinner will be served in the first-floor courtyard outside the Borderland's Cantina. If you have not been registered, you will not be served. Please take this opportunity to register at a Home Store. Dinner service will end at seven p.m. sharp."

Maddie hopped off the cot. "I'm so hungry, I don't even care what they're serving."

Lexi hauled her butt up to follow Maddie, but stopped when she saw her dad, Arthur Ross, hobbling toward her.

"Hey girls," he said, cheery as ever. "Lex, I finished the database, but now I need help inputting the information collected at the Home Stores. Can I borrow you?"

Lexi's stomach growled. "Can I start after dinner?"

Her father checked to see if anyone was looking (no—everyone was shoving their way downstairs to grab some grub), then pulled a box of frozen burritos from his satchel. "A special treat for working through a meal."

Maddie perked right up. "Can I help?" she asked, eyelashes batting. She grabbed Lexi's arm and gave her a pleading look. "Don't leave me alone to eat the camping food."

Maddie could seemingly turn her friendship off and on whenever she liked. A minute ago she'd looked at Lexi like she was no better than the crap being sucked out of the toilets; now she clung to her like they were best buds. But Lexi told herself that she was just being sensitive. Maddie was her friend. They'd been having a great time right up until like five minutes ago.

"Of course I won't leave you," Lexi said.

Maddie snatched the box of burritos. "Knew I had you whipped," she said, kissing Lexi's cheek. "Now, where's a micro when you need one?"

After nuking the food, Lexi and Maddie wolfed their burritos as they followed Arthur to the first floor. Dad had a laptop set up on the folding table serving as the entrance to the JCPenney. Beside it sat one of the guards responsible for checking people in.

There was a healthy line snaking away from the counter. It had taken several hours, but people were finally convinced that it was safe to come out into the open. Or maybe they were just that hungry. It didn't matter. Each gave the guard her name, and in return was handed a special white mask that fit like a dome over the nose and mouth, and small bottle of hand sanitizer.

"Of course they show up after we've cleared the whole place and set up their beds," Maddie snarked, scarfing the last of her burrito.

At least they've decided to join the forces of good, Lexi thought. If her mother's orders had failed to rally people, what then? She refused to think of it. Maddie was wrong. The Senator was in control—look how people followed her commands! There would be no more riots. She would not end up buried under the rubble again. She had Maddie to watch her back. *Right?*

Maddie picked up the first sheet in the pile beside the laptop and Lexi positioned herself in front of the screen. Maddie read the names and Lexi clicked the box in the database to indicate the person had checked into a Home Store, and then the box indicating which of the three stores they were in.

After a half hour of droning on, Maddie interrupted her recitation. "She's here."

"Is that a name?" Lexi said, scrolling through the list.

"Ginger," Maddie snarled. "She's here."

Lexi's jaw tightened at the name. Ginger had abandoned her, leaving Lexi to try to save the kids in the Abercrombie alone. Ginger had made her use the CB radio to call Ginger's dad, who caused a riot outside the mall and got Lexi in trouble with her parents, and Darren, her parents—everyone—in trouble with the Feds. Ginger had ruined everything. And now she was back.

Lexi cracked her knuckles. "We shouldn't be surprised. Where else would she go?"

"Stay in whatever hole she'd crawled into when she left me to die in the Abercrombie? All it took was one mall apocalypse to wreck a lifelong friendship." Maddie snuggled against Lexi's shoulder. "At least some people are real friends."

Lexi felt a warmth spread over her cheeks. *Real friends.* She didn't want to show Maddie how much those words meant. She straightened her back, jostling Maddie, who sat straight.

"Back to the grind," she said, sighing, and read the next name.

Someone coughed in the line. The sound echoed like a bomb blast around the emptiness of the hallway. The guard at the table next to them looked up.

"Who coughed?" he shouted. It was the guy who'd seemed so lost this morning. Now he looked like a wolf with a scent.

No one responded. Then a youngish woman waved an arm. "She did!" she yelled, pointing to a mom-aged woman in a flowery dress.

The older woman froze, glanced around her. "I feel fine," she squeaked. "I just need a sip of water."

The rest of the people in line backed away from her. Two guards, faces in masks and hands covered in plastic gloves, closed in from the hall.

"Really, I'm fine," she said, then, as if her body wanted to betray her, she coughed again.

The guards grabbed her arms and led her out of line. The guard next to Lexi pulled antibacterial wipes from a container. He waved them in the air. "Miss," he yelled.

The girl who'd sold out the woman pointed to herself.

"Yeah, you," the guard said. "Take these and wipe down your hands and face, and give one to everyone around you, then wipe the barrier where the woman was standing."

The girl's eyes were wide, her mouth a thin, trembling frown. She obeyed, skipping forward on her tiptoes, and then scuttled back to where she'd been. The others in line took their wipes and began cleansing the space.

The guard turned to Lexi, sliding two masks across the counter. "Put these on."

Lexi slipped the thing over her face and passed the other to Maddie, who followed suit without making a peep.

Shay was shaken awake by Jazmine. "Dinnertime," the nurse said, holding out a plate. A pile of what looked like reconstituted barf slid across the surface.

"I'm going to be sick."

Jazmine smiled and dropped the plate onto the metal table between Shay and her sister. "You had a visitor this afternoon. Some boy."

Shay's heart rate increased. "Oh?" But then she reminded herself that it was Marco, had to have been; Ryan, even if he was still in the mall, had no idea that she was in the med center. Only Marco knew that. Her heart rate sank back to normal. "He's just a friend."

"Seemed pretty friendly," Jazmine continued, the smug smile on her face visible beyond the borders of her mask. "He kissed you."

Gooseflesh prickled across Shay's skin. Marco *kissed* her? No, that was against the rules. If she had kissed him on the cheek, that was only to be friendly. He was taking things out of context. He was reading into her actions. Not that she could really blame him. She had been, in essence, leading him on. But what choice did she have? She had a sister to protect. She needed an ally. And to keep him, she would do whatever she had to.

But she would say something to him the next time she saw him. There would be no kissing, especially while she was passed out. Or if he really needed a kiss, then only on the cheek. God, this Marco nonsense was the last thing she wanted to deal with. Why were boys so freaking needy?

Jazmine laughed. "You look like you're deep in thought, so I'll let you think." She stood.

"No," Shay said, not wanting to be left alone now that she was awake. "I was just thinking about the boy. Do you have a boyfriend?"

Jazmine settled back on the gurney. "I'll tell if you eat something." She nodded at the plate.

Shay lifted the sagging paper dish. "What is it?"

"Chicken something," Jazmine said, eyeing the plate. "I had some. It's edible."

"Are the white lumps chicken?"

"A safe bet," Jazmine said. "I say just close your eyes and shovel it in. You need to eat."

Shay held up her wrist. "I have my trusty IV."

Jazmine frowned. "You planning to spend the rest of your life with that in your arm?"

"Who knows how long that even is?" Shay wasn't

sure why she said that. She didn't want to be negative. But it felt true, once said. She could die tomorrow. And wouldn't that be better than facing another nightmare day in this place?

Jazmine's face softened, but still looked disappointed. "You have to stay strong," she said. "You have a sister to watch out for." She squeezed Shay's hand. "Things are going to get better from now on. This senator lady has got people working together."

For how long? Shay had never been a bitter person, but now it felt like all that was inside her was bitterness. She pushed it down, conjured some happiness.

"That's great."

Jazmine smiled. "That's my girl."

Shay shoveled a spoonful of chicken slop into her mouth and forced herself to swallow it down. "It's actually good," she managed, stifling a retch.

"Now I know you're lying," Jazmine said, chuckling. "Here." She pulled a small leather notebook from the pocket of her cardigan. "I found this in the PaperClips and thought you might like it. You look like a journal girl."

Shay laid the spoon aside and took the notebook. It was a business thing, the kind of little book her dad used to take to conferences before he got an iPad. Opening it, Shay saw that the pen was one of those special ones that had a built-in light in the pen tip and a highlighter on the other end. She ran her fingers over the paper, which was smooth and blank.

"Maybe you can write something about your grandma and show it to me?"

Shay glanced up from the beautiful blankness of the paper, tears turning the world to water. "Yes," she said, her voice catching on the word.

Jazmine smiled and patted her leg through the thin blanket. "Then you finish your food. I'll be back in a half hour to check you out." She took Shay's wrist and gently removed the IV.

Panic gripped Shay. "Don't I need that?" Why was Jazmine taking away her medicine?

"It's just saline," Jazmine said. "And you're conscious now, so you can feed and hydrate yourself. We have to conserve what resources we have, now that we're on our own."

"But what if I pass out again?"

"Honey, that was the effect of a sedative I gave you. One of the security guards said you looked panicked, so I gave you something to help you relax. But you're all better."

Gave me a sedative? Like Shay wasn't already feeling totally out of it, this woman thought it was a good idea to drug her? And "all better" seemed a long way off if sedatives were on the table as treatment. Unless this was all some ploy . . .

"Are you kicking me out?"

"We need the bed for people who are in recovery."

"But what about Preeti?"

"She'll stay for another twenty-four hours for observation, but then she can join you at the JCPenney."

Shay's mind raced. She would not be turned out into that madhouse. She would not be left alone to be crushed by the masses. Where was Marco? She began to cry. It was all she had left.

"Don't make me leave."

Jazmine squeezed her shoulder. "You're a strong girl," she said. "Things are safe out there now. I wouldn't send you into harm's way."

Shay did not trust this woman. Who was she, really, but a stranger who'd pretended to care, just like everyone else? Shay was just another body to be moved around. She had to find Marco. He would help her get Preeti out of here. He would help them find somewhere to hide.

Jazmine continued spouting her plans for Shay's release. "A guard will take you to the JCPenney if you want."

"No," Shay blurted. "I can do it." She would not get trapped by one of those lunatics with a Taser. She'd seen them blast people if any of their orders were contradicted.

Jazmine brushed off her pants. "If that's what you want." She walked to Preeti's bed and checked her over—pulse, temperature, blood pressure, lung sounds. "Your sister is doing just fine. You can come back and see her in the morning."

Shay was barely paying attention. She needed a plan. She was still wearing the T-shirt and jeans she'd stolen from H&M. Maybe her bag was under the bed?

Jazmine, as if reading her mind, handed her her bag. "What did I say this morning?"

Shay snatched the strap.

Jazmine grasped her shoulder. "I told you that you have to trust someone."

Shay nodded because that was what Jazmine wanted, but the woman was wrong. Shay would not trust anyone but herself. Who else could she really count on?

"Can I finish my food?" She needed some more time to come up with a strategy.

Jazmine sighed. "Take your time," she said. "I'll be back in an hour to check you out."

Good. An hour to plan her actions. She scooped the rest of the chicken mush into her mouth. She wasn't sure what food existed outside the med center; who knew when her next meal would be? She dumped out her bag and sorted the items: wallet, iPod, headphones, dead cell phone, contact solution and case, children's Tylenol . . .

The bottle stopped her brain cold. She'd last held it to Nani's lips in an attempt to drive back her fever. How deeply she'd failed Nani. What an idiot she'd been to think she could save her. What good were her plans, really? She'd screwed up everything, killed her grand-mother, nearly killed her sister. Better to just lie back and let the mall take her.

Preeti stirred. "Shaila?"

Shay froze, caught between the sadness inside, suck-ing her against the bed, weighing her body down, and the need to show her sister everything was okay.

"Shay?" Preeti's voice trembled. "Are you here?"

Jazmine was right about one thing: Shay had to be strong for Preeti. She sealed up the sadness like a sand-wich bag. *Poof!* The emptiness felt like joy.

Shay sat up. "I'm here."

Preeti, who hadn't even really been awake, rolled over. "Tell Mom I'm not going to school."

"Okay," Shay chirped. She stuffed all the crap back into her bag. Her hand stroked the smooth surface of the notebook, nestled amid the sheets. Did she even need it? She felt so clean inside. *Take it,* whispered the sadness. Shay slipped it into her bag.

■　■　■

Ryan tapped the pill bottle against his legs as he padded through the service halls back toward the Grill'n'Shake. At least he thought he was heading back to the Grill'n'Shake. Ryan tried to stick to the path Marco had taken, but all the halls looked alike and, without Marco's card, most doors were closed to him. He was beginning to consider the possibility that he was lost.

There were store names printed in block letters on some of the doors, but that information was of little use to Ryan. It's not like knowing he was outside the Candy Hut gave him a clue about where he was relative to the Grease'n'Suck. He wasn't a big mall person, not like other people. Funny, to go to the mall maybe five times in a year and end up getting quarantined on one of those visits. *Typical Murphy Luck.*

Ryan's older brother, Thad, had a theory about Murphy Luck. Murphy Luck was always to blame for an interception. Murphy Luck explained why Thad could drink a twelve-pack of light beer and not even get buzzed. Murphy Luck was why Dad was such a dick. The man couldn't even keep a one-day construction job without pissing someone off. Crap like getting lost in the service halls of a mall qualified as undeniable Murphy Luck.

Voices echoed from around the corner. Not wanting to find out if they belonged to security, Ryan pushed open the nearest exit door. It opened into the second-floor hallway next to the Sports Authority. Feeling like perhaps Murphy Luck had taken a time-out, and that he should not be in the hall, Ryan decided to upgrade from his crusty climbing clothes.

The store was empty—no salespeople, no shoppers, and most importantly, no insane looters with guns. Things seemed normal, like there had never been a riot. Were people really following the mall leader's orders?

Not that it mattered to Ryan. Mike had made the call that they were staying under the radar. Ryan was not going to rock the very small boat of protection he'd found in this hellhole, even if it meant also staying under the thumb of Marco. Mike had watched his back from minute one of this nightmare. Ryan owed it to him to stick with his plans. They were teammates, and a team was a powerful thing. He would find some way around the Marco-Shay situation.

He grabbed a pair of basketball shorts and a T-shirt, then decided, why stop there? They were obviously taking up residence in the place and might want a change of clothes. He grabbed a duffel and packed it with some T-shirts in his size, then a bunch larger for Mike and Drew, shorts, socks, and boxers. He went into the back to look for some sneakers.

As he rounded the corner of one floor-to-ceiling shelf, he discovered a person who'd not been as lucky with the flu. It was a man. Old. His dad's age. His face was bluish and blood had dried in thin trails from his nostrils. Puddles Ryan did not want to know the origins of pooled around his legs. He smelled terrible.

Ryan scrambled back to the other side of the shelf. His second dead body in as many days. Why was this happening to him? To any of them?

Forget about it. There was nothing he could do to help that guy or Mike or himself, any of them. Best to just forget about it. Move on. Find the sneakers and get the hell out of there.

He found a pair of sneakers in his size. The things cost two hundred dollars. In the real world, he couldn't have ever hoped to buy them. *Screw the Shops at Stonecliff.* The place owed him some freaking nice sneakers for all the crap he'd been through.

The coast was clear outside the store. Ryan heard voices down below, but just regular talking. He checked over the railing and saw people sitting on the floor with paper plates. There were dead bodies lying around and these people were at a goddamn block party. It was like bizarre-o-world.

The ground seemed to pull away, and Ryan felt a wave of nausea course through him. He found a bench and parked his ass on it.

He was not fully recovered from the flu. He pretended he was fine, but there was a constant ache in his muscles and his brain went fuzzy if he moved too fast. He should get back to the Grease'n'Suck. He waited for the nausea to subside, then shouldered the bag and tried to look as inconspicuous as possible.

There was no one on the third floor, so Ryan walked faster, nearly running into the Grill'n'Shake. The dining area was empty now. Ryan headed straight into the kitchens.

Mike and Drew were sitting beside a small pile of boxes overflowing with bags of defrosting chicken strips, crackers, and what appeared to be a handle of vodka.

"Looks like you've got all the food groups," he said, dropping the duffel.

Mike looked up. "What the hell took you so long?" He stood and grabbed the back of Ryan's head, pulling him into a hug. "You okay?"

Ryan shrugged him off. "Fine." Mike's caring was a little intense. "I'm not at death's door."

"You were at death's door, idiot." Mike shoved Ryan's head.

"I'm fine, really," he said, trying to ignore the throbbing Mike's jostling had ignited in his skull. "I got us some clothes."

Drew rifled through the duffel. "Packers!" He pulled out a jersey.

"What kind of crap are they selling in this mall?" Mike said, grabbing the bag.

It was the one point of dissention between Mike and Drew. Mike was a Giants guy and Drew had been raised a cheesehead like his dad. The only fight Ryan had seen between the two started when Mike in a drunken haze pissed on Drew's cheese-wedge hat. Drew had tackled him, busting a hole in his basement wall. The fight ended when Mike promised to not only buy a new hat, but to wear a Packers jersey for a week.

"Don't get your jocks in a twist," Ryan said, rubbing his temples. "There's something for everyone."

Mike dug out a Giants jersey and pulled it over his head. "Now we're in business."

"Jumbo Shrimp comes through in the clutch." Drew tugged on some new socks.

Ryan ducked into the bathroom to change and splash water on his face. He slurped some from his cupped hand, then examined himself in the mirror. He didn't look good.

Pale. Bags under the eyes. He'd bench himself. But this was no game. There was no bench to rest on.

When he came back, Marco had rejoined their crew and was skulking in the corner. He was smiling, but still looked pissed off. The guy was weird.

"Now that the whole gang's back together, let's mosey to our new quarters." Marco clapped his hands like this was some class trip.

Ryan was not ready to follow Marco blindly. "What did the senator want to see you about?"

Marco gritted his teeth. He had not wanted to share that particular tidbit with Mike, but it figured the douche wouldn't allow even that small lapse in information. Perhaps he'd twisted the knife too hard on the whole Shay issue.

"She asked me if I had a stolen card key. She'd seen me in a back hall during the riots. I was trying to save my friend's life." Marco looked purposefully at Ryan, who looked a bit peaked. "The senator was suspicious, so I gave her my old one from the Grill'n'Shake." It was a decent lie. The douche did not question him further and slogged over to a duffel bag.

Mike nodded. "Nice thinking."

"I thought so." Marco was impressed with himself. Everything was coming up Carvajal today. If you discounted the whole trapped-in-a-mall-with-a-deadly-virus thing.

The mall speakers squealed and announced the end of dinner in fifteen. "Please return to your Home Store for distribution of new clothes and toiletries."

Marco checked his watch. It was six forty-five, a little

early for curfew, if you asked him, but nobody was asking, so he'd better get this show on the road. "I have to get back before anyone cares that I'm gone."

"Calm down, Taco," Drew muttered, pushing himself to standing.

"Marco." Marco would not let that nickname back into their vocabulary.

"*Mar*-co."

The nickname had sounded kinder.

The Three Douches hefted their boxes of nutritionally dubious food and followed Marco into the service halls. Marco decided to risk the elevator—he was now a sanctioned mall employee of sorts; who was going to stop him? He led them down to the parking garage, then wove through the rows of cars to the far wall where he knew of a storage closet for cones and other parking-related crap.

The door to the room wasn't even locked, so Marco swung it open and was greeted with a cloud of stale air. He flipped on the light. The space was the size of a minivan and was empty save for a stack of cones and some sandwich board signs used for indicating that the lot was full.

"There's no window," Ryan said, poking his head through the doorway. "How are we supposed to breathe?"

Mike pushed past him into the space. "It's perfect. No one will bother us here."

"Glad I packed the vodka," Drew said, pulling the bottle from the box.

"I'll come back in the morning to check in," Marco said, dusting off his hands. He didn't want any residue from that hole following him up into the mall.

"What are we supposed to do for a bathroom?" Ryan's voice sounded squeaky, like he was about to cry. Marco would have liked to see that. He would have liked to record it for Shay. *Here's your big strong boyfriend* . . .

"The parking garage is your oyster," Marco said, waving a hand.

Mike grabbed Ryan by the shoulders. "We'll manage."

Mike held a hand out for Marco to shake.

Marco took it. "See you in the morning," he said, then shut the door on them for the night.

E
I
G
H
T

P.M.

exi had finished typing in the last entry when a
guard approached with a late arrival, fresh from the
med center.

"She's a riot intake, not flu," the guard said. This
diagnosis seemed hasty to Lexi. The girl did not look well.

"Shaila Dixit," she mumbled, eyes bloodshot and scanning the inside of the JCPenney as if ready to run at the
least provocation.

Even through the mist of sick and crazy the girl was
giving off, Lexi could tell she was gorgeous. Much prettier
than Lexi. But wasn't everyone?

"I can't really check people in," Lexi said. "There's a
guard."

"I'm not waiting," the guard said, and left.

The girl kept sweeping the room with her eyes.

"I guess I can just tell him when he gets back," Lexi
offered.

The girl glanced at her. "It looks safe," she said. "Is it safe?"

Lexi shrugged. "Compared to what? We're in a mall with a lethal virus."

The girl was not amused. "What do I do? Just find somewhere to sleep?"

Lexi checked the list. The guard had left his clipboard on the counter when he went to the bathroom. Maddie had said she had to go too, and would he show her where they were? That had been like a half hour ago. It did not take much imagination to picture what had caused the intervening delay. The guard had been on the "youngish and cutish side"—Maddie's words.

"You're cot number fifteen-twenty. That means first floor. Look for a cot with a five-twenty on it." Lexi reached under the counter, where perfumes had once been stored, by the smell of it. "Here's a nightgown."

The girl took what looked like a nightie Laura Ingalls Wilder would have donned on the prairie.

"And here's some soap, hand sanitizer, a mask, and I think a toothbrush?" Lexi passed a plastic bag across the glass.

"Thanks," the girl mumbled, taking the items and stuffing them into her shoulder bag. She all but tiptoed into the store, head turning this way and that, as if watching for ghosts haunting the empty cosmetics counters. For all Lexi knew, they were—who knew how many had died in this very spot?

The question having been posed, Lexi realized she now possessed the power to answer it. In front of her, on her laptop, was a database of the entire population of the mall. Her father had set up an intranet linking Lexi's laptop with a server in the mall offices. He had entered all the names from the med center himself instead of letting Lexi do it—some lame attempt at preserving people's privacy or something. All she had to do was run a search for all the entries that had not been checked in to one of the Home Stores or the medical center and she would get—one thousand five hundred and thirty-five.

ONE THOUSAND FIVE HUNDRED AND THIRTY-FIVE?

Her father must not have finished entering his names. No way there were over one thousand dead. First of all, where would the Senator have put them?

Maddie trotted back to the counter. "What'd I miss?" Her shirt was disheveled. Her cheeks were flushed. Her face mask hung like a necklace around her neck.

"You know, my mom made an announcement about minimizing contact to prevent the spread of disease." Lexi canceled her search, erasing the impossible number.

Maddie poked her in the arm. "But I already *had* the disease, so that rule totally does not apply to *moi*." She winked at the guard as he passed to begin shutting the security gates.

Lexi rolled her eyes and closed the laptop. "I'm going to check on our new home."

Maddie brushed her hands over her shirt. "Excellent. I want to use the bathroom." She replaced her mask.

"You just came from the bathroom."

"Oh," she said. "Right." She laughed. No, cackled. Lexi was not sure how to respond, so she kept silent.

Their cots were on the second floor in what had been an evening gown display. Lexi had pulled rank and gotten them these digs. The area was a small bubble off the main floor, offering them an iota of privacy, something the rest of the floor lacked. There were two other cots in the space, both occupied by older women who were already prone and staring at the ceiling.

Lexi had left her assigned Ziploc bag and pajamas on the cot closest to the wall. Maddie had moved both one cot over, giving herself the cot next to the wall.

"You moved my stuff," Lexi said.

"Is that okay?" Maddie asked. She grabbed her stuff and sashayed out of the bubble.

It was okay, Lexi guessed. But Maddie should have asked. Maybe she'd thought it was someone else's stuff? No, Maddie had seen Lexi's assigned paisley boxer pj's after dinner check-in. *Whatever.* It didn't matter. One cot was as good as the next. And it was better than sleeping with her parents in the mall offices. That was the message the Senator had relayed after dinner via the guard's walkie-talkie. "Please ask my daughter if she would please sleep up here with her parents." Just the words every girl longs to hear. She told the guard to reply in the negative.

Lexi grabbed her stuff and headed for the dressing rooms. There were lines for the bathroom and she wanted out of this hairy nightmare sweater ASAP.

Shay sat on the cot marked 520. There were far too many people in this room. The nearest cot was a mere foot away and the woman on it was already snoring.

The guard had closed the security gate over the exit to the rest of the mall. Was this supposed to make her feel safe? She felt trapped, caged. There was no running back into the mall through the front entrance. To escape, she was going to have to go out the back.

As if to emphasize the prison aspect, a security guard stalked by her cot, stun baton swinging beside his leg and Taser in its holster. There were only a few guards. After Lights Out, it wouldn't be hard to sneak by them. Shay tried to memorize the path from her cot to the stockroom door. Once she was in the stockroom, she could use her key-light to find the service door. After that, she was home free. She would fetch Preeti from the med center under cover of darkness and then hide out in a nearby stationery store until morning, at which point she would find Marco and they would hole up in some back-room fortress until the government decided to open the doors.

Now the only difficulty was the waiting. She did not know how long she had until Lights Out. How to kill the time? She went to the bathroom and brushed her teeth. Some other women were washing with wet paper towels, splashing water over their faces and hair. Shay decided to follow suit. She bent over her sink and tried to get her hair under the faucet.

"It's easier if you use your Ziploc bag like a bucket," the woman next to her said. "If you want, you can use mine." She held out her plastic bag.

The woman had a nice face. She looked old, but not Nani old.

"Thanks," Shay managed, and took the bag.

The woman returned to running her fingers through her mane of brown hair. Shay wondered if the bag was okay—was the woman infected? It was too late now. Shay filled the bag, added some soap, and doused herself, then passed it back to the woman. Only afterward did she real-ize that she'd failed to remove her T-shirt, the top quarter of which was now soaked. She would have to change into the wretched nightgown she'd been given: red plaid with small blue flowers and a lace-trim collar. It fit her about as well as a garbage bag and was only slightly more comfort-able. The fabric was a weird polyester that crinkled with her every motion. She left her jeans and boots on.

Another fifteen minutes were consumed in the finger-combing and braiding of her hair. Shay contemplated hacking the mess off, but the mere idea of losing her hair brought tears to her eyes. She found a stray elastic in her bag and wrapped it around the end of the braid.

The lights still glared down at her. There was more time left to kill.

The notebook found its way into her hands. She flipped it open. She clicked the pen light on and off, on and off. No words came. Normally, she couldn't write fast enough, the words poured so rapidly from her brain. Nothing. She put the pen tip on the page, wondering if mere proximity would inspire, but no. Still nothing. Her words had died.

She closed the journal and dropped onto the cot, which was a mistake, as the thing was barely softer than the cement floor. Her head throbbed. She closed her eyes and concentrated on the pain. At least in it there was some-thing to hold on to.

"Pass the crackers," Ryan said into the black. Mike had ordered the lights be left off to keep their hiding place inconspicuous.

A bag hit him in the side of the head.

"Nice aim," he grumbled, rubbing his cheek. His head could not withstand much more abuse.

"I am like a freaking laser guided missile, J.S.," Drew said from somewhere off to Ryan's right. He sounded drunk. Ryan wondered how many handles of vodka the two had stowed away and whether there was anything of a non-alcoholic variety available. He was not going to risk a flu relapse by getting hammered.

Munching stale saltines, Ryan contemplated his options for reconnecting with Shay. He could sneak out tomorrow during a bathroom break and try to locate her in the med center again. Maybe just seeing him would be enough to bust up whatever she had going with Marco. Taco had said she'd come to him for help. *I can help her now.*

The thought made him laugh. How could he help anyone from a dark closet in the parking garage? And what, was he going to propose that she live with the three of them in this tomb? He wasn't even sure he'd make it through the night. The floor was cold and kind of wet, and the air smelled of exhaust fumes and was thick with dust.

Plus, would Marco retaliate if Ryan made a move for her? Not like things could get much crappier. He could move them to an even dirtier hole in the parking garage, but Ryan doubted such a place existed. He could rat them out to security, but if he hadn't done that already, it seemed unlikely. Mike had mentioned something about them watching out for Marco. Maybe the weasel needed them more than he needed to keep Ryan away from Shay.

Ryan's brain throbbed. He was not known for his strategizing skills off the field. Ryan's plan was just to be nice enough to people, to pass his classes, and generally not make any waves outside of the football arena. Mike was the guy who was always running some scheme. Maybe he could help with Shay?

It would have to wait. Ryan's head was killing him. He pulled the pill bottle from his pocket and decided to take two. Whatever they were, they had to help. His head couldn't feel any worse.

"I need a drink," Ryan said, palming the pills.

"I've got a bottle of joy juice with your name on it." Mike's voice sounded like it was coming from the floor. Was he already flat-on-his-back drunk?

"Anything of the less flammable variety?"

"You can't light vodka," Drew mumbled, like Ryan was such an idiot for not knowing this.

"Water," he said, growing more tired of this stupid plan by the second. "Do we have any water?"

"You need Bacardi 151, something serious," Drew continued.

"Shut up," Mike drawled. "Any drink you make, I can light it. You just have to hold the freaking lighter over the glass for more than two seconds."

"Like you know anything."

"Like *you* know anything."

Ryan slapped the pills into his mouth and choked them down with spit alone. He curled up on the gross floor, head on his duffel, and prayed that whatever he'd just taken didn't kill him. This could not be how he lived for the rest of his potentially shortened life. There had to be a Plan B. Plan A sucked.

■　■　■

The line for the bathroom was no shorter when Lexi emerged from the dressing rooms in her boxers and T-shirt. It snaked around the perimeter of the sales floor. The women in line chatted with those seated on cots. Everyone seemed happy, some even laughed, like it was okay to joke around again. The mall, well, the JCPenney felt safe. Like no one would leave a girl trapped under a corpse beneath a pile of garbage ever again.

Even with all the women using it, the bathroom was relatively clean. One girl tossed her paper towel into the trash only to miss. Instead of walking away, she trotted over and put the crumpled sheet into the bin. It was like people cared again. Had Lexi's mom actually pulled this thing off?

"Hi."

Lexi had just splashed water on her face, so it took a second for her to wipe her skin dry and address the person belonging to the voice. She knew who it was, though. It was undoubtedly Ginger Franklin's tremulous warble.

"I'm so glad you're okay." Ginger twisted a strand of her hair around a finger.

Ginger had a bruise on her cheek. Lexi did not really care how she got it.

"No thanks to you," Lexi said.

Ginger looked like she was tearing up. *Good.*

"I'm really sorry," Ginger said. "I was just so scared. I don't want to die in here."

"Really? Because everyone else is totally lining up for the chance to kick it in the Gap."

"I suck, I know it. What can I do to make it up to you?"

"Go away." Lexi turned back to the mirror and dug the mini toothbrush out of her bag.

Ginger wiped her eyes with her hand. "I never took you for a mean girl," Ginger said.

"No, you only took me for a loser you could use and then abandon."

"I never took you for a loser." Ginger disappeared from Lexi's mirror.

Lexi didn't need Ginger. Ginger had bailed when Lexi needed her most. When her supposed best friend needed her most. Friends like that were no friends at all. Still, Lexi felt like a jerk. She wasn't used to being pissed off at anyone except her mom. Her computer nerd friends, or friend, really—Darren and her, they never fought.

Lexi allowed herself to wish Darren were here. Yes, it was kind of a death sentence, but it would have been great to have had one of her people stuck in here with her. Darren would have been the perfect partner for spying on the Senator. Darren would never have ruined everything by calling his dad and starting a riot outside the mall.

Lexi finished brushing her teeth. The fantasy swirled down the drain with her spit. She was trapped in here with one friend who was kind of a bitch and another who was no friend at all. *Welcome to your life.*

Back at the cots, Maddie was flipping through a magazine.

"They came by with books and stuff," she said. "I got us a *Cosmo* and *Us Weekly*." She waved two magazines. "Can I take *Us Weekly*?" It was the one she had in her hands. Lexi nodded.

Maddie went back to reading. "It's a week old," she groaned. "I already knew about this breakup."

Lexi had never even flipped through a *Cosmo* before. There were lots of skinny white girls in clothes that looked less comfortable than the sweater from hell Lexi had spent the day trapped inside. These were not her people.

"I'm going to walk around."

"Let me know if you find a copy of *Lucky*."

What in the name of jeebus was *Lucky*? "Roger that," Lexi mumbled, and made for the stockroom.

LIGHTS OUT

At ten, the lights went black. All of them. The men around Marco grunted—"Hey!" "What the hell?"—and the shrieks of women could be heard from the JCPenney down the hall. The mall speakers bleeped and the not-quite-reassuring voice of the senator apologized and ordered that some lights be left on for safety's sake. Within five minutes, a fluorescent light buzzed to life somewhere behind Marco's head.

Marco had preferred the black. He had covert ops to run. Light just made everything that much more difficult.

After storing The Douche Corps in the parking garage, Marco had signed in to the Lord & Taylor, which was where all the unaccompanied men were supposed to live together peacefully. Whoever devised this plan had clearly never been to an all-boys camp. Some total dick had pissed all over the seat of the john Marco had gotten stuck with, and in the time he'd taken to do the round-trip tour through the facilities, some asshole had stolen his pillow. At least no one had crapped in his cot.

Marco had gone to camp. Once. His parents had signed him up for a community day camp one week, at the end of which all the campers went on an overnight to Bear Mountain State Park. Marco was supposed to share a tent with one of the other kids, but some false claims were made about Marco's sexual orientation, which prompted the boy to abandon Marco after lights-out to bunk with his friends in another tent. Marco's solo enclosure was excreted upon at random intervals throughout the night. He listened to the sound of piss spattering on his tent and prayed that the walls truly were waterproof. After each golden shower, there was an explosion of laughter from the other tent signaling the piddler's return to his partners in pee.

He'd cried. Not like anyone was there to call him a pussy over it. In the morning he packed the tent in its bag, then washed his hands over and over, never really feeling clean. When the bus dropped him off, he informed his parents that he hated camp and didn't ever want to go again. Money always being an issue anyway, the funds were never again wasted on summer programs.

At least this time, it didn't matter. He would not be at the mercy of these assholes. He had the key to the entire mall. And he was out of here the second that security guard cleared the area.

Shay was beginning to regret her plan. Here she was, in some back hallway behind the JCPenney, and there were no lights except the tiny LED on her key and the glowing red of a distant exit sign. Voices echoed down the hall, from where, Shay was not sure, but they scared her. She did not like being alone in this hallway, and definitely did not like the idea of *not* being alone in the hallway.

Stumbling forward, Shay kept one hand on the wall, the other waving the small light back and forth across the ground in front of her. Knobs on pipes winked at her. Her hand dropped into a doorway and she staggered, falling against the metal door. She fumbled her key ring, which clattered into the black below.

Shay knelt on trembling legs and patted the cement. The echoes were closer now. Or were they simply coming from the other direction?

Her hand hit something soft, not keys. Shay dared to let her fingers explore the softness. It felt like jeans. Something groaned. Then claws clasped her wrist.

Shay screamed, punched and kicked the softness, which groaned again and let go.

"Help," it may have said.

Once freed, she thrust herself away, hit the opposite wall, then clambered to her feet. Running blind through the dark, Shay took whatever turns the hall presented; she just needed to be away from whatever had groaned. Visions of Nani's blackened, gaunt, dead face, eyes glistening, flashed in the darkness. She ran from the visions, had to escape these ghosts. *Exit.* She needed an exit.

Red signs were her only guide. EXIT. EXIT. Her hands slammed into a dead end. From the cold and the corrugation, Shay guessed it was a sealed-over freight delivery door.

Shay banged on the metal. *Let me out!* she screamed in her mind, afraid if she spoke in real life, the echoes would materialize into people. That the ghosts would be real.

The freight door didn't give when she struck it. All the doors from the mall to the world must have been sealed over with concrete, permanently shut. She would die in this place. All of them were being left to die in this place.

Marco rolled off his cot and crawled down the narrow aisle to the far wall. He traveled light, just his card key, wallet, and iPod—no way he was getting rid of it, even though without Internet or a charger cord, once the battery died, it would be dead weight. He'd never changed into the boxers and shirt he'd been given to sleep in—like he was going to go nighty-night amidst that pack of wolves? *Hells to the no.*

He made it to the nearest stockroom door and slipped through it unnoticed. There were no lights on. The place smelled weird. Then Marco saw a lighter flash in a far corner. *So this is where the party's starting.* Marco had wondered how people would take going from complete freedom to incarceration. Apparently, incarceration had won out for a few hours and now the natives were restless. He was glad to be getting out while the getting was good.

The door to the service hallways was thankfully closer to him than to the lighter flame, so he escaped without incident. Alas, the halls were dark, which made everything suck that much more. Marco groped along the passage, hoping to find an exit before something found him.

No such luck. Footsteps slapped toward him. Then arms slammed into his back.

"Out of the way, loser!" a voice cackled, tearing past Marco.

Okay, maybe this was worse than the Lord & Taylor. At least there were a few security guards in the Lord & Taylor.

As Marco weighed the pros and cons of returning to the at least semi-policed chaos of the men's Home Store, a familiar voice echoed down the passage to his right.

"Help," Shay whispered. "Someone? Help."

Marco ran through the black toward her voice. What the hell was she doing here? Shouldn't she be in the med center? She had a serious head injury!

He turned a corner and heard a door rattle. Marco dashed toward the noise and ran smack into Shay. She screamed and Marco jumped back.

"Shay, it's me! It's Marco!"

She burst into tears and threw her arms around him.

He stroked her hair. "You're okay," he whispered. "I'm here. You're safe." He was not sure why he said this. Like he could protect her from anything.

Her body went limp, as if her bones had evaporated. "I'm so scared," she whispered.

"Let's get you back to the med center."

"Kicked me out," Shay mumbled.

"Then the JCPenney," Marco said, assuming she had been thrown in with the rest of the *chicas*.

Shay nodded against his chest.

Marco used his iPod as a light, flashing it for brief moments to find landmarks—a name on a door, a corner— and managed to wind his way through stockrooms and passages to a door marked JCPENNEY. Shay clung to him like she couldn't take a step without support.

"Why did they kick you out?" he asked, trying to take her mind off whatever had happened to her in the tunnel before he found her. He prayed it was just the dark. If it was something worse, he would find whoever hurt her and kill the bastard.

"No room," she said, her voice barely hissing beyond her teeth. "I'm all alone in there."

Marco slid his card through the reader and opened the door. "It's safer in here," he said, leading her into the stockroom. "Just stay the night, and tomorrow, I'll find us someplace to hide."

She nuzzled closer to him. Warmth flared over his skin.

"And Preeti?" she managed. "We have to protect her."

Marco stopped in front of the door leading to the sales floor. "And Preeti. I am going to take care of you both." He liked saying the words. It was as if by saying them, they could be true. A dream blinked into his brain, him and Shay and Preeti hiding out in a stockroom, all the food they needed, no one bothering them, safe until whenever this nightmare ended. Him and Shay. Together.

Shay leaned her head against the door frame. "'Til tomorrow, then," she said.

Marco, unable to control his lips, leaned forward and pressed them to her forehead.

Shay stiffened. "Please," she said, pushing him away. "I can't."

And a part of Marco seethed. *She can't with me.* But the better part won out.

"Okay," he said, pulling back. "I'm sorry."

"I'll see you tomorrow?" Shay said, smiling.

"I'll find you after Lights On."

Shay nodded and slipped back into the neat, quiet rows of sleepers.

Marco tracked back to the service door only to hear voices on the opposite side. Not wanting to risk another encounter in the black, he padded to the opposite side of the stockroom. There were several different large rooms back here, all of them stuffed with the original contents of the sales floors. Sequins sparkled in his dim light, and his pants caught on errant hangers and poles from the haphazardly disposed-of racks.

Lexi sat on a desk in an office of some sort. She'd wandered after leaving Maddie and found her way into the stockrooms. When Lights Out was announced, she'd stumbled into this office, closed the door, and flipped on the light. Searching the room, she came upon two significant prizes: (1) an old CD player with a cache of not-too-terrible CDs, and (2) a bag of peanut M&M'S. Satisfied this was the best the place had to offer, she'd turned the lights off and enjoyed her feast with a Beatles accompaniment playing softly. She was halfway through *Revolver* and had two M&M'S left when someone slammed into the other side of the wall against which she was leaning.

Unable to leave well enough alone, Lexi slid off the desk and tiptoed to the door. Peeking outside, under the dim light of the one bulb left burning in the stockroom, she saw a boy wrestling with a display rack.

And not just any boy. A lanky, nerdy-looking guy. And judging from the amount of space he'd covered before becoming ensnared in the racks, at home enough in the dark that he probably spent too much time indoors, perhaps playing video games; this was his element. This was also Lexi's element. This boy was her people.

She suddenly wished she was back in Maddie's outfit. She wanted to look hot for this guy, even if it meant breaking out in a sweater-induced mega-rash.

What would Maddie do? Say something flirty, be confident.

"I think you won," Lexi said.

The guy gave his cargo pants one final jerk and freed himself from the wretched rack. Looking up, he squinted at her, then smiled—he wasn't wearing a mask. *Does that smile mean he likes what he sees?*

"I would hope I'd have the advantage over a clothes hanger," he said.

Lexi liked his face. It wasn't model-nice, but wasn't bad, either. "Don't get cocky," she said. "I had my money on the rack for a few seconds."

"The thing did rip my cargo pants," he said. "I guess we'll call it a draw."

Lexi didn't get a slick vibe from him. He wasn't giving her a line. Sarcasm was his normal mode. It was also Lexi's. She kind of didn't want him to go. "So what brings you to the JCPenney after Lights Out? Did a girlfriend let you in?" She might as well find that out now.

He considered his answer a moment longer than Lexi would have liked.

"A friend who is a girl let me in," he said. "We have been helping each other out and she asked me to check on her. She was scared to be separated."

Lexi did not buy this excuse. How did they know when to meet? It was a long time after Lights Out. And how did he find his way through the service hallways to get from the Lord & Taylor to here? And why lie to her?

"That smells like a load of crap, but whatever. I don't really care. Go on with your operation." She let him hang on that line, turned and went back into her office.

He followed her. "Is this your room?" he asked, flipping on the light.

Lexi couldn't help but smile that he'd followed. "It is now," she said, hopping onto her desk. She held out the last two M&M'S. "Want one?"

"Thanks," he said, and popped it into his mouth. He chewed slowly, luxuriously.

Lexi slid the yellow M&M between her lips. If neither of them could speak, then he couldn't leave. The candy was gone all too quickly. "You going to tell me the truth now?" she said, trying to keep up her confident front. "Like what you're really doing in the back of the JCPenney after eleven on a Saturday. I mean, the place closes at nine according to the sign on the door."

He laughed. "You got me. I'm into women's clothing and needed to stock up on evening wear for the Halloween drag ball."

Lexi had completely forgotten about Halloween. How sad was that? Not that she dressed up. She and Darren hadn't dressed up in years. No, they liked to hide in the bushes outside his house and scare the crap out of the little trick-or-treaters (obviously the Senator allowed no pranks to be played on her government-funded lawn).

"I'm just kidding," he added.

Lexi came back into the present. "Sorry," she said. "Very funny. I just had forgotten about Halloween. Weird how it feels like time should have stopped, like the world should be on pause until we're out of here."

"Yeah," he said.

Had she said something wrong? He had withdrawn into himself, shrunken like a raisin. "I'm Lexi," she said, wanting to bring him back.

"Marco," he said, then seemed to regret it.

There was a knock at the door. They looked at each other. Lexi kicked out the desk chair and Marco dove into the darkness under the desk. Lexi dragged the chair back with her feet as the door opened.

"What are you doing back here?" the guard said. He glanced around, suspicious.

Lexi weighed playing dumb against pulling the mom card. She decided on the mom card. "I'm the Senator's daughter."

"Oh," the guard said. He seemed to weigh options himself. "You can't be back here after Lights Out."

Lexi slid off the desk. "Oh, okay," she said. "My mom had said I could take a break back here if I needed to."

"I never heard about that."

"I guess she forgot to tell people," Lexi said, walking toward the door, opening it for the guard. "I'll be back here every night after Lights Out." She hoped Marco got her message—*I'm here if you want to hang out*. However he'd gotten in here, she felt pretty sure he could get in again.

The guard took the door and held it open for her. Lexi walked through, wishing she could have said good-bye. But really, where was Marco going to go? They were trapped in here. She would see him again. The thought brought a smile to her lips.

Maddie was still awake when Lexi returned to the cot.

"Where have you been? I'm wired and there's nothing to do."

"I found a boy in the stockroom," Lexi said, unable to keep it to herself. She'd met a *boy*.

Maddie was all ears at the mention of boys. "Are you telling me there's a party in the stockroom and you are just letting me in on it now?"

"*A* boy, singular." Lexi stretched out on the cot, hands behind her head. "And he wasn't your type."

"At this point," Maddie mumbled, flopping back on her pillow, "any boy is my type."

"Well, he's gone now. And we just talked."

"What a waste."

It hadn't been a waste. Lexi would find him again. He was her people. She'd finally found her people.

Marco waited five minutes before crawling out from under the desk. He crept to the door and cracked it open. With only the one lit bulb, it was hard to know if the coast was clear, but he needed to get out of there, so he just ran for it.

"I knew she wasn't alone in there." The guard emerged from the shadows.

Before Marco had a chance to utter a syllable, the guy fired the Taser and a jolt like fire in the blood sent Marco into a swirl of darkness.

DAY

EIGHT

LIGHTS ON

Lexi had just finished brushing her teeth when an announcement beckoned her to the mall offices.

Maddie, who stood at the next sink, splashed water at her. "Uh-oh," she said, miming concern, "did Mommy Dearest find out about your new boyfriend?"

Lexi froze. *Supercrapafragilistic.*

"Hello, I'm joking," Maddie said, drying her hands on her shirt. "Breathe."

Lexi took a breath. "My mom and I have issues." Like that began to cover the minefield that was Lexi's relationship with the Senator.

"Join the club," Maddie said. "See you at break-slop?"

Lexi groaned thinking of her first freeze-dried slurry meal. "I guess."

She had to ask where exactly the mall offices were, but once inside, she knew where her mother's office was located. The Senator's screaming voice emanated from the room at the end of the hall.

"I said I did not want a police state!" she barked. "We need to develop trust and you have your men out Tasering every breathing body they find!"

A guy who looked to have gorged too often on the potato chips sat opposite her mother. His arms were crossed over his broad chest and his face looked like a cartoon of a face, all round and red with beady eyes under bushy brows. He cleared his throat before responding.

"You have a rat problem, Senator," he grumbled. "And you have to put rats in cages."

"They're kids, Hank," her mother said, "not rodents. I want them to fall into line and your policy is not helping with that goal."

Hank put his hands on his thighs and pushed himself to standing. "It's your call," he said, "but you invite rats to dinner, you can't complain when they sh—" He noticed Lexi in the doorway. ". . . crap all over the carpet."

The Senator waved Lexi toward her. Lexi obliged, and even let her mother kiss the side of her head. "Good morning, sweetheart," Dotty said, her voice sounding tired. Her mother's eyes looked bruised. *When was the last time she got any sleep?*

"You called for me?" Lexi said.

"I need you to go with Hank to check in all the young people his team collected last night." The Senator handed Lexi a laptop bag. "Your father hasn't trained anyone on the system yet and he can't type as fast with only the one arm."

Lexi glanced at Hank. He was giving her the once-over

too, and did not look that impressed. Lexi straightened herself and put on her serious face.

"Sure," she said, "no problem."

"She needs clothes," Hank said. "That shirt is see-through."

Lexi hugged the laptop to her chest. *If the shirt is see-through, that means the guy last night might have seen . . .* How many times in one week can you wish yourself deleted from the universe?

"Here," Dotty said, handing Lexi a hoodie. "Put this on and get going."

Lexi kissed her mother, not caring that this was the first time she'd done so in weeks—she was that grateful for the sweatshirt. She tugged it on, zipped it up, and pushed past Hank into the hallway.

Marco was kicked awake by a passing boot. He coughed, then fished a splinter of wood from his mouth—how that had gotten in there, he did not want to know. Patting down his clothing, he found that his person was unmolested. More importantly, the universal card key was still safe in his pocket. Perhaps that was the best he could hope for considering with whom he'd been sharing a cell.

He'd spent a miserable night in the old med center/ PaperClips surrounded by just the sorts of people you'd expect to find in the drunk tank of a local lockup. There were a few older guys, most looking wary of their fellow inmates, but by far the majority of this crowd was teens and college-aged kids, grouped according to clothing type: goths in black pleather, jocks in jerseys, would-be ganstas in baggy shorts with 'do rags on their heads. All kids Marco would have hated had they met at school—he could tell just by the looks they gave him.

He curled his knees in and sat pressed against the wall. He figured if he made himself small, he'd stay off people's radar. The room felt like the Thunderdome—they'd all entered, but only one would leave.

If this was what he'd face in the service halls every night, he needed to rethink his entire plan. He needed Mike with him at all times to defend against these dickheads. But how to convince paranoid Mike to leave his nice little bunker in the garage?

"Get up, people!"

The heavyset guy from yesterday in the senator's office pushed through the double doors from the stockroom. Behind him were two guards in full riot gear and the senator's kid. *Lexi.*

"I am chief of security Hank Goldman. I need to confirm that all of you are registered, and then escort you in groups back to your Home Stores for assignments." He pointed a finger at the exterior wall. "Get your backs against the glass and we can start this process."

"Or what?" some idiot shouted.

"I will personally beat the living crap out of any troublemakers."

As if hoping to serve as an example, two goth kids rushed the four of them. Hank smacked the first in the chest with a nightstick, then smacked the second in the back of the head with it on the downswing.

"Any more of you assholes want to test my resolve?"

Apparently not. Everyone shuffled toward the wall and formed a single-file line. The goth kids were left unconscious on the cement. Marco stepped over them as he approached the table.

"Marco Carvajal," he said, looking purposefully at the daughter.

Lexi glanced up, then back at the screen. She seemed to be blushing. Did she regret sharing the M&M'S?

"I'm so sorry," she said.

"It's not your fault I got nabbed." She seemed genuinely ashamed. Could he use this guilt to some advantage? Perhaps she could be useful in solving his Mike problem. Perhaps she could feed ideas to her mother . . . *Check and mate.*

"You're already registered," Lexi said, distracted. Then she swallowed. "I still feel bad you ended up in here"— she nodded her head at the line—"with *them.*"

"Oh, these gentlemen were charming bunkmates," he said. Marco tried to glance over the top of the computer to see his file. Just what did Lexi know about him?

"Any of them you want me to send to bathroom cleaning duty?" Lexi waggled her eyebrows, then blushed deeper, as if horrified by her own eyebrows.

Hank stepped forward. "Is there a problem with this one?"

Lexi closed the laptop. "Nope, everything's fine. Next!"

Marco gave her a two-finger salute and joined the guard who was waiting to lead him back to the Lord & Taylor. He hadn't gotten a peek at his file, but he doubted the senator would put their little deal on the books. It was safe to assume Lexi was in the dark. He could play her like a goddamn n00b.

■   ■   ■

Shay appreciated the regimented schedule the new mall order imposed on her. If every fifteen minutes there was another announcement telling her to use the facilities before breakfast, or to line up for breakfast, or to finish breakfast so that she could line up to receive her work assignment, there was little time in between to dwell on the fact that she could not scrape the image of Nani's blackened, bloodshot face stuck through with tubes off the inside of her brain.

There were other distractions too, like the fact that her frontier-woman nightshirt itched like a scab and she had to pretend with every bite that she was eating oatmeal and not the "Southwestern Omelet" the guard claimed he was scooping onto her plate. There were all the people jostling for places to sit around the first-floor courtyards, and all those germ-ridden bodies made her break out in cold sweats. So much to worry about. She had barely enough time to obsess over her misery.

But what was she so miserable about? She was one of the *survivors*. Everyone around her was muttering about this. They had survived. Life was a gift. Each day was so precious. Shay tried to agree with them when they looked at her, bobbed her head as was expected, said, *Yes, a blessing,* when it looked like they needed more. She ate her "Southwestern Omelet" because that's what you did when you were alive: eat, breathe, sleep, wake.

She snaked through the line toward the registration table at the entrance of the JCPenney. There were security guards everywhere. A man who was caught without his mask was yelled at until he tugged it on. Two teens caught holding hands were pulled apart and reminded of the ban on non-necessary touching. Was this really living?

"Name?" the guard said when she reached the table. He now had a laptop instead of a clipboard and sheet of paper.

"Shaila Dixit," Shay mumbled.

"Spell that, please," the guy said.

She gave him the letter-by-letter, and he informed her that she'd been assigned to supervise at the school, which had once been Baxter's Books.

"Supervise?" Shay was confused. She was a student herself.

"Everyone over the age of fourteen gets a job," he said. "There won't be new clothes until lunch, so just head up to Baxter's now."

Shay did as she was told. A few of the escalators were back online, so she only had to tromp up one flight of steps to reach the third floor. There was a guard standing at the information desk to Baxter's.

"Student or teacher?" he asked.

Shay wondered whether the fact that he couldn't tell spelled doom for her tenure at the school. "Teacher," she replied.

"Movies." The guard nodded toward the CD and DVD section of the store.

Inside the walled-off area were some other kids around her age, but most people there looked like grandparents. One harried-looking woman with blond hair and cat's-eye glasses stood in a corner sifting papers from a stack in her arms into piles. Instinctively, Shay wandered over to her.

"Can I help?"

The woman glanced up. "Yes!" she gasped, dumping a

load of paper into Shay's arms. "I'm Alison Chase, director of this whole school experiment."

"Experiment?"

"God knows if this thing is going to work," Alison muttered, sweeping a stray lock behind her ear.

She asked Shay to finish collating the stack, then shuffled over to where she'd piled books into different groups. Perhaps due to Shay's example, some other people approached her and offered to help sort the books. A tiny flicker of warmth sprouted in Shay's chest. She had done something good.

Just as Shay sorted the last page into its pile, Alison clapped her hands for everyone's attention. She introduced herself, then began explaining what they were all doing there.

"I was asked by the senator to help organize a school for the young children with us here in the mall. I am the head of a private elementary school, and thus have some experience with this kind of thing. Still, we are operating by the seat of our pants. I am going to assign you into teams of two, and give each team five to ten children." She pointed to Shay. "This young woman is standing next to the packets I've put together for each team. Hopefully the instructions contained therein will help you manage your charges. Then again, I wrote it in the wee hours last night, so no guarantees."

Some people laughed in response. Shay glanced at the pages, becoming more nervous with the woman's every word. Who thought it was a good idea to put her in charge of anyone, let alone *children*?

Alison answered her question as if reading her mind.

"You were all selected for this job based on what little we know about you—either you have a child or younger sibling here in the mall with you, or you indicated that you were a teacher, camp counselor, or babysitter at some point in your registration. Our main job is to keep the children happy. Any ideas you have for how to accomplish this, please bring them to me. I am open to any suggestions. We basically have the entire mall at our disposal.

"I figure that the older children might respond to some sort of academics, so I've put the teachers and parents in charge of them. For the younger kids, I planned that the teams would take them to the food court, which needs to be cleared of tables and chairs. We can use it as a big field, and we have the two rides that the kids can play on.

"Unfortunately, this is as far as I've gotten with the planning. Again, please come to me with any suggestions. I really appreciate your helping to take care of these kids."

She began to read off the teams. Shay picked up a packet of paper and flipped through the paragraphs. The instructions seemed highly vague.

"Shaila Dixit and Kristian Olivier. Five-year-old Group C."

Five-year-olds? What was she supposed to do with a five-year-old? Did they use diapers? She hadn't changed a diaper . . . ever.

A guy who appeared to be around twenty-five walked toward her. "Hi, I'm Kris," he said, holding out a hand.

"Shay," she said, handing him the papers. "I think you should be in charge."

"Because of my evident charm and wit? Or was it my spectacular outfit that gave my leadership credentials away?" He tugged on his T-shirt, which featured Tweety Bird giving the finger.

Shay smiled despite herself. "Because anyone is better than me."

"Let's not get ahead of ourselves," he said. "I mean, I'm an actor-type. Known shady element of society."

"You're an actor?" Shay found herself interested— she hadn't thought anything would be interesting ever again. "I was Titania in my old school's production of *A Midsummer Night's Dream*."

"You've been a fairy queen and claim to have no leadership skills? Oh, modesty. For shame!" He swept a hand against his forehead. Then he bowed deeply. "Way back in high school, I played that 'merry wanderer of the night' Puck, my lady."

Shay felt giddy. She tried to recall a single line from the play, from anything, from Tagore even, and failed. "So what makes you a good teacher?"

"I run an after-school theater program at Alison's school. You know, after all-day auditions and answering all the fan mail and before I escape to Broadway for curtain call, etcetera, etcetera." He rolled his hand and fake yawned.

"And the Tony goes to . . ." Shay said.

"You're too kind." Kris kissed the air to his invisible fans.

Alison interrupted them. "Kris, your kids await." She shooed them toward the store proper.

"All right, bossy," he said, giving her a playful shove. "Man, you'd think this was like some crisis situation or something."

"No touching," she said, playfully shoving him back.

Shay felt tears in her eyes. She liked these people. They seemed so normal. Where had normal been hiding?

Ryan had had about enough of the parking garage. It was nearing ten in the morning and Mike and Drew were still passed out after last night's bender. He'd stayed in the rat hole with them for an hour after waking up, then had to bolt or risk losing his mind in the dark. Not that the rest of the garage offered much in the way of light. Every exit was permanently sealed over, as he and the others had found out the hard way after crashing their cars into what had seemed like flimsy gates. Every window or hole to the outside world was blocked. The only light came from the glassed-in central pavilion. Security must have cut all the fluorescent ceiling lights to discourage people from coming down.

Ryan circled the perimeter, first at a walk, then, once he was sure his head could take it, at a light trot. He only lasted a few strides, but it felt good to stretch his legs. He missed running. Every day, he pounded the pavement. It was part of his training, but it was also something he loved. Like rock climbing, it was something he could disappear into, where he was only competing with himself.

How long would it take to completely recover from the flu? Maybe he could sneak up to the medical center and ask one of the doctors.

He made it to the opposite side of the garage before hearing any noise other than the squeak of his sneakers on the pavement: A door shut on a car. Ryan scanned the nearest cars and saw a giant SUV rocking.

Ryan crept up on the SUV from its rear blind spot. He wondered if he should wake Mike or Drew. It was probably not the wisest move to be ambushing a potentially hostile individual alone. He ducked down and crawled the rest of the way to the bumper. He heard voices inside. Sliding up to standing, his back against the chassis, Ryan peered in through the side window.

A child screamed and the car rocked again. The door creaked open on the opposite side of the car and Ryan heard footsteps. He rushed around the back of the SUV and saw two small heads disappear into the next aisle.

It was easy to catch up to the kids—one boy and one girl. They kept looking behind them and tripping over their own feet. Ryan guessed they were kindergarten age by their height relative to the car bumpers. He grabbed the backs of their shirts, jerking them to a halt.

"Let go!" the boy cried. He had curly blond hair and freckles, the poster child for cute kids. And he was literally crying because of Ryan. Ryan wondered how bad he looked—in general, people did not think his face was scary.

"Calm down!" Ryan said. "I'm not going to hurt you!"

The kids stopped struggling. Ryan let go of their shirts and squatted to be on their level. As he did, the girl kicked his shin and both ran. What had happened to these kids?

"I just want to help you!" he shouted, deciding against chasing them, mostly because his head had begun to throb again. "Where are your parents?"

The footsteps stopped. Ryan heard whispering. Then, from off to his left, "They got sick." It was the girl's voice. "They told us to hide in the car until the police told us it was safe to come out."

Holy crap. How long had these kids been down here? "When did your parents get sick?" Ryan took a few slow steps toward the voice.

"Wednesday, I think."

"You've been in the parking garage since Wednesday?" If the parents had been gone that long, they weren't coming back.

"We have a bunch of groceries in the car," the boy said, stepping out from between two cars. "We're fine down here. Leave us alone."

"The fact that you're telling a complete stranger about your supplies in a life-or-death situation like this tells me you are anything but fine."

The boy looked at his sister. A tear ran down his cheek.

"Crap," Ryan said, kneeling again. "I didn't mean to scare you. It's just that I don't think the police are going to come and get you for a long time. Do you have enough food to last a while?"

The girl, who was taller, slung her arm around her brother. "We ate most of the good stuff," she said. "And some of it started to smell bad, so we threw it out." She pointed to where the overflowing Dumpsters had been moved. The girl had dark hair, and what little light there was winked off the spangles in her headband.

"That was really smart," Ryan said, trying to both calm the kids down and figure out what to do with them. He could not leave them in this garage. It was one thing for him and Mike and Drew to choose this hell, it was another for these kids to be stuck here on their dead parents' orders.

"Mom told us to stay here," the boy said. "I don't want to leave the truck."

"Are people still getting sick?" the girl asked. She sounded older than the boy. But not much older.

"I don't know," Ryan said. "I would think so."

"Then we'll stay down here." She released her brother's shoulder and took his hand. They began to walk back toward their car.

He had two options: One, wrestle both kids up to the main floor and turn them over to security, which was not only risky for himself, but might expose the kids to the disease, or two, leave them in their SUV, where they had been fine until he scared the crap out of them. The decision was clear.

"My name is Ryan," he said, backing out of their way. "If you need me, I'm staying with friends in a closet on the other side of the garage."

The girl stopped and nodded at Ryan. "I'm Ruthie, and this is Jack." The boy waved.

"If you need anything," Ryan said, "just remember—Ryan, in the closet."

N O O N

It took Lexi the entire morning to process the delinquents in the PaperClips. By the time the last one was escorted out, Hank told her to take the rest of the morning off until lunch.

"Isn't lunch at noon?" Lexi asked. According to her phone, it was eleven fifty.

"Enjoy your ten minutes of freedom," he said, taking the laptop from her and exiting through the stockroom.

This was the thanks she got for working without a break since eight in the morning? She cracked her knuckles, then flopped onto the table. Alone in the Paper-Clips yet again. At least this time she wasn't buried under anything. And there were no bodies.

At least not on the floor in front of her.

There were over fifteen hundred unregistered names according to the database last night, and this morning, she'd only accounted for fifty of them in the PaperClips.

Where were the rest of the missing? Maddie could not be right in thinking that they were all dead. But in these ten minutes of freedom, Lexi decided to count the few bodies she knew about.

The hole in the wall leading from the PaperClips to the Pancake Palace was still covered over by a sheet of plastic, though the material now sported some holes and was so wrinkled it was no longer transparent. Lexi pushed it aside and stepped into the Pancake Palace. The lights were off, so she followed the wall toward where she remembered the doors to the kitchen to be. Beside the swinging kitchen door, she found a light switch.

The lights shone down on an empty space. Everything that had been in the Pancake Palace—the beds, the boxes of supplies from the government, the patients—had been taken out. Lexi pushed through the swinging doors and entered the kitchen. The door to the freezer was closed, but there was no evidence of it having been sealed over as her mother had ordered. *Which means they haven't gotten to it yet, which means I'm in business . . .*

Lexi pulled on the freezer's handle. With a thunk, then a rush of air, the door released and swung toward her. Cold air kissed her face. The freezer was empty.

Lexi stuck her head inside. Empty. Nothing. The freezer contained shining steel walls coated in a dusting of white frost, that was it.

Had she dreamed the bodies she saw in there? No. Her mother had screamed. There had been bodies. Stacks of them. The mall manager. Lots of people. All dead. All frozen.

Where were they now? Who had taken them? Was the government somehow sneaking the dead out? Did her mother know?

Lexi slammed the freezer shut and scrambled out of the Pancake Palace. In the halls, she blew by people carrying giant bags of popcorn, pushing dollies stacked with towels and bins piled with clothing, a line of children marching and singing "Ten Little Pumpkins." None of that mattered. Where were the bodies?

At the mall offices, she had to lie to the guard about finding a computer glitch to get inside, but what was one lie compared with the disappearing dead? She had to get to her mother. She had to know.

Hank Goldman was sitting talking to the Senator when Lexi burst breathless into the room.

"Lex, what happened?" her mother said, standing. She even came out from behind the desk and took Lexi into her arms.

"The bodies," Lexi said, trying to regain her breathing. "The freezer. Empty."

"We can talk later," Hank said, getting up to leave.

"No," the Senator said. She pushed away from Lexi, held her by the shoulders, and glowered into her eyes. "Baby, I need you to forget about the bodies. I have that situation under control."

"But Mom," Lexi retorted. "The ones in the Pancake Palace. They're gone."

"I know," her mother said. "I had them moved for sanitation purposes."

Her mother moved the bodies. The government was not meddling. Her mother was moving bodies without anyone's knowledge. "What's more sanitary than leaving them frozen and sealed in a freezer?"

The Senator released Lexi and shuffled back behind the desk. "Please, trust me. I have this situation under control." She sat in her large leather chair. "Just relax and go be with your friends. I gave you three an assignment you should like—clothing sorting."

Three? This was how out of touch her mother was—she still thought Ginger was her friend. "When was the last time you saw me clothes shopping?" Lexi asked, not even trying to hide her snark.

"Your friend Maddie requested the job this morning," her mother said. "I thought you'd be grateful I gave you an assignment together." The Senator turned her attention back to Hank. "So you were saying about an alternative for the rats?" The interview was over.

Lexi wandered out through the offices. Her mother was stonewalling her on the bodies, a secret they had shared not twenty-four hours ago. And apparently there was a rat problem.

Out in the hallway, Lexi heard the crowds gathering for lunch. It took her ten minutes to find Maddie in the chaos of the first-floor courtyard. There were a few tables set up, but most people were still camping out on the floor with their plates of freeze-dried goop and bottles of water.

"Hey, stranger," Lexi said, sidling up to her on the food line.

"Girlfriend!" Maddie gave her a one-armed hug. "You missed it. I complained about my original assignment to, get this, mop the freaking floors, and got upgraded to clothing sorter. I just said that I was friends with you and *voilà!* We're clothing sorters."

"Yeah," Lexi murmured. "It's good to know the boss's kid." She wasn't sure why, but it felt a little gross to have Maddie using her name to get better stuff. It was one thing for Lexi to use her influence, and another to have it used by proxy.

"Turn that frown upside-down," Maddie said. "We have the best gig in this hellhole."

They reached the guy guarding the Borderlands Cantina, which was where whoever was assigned to cooking duty was reconstituting the freeze-dried rations. They gave their names, which the guard checked against the database. He grunted an okay and waved them in.

Trays of goop in hand, Lexi followed Maddie through the crowds toward the central fountain.

"Okay, don't freak out," Maddie said, "but we have a bit of a leech problem."

Lexi glanced at the fountain and saw Ginger already seated on the stone wall. "That's some leech."

Maddie sighed. "She got placed on clothing sorter duty too, and has been hanging on me, begging forgiveness, blah, blah. She asked if she could eat lunch with us and I told her it was a free country."

Maddie did not sound quite as pissed off as Lexi felt. "She bailed and left you to die."

Maddie shrugged. "We're all going to die."

Ginger shuffled over to make room for them. "I had to tell two old ladies to take a hike to save the spaces." She smiled this big grin, like saving seats on a wall made up for anything.

Maddie plopped down beside her. "I'm not sure I can choke this crap down."

"They said it was veggie chili." Ginger smoothed a lumpy section with the back of her spoon.

"It's food," Lexi said. Was she supposed to just laugh, let bygones be bygones, forget how Ginger had slunk away from her when she'd asked for help trying to save people, *people* here including her alleged best friend? Which person, strangely enough, seemed to have completely forgotten said abandonment. Lexi shoveled a mouthful in and instantly regretted it. "Nuhpken," she managed through closed lips.

Ginger passed her one.

Lexi took it grudgingly and spit out the food. "This meal must be ingested in small bites."

"And with lots of water." Maddie passed her a bottle.

As the minutes ticked by, Lexi had a harder time maintaining her level of maximum annoyance. Ginger was apologetic to the point of ass-kissing: "I'm so sorry I left you, I was just completely freaked out." "I'm a total hypochondriac, I know it's no excuse, I'm pathetic." "You were such a superhero, Lex, I wish I were as strong as you." It was easier to just talk to her than keep up the force field of anger.

But there was something else. As Maddie recounted their morning of sifting through clothes, how it was so unfair that someone was going to be given this amazing pair of 7 for All Mankind jeans and would they even appreciate them the way Maddie would, Lexi felt the power of the bond between Maddie and Ginger. Ginger, for example, knew what 7 for All Mankind was. She agreed with Maddie about how there should be a clothing hierarchy, where people who knew about designers got the designer clothes. The two were "besties," always would be, no matter what. They had what Lexi had with Darren. So what if

Lexi had saved Maddie's life after Ginger left her for dead? Whatever had happened, Lexi sensed that she would always be their third wheel.

And so when Maddie turned to her and asked where she'd been all morning, Lexi told her about the Paper-Clips, about the people who'd gotten Tasered for sneaking out at night, but said nothing about the missing bodies. She would find someone else, someone more like her, someone, maybe, like Marco, to help her with that project.

"Alexandra Ross," her mother's voice boomed from the loudspeakers, "please come to the mall offices."

Lexi pounded the last of her water. "Break time's over."

"We'll catch you later?" Ginger asked, smiling.

Lexi did not miss her use of *we*. "Yeah," she said, and went to see what Mommy Dearest wanted.

Ryan had taken the rest of the morning to hunt through the parking garage for other stowaways. He found two bodies, one in the front seat of a sedan, seat-belted in as if ready to drive off, the other stretched across the back of a station wagon. Most people had decided that whatever was going on aboveground was better than going it alone in the dark. He saw the appeal of that decision.

But better than other people, Ryan found people's stuff. It seemed that a number of shoppers had stowed goods in their cars. And as Ryan was already Stonecliff's Most Wanted, he did not see any reason not to bust open some windows and collect the gear. He found a laptop and a bunch of DVDs. There were some children's clothes in the back of an SUV. One wagon had a huge box of crackers stashed in the tailgate. Arms full, he went back to Ruthie and Jack's SUV.

The two were curled up in the dark with the door cracked open. Ruthie was whispering something to her brother. "And then, Peter threw dust from Tinker Bell on Wendy and her brothers, and they could fly!"

Ryan felt like Santa Claus. "Delivery for Ruthie and Jack," he said, stepping into the doorway.

"Are those crackers?" Ruthie dove for the box, nearly pushing Ryan over.

"You guys have any light?" he said, releasing the crackers and nearly dropping everything else.

Ruthie shuffled into a sitting position. "We stopped using the car's light two days ago. That way, when Mom and Dad come back, we can drive home."

These kids had been trapped down here with no lights for two days, they thought Mom and Dad were coming back—they really needed his help. "Here's some clothes and a laptop and some DVDs for when you get tired of telling stories," he said. "I didn't find anyone else hiding out down here, but that doesn't mean someone won't show up, so keep this door mostly closed. How much more food do you have?"

Jack held up a bag of chips. "I'm saving this for lunch."

"We could use some more food," Ruthie said, mouth spewing cracker crumbs. "And drinks. Juice boxes?" She sounded excited, like maybe they could go shopping. Ryan sensed she was desperate to no longer be in charge of things.

"Let me see what I can scrounge for you," he said.

Ruthie threw her arms around his neck. "Thank you."

He pushed her off, uncomfortable with being thanked before he actually did anything. "Just keep the door mostly shut until I get back."

She nodded and pulled it halfway closed, blocking the two from Ryan's sight.

It felt good to have a mission, to be doing something he was sure was right for a change. He would get them flashlights and juice boxes—there had to be some left in the wholesale place—he would give them everything they needed. He would take care of them.

The only way back into the mall—aside from Marco's magic key—was the central pavilion. Ryan rolled the dice on whether anyone would recognize him or even care if they did. He pushed open the glass door and took the steps two at a time up into the blinding light of the central courtyard.

Two security guards had brought trays up to the food court, so that Shay and the others in the school could eat lunch separate from the masses. The children ate what they were given, though some made fun of the way the food squished. The fact that everyone had the same thing seemed to make eating it all the more acceptable.

Shay had to admit that it was nice being around the kids. She even missed Preeti, whom she normally found annoying. It would be nice to be annoyed by Preeti instead of worrying about whether she really would be released from the med center this afternoon. She imagined Preeti being once again like these kids, happy to run around in the empty food court, playing freeze tag or jumping rope. They appeared to have forgotten that they were trapped in the mall. Even if she couldn't feel that happiness or forget the walls locking her in, it was calming to watch those who could. People like Kris, who it turned out was just an overgrown five-year-old.

He had found a large blue plastic bottle of bubble solution and was waving its giant orange wand in slow circles. The bubbles were not floating far enough for his taste, so he began dancing in loops. The kids—all different ages, whoever had finished their lunch—orbited him, unable to escape the palpable gravity of the bubbles.

Kris began to wave the wand in larger circles, to run, trailing a stream of bubbles. The children pranced, laughing and squealing, under the shimmering orbs as they glided up toward the glass ceiling. Kris was unable to keep from giggling right along with the kids. He ran back through his bubbles, slapping at them with the wand, causing the kids to shriek with delight. The bubbles formed a gleaming cloud around them. *Bubbles on clothing, bubbles in hair, bubbles, bubbles everywhere.*

Shay watched the rainbows swirl on the surface, followed the soap-sacs as they drifted up, up, and finally burst against the glass. For all the joy around her, all she saw was that death, the final gasp and pop of the bubble against the wall that divided picture of sky from sky.

Marco scarfed his lunch so he would have a few extra minutes to sneak down and make his pitch to the douches in the basement before being hauled back into his indentured servitude. He'd been assigned to construction. A kid who'd never hammered more than a birdfeeder together was being asked to build wood frames for showers. More importantly, the showers were going to be built in the goddamned parking garage. Apparently, it was the only place with proper drainage.

This presented Marco with an ideal argument for why Mike should move with Marco to a more central location. After last night's terror in the hallways, he knew he would not survive without having Mike nearby at all times.

The problem was that there was little chance that the showers would be built anywhere near the closet where he'd stashed Mike and the others. Marco could only hope that the construction would be noisy enough to scare them into moving. Perhaps Marco should suggest that security might start taking an interest in the parking garage in general, given its usefulness in the shower department. That might convince Mike.

Of course, this left the problem of what the hell to do with them aboveground. But Marco would think of that later. First things first: Convince douches to leave basement.

Marco emerged from the service stairwell into the black of the garage near the closet. From the complete blackness of the wall, he guessed that the lights were not on in the closet. *Could the douches still be asleep?* He felt around until he found the handle, then knocked. No answer. He knocked again. Nothing. "Guys, it's Marco," he said, then again, louder. Still nothing.

He quickly prayed that Mike would not shoot him in the head and opened the door. He heard a fart, then a snort. Marco flipped on the light.

Both Mike and Drew were passed out. An empty handle of vodka rested next to its half-empty twin between their prone bodies.

"Mike?" he said. "Hello, Mike?" He kicked Mike's sneaker.

"Wha?" Mike winked an eye. "Turn the freaking lights off, dickhead."

"It's noon," Marco said.

"Who gives a rat's ass?" Drew rolled over, pulled his shirt over his head.

"You need to move out of here." Marco was going with the direct approach.

"Like hell," Mike said. He shuffled up on his elbows and squinted at Marco from under the visor of his hand. "You said this was the safest place to hole up."

"That was before they decided to build showers down here."

Mike dropped his head back and uttered a string of barely comprehensible profanity. Then, as if seeing the room for the first time, asked, "Where's Ryan?"

"Bathroom?" Marco suggested.

"Go check," Mike said.

"I'm not your errand boy," Marco said.

"Actually, that's exactly what you are," Mike said, pushing himself to standing. "That's our deal—you help us hide and survive, we help you not get killed." He walked to the door, only wavering slightly, and scanned the darkness outside. "Shrimp!" he barked. No reply echoed back across the garage. Mike punched the door frame. "I've got to find him," he said. He knelt by the food box, dug around, then emerged with a bottle of Sportade and started sucking the red liquid down.

This was not good. Mike was sure to get himself into some altercation with the guards. This would not only get Marco into trouble with the senator, it would jeopardize his only means of protection in the mall.

"I'll look for him," Marco said.

Mike finished the bottle and wiped his mouth with his forearm. "I thought you weren't my errand boy."

"I can't afford to let you get caught."

Mike nodded. "What about this shower situation?"

"They're going to start putting stuff together this afternoon. Just lay low and I'll find you somewhere new to hide out."

"With more booze," droned Drew from the floor, "and girls."

Mike glanced at Drew and shook his head. "Just find somewhere out of the way," he said.

Kris trotted to where Shay was sitting under a potted tree, bubble wand hanging by his side. "I cannot keep up with these kids," he said, flopping beside her. "You have to take a turn." He held out the wand.

"You've only been at it for an entire hour," Shay said. "I think you're selling yourself short."

"Well, I do love me some bubbles." He stood up. "But you have to stop moping or I'm telling them that you sing Raffi songs if tickled."

"You wouldn't dare!" Shay said, slapping at his calf.

"Oh, try me," he said, holding his hands up. "I give you five seconds and then you will be a target."

Shay felt a smile pinch her cheeks. Weird, how you could smile but still feel wretched. And then she saw him: Ryan was behind the counter of the Magic Wok. And then he wasn't. Where had he gone? He couldn't disappear again. She jumped to her feet and bolted toward him.

"You didn't have to run!" Kris yelled after her.

"Ryan?" Shay said, slamming into the counter.

He stood slowly, emerging from behind the wall of glass. He looked ragged and tired and his chin bore the scraggly beginnings of a beard, but god, he was beautiful. The most beautiful thing she'd seen in days.

"You're okay," he said.

Shay hitched herself up onto the counter and slid over into his waiting arms. "I've missed you," she whispered, tears stinging her eyes.

"You're okay," he said again.

In his arms, everything felt lighter, the sadness, the guilt. She felt weightless. She hugged him tighter.

"I saw you in the med center," he said. "Marco told me you got hurt in the riots."

Marco told him? Marco knew Ryan was here and hadn't told her?

"I'm fine," she said, not wanting to remember. They pulled apart, though Ryan held on to her arm. "And you? Where have you been?"

He hesitated—she could see him disappear for a moment, felt his grip on her loosen. "Hiding out," he said, finally, "with Mike and Drew."

"And Marco?" Something was off. Why would Marco be involved with the guys who'd tortured him?

"He's helping us."

Shay wondered just how many people Marco thought he could help. He'd promised to find somewhere for her and Preeti to hide, but she hadn't seen him all day. "He said he would help me find somewhere to hide."

"Maybe we can hide together?" Ryan perked up, squeezed her arm.

Shay caught sight of Kris in a cyclone of bubbles. At Lights On, no question, she would have said yes, but now, she wasn't so sure. But she didn't want to disappoint Ryan, so she said, "Of course."

Ryan let go of her arm and leaned on the counter. "I should tell you that I'm currently hiding out in a window-less room in the garage with two guys who are completely hammered out of their minds."

"Sounds charming," Shay said, nudging him with her elbow, just wanting to touch him.

"Actually, I should get back down there," he said, standing, pulling away from her. "I kind of left without saying anything."

"Oh."

"And that guy over there keeps giving me dirty looks."

Shay looked where Ryan nodded and saw Kris staring at them. "He's my co-teacher," she said. "He's harmless."

"Still"—Ryan glanced around like Kris was the least of his worries—"I'm kind of in trouble with security."

Shay wondered if he'd been in the halls last night. She'd heard that some people had gotten caught by secu-rity. And just like that, at the mere thought of that dark hallway, the ghost image of Nani's dead face flashed in her mind. Her knees buckled.

"Are you okay?" Ryan said, pulling her back to stand-ing. "What just happened? Do you need to go back to the med center?"

"No!" Shay said, too forcefully. She would not go back there. "No," she said, more calmly. "Just lightheaded. I had a mild concussion."

"I've had one or two of those," Ryan said. He stroked her head.

Shay melted against his body, let him stand for her. "Stay with me."

Ryan pulled away again. "I'll come back here," he said. "Tomorrow. This same time?"

Tomorrow. Would there even be a tomorrow? What if he died before then? "Fine," she said.

He held her hand, looked at her like he wanted to do something more. Shay wasn't sure what was holding him back. He then gave her a weird little wave and ducked out the back of the kitchen.

Shay slid over the counter and wandered back toward Kris.

"Who was *that* hottie?" he asked, whipping the wand in front of her, showering the air with soap. "Does Shaila have a boyfriend?"

Shay shrugged with a noncommittal smile, like she was keeping a secret, but the truth was she wasn't sure if she did. When they'd last been together, Ryan had kissed her. Now she got a wave. What had changed? Suddenly, she couldn't remain standing and slumped to the floor.

"Hey kids," Kris said in a singsong tone, "I think Miss Dixit will sing—"

"I'm up!" Shay yelled, jumping to her feet. "Give me the bubble wand, you traitor."

Kris smirked and passed her the plastic. And strangely enough, as she ran with the bubbles, between the sunshine and the soap film, she was almost normal.

F
I
V
E
P.M.

Marco had to haul ass to make it to the senator's office on time. He'd been hauling ass all afternoon—running shower materials from the HomeMart to the garage, sneaking off whenever possible to scout stockrooms as potential hiding places—and he was feeling ragged around the edges. With having to fit in this little meeting, he'd have to skip dinner entirely to move Mike and the others to the back of the bowling alley before evening check-in at six.

It was a kind of brilliant idea. The bowling alley wasn't currently in use, so Marco had been able to explore it without interruption. There was a storage room for mechanical stuff and extra chairs in the very back that connected via a door to a narrow walkway behind the pin-setting machines. Mike and the others could hide in the storage room, and if anyone came knocking, could sneak onto the walkway until the coast was clear. Even better, there was a food storage room next to the room where Marco planned to shove Mike, and the food people hadn't cleared it out yet, meaning Marco didn't have to worry about dinner for the douches. Finally, the storage room was opposite the door to the fire stairwell, meaning should Marco ever have a problem, the douches were easily reached.

The only string left dangling was Ryan. He was nowhere Marco had figured him to be: not the climbing place in Shep's, not hiding out in the men's dorm, not in the med center looking around for Shay (Ryan didn't know she'd been transferred). So in addition to moving the douches, he had to sniff out the one who'd gotten away or risk Mike taking on the task and getting locked up by security.

"Marco Carvajal to see the senator," he told the guard behind the glass.

The guy nodded and buzzed him in.

The offices were more crowded than they had been yesterday. Regular people in sweats and T-shirts sat filing paperwork into binders. In the computer room, four people sat at terminals typing. There were only two security guards in the place: the guy manning the front desk and the guy in the camera feed room.

The senator was chatting on what appeared to be a giant cell phone. "I'm glad the house arrest program has isolated any potentially infected people, but that really doesn't do me any good in here. I need information. Have the antivirals had any effect?"

Marco held off on knocking.

The senator dropped her head into her hands. Her shoulders heaved, then she lifted her face, which was

again all business. "Let me know if anything changes."
She laid the phone on her desk.

Marco lurked in the doorway. What did it mean that
antivirals had no effect? Who was being held on house
arrest? Had they found the person who planted the bomb?

"Should I come back?" he offered.

The senator didn't even glance up. "I know you heard
me," she said, "so let me explain. The government, on
my husband's suggestion, scanned all the security footage
of the parking lots and exits to identify anyone who may
have been exposed to the virus, but got out of the mall
before the quarantine. The government has put them on
house arrest. Second, the CDC has been testing antivirals
to see if anything can be done to help us, and have so far
come up with zip. Now you." She leaned toward him and
pointed at her chair. "Was it your friends who led the little
hallway romp my security team corralled last night? I saw
your name on the list of those captured."

"I have no friends, so no," Marco said. "I can, however,
guarantee for you that the individuals you asked me to
monitor were not involved in the 'hallway romp.' They
spent the night in the parking garage closet I left them in."
Marco recalled their state of inebriation from earlier this
morning—they were barely capable of speech, let alone
romping.

"Aren't we serious?" The senator smiled creepily. She
reached into her drawer and pulled out something. She
slid it across the desk. It was a granola bar. "Do you like
these? They hurt my teeth."

Marco snatched the bar and nearly ate the wrapper,

he was so hungry. It took him a few seconds to recover from the animal ferocity of his hunger to realize he should thank the woman. "Thunk oo," he managed.

"I'm not your enemy, Marco," she said. "I am trying to save lives here." She leaned back in her chair. "I am interested to hear your suggestions for how to manage this nighttime restlessness among certain mall residents."

"Why are you asking me?" Marco wiped the crumbs from his mouth on the back of his hand to appear slightly more professional.

"Because you were out in the halls last night. Why were you running around? Checking on the individuals I asked you to monitor?"

Marco wondered if telling her about Shay would be a good idea. Would she help him hide her? No, of course not. The senator thought her Home Store plan was the safest thing going. Of course, she hadn't had to sleep in one of them.

He cleared his throat. "Yeah," he said. "I checked in with them. Then I got busted by security."

"So the report that you were in the back of the JCPenney with my daughter is a lie?"

CRAPcrapcrapcrap . . . "I was exploring." *Lamest lie ever—check.*

"My daughter?"

CRAPCRAPCRAP! "The mall. The hallways. I ran into her by accident. I didn't do anything!"

The senator smirked. "Let's assume for the moment that I believe you. Most of the people caught by security were caught in compromising states of undress with members of the opposite sex. Or simply running around in the dark like idiots. I sense that these individuals are not thrilled with my curfew or my notions of how to prevent the spread of contagion. As a result, I'm thinking of opening the bowling alley to these kids until midnight and having the place supervised to prevent as much contact as possible. What do you think?"

This was a terrible idea. Not only did this obliterate his entire plan for where to store Mike & Co., but from the looks of the assholes in the PaperClips this morning, a chaperoned event in a bowling alley was not their idea of a good time.

"That idea sucks," he blurted, then reconsidered his approach. "I mean, it's not going to work. The people in the hallways last night didn't seem like the types that go to school dances."

"You have another idea?"

"They just want to fool around and get loaded. Give them a dark room and a keg and let them go at it."

"And the flu?"

Marco shrugged. "You can't save everyone."

The senator rubbed her temples. "I can't believe I'm even considering this."

Marco could not believe it either.

"Okay," she said, dropping her hands on the table. "I will give you your keg and until midnight to have your party. You spread the word that you're running this thing— I can't be involved. But you tell me where it's going to be. I'm going to have security raid the party at midnight and shut it down."

Marco's brain seized up at the mention of "your party." Marco had never thrown a party before. Ever. He, in fact, had never consumed alcohol. The last party he'd attended was a fifth-grade pool party and he'd gotten almost drowned on purpose by a bunch of assholes. Why would the senator think it a good idea to put him in charge of this?

No, the person to host a party was Mike Richter. He threw all the good parties at West Nyack. But Mike wanted to stay hidden. He would never agree to host a party in this place. And even if Marco sold him on the idea, how could Marco cover up the fact that he was doing this on behalf of the senator?

But then he recalled Drew's request—more booze and girls. What if he had the senator put this keg in the storage room and just casually mentioned to the Douche Squad that he'd heard there was going to be a party there? Drew at least might want to check it out and then Marco would have half of his team of bodyguards with him in case things went south.

"Leave a keg in the bowling alley," he said, finally. "Tell security to invade the mechanical storage room."

The senator nodded as she said, "I have no idea what you're talking about." She waved him out.

Marco stood. He was sweating all over. So he'd have to find a new hiding place for Mike. He could do that. Also, he'd have to talk to his peers to invite them to this party, wouldn't he? A potentially awful interaction, but he could survive it. And running a kind of double bluff where Mike didn't know the party was rigged or that Marco was its host? No problem. Or, manageable problem. *I hope.*

■ ■ ■

Lexi had about reached her limit on helpful daughter stuff. She'd spent all morning logging degenerates, and all afternoon setting up a CB call center in the old Silver Screen store so that people on the inside could communicate with family on the outside. Now, instead of being able to catch up with Maddie and Ginger before dinner, she was being called in by her mother *again* to handle something that some other person surely could manage. She didn't even need to know what her mother wanted done. Whatever it was, someone else could do it. This was total child abuse. Were there any other authority besides her mother, Lexi would have totally ratted her out to them.

She stepped off the escalator nearest the offices and nearly ran into Marco. *Of all the escalators in this mall, he's at the top of mine . . .*

"It's you again," he said, flustered.

"Me again," Lexi said, not sure if he was happy. Not sure about the exact implication of *again*. She didn't want him to go. "Sorry about last night," she sputtered. "And this morning."

"Not your fault I got busted," he said.

"It's a little my fault."

He looked at his iPod. "I should go."

"Wait," she said. "I need your help."

He raised an eyebrow. "The daughter of the leader of this mall needs *my* help?"

Lexi was all nerves—yes, she wanted to tell him about the bodies, but her mother would kill her if she found out; then again, her mother was being kind of a jerk about the whole bodies thing anyway (weren't there not going to be any more secrets between them?)—and so she just blurted it out: "I think my mother's hiding dead bodies."

Marco stepped closer. "How am I supposed to help you with that?"

"I thought maybe, you know, tonight, we could, maybe, meet, and, you know, look for them?"

"Why would I want to find dead bodies?"

He had her on that one. "It's a mystery?" Lexi said, trying out the concept. "There were some bodies in a freezer in the Pancake Palace, and now they're gone. I want to know what happened to them."

He glanced over his shoulder, then walked to a corner. Lexi followed.

Marco leaned in toward her. "Do you think the government's taking them out? Like there's some exit still open?" His breath tickled her hair. Her skin sizzled.

"No," she said, but he pulled away at the word, so she corrected herself. "I mean, maybe. We could find out together." She put on her charming smile, or the smile she thought looked most charming. She was so not good at this.

Marco was looking past her, so she turned her head to see what he was staring at. It was the ice-skating rink. Which was closed. There was a little printed sign on the door: COOLANT FAILURE. CLOSED UNTIL FURTHER NOTICE.

"You thinking what I'm thinking?" Marco said, glancing at her.

"It would be the perfect place to hide them." Lexi couldn't help noticing how close they were. She could feel the pull of his body like gravity.

He held out his hand. "I'll meet you in your office after Lights Out."

Lexi slid her hand into his. "See you then." His hand

felt kind of sweaty as he gave hers a shake. It wasn't sexy, but at least they were touching. She liked the touching.

He dropped her hand and trotted away, leaving Lexi in a state of minor meltdown. She had a date. To find dead bodies, fine, but whatever. She was meeting him again. It took her a full minute to remember why she'd even come to the third floor. Refitting the armor of snark she always favored when meeting her mother, Lexi tromped up to the office door and asked to be let in.

Three plastic trays of frozen dinner—not reconstituted freeze-dried slop, but Lean Cuisine—steamed on the Senator's desk. Her mother was smiling in her chair. "I thought we could have dinner," she said, "as a family."

Dad was seated in the other chair opposite the desk. "We have stir-fried chicken!"

Lexi sat down in front of her tray. The smell was beyond delicious. Her mouth hurt from how much she wanted to just wolf the food. "Is everyone getting stir-fry tonight?" Maddie would freak out over this.

"It's just a special treat for our hardworking girl," Dad said.

"I really appreciate your pitching in while your father's recovering," Dotty said.

Lexi smiled, said it was nothing, and she even actually appreciated her mother doing something nice for her after asking her to do all that extra crap, but it still felt wrong to have this amazing feast. Not wrong enough not to eat it in two bites, but wrong nonetheless.

"I think things are finally turning around," Mom said. She seemed honestly happy. "People are really getting on board with the whole Home Store concept and the work crews are functioning pretty smoothly. We've only had a couple of complaints, and those people came around eventually."

"I told you people would see the light," Dad said.

"I'm told by this evening, there should even be showers in the parking garage." Her mother crossed her arms over her chest, gloating like she'd invented the concept.

Lexi felt like both her parents were waiting for a response. "What about the missing bodies?" she asked.

Her mother's face deflated. "I told you," she said, all business. "Don't worry about the bodies. I have everything under control."

Lexi felt like a bitch for killing the moment. "I think people will be psyched about the showers."

Her father smiled. "I know I'll be happy to use them."

Dotty raised her water bottle. "Here's to a good day."

"A good day," her father said, lifting his own.

"A good day," Lexi repeated, and tapped her bottle against theirs.

They finished their meals accompanied by Dad's anecdotes about training some mall inmates to use the computer system. Oh, how the uninitiated were foiled by things like a macro! It was Dad's usual method of peace-making between Lexi and her mother. He always had some non-confrontational filler conversation at the ready. Both Mom and Lexi laughed at appropriate times, knowing that's what they were supposed to do. It was hard now, though, what with their being kind of in the middle of an apocalypse, to just pretend things were cool between them. Lexi wanted to know what was really going on with the mall—were people really getting on board? All those degenerates she'd logged this morning in the PaperClips seemed a rather stark argument to the contrary. And why was her mother being so coy about the bodies? *I guess I'll find out soon enough . . .*

Lexi offered to clear the trays, and when she came back, her mother had resumed examining her papers. "I need one more favor from you, Lex."

All the muscles in Lexi's shoulders tightened. "Another favor?"

"I got you stir-fry," her mother said, head tilted and eyebrows raised, like this alone was compensation enough for eons of slave labor.

It wasn't too awful a request. Apparently, TVs and DVD players and even some game systems had been set up in all the Home Stores to provide people with entertainment. Lexi was to hook all the stuff up correctly and load the first round of DVDs and games into the machines.

"I really appreciate your helping me," her mother said, standing and coming out from behind the desk. She put her hands on Lexi's shoulders, then pulled her in for a hug. "I feel like I can't trust anyone but you and your dad."

Lexi hugged her mom back, in part because that's what you did when someone hugged you, and in part because she felt bad about her intended investigation later this evening with Marco. She told herself, *I'm not really breaking my mother's trust in checking out the ice-skating rink.* She told herself, *It serves Mom right for not telling me about the missing bodies.* But she knew, under all that, she was doing wrong by her mom. And worse yet, she knew that she was still going to do it.

■   ■   ■

The Sam's Club was crawling with people. Ryan couldn't hope to snatch anything from it without getting caught. He tried to approach a giant stack of chips and this old lady got in his face about what his assignment was and that if it wasn't food consolidation, he had better mosey on back to where he came from. There was definitely something funky going on with all the regular food in the mall. Any stores that stocked some type of food (candy places, restaurants, Target) were gated over like they contained piles of gold and not bags of Doritos.

Ryan would not let these minor setbacks throw him off course from his goal. He had to find stuff for Ruthie and Jack. Though the rioters had cleaned out most edible things from the food court, he scrounged a bag of fried noodles from the Chinese place and a giant can of refried beans from the taco joint. He found a box full of individual packets of fruit snacks in the movie theater, and stole four water bottles from where some workers were building showers in the parking garage. This haul, plus two flashlights and a DVD box-set of Disney movies, filled a backpack, which Ryan carried with no small amount of pride back to the SUV.

"How are we supposed to open this?" Ruthie asked, turning the giant can of beans over in her hands.

Neither of the kids were as psyched as Ryan had anticipated. He had pictured tears of joy, more hugs. All he got was a complaint from Jack that he liked Thomas the Train Engine better than Disney and this insight from Ruthie.

"Here," he said, snatching the can from her. He placed it on the ground, took a toy airplane he saw lying on the floor of the car, and smashed the top of the can. The can remained sealed. The plane, however, snapped in half.

"That was my favorite airplane!" Jack wailed.

"Quiet!" Ryan whispered, nodding his head toward the workmen. "I'll find you a new plane."

Jack shut his trap. He looked miserable. Ryan felt miserable. Why were they making this so hard for him? He was trying to help them, for crissakes!

"I'm sorry," Ryan said, handing the pieces of plane to Jack. "I'll find something else to open the can."

Ruthie flicked the flashlight on and off. "At least we won't be in the dark."

"And I'll find you more food tomorrow."

"Thanks," she said.

Finally.

Footsteps echoed from nearby. Ryan scanned the darkness.

"What the hell are you doing?"

It was Marco's voice.

"Nothing," he said. He glanced at the kids, placed a finger to his lips, and pressed the door to the truck closed.

Marco tapped his back. "Not too stealthy an operation you have going here."

Ryan swallowed the anger that crept in, tightening his fists instinctively. "It's just some kids. They asked me to help them."

"Just send them upstairs."

"They don't want to go upstairs."

"They want to stay in the parking garage?"

"They feel safe here."

"Well, they're not. Send them upstairs."

Ryan gritted his teeth. "I told you, they don't want to go upstairs."

"They're not your freaking pets, Ryan. Let the adults take care of them."

"I saw Shay today," he said, changing the subject to avoid smashing his fist into Marco's smug mouth.

Marco's scowl altered slightly. "So?"

"So I don't think she's your girlfriend." If she were with Marco, she would never have dove across the counter when she saw him. Though he was not as sure about this as he was trying to sound.

"I don't care what you think," Marco snapped. "I'm the one who's been there for her every time she needed me."

Ryan would not let Marco off with that lame excuse anymore. "I can be there for her now."

"Great," Marco said. "May the best man win."

Ryan smiled. *I already have.* No way that hug was just friendly, especially now that he'd seen Marco's face. The guy was making the whole relationship thing up. Ryan could smell the lie on him.

Marco shifted slightly to get a better look in the van. "So how many do you have in there?"

"Two." Ryan was not pleased to have the conversation turn back to the kids.

"Mike know about this little pet project?"

Ryan's fists tightened again. "I haven't told him yet."

"I don't imagine he's going to agree to adopting two new teammates."

"He might."

"Well, how about I make you a deal? I don't tell Mike about the contents of this SUV or your extracurricular activities stealing food for them in the mall, and you do me a favor."

"What?"

"When I saw Mike and Drew earlier—who, by the way, are very worried about where you ran off to this morning—Drew indicated that he was in need of some female companionship. So I was thinking that maybe you could invite some girls to the new hiding place I found you."

"Girls?"

"You've heard of the species?"

Ryan was about thirty seconds from decking the asshole. "Where do you want me to invite them to go?"

"The storage room in the back of the bowling alley. I've even snuck a keg in there for you—that might help get the girls' attention. If they sneak out into the service halls after Lights Out, they can exit into the main part of the mall and then run up to the bowling alley."

Ryan actually liked Marco's idea. Maybe he could invite Shay to come? Though he wasn't sure he wanted to invite her to party with Mike and Drew in a storage room. It didn't seem like her kind of hang.

"Fine," Ryan said finally.

"Glad we could come to an agreement." Marco turned and walked back into the dark.

Ruthie pushed open the door. "Who was that guy?"

"A friend."

"He didn't seem like your friend."

"He's more like a friend of a friend."

"He won't tell on us, will he?"

Ryan patted her head. "I told you I'd keep you safe."

Jack flashed the flashlight under his chin, lighting his

face with ghost-story shadows. "And you said you'd get me a new plane," he growled in a monster voice.

"New plane, got it."

"See you tomorrow?" Ruthie smiled.

"Sleep tight."

Marco ran across the parking garage. If this completely fraked-up plan of his was going to work, he had to get to Mike and Drew before Ryan showed up. He'd saved himself the stress and embarrassment of actually having to invite anyone to this stupid party. Now, though, he had to get Mike and Drew to come to the party of their own volition. He hoped that having spent nearly twenty-four hours in the dungeon of the parking garage closet would be motivation enough.

He was out of breath and sweating by the time he reached the closet. He knocked on the door.

"Get the hell in here," Mike grumbled.

They sound ready to change venues. Marco opened the door. They'd turned the lights off and were again sitting in the dark.

"Can I turn on the lights?" he asked.

"How close are the shower people?" Mike asked from the corner.

"They're on the other side of the garage, which is what I came to tell you. I think you're safe here for another night."

"Like hell." It was Drew this time, from the opposite corner.

Marco flipped on the light, blinding himself momentarily.

"My head just split open," Drew groaned. He was

sprawled in the corner to Marco's right, vodka bottle between his legs.

Mike had an open bottle of Sportade and some empty cracker packets in front of him. "Did you find Ryan?"

"Yeah," Marco said. "He was just tooling around the parking garage."

"All day?"

"I guess," Marco said, shrugging. "It's not like I had a GPS tracker on him. I just saw him as I was coming here. He said he was on his way back."

Mike dribbled some vodka into the Sportade bottle and took a swig. "So we'll see you in the morning."

Marco screwed his courage to the sticking place. "Not that you care or anything, but I heard about this party up in the bowling alley."

Drew started as if electrocuted. "Party? You're kidding me! Here?"

Mike was not so excited. "How the hell is anyone planning a party?"

"I don't know," Marco answered truthfully—after all, he was planning it and had absolutely no idea what he was doing. "But I heard that some kids had gotten their hands on a keg and had stashed it in a storage room at the back of the bowling alley." He swallowed down a small ocean of saliva and tried to control the jiggle in his foot. "I could take you guys up there," he said, "if you wanted to go."

"Hell yeah, we want to go," Drew said, standing as if ready to be led to the place that minute.

"Sit your ass down," Mike barked. "We made an agreement to keep away from everyone to avoid contaminating ourselves."

Drew slammed the wall with his fist. "Screw that, Mike!" he yelled. "I cannot spend another night in this hole. All the vodka in the universe can't make this place anything other than hell on earth."

"You want to die, Drew?" Mike said, standing. "This isn't a joke. You make out with the wrong chick and you end up dead."

"Ryan didn't die."

"That was a lucky break on his part."

"This isn't living, Mike." Drew was quieter now. "And how do we know we don't have it already? We breathed that same crap air that everyone else did. These could be our last freaking days on earth. It seems stupid to waste them hiding in the basement."

This was going better than Marco had planned.

Mike and Drew faced off for a few seconds longer, then Mike hurled his Sportade bottle at the wall, spraying them all with red juice.

"Fine," he yelled. "Screw it. Fine." He glared at Marco like this entire thing was his fault. "We'll go."

Marco did not like that look. "Hey, I didn't mean to screw with you," he said, backpedaling. "I just thought—"

"Stop talking," Mike said. "Just tell us when you're coming to take us to this goddamned party."

"Lights Out," Marco said, trying to breathe normally. "Ten o'clock."

"Yes!" Drew said, punching the air.

"Turn the lights off," Mike said, slumping back in his corner.

Marco left while the getting was good.

■   ■   ■

Shay had not realized how far the sadness had drifted from her until the mall loudspeaker requested that she come to the medical center in Harry's to reclaim her sister, at which point it swept back in like a tide. She handed the jars of paint she'd collected to Kris—they were cleaning up from the afternoon's activity of painting a mural of fall trees. It had been Kris's idea. He thought people would like to see the flaming colors of fall around them. "It'll be a kind of reminder that there's a world outside," he'd said.

Painting had soothed her mind. But now, as she rode the escalator down to the first floor, her brain fritzed.

Harry's, now the medical center, was only open on the first level, like the Home Stores, with the gates pulled across half of the wide entrance. The other half was mostly blocked by a phalanx of cosmetics' counters. A bored-looking woman sat at one and flipped through a magazine. No need for a security guard, Shay guessed, to keep people from invading the disease ward.

Preeti was sitting in a chair by the front desk. She hugged her purse to her chest and stared at the floor. The girl looked like a skeleton. Her eyes were ringed in shadows and her lips bore a fringe of cracked and peeling skin. The shirt they'd dressed her in was either two sizes too big or Preet had shrunk that much in a span of days.

Shay put on her most confident face and opened her arms. "Hey, stranger."

Preeti glanced up, a smile briefly turning her lips, but it instantly fell away. "Where's Nani?"

They didn't tell her.

The person at the counter spoke. "Are you Shaila Dixit?"

Shay nodded.

"Your sister is being released into your care. You should watch for signs of relapse."

Shay nodded again, barely able to concentrate. They hadn't told Preeti. Meaning she would have to tell her.

"Any coughing or sneezing, thick green mucus, a fever—if she exhibits any of these signs, you must bring her back here."

The woman's words began to sink in—they wanted her to take over caring for her sister. She was going to have to keep Preeti alive again. She could barely keep herself alive.

The counter person handed Shay a medical mask for Preeti. "Keep the mask on at all times. Good luck." The woman nodded toward Preeti, as if prodding Shay on.

Preeti was staring at her.

"Here," Shay said, holding out the mask.

"Where's Nani?" Preeti asked again. She did not take the mask.

Shay found it hard to keep her hands from shaking. "She." What words to use? There were none. "She's dead." She spat the word out like poison.

Preeti looked confused. "She had the flu. I had the flu. I'm alive."

Shay sat in the chair next to her, thinking it better to sit before she capsized. "She was too old."

A sob shook Preeti's shoulders. She fell forward into her own lap. After a few moments, she sat up. "How can you just say that like it's nothing!"

Shay felt herself retreating, as if there were doors inside her that could be closed, sealed over, better than a Ziploc, leaving only this shell to respond. "It's not nothing."

Tears ran down Preeti's face. She glared at Shay for a few seconds longer, then stood. "I want to talk to Ba."

There'd been an announcement in the afternoon that CB radios had been set up in the old Silver Screen store. People were invited to sign up to use them to call their families. Someone in the med center must have told Preeti about it. *Probably that traitor Jazmine.*

"There will be a line." It was dinnertime, and Shay was sure that everyone would be trying to call out. Everyone, of course, except her. Like she could face her parents right now.

"I don't care." Preeti snatched the mask from Shay's hand and started walking.

Shay followed.

There was a line at the table for the CBs, as Shay had predicted. Preeti was undeterred. She stomped to the end of the line and stared at the prodigious rear of the man in front of her rather than look at Shay. Shay did not mind. The last thing she wanted was to fight with Preeti about whether or not she was showing the appropriate amount of remorse for letting Nani die. Like there were measures for such things. If only Preeti could see the desolation inside her. Would that begin to pay her debt?

When they reached the front of the line, Preeti spoke for herself. "I need to call my mother."

The man behind the table slid a clipboard toward her. "Write the name and the home and cell phone numbers, address, and then your name. The guard will contact the government on the outside, and they will call your mother and tell her to come to the mall. Once she arrives, they will contact us here and an announcement will be made over the mall's PA system. Return to this location when you hear your name over the PA. All calls are monitored by the federal government." From his deadpan tone, Shay could tell this was a speech he'd given one too many times.

Preeti began scrawling information onto the blanks. "We'll wait here," she said.

"There is no waiting area."

She handed him back the board. "That's okay," she said. "We'll find someplace."

The guard looked over the form. "Suit yourself." He then picked up his walkie-talkie and read out Shay's parents' names and their home address and phone number.

It was bizarre to hear the words. To be reminded that there was a house on Walnut Street with a room just for her. That all her clothes, her books, the scraps of her life still persisted beyond these walls. For some reason, the thought of them made her sick. That didn't feel like her life anymore.

Preeti hunkered down against the glass wall that had once been the Silver Screen display window. It was covered over now with Kris's mural of handprint trees. The image felt like a cruel joke. There was no world outside, not for them.

After only fifteen minutes, the guard called them. "Pretty Dixit?" he shouted.

Their mother must have raced to the mall—their house was close but not that close.

Preeti jumped up. "Preeti," she corrected. "Long *e*'s."

The guard handed her a CB. "Station five," he said.

"You have twenty minutes." He waved her in. "Have a good visit, Preeti."

Shay followed Preeti into the store. The guard didn't even acknowledge her passing. It was better that way. Shay wanted Preeti to make the call without even mentioning her presence.

"Ba?" Preeti asked, voice cracking on the one syllable. She fell into a folding chair in front of the table with a number five taped to it. There was a second chair. Shay remained standing. Posters with scenes from famous movies lined the walls. Nearby stood a cutout of a handsome vampire. Oh, to have the blood sucked out of her body. By him, by anyone.

Preeti asked the machine for her mother again. This time, her mother's voice boomed in answer. "Shaila?"

Preeti lowered the volume. "No, it's Preeti."

Ba started crying. Bapuji's voice took over. "It's so good to hear your voice," he said.

They began speaking in Gujarati. Preeti cried as she told them about what had happened, how she'd gotten sick, how Nani was dead.

Ba cried out. Bapuji didn't say anything for a moment. "And Shaila?"

"She's fine," Preeti said. "Here." She held the CB out to Shay.

Shay backed away from the thing.

Preeti looked at her like she was crazy. "Just say something so they know you're alive."

Shay shook her head. She couldn't even mutter the word *no*.

Preeti rolled her eyes. "Shaila-bhen is acting weird," Preeti said into the CB. "The nurse said she hit her head during the riot."

That got Ba screaming in English. *Riot? I'll sue them! How could they?* Suddenly the channel squealed and went silent.

Preeti pushed the volume buttons. "Ba?" She squeezed the talk button. "Bapuji?"

Another voice interrupted the call. "This call has been censored by the Federal Bureau of Investigation."

"No!" Preeti screamed. She marched up to the front and held the machine out to the guard. "I still have ten minutes," she yelled. "Get my parents back."

The guard took the CB and shut it off. "If the channel gets cut off by the Feds, it means we can no longer use that channel for a set period of time."

"So give me another channel." Preeti crossed her arms and set her face in a scowl. Shay knew this pose. The guard had no idea of how stubborn Preeti could be when challenged.

"The FBI now considers that receiver off-limits. They will investigate the violation, then contact us, after which time you may reestablish connection. The process is expected to take a minimum of twenty-four hours."

Shay knew she should get angry. That she should tell the guard off, help her sister. But no anger came. She felt the mildest tingle of anxiety, like a skittering light through the black.

Preeti started to cry. The guard apologized, then called another name. The second guard, stun baton in hand, approached Shaila and told her to move her sister away from the station before she caused trouble. Shay followed the guy's orders. She walked to her sister, wrapped an arm around her shoulders, and told her they'd come back tomorrow.

Preeti snuffled loudly, wiped her hand under her mask, then walked where Shay led her, toward the JCPenney.

Preeti shrugged out from under Shay's arm. "Why didn't you say anything?" she asked, her words catching on a sob.

"The guard said you could call back tomorrow."

"To Ba," Preeti corrected.

Shay didn't answer.

"What's wrong with you?" Preeti asked.

Shay didn't answer.

Preeti stopped. "Shaila-bhen." She glared at Shay.

"I'm tired," she said finally.

Preeti turned and stormed to the guard at the entrance to the JCPenney. "I need to register or something?" she asked.

Shay, frozen in the hallway, watched as Preeti took the bag of toiletries and stack of clothes the guard gave her and disappeared into the store. The emptiness would devour her if she let it. But Preeti needed her. However ridiculous that need was—like Shay had anything to give—it was a tether to reality.

She approached the guard and gave her name, then trotted to where Preeti had slumped on a cot near Shay's own.

"I'm sorry," she said. "We'll call Ba tomorrow. I'll talk."

"Promise?" Preeti said.

Shay forced herself to nod. "We still have a couple

minutes to get dinner." She held out her hand and Preeti took it.

The last thing Lexi wanted was to face the happy couple of Maddie and Ginger after slaving all day on her mother's projects, and yet there they were, hunkered down on neighboring cots in the alcove Lexi had procured for her and Maddie. They'd even wheeled one of the small TVs in there and were watching some series involving very pretty, very skinny girls and oily guys with no chest hair.

"Hey, stranger!" Ginger said, waving as Lexi approached.

Maddie held out a Ziploc bag containing popcorn. "They handed out popcorn to everyone. They said it was to thank us for a *great first day of work*!" She said the last words in a squeaky voice, arms scrunched in and fake grin on her face.

"Thanks," Lexi said, surprised that they saved her a bag. She wouldn't have put it past them to eat her share and not tell.

Ginger stretched out on her cot. "Lexi, are you okay with me moving in here with you guys? There was an extra space, so I dragged my bed over."

"Of course she's okay," Maddie said, play smacking Ginger's leg.

"Yeah," Lexi said. "Of course." *Like I have a choice . . .*

"Where were you, by the way?" Maddie said, munching kernels from her bag.

"My mom had some stuff she needed me to do."

"Well, you missed some choice clothing sorting," Maddie said, sarcasm dripping off the words.

Ginger lifted her T-shirt to reveal a sequined tube top. "We *borrowed* some stuff that the head sorter said to throw away." She snapped the edge of the top against her rib cage. "How could she expect me to throw this away?"

Maddie grabbed Ginger's shirt and tugged it back over the top. "You want everyone to see?" she growled.

Ginger blushed hard enough that her face matched her hair. "Did anyone notice?"

"You're fine," Maddie said, and flipped back on the show.

Lexi had never seen this particular sexy-teen soap opera, but from Maddie and Ginger's running commentary, it was clear they were watching it for a fourth or fifth time. She munched her popcorn, feeling alone even with the two next to her, and wished the minutes to fly by so that she could escape into her office and meet Marco.

Marco slapped another glow-in-the-dark star sticker against the wall. They were barely visible in the fluorescent light of the service hallway, but after Lights Out, they'd shine.

He was putting down the final bread crumbs that would lead his would-be partiers to his makeshift party. He'd started at the exits to both the JCPenney and the Lord & Taylor and snaked a path marked in star stickers to the fire staircase between them, then through a passage to the exit across from the bowling alley. They would have to make a run for it from there across the open mall walkway, but Marco figured few guards would be patrolling the third floor, since after Lights Out it was supposed to be empty, and honestly, if some kids got caught, he couldn't give a crap.

Ryan had better have held up his end of the bargain. The party would definitely not happen without his spreading the word. True, Marco should have done the spreading himself, but when Fate hands you a gift like having leverage over someone who is obviously much more qualified to talk to your peers about a party, you take it. Why hot girls specifically? Marco assumed that if you told hot girls there was a party somewhere, they would spread the word faster than this virus. This assumption was mostly based on bad movies he'd watched on late-night television. He hoped it was true.

On the subject of hot girls, Marco wondered if Ryan would invite Shay to the event. He could not hope to keep his girlfriend bluff going with her right there in front of them. How could he convince her to choose him? *Screw it.* It didn't matter. Whatever he did, of course she would choose the douche over him. Like he had anything to offer a girl in the boyfriend department.

This party was not destined for success. He'd found the keg the senator had promised him and it looked small. With the way Mike and Drew had been sucking back vodka, Marco imagined this thing would be gone in ten minutes flat.

The space, though larger than the parking garage closet, could hold maybe ten people comfortably. Assuming that comfortably included sharing the space with stacks of chairs and parts for the pin-setting machines.

Marco did what he could to improve things. He threw what scraps of material he could find over the machinery. He unstacked some of the chairs. He stole a CD player with an iPod dock in it from the back of the BathWorks and plugged that in opposite the keg for safety's sake. And, in his one effort at making the place cool, he'd also filched a strobe light. If that didn't say party—well, what the hell did he know about parties anyway?

He reached the door to the main hallway and stuck a star to it. It was out of his hands at this point. If people came, great. If not, well, it was the senator's dumb idea to begin with.

The senator. Lexi. *Crap.* He had promised to help her investigate the ice-skating rink for bodies during the god-damned party. How the hell was he supposed to host a fraking party and play Sherlock Holmes with the daughter?

He needed a personal assistant at this point to keep track of his schedule. Time-management was not his forte. This had never before posed a problem, as he was used to no life at all, no friends, no one giving a crap about what he was doing ever. But now he had three different—no, four scams running at the same time. What the hell was he thinking?

Calm the frak down. He could do this. Get the douches and drop them at the party. Then sneak away while they get blitzed and meet Lexi. Be back before the midnight raid. Save the douches' collective ass. And the senator will never be the wiser. *All in a day's scheming.*

LIGHTS OUT

It was a relief to lie on her cot in the black after keeping up appearances for Preeti all evening. All her energy had gone into smiling and chattering on about happy things to keep her sister in good spirits. At dinner, she'd found Kris and introduced them. He'd been wonderfully normal, as Shay had assumed he'd be, and his normalcy took some of the pressure off. But once dinner was over and they returned to the JCPenney, Shay was again a one-woman act.

She tried to sleep—she was exhausted, it should have just happened—but closing her eyes did not stop her mind. It was like, having shut away the sadness, her brain was scrambling around for its missing parts. Every noise startled her. The walls felt too close. She needed a drink, to go to the bathroom, a breath of fresh air.

Off to her left, toward the front of the store, someone coughed. Big hacking coughs. They didn't stop.

A flashlight beam cut the black and closed in on a woman hunched in her cot.

The guard holding the light, his face in a serious full-coverage, hard plastic mask, like the one firefighters use, grabbed the woman's arm and injected her with something that knocked her flat. Another guard materialized from the black, and together they hoisted her cot up and across an aisle, then out the front of the store.

Shay couldn't look away from the empty space on the floor left by the missing cot. How many more would be gone by morning?

Some people whispered. Then Shay heard Preeti sniffle. Slipping off the side of her cot, Shay crawled to Preeti. Without a word, she slid her body up onto Preeti's cot and wrapped her arms around her sister. Preeti curled against her, spine to sternum, and cried.

This kind of being with her sister was easy. It took no effort to hold Preeti as she cried. Just her body there, solid. It had to be somewhere, so why not here? Shay's mind, though, scrabbled around, restless. Preeti quieted, her breathing fell into a rhythm, all around became a symphony of snores, but Shay's brain raced on. She stared at the one light left burning until it shone in green relief against the insides of her eyes.

Marco banged on the door in the garage until it opened.

Drew was the first out. "Let's get this party started."

Mike followed bearing a handle of vodka. Noticing Marco's gaze, he said, "I always bring my own. Who knows what bathtub crap they're going to be swilling at this dive."

Marco swiped his card and opened the door that led into the fire staircase nearest the bowling alley. He grabbed Ryan's arm before he followed Mike and Drew into the stairwell.

"You spread the word?" Marco whispered.

"I told a girl who looked like a partier, if that's what you mean."

This was not encouraging. He let go of Ryan's arm and tromped up the stairs behind the three. At the top, he swiped his card into the door marked BLAZING LANES.

"After you," Mike said, clasping the door.

Marco led the way into the bowling alley and opened the door to the storage area. Two girls stood over the keg trying to jam the tap into its top.

Drew shoved Marco out of the way. "Might I assist you lovely ladies?"

Mike unscrewed his bottle and took a swig. "This is supposed to be a party?"

Surveying the room through the lens of Mike's sarcastic drawl did not improve matters. The strobe light pulsed lamely from its corner, but did little more than annoy the eyes with the overhead light on. There was no music playing—Marco had forgotten to put in a CD. And the two girls were not exactly the hotties Marco had been hoping for.

Ryan slumped into one of the chairs. "It's better than spending another night in that dungeon."

"I'll give you that." Mike passed him the bottle, which Ryan declined.

Drew managed to finally tap the keg and in a sputter of foam, got the beer flowing. The mood lightened signifi-

cantly with this fortuitous event. Upon the discovery that
there were no glasses (*HOW COULD I FORGET GLASSES
OF ALL THINGS!?!*) Drew suggested they all suck it
straight from the tap, which apparently made everyone
the merrier.

Ryan held a keg stand for longer than either of the girls,
and Drew for longer than everyone. Mike remained by the
CD player, into which he had inserted his own iPod and
which now blared some drum-and-bass rap song. Marco
tried to remain invisible by the door.

"Taco!" Drew yelled. He waved for Marco to approach.
"Get your ass up here!"

Marco had never imbibed alcohol of any sort. A keg
stand seemed like the wrong way to begin the process of
acclimating to the stuff. "I'm good."

"That was not a request!" the doofus barked, and strode
across the room.

He hefted Marco's struggling body over his shoulder
and planted him on top of the keg. One of the girls jammed
the tap into Marco's mouth and what tasted like liquid
stale Triscuits flooded in. Marco swallowed too late, and
beer shot out his nose.

"He's totally snarfing!" the girl shouted.

Ryan pulled the tap from Marco's lips. "Don't drown
him."

Drew planted Marco back on his feet, and he stumbled
until he landed on his ass near where Mike surveyed the
scene.

"You popped your cherry," Mike said, swilling more
vodka.

"I'm going to be sick."

Marco staggered for the door and was thrust aside by more revelers in search of the rumored keg. Ryan had done his job. The senator would have to be happy with Marco's effort.

The door next to the storage room was marked JANITOR, and inside, as Marco had hoped, there was a large sink. He shoved his face under its faucet and took big gulps. He had to wash that Triscuit taste out of his mouth. The water did something to calm his stomach. He belched, adjusted his shirt, and stalked off to meet Lexi.

Lexi had to fake going to the bathroom to get away from Maddie and Ginger. Why they were pretending to care what was going on with her was beyond Lexi's imagination, but it didn't matter now. Now she was seconds away from seeing him again. Her real friend. *Boyfriend?* Potentially.

Lexi kept wanting to check her phone, but it had died, and so the only marker she had for how much time had passed was the incremental increase in her anxiety with each passing heartbeat. First, her leg began to jiggle— classic Lexi move; her mother was always telling her to stop jiggling lest she vibrate dinner off the table. Next, nail biting. Once she'd managed to tug a hangnail to bleeding, she moved on to pacing. Pacing didn't last long; Lexi transitioned to spinning in the desk chair. She was nearing the nausea point when the knob turned.

"Marco?" she whispered, trying to stop her brain in its spin cycle.

"You expecting someone else?" He slipped in and shut

the door behind him. "No security escort tonight, Your Highness?"

"Hey, I didn't ask that guy to Taser you."

"Not yet," Marco said.

Lexi wondered if he was implying something of a sexual nature. A twinge of fear tickled her spine, but then he smiled a crooked smile and she laughed a little too loudly to show that she had totally gotten that he'd been joking the whole time.

They entered the service halls and soon were faced with a locked door.

"Dead end," said Lexi.

"For some," whispered Marco. Then he slipped a card through the reader and it opened.

"You stole a card key?" Lexi asked, feeling something between anxiety and awe.

"Don't freak out. I used to work here," Marco clarified, holding the door open. "The card was a privilege of employment."

They took the back hallways the long way around the mall, which took for-freaking-EVER, but Marco was jumpy about crossing the "public areas" of the mall when using his card key.

"You haven't yet had the pleasure of feeling your nuts burned off by a Taser," was his explanation.

When they reached the vicinity of the ice-skating rink, the elevator dinged as they were about to unlock the security door. They bolted down the service hall and hid around a corner, then watched as a shrouded gurney was wheeled out of the elevator and through the doors.

"We were right," Lexi whispered.

"*I* was right," Marco retorted.

As soon as the gurney was gone, Lexi and Marco snuck over to the door. Beyond it was a hall that led to the cavernous storage room for the Zamboni. The retractable doors between the rink and the storage room were open, meaning the air was so cold, Lexi's eyeballs hurt. She and Marco ducked from pile of crap to pile of crap until they reached the far end of the storage room and peered out the doorway.

There was no more ice-skating rink. There was merely a gigantic pile of bodies. It was like a garbage dump, just heaps of bodies tossed one on top of the other. The glassy eyes of one man seemed to be staring right at Lexi. She whipped back around the wall and threw up on the cement.

"Frak," Marco said, pushing himself flat against the wall. He stared at the huge barrel in front of him as if it might provide some explanation for the body dump.

Lexi knelt against the pavement, then pushed herself away from her own sick and leaned against the wall. "We're screwed," she said. "All of us. Screwed."

Marco suddenly dropped and threw himself over her, finger to his lips.

The wheels of the gurney squeaked past.

"That makes one fifty today," said the person steering the now empty gurney.

"Better than yesterday," the other said. "We had two hundred yesterday."

His forehead pressed to Lexi's. His breath misted against

her cheek. She felt shimmery tingles dart over her skin.

The door slammed closed. They were alone with the corpses.

Marco flung himself away from her, careful not to expose himself to another glimpse of the rink. "I should have known."

"Known what?" Lexi asked. "That my mother was piling a billion bodies on the ice-skating rink?"

"That this virus was some freak killer flu. Essentially, that the majority of the mall was screwed. Why else would they trap us in here? To keep the good people of Westchester safe in their McMansions, that's why."

Lexi's mind kept drawing a blank. "This many people can't have died. There were only maybe seventy in the freezer. There are—"

"Thousands. That looks like a freaking Bieber concert worth of bodies."

"We can't tell anyone," Lexi said, only realizing after she'd spoken that she was repeating her mother's words.

"Of course we can't," Marco said, standing and beginning to pace between the barrel and the wall. "People would lose their shiznit if they knew this many people had died."

"So, what? Do we just do nothing?" Lexi hoped Marco had an answer, because she was freaked out beyond the capacity for rational thought.

"I'm going to start taking extra precautions. No more interpersonal interaction. I am staying ten feet from every freaking disease-carrying douche in this mall."

It took Lexi a moment to realize that this most likely foreclosed any further touching between the two of them.

"Does this mean we're not meeting in my office anymore?"

Marco smirked. It wasn't exactly a cute smirk, more like a calculating smirk. "You have any more mysteries in need of solving?"

"I won't know until tomorrow."

"Then I guess I'll see you tomorrow night."

They snuck back to the JCPenney in silence. Strangely, Lexi could no longer remember what the rink exactly looked like. She could recall the beams of the ceiling, the general level of freaked out she'd felt, but not the bodies themselves. *Whatever.* Better that she couldn't. Who wants to remember something like that?

She bumped into Marco when he stopped suddenly at a door. She tried not to obsess about how much she liked being pressed against him, even for a second.

"Sorry," she whispered.

He didn't answer, just opened the door for her. She walked through. He didn't follow.

"Aren't you coming?" Shouldn't they talk more? Didn't he want to hang out?

"I don't live here," he said coolly.

"But I'll see you tomorrow?"

"Yeah," he said. "Tomorrow." And let the door slam.

Lexi slunk back to her cot in the alcove. Why didn't he want to hang out more? Of course, for him even entering the JCPenney was risky. Maybe he was afraid of getting Tasered again? She couldn't blame him for that. And he said she'd see him tomorrow. That was good. He would see her again. That was almost a promise of a second date.

"Off with your boy again?" Maddie's voice hissed through the dark.

"Where'd Lexi find a boy?" Ginger was on Lexi's other side.

"Just taking some alone time," Lexi lied. She would not tell anyone about the bodies. As insane as she felt admitting it, her mother was right to not let that tidbit out.

"With the boy?" Maddie would not let it go.

Lexi decided to throw her a bone. "Maybe." She smiled to herself in the dark. She had something neither Maddie nor Ginger had: a boy.

"You're going to have to do better than that over breakfast, so think of some juicy details or I strangle you with skinny jeans." Maddie shifted in her bed. "I am dying for gossip and you're the only one who's got any."

A part of Lexi wanted to gossip with them. She'd never felt this way about a boy before, never found excuses to bump into a guy (literally) before, never felt a fire under her skin when he spoke. Was what she felt normal? Was she making a fool of herself? But Lexi wasn't sure Maddie and Ginger wouldn't make her the butt of their jokes, they who'd played Truth or Dare enough times to know the rules. Surely tingles from a boy's platonic touch held little in the way of interest gossip-wise to them. So she rolled over onto her stomach and remembered the feel of his breath on her cheek and said, "Maybe," so quietly, she wasn't even sure Maddie had heard.

Ryan surveyed the party from a chair in a corner. Mike had taken over and turned what had been a lame group of people with a keg into a legit party. *Leave it to Mike.* He could take even this crappy excuse for a party and make it into a scene.

Much of the work was done by simply having the overhead lights out, but Mike had also found some flashlights, which he jammed in the corners to provide some "romance," as he'd said. That plus the strobe plus some decent music equaled not bad.

The music transitioned to a dance beat and the girls writhed around Drew, who looked happier than Ryan had seen him in days. Other people had shown up, and they mostly kept in their little groups, dancing or hovering around the beer. Someone had stolen some glasses from the bowling alley bar, but even though the drinks were now mobile, there were always those guys afraid to let the keg out of their sight.

Mike remained on the sidelines, as always. He never really attended his parties. Mike preferred to observe people, then saunter through after people were drunk to receive their congratulations for throwing another awesome party. Drew was the guy calling the shots at the event itself. That was the way they worked—Mike set it up and Drew carried it out.

At a regular Mike party, Ryan hung by the TV half watching whatever sport was on—there was always some game playing. Parties were all about dancing and drinking, and he wasn't much of a dancer and tried to avoid the drinking games because they always became a little too intense. Never play beer pong with football players. When his girlfriend of the moment showed up, they'd find some place to hook up. All told, parties were not that great, but they were better than nothing.

However, these regular complaints weren't what had his butt glued to the chair. Tonight, he simply wanted to

be somewhere else. With someone else. Specifically, anywhere with Shay.

The song changed and a bunch of the girls squealed.
Drew picked two up, one in each arm, and spun them,
thwacking a random dude in the face.

"Hey, dickhead, watch yourself!" the guy shouted.

Drew dropped both girls—no joke, dropped them—and
turned to the shouter. "What did you call me?"

The guy, who looked about twenty-five, stood taller.
"You hit me in the face, *dick*head."

Drew shoved the guy in the chest, and that was all
it took. Three guys launched themselves at Drew and he
went down. Girls screamed. People pushed back to give
the fight its due space. Mike paused the music and stood.
Ryan sensed something awful coming.

Where the hell was Marco?

Mike pulled something from his waistband.

Ryan bolted out of the chair and threw himself into the
fight. "Get off him!" he shouted, pulling at every limb he
could get a grip on. With his help, Drew was able to shove
the mob off him, kicking one in the gut so hard he puked
and fell to the floor. Drew squared his back to the wall and
Ryan stood beside him, fists up.

Drew grabbed a chair and wielded it in one hand. "Get
out of my party before I have to get angry."

The fighters looked ready to test Drew's resolve until
Mike joined the two of them, gun in hand.

"You heard the man," he said.

The guys did not look happy. "Be seeing you," one said
with a menacing chin thrust.

"Any time," Mike snarled.

The four left. Mike shoved the gun back in his pants.

"Anyone else interested in a fight?"

People hung back, clutched their beers.

"Excellent." Mike went back to the CD player and turned on the music.

Ryan put a hand on Drew's shoulder. His shirt was soaked through with sweat. "You okay?"

Drew set the chair down. "Better than okay, J. Shrimp." He smiled and Ryan noticed two of his teeth were dark with blood. He pushed past Ryan and rejoined the dancing girls.

Ryan went over to Mike. "Where's Marco? Shouldn't he be keeping things cool?"

"Why would Marco be in charge of keeping anything cool?"

So Mike had no idea this was Marco's party. What else did Mike not know about Marco?

Mike pointed to the door. "Shrimp, you monitor guests for the rest of the night. Keep the assholes out."

Ryan nodded, not sure how he was supposed to spot the assholes. He made a rough assumption that anyone who looked like a person Mike wouldn't invite to one of his parties was out.

The best way to turn assumed assholes away was to tell them the keg was kicked. When Ryan saw an asshole in a group of non-assholes, he turned the whole pack away— better safe than sorry. As the night wore on, however, even with turning away a large number of potential assholes, the room was packed beyond capacity. Ryan was not even sure another body could squeeze into the space.

Footsteps slapped their way toward him. "Sorry, dude, party's full," Ryan said.

"It's me," Marco said. "And what the hell are you—Oh." He looked in the doorway. "Crap."

"I've been turning people away, but still—"

"You've been turning people away?"

"Some assholes attacked Drew, so Mike put me on watch to keep any other potential assholes out."

Marco swore something vicious under his breath.

"What, you were hoping for a fight?" Ryan was not sure why turning people away would be such a bummer. *Another thing I don't understand about this guy.*

"It doesn't matter," Marco said. "You and Mike and Drew have to come with me."

"Why?" Ryan saw a flashlight streak across the wall at the far end of the hall. That could only mean one thing. "Did security follow you?"

Marco looked confused, then, glancing down the hall, nodded. "We have to get you out of here."

"We can't leave Mike and Drew," Ryan said.

He shoved his shoulder into the mass of people by the door and began driving his way toward the music. The music was deafening next to Mike, but Ryan managed to communicate the approaching security problem by screaming directly into Mike's ear.

Marco popped out of the crowd just as Mike nodded his understanding. "You'll never get out that way," Marco yelled. "Follow me."

Some people started to scream, but Ryan couldn't tell if it was because of the party or because security had arrived. He didn't bother turning to look. Marco led them to a narrow door at the back of the room and pushed both Ryan and Mike into it.

"Where's Drew?" Marco asked.

Ryan pointed to the dance floor.

Marco rolled his eyes and shoved his way back through the crowd. There was more screaming now, definitely a sign that security had arrived. Suddenly, Drew's body crashed against the door frame.

"What the hell?" he shouted.

"Get in there and be quiet." Marco pushed Drew through the doorway, passed something to Mike, and slammed the door on the three of them.

They were in some mechanical space. Three steps led up onto a metal bridge over the long shafts and gears of the machines. Dangling in the air to his left were bowling pins, all organized in the pinsetters.

Mike flipped on whatever Marco had passed him. It squealed, then began speaking. It was a police radio. From the chatter, it was clear security was busting the party.

"We'd better get away from the door," Mike said, creeping up the stairs.

The three tiptoed down the catwalk to the far end of the space and listened to the muffled shouts and screams from the remains of the party on the other side of the door.

Marco slammed his back against the door. Before him, the party-goers were roiling like flies against a window. So much for his vow to stay away from people. Security stood at the exit—the only way out save the dead end mechanic's passage over the pinsetting machines in front of which Marco stood. There was one man in full riot gear in the open doorway to the hall, but the overhead lights glinted off the helmets of others behind him. Still, the revelers scrambled from wall to wall and climbed on chairs in an attempt to escape their fate.

"Everyone, calm down. You will not be harmed. We are here to confirm your registration and escort you back to your Home Stores."

It took several more announcements of this nature before people stopped raging. Security did not enter the room, but rather ordered people to come out single file to check in. Marco got into the line along with the others. He did not want to draw any attention to himself or the narrow door to the walkway. The only important thing was to keep them from finding Mike & Co.

At the exit, a man with a stun baton forced Marco against the wall. He shuffled forward with the line until he reached another stun-baton-wielding guard. The baton flipped down in front of him, halting his progress. A second person jammed something into Marco's ear.

"What the hell?" he asked.

"Normal temp." It was a woman's voice. "Asymptomatic." The baton lifted.

Marco shuffled forward. Near the end of the hall stood three more guards, one of whom had a tablet.

"Name?" said the tablet bearer.

Behind him, Marco heard shouting.

"One-oh-one. Tag him." The woman's voice.

"I'm not going in there!"

Marco turned and saw a guy get shoved into what Marco knew to be the food storage room for the bowling alley. The door was slammed. The guard flipped down the stun baton in front of the next victim.

"Name?" the tablet guy repeated.

Once Marco was identified, he was led by another guard to a table in the restaurant. The metal gate blocking it and the bar area off from the rest of the mall had only been raised halfway, so Marco had to duck under it.

"Take them down," Marco's guard said, pushing him forward toward the table, where there sat four other guys surrounded by two guards.

On the short journey back to the Lord & Taylor, the others complained about security busting the party, but otherwise seemed pleased with the evening. Marco gave himself a mental pat on the back for having actually pulled the night off. So a few people were jailed for having mild fevers. Given Marco's recent revelation of the death rate from the flu, he was prepared to accept the willy-nilly bagging and tagging of anyone with even the remotest sign of having it.

Flopping down on his cot, Marco slathered all his exposed skin with hand sanitizer, then finally allowed himself to relax. In that momentary pleasure, he thought of other pleasurable things, like Shay, and recalled that he had totally bailed on helping her find a place to hide like he'd promised the night before. Leave it to him to screw up the one thing he actually cared about.

He would make it up to her. Tomorrow. He would find

her and do something—steal her some food from where they were stockpiling everything in the Sam's Club. Yes. She might like that.

He could handle this. He could keep all the balls in the air. He would handle this. He was in control.

DAY
—
NINE

LIGHTS ON

The glare of Lights On woke Shay after what felt like mere minutes of sleep. Her body was stiff, like an old puppet's, and her head swam. She was still in Preeti's bed, and her sister lay rigid in her arms.

"I don't want to be here," Preeti whispered. "I want to go home."

"Yeah," Shay answered for lack of something better.

"I dreamed of that coughing." Preeti hunched tighter against Shay. "Coughing everywhere and men in black trying to catch me. All I could do was crawl. They were always right behind me."

"It was just a dream," Shay said.

"But it wasn't," Preeti said, sitting up. She pointed to the empty space where the missing cot, and missing woman, should have been. "There really are men in black."

Shay shuffled up on her elbows. Moving hurt her head like a blow. The pain focused to a laser point just above her right eye. "That woman was sick," she said, wincing. "The men took her to the med center. To protect us."

Preeti didn't answer right away. "There are more," she said. "I count ten more spaces."

Shay glanced around. There were odd breaks in the lines of cots, more missing women, missing girls. She wondered why they took the cots. Did they not expect the women to return? Of course they didn't expect them to return.

This was not helping anyone. Preeti needed normal. She needed to get out of bed and do something other than stare at empty spaces.

"We should brush our teeth," Shay said, sitting up. A red-hot poker ran through her skull. She ignored it. "We should get breakfast."

"I don't want to go out there," Preeti mumbled. She pulled her knees to her chest and wrapped her arms around them.

Shay stood, forcing her awkward limbs to function. "You just need to get out of here," she said, pulling Preeti's arm. "This place is depressing. You'll like school."

"School?" Preeti asked, incredulous.

"It's what they're calling running around the food court with your friends."

Preeti perked up at the word. "Do you think Lia and Sahra are still here?"

"You'll have to see," Shay said, shrugging playfully, happy for the mask so she didn't also have to fake a smile.

It was hard to tell how many people were missing at breakfast. Yesterday, some team had moved tables—every-

thing from cheap plastic and metal backyard sets to fancy
carved-wood dining room displays—into the first-floor
courtyard, but there were not enough seats for everyone
and no assigned tables. It looked like the same crowds as
had eaten dinner, but maybe with so many people, no one
noticed ten, twenty, a hundred missing bodies.

"Can we ride the Ferris wheel at school?" Preeti asked.
Her fears seemed to have dissipated with the promise of
school and friends.

"You can do whatever your teacher says." Shay poked
a pile of what she'd been told were grits. How could grit
be food?

Preeti ate what she'd been given like a thing starved.
Spoonful after spoonful went into her mouth. "You going
to eat yours?" she asked, scraping the last grits from the
plastic.

Shay shook her head, pushed the plate toward her sister, and refit her mask over her mouth.

It was disconcerting how quickly Preeti had recovered.
Where was the sadness, the anger of yesterday? She hadn't
even mentioned calling Ba. Not that Shay was interested
in reliving that torture. Her head throbbed. She needed
to go to the med center. But not before getting Preeti to
school. Preeti would only freak out if Shay told her she
felt like crap.

Ryan snuck from car shadow to car shadow through the
parking garage. With the showers now on this level, whoever was in charge had all the lights turned on. Keeping
Ruthie and Jack a secret was going to be harder. Their SUV

was too close to the new shower establishment. Maybe he could convince them to move into the closet? No, that would be worse. And what if Mike or Drew went back there to get something?

Mike had decided that he liked living in the bowling alley. They'd discovered a walk-in fridge, just like the one in the Grill'n'Shake, in the room next to the place where the party had been. The metal door had been padlocked, but a few blows from a fire extinguisher had smashed both it and the handle. Mike and Drew pried the thing open with metal bars scrounged from the party room. Inside, they'd found a meager selection, but still. It was food.

Ryan had made off with a bag of rolls and a can of mandarin oranges. He'd also found a can opener in the bar, so there'd be no broken toys this morning. To get away without Mike and Drew freaking out, he said he'd forgotten something in the storage room. A clean shirt or whatever.

"Bring one back for me," Drew had muttered, crumbs spewing from his mouth.

Ryan felt warm inside, seeing the SUV. He knocked on the door using the special three-knock code they'd developed—one short, one long, one short. Ruthie pushed the door open. Her eyes were red with tears.

"Jack's sick," she said.

Ryan's first thought: *I did this.* He'd had the flu. Maybe he was still contagious when he met them.

He crawled into the van and looked over the first row into the way back. Jack was curled like someone had kneed him in the groin.

"Hey, buddy," he said, putting a hand on Jack's shoulder. "I brought you some rolls."

"My tummy hurts," Jack moaned.

A stomachache was not coughing. This was not the flu. *I didn't kill him.*

Ryan was suddenly able to think. He pulled the can opener from his pocket and passed it to Ruthie. "You need to eat," he said. "See if you can get him to at least eat a roll or something. And drink. If it's a stomach problem, he needs lots of water. I'll go to the med center and see about getting some Pepto or Tums."

"And he'll be okay?" Ruthie was clearly freaking out.

Ryan grabbed both her shoulders and stared into her eyes. "Chill," he said. "Jack is going to be fine." He opened the bag of rolls and handed her one. "Just take care of yourself. I'll take care of Jack."

Ryan pressed the door closed and slunk toward the showers. Thinking this was an ideal opportunity, he crept to the end of the line and joined the crowd. The guard on duty down here was merely an old dude passing out towels and chunks of soap. When Ryan reached the head of the line, he was given a towel and white wedge.

"When you're done, throw the soap on the ground and put the towel in that bin." A large, wheeled canvas container stood near a parked wagon.

"Are there razors?" Ryan asked, rubbing his prickly face.

"Safety razors are in the Home Stores. Ask a guard."

So that was a no for him. Whatever. He didn't have much facial hair to begin with. Maybe Shay liked her men fuzzy. Or could grow to like *him* that way at least.

After showering, which felt like goddamned heaven, he changed into his other pair of clothes from the duffel in the closet and joined the rest of the mall on the first level. People were sitting at tables eating breakfast. This totally normal event made Ryan sad. Why couldn't he be a part of this? Why was he an outcast just for trying to escape? Like every one of these people hadn't thought about it.

That was when he saw Mr. Reynolds. The jerk was holding court at an iron backyard dining set, a crowd of guys his age—old and gray-haired and rich-looking, even in their mismatched clothing—nodding along with whatever he was saying. Ryan ducked behind a crowd of women to avoid getting spotted. No telling what that bastard would do if he saw him.

Why did Reynolds get to live like a normal person? He was the asshole who got Mike and Drew and him into this mess. It had been Reynolds who convinced Mike to try to escape out the garage, who got them all in trouble with security, who would have left Ryan to die of the flu, and who blew their escape out the roof by only thinking about himself. And yet it was Mike, Ryan, and Drew who got stuck munching soup crackers in a dark closet like a bunch of outlaws? It was completely unfair. Like everything else about this place.

Ryan had to focus. Get to the med center and get back to Jack. He had people depending on him. He wasn't a smug, sell-out, selfish ass pretending to be some big shot. Ryan mattered, at least to Ruthie and Jack.

The med center was guarded by a mom-aged woman.

She ate her breakfast while playing Scrabble on a tablet. "Sick or visiting?" she said, without looking up. "There are no visitors for flu patients."

Ryan decided that saying sick might get him admitted and saying helping someone sick might invite too many questions, so he said, "Visiting."

"Name?"

That had him. "Dixit," he said. "Preeti Dixit."

The woman abandoned her game and switched to a different program, some sort of spreadsheet. "She's not here anymore."

"Um, well, yeah, but she told me that she forgot something, and wanted me to pick it up."

The woman shrugged. "The lost-and-found is in the back," she said. "But it's only phones and stuff, anything that could be wiped down. No clothing, no books."

Ryan nodded. "It was her phone. Can I check if it's here?"

"Enter at your own risk," she said, pointing to the hall between two rows of curtains. "Take that path to the back wall, then through the door marked STAFF. Box is on the shelf on the right."

Ryan glanced into the rooms created by the curtain system as he passed. There were few people in here, all of them looking normal save for the odd air cast or bandage. None of them looked like a flu victim.

Ryan saw the top of a head over the curtain wall coming his way, so he ducked onto the escalator, which was off, and ran up it. The second floor was entirely different from the first. The only curtains here were a row of them

against the security gate at the entrance to the mall, blocking the view out. The rest of the floor—a whole department store's worth of floor—was just people on cots.

Each person had on a mask, except for those with tubes
in their mouths hooked up to machines. But there were
few of them. Those people were in a row on actual gurneys near the back wall. Most people lay still on their
cots, inches from the floor and a foot from the next patient. Every few seconds, one would start convulsing with
coughs, then another, like there was some timer controlling them all.

But the worst part was the area next to the gurneys.
An area the size of half an end zone was covered in what
looked like mattresses, and piled on these beds were bodies. Dead bodies. Had to be. Not one moved. There were
a bunch of them lying there. Like some gross sleepover.

"You shouldn't be up here!" A woman strode toward
him, a surgical mask over most of her face.

"I-I hurt m-my ankle," Ryan stammered, trying to pull
his eyes away from the mattresses.

"Get a mask on and wait on the first level!" The woman
forcibly turned him around and pushed him down the
stairs.

Ryan stumbled down, trying to make sense of what
he'd just seen. It didn't look like a place anyone expected
to leave. You went from cot to mattress to where? Was the
stockroom on the second floor packed with corpses?

Bile burned his throat at the thought. This was like
some death factory. He would never let them take Jack.

Ryan loped down the hall toward the exit.

"Find your friend's phone?" the woman at the entrance asked.

Ryan kept running, needing to put some distance between him and that place. He would find stomach stuff somewhere else, anywhere else. He would never go in that place again.

Marco sat outside the senator's office contemplating what the hell the woman could ask of him next. He figured he deserved a major thank-you for last night's festivities. Anything after the thank-you that didn't include *And here's a fried chicken basket as a reward* was going to set him to screaming.

The security guard had woken him from his cot some brief moment after Lights On. "The senator needs to see you," was his only introduction. Marco figured she was eager to hear how he made such a success of this party insanity. He would try not to blurt out *Dumb luck*.

He peered into the office to see what was taking so long. The senator had a half-eaten bagel on her desk and the fat cell phone was again pressed to her ear. *Where did that woman get a* bagel? Marco salivated at the word.

"Well, that's discouraging," she said into the phone. "Chen tells me he's gotten nowhere in here. But my hygiene initiative seems to be working. Only three hundred new admits yesterday."

Three hundred. All destined for the ice-skating rink. How many more could be piled on before the whole thing cracked and crashed down into the medical center below?

Maybe that would be better, save the trouble of transporting the bodies up a floor.

"I need more than twenty-four hours. Give me seventy-two at the least. I can show you real results in seventy-two."

She sounded like she was bargaining. With whom? For what?

"I suppose I should say thank you." She bit her bagel and chewed slowly. "Tomorrow, then." She put down the phone but remained staring out the square of window.

Marco decided to knock. His stomach was growling. Maybe she'd share the bagel.

The senator glanced at the door, then swiveled in her chair to face him. "You failed me, Carvajal," was how she began.

"I threw the party," he said, confused. "Security came. Nice move checking people's temperatures, by the way. How many sick did you sentence to the medical center?"

"Security did an excellent job controlling the party itself," she said, patting her mouth with a napkin and replacing her mask. "I want to talk to you about the twenty or so people they found rampaging around the mall after being kicked out of the party by 'some kid.' I'm assuming this kid is you?"

That goddamned Ryan Murphy was screwing up everything in Marco's life. Couldn't the flu have killed him when it had the chance?

Marco cleared his throat. "It wasn't me," he said, banging together a plausible excuse. "I went to the can and some kid took up bouncer duty by the door."

"These people you let escape? They smashed the front windows of the Jessica McClintock store and were caught defacing the mannequins. How do I explain this to the other mall residents? This makes it look like we don't have control."

"You *don't* have control." Marco wondered why this was such a revelation.

"If we don't provide the illusion of control, we'll have anarchy. Your job is to help me project this illusion. And if you can no longer manage your job, I am going to have to relieve you of your card key and all privileges of non-compliance that up until now you have enjoyed."

She will pry this card from my cold, dead fingers.

Marco shifted to sit taller. "You told me to throw a party, I threw a party. I did everything you asked."

"Tonight, you make sure to go to the bathroom *before* the party. Let me know at our evening meeting where to deliver the keg." She picked up the bagel and pointed him to the door. "And do a better job of working your mall assignment. I got a complaint report from your coworkers on construction that you were slacking off."

Screw construction. Screw her and her job. Like Marco needed this crap in his life. But without the card key, he was a sitting duck like the rest of them, fodder for the medical center, another body on the ice. *Not a lot of options trapped here in Suck City.*

He had to problem solve. He'd completed an experimental party. What had he learned? Mike and Drew were a liability. Mike had control issues. Everyone had control issues. Marco would control their control issues. They were not invited to tonight's event. He would provide his own security by not attending the party—no chance of facing a beat-down if he wasn't there.

First job was to find out who got tossed from the party last time. That douche Ryan would be able to identify them. Marco would get them to sign on to this new party—he had to find a new spot for it, a bigger place, better decorations, decent music. Then those guys would spread the word. He just had to keep Mike from hearing about it. Which meant finding Mike. *So much plotting, so little time . . .*

Lexi noticed several solutions to the problem of what to do with your mask while eating. Some wore it like a party hat on their heads, others like a necklace. She saw one guy with it balanced on his beard, just below his mouth. Another woman had hers on her forehead like a stunted horn. Lexi decided to go for the utterly original mask-on-ear look.

"Now that's a fashion trend I see sweeping the runways this spring," Maddie mused from across the picnic table.

"It's a hat plus an earring," Ginger chirped. "Very chic." She pulled her mask necklace over her ear.

Lexi had never envisioned herself as a trendsetter, but here she was, blazing fashion trails. She'd never imagined herself with a boyfriend either, but she had another date for after Lights Out. The world of the mall was like another dimension, an opposite world, the mirror reverse of reality. And Lexi liked life in the mirror.

"So about this boy," Maddie said, swallowing her mush.

"Where did you find him?" Ginger asked, leaning toward Lexi, elbows on the table.

"Why is he in our Home Store's stockroom?" Maddie pointed her spoon at Lexi. "Are you hiding him? Does he have the flu?"

"I'm not hiding him," Lexi said, half annoyed by the interrogation, half thrilled.

"So how does he get in?"

"I let him in," Lexi lied.

"You bad girl!" Ginger squealed.

"Does he have friends?" Maddie was practically crawling across the table. "Would he like to share those friends with two eligible hotties?"

"Is he here?" Ginger looked around at the other tables. "Is that him?"

Lexi tried not to be insulted by the fact that the guy she picked looked like a loser. "No way," she said. "Not in his dreams."

"What about him?" Maddie pointed to a hulking guy who looked to be near thirty.

"Ew!" Lexi squealed. (*Squealed!* She was squealing! Who was this squealing person?) "He's old. Gross."

The game carried them through breakfast. After dropping their plates in the trash, Lexi followed Maddie and Ginger to start work as a clothing sorter back in the JCPenney, which was where women's clothes were dumped. Men's were in the Lord & Taylor, children's in the HomeMart.

The first-floor stockroom was filled with piles of women's clothing from all over the mall. There were fifty sorters assigned to women's clothing, five supervisors (old ladies too frail to do any work), and two guards. The sorters were divided into three groups: nightgowns and lingerie, shoes, and all other, the latter being the largest group. Today, Lexi, Maddie, and Ginger were assigned to shoes.

"They want us to throw away a pair of seven-hundred-dollar Jimmy Choo heels?" Ginger said, clinging to the strappy pair like life itself. "I just can't do it. They can't make me do it." She stuffed the shoes into the corner.

Lexi had never understood high heels. They were painful—she'd worn a pair to a bat mitzvah of some work friend of her mother's and had gone barefoot after an hour. Life was so much nicer in a pair of sneakers. Maybe not sexier, but more comfortable.

Maddie had a pair of stacked stripper heels strapped to her feet. "Is this a good look for me?" she said, finger to chin as she admired her feet. She had her sweats bunched around her knees and had tied off the front of her turtleneck through the neck to bare her midriff.

"It's a winner for sure," Lexi said, throwing a ballet flat at her.

Ginger began tugging at her T-shirt. "I think we can start a trend," she said, pulling the hem of her shirt through the neck hole. "What do you say, Lex?"

Lexi threw the other flat from the pair at Ginger. "I would rather catch the flu than that trend."

"For shame!" came an old lady's voice from around the corner. She appeared shortly thereafter, waving a finger at them. "I will not have any joking about our terrible predicament. Now get those shirts back on right and put on your rationed shoes, then get the sorted pairs out to the registration area before the lunch break."

Maddie and Ginger could barely control their laughter as they straightened their shirts and retied their sneakers.

"Like I'm parting with these babies," Maddie said, sliding the stacked heels into the corner where Ginger had stowed the Jimmy Choos.

Once the three of them had moved several stacks of

approved shoes out to the registration area, Maddie and Ginger signaled for Lexi to sneak one of the pairs they'd siphoned into their corner under her sweatshirt and follow them. They led her into a dark section of the stock area, where the unsorted clothes were left until needed, then through a door and into the loading area. A corrugated metal door filled most of one wall. An almost magnetic pull tugged on Lexi, whispering, *Outside . . .*

"Ta-da!" Ginger said, waving her arms at the other walls.

Ginger and Maddie had hung slinky dresses, tube tops, and mini skirts around like decorations. All the items were expensive-looking. They dumped their haul of impractical, uncomfortable, ridiculously high and strappy heels on a table above which hung a strapless green velvet cocktail dress.

Lexi could not believe the amount of stuff they had stolen. "You guys are going to get in trouble," she said.

Maddie looked at her like she'd grown hooves. "Why? They want us to throw the stuff out and we're simply rescuing these trifles from the Dumpster."

"But what if someone found out? Like the other people in the mall who like Jimmy Choos or whatever?"

"How would they find out?" Maddie asked, stepping toward Lexi. "You're not thinking of enlightening anyone about our little stock here?"

"No," Lexi blurted. "I mean, of course I wouldn't tell on you." She felt like she did the time she stole her mother's lipstick to write on the wall. The offense was written everywhere in red and yet still, her mother questioned her, like she was hoping to catch her daughter in a lie.

Ginger intervened. "She gets that this isn't stealing, Mad. Lay off."

Maddie backed off. "So long as we're all cool with things," she said, "why don't we try some goodies on?"

Ginger clapped her hands, then tugged off her tee. "I've been dying to try the Alice and Olivia!"

Lexi could not stop feeling like the loser in the room. "Isn't that old lady going to wonder where we went?"

"Who, Betty?" Maddie asked, sliding a shimmery black dress over her head. "That old bag wouldn't know if a year passed between checking on us. Yesterday, she asked me three times in as many minutes how soon until lunch."

Lexi tried to relax, be cool, but she felt like any second her mother would bust through the door and catch her. Should she tell Maddie and Ginger about the bodies on the ice? Would knowing that they were all on the edge of death get them to follow the rules?

But did you really need to follow *all* the rules to keep things from falling apart? The new mall order would not crumble over a couple of hidden prom dresses.

And so when Ginger pressed a blue dress into Lexi's chest and begged her to try it, that she would look "so amazing" in that color, Lexi took off her clothes and put the thing on. It didn't fit, but what did that matter? Ginger told her she looked gorgeous and even Maddie gave the outfit a nod of approval.

"We'll find some things in your size," Maddie said.

Lexi said thanks and tried to look grateful.

NOON

Shay counted five kids and two teachers missing. And that was without really knowing anyone.

Preeti had run off the second Shay checked her in with Alison at the information desk in Baxter's. Preeti's "class" did in fact contain her two friends from before the riots, before she'd come down with the flu. Preeti had seen the girls in the children's book section—Preeti's class was old enough to actually try to teach them something—and they'd met, grabbing hands and squealing as if this was an average day at their regular school.

How could Preeti be so normal? How was anyone pretending that life was not simply a waiting game to see who dropped next?

Take Kris, for example. Lunch was late, so he was leading a game of duck-duck-goose. Duck-duck-freaking-goose. The kids loved him like a god and jumped on him every chance they got. "Goose" would topple into Kris's lap and he would cry out like he was shocked by the attack, then start tickling. Everyone ended up laughing— the ducks and the geese. Shay made a good show of merriment, laughing the best "I'm having a good time" laugh she could muster. But Kris, he was really laughing. He actually was having a good time. What was his damage?

Duck-duck-goose ended and Kris waved for Shay to help him collect one of the art bins Alison had spent the night putting together. "We'll make masks," Kris said, holding up a Popsicle stick and paper plate.

"A mask to wear over our masks," Shay said, hefting a tray of paints and brushes.

"Decorating their face masks!" Kris exclaimed, missing her sarcasm entirely. "I love it. We'll get stickers and do it after lunch."

After they'd set down the materials and gotten the kids started gluing sticks to their plates, Shay asked—no, begged, "Tell me. Please. How do you do it? How can you stay so happy when we're missing five kids—five, just in one day?"

Kris knelt back on his haunches, then sat and propped his arms behind him. "It's a choice," he said. "The way I see it, you can look at this as a giant suckfest of death or you can decide to make the best of things and live. Why not stay positive?"

Shay looked at him like he'd just peeled off his skin to reveal the alien hide beneath.

Kris elbowed her. "Don't look at me like I'm insane," he said. "It's not like I'm not scared or sad or kicking myself for coming here that fateful Saturday, but that's all stuff I can't change. What I can change is how I react to it, and I choose to stay positive." He shuffled over to a girl who was having trouble with the glue and getting it in her hair. When he returned, Shay was still gawking.

He mimicked her look back to her. "I sound that nuts? Let me try again.

"My mom died of cancer a couple years ago, just as I was graduating from Tisch. I was really pissed about that. I would look at what was happening to her—she was young, really young, like in her forties—and I felt all this rage at god, the universe, everything. My dad became a wreck, stopped going to work. The law firm ended up giving him an extended leave of absence, but he's never gone back. My mom, though, she was like a saint.

"One day I said to her, Aren't you freaking pissed off? And she said, Oh, I'm pissed. This sucks—she said *sucks*—but I don't want to spend my last days angry." He picked a dust bunny from his jeans and flicked it into the air. "That was before things got really bad. By the end, she was miserable and cursing everything, but before, she chose something else."

Another kid screamed for Kris and he went trotting over to the rescue. Shay felt around inside herself, looking for that energy necessary to break orbit from the emptiness, to choose life, and found nothing.

To keep from getting crap from the other construction people, Marco had to party plan during meal and bathroom breaks. He'd scrawled some ideas on toilet paper, only to have the sheets dissolve in a deluge while helping some old guy repair a busted faucet on the second floor. This was the kind of crap day he was enjoying.

He'd decided to host this party in the IMAX theater. It was separate from the other theaters, which were being used by the school during the day for child placation and in the evenings for general entertainment of the masses, and he'd confirmed with a guy on security that the IMAX was abandoned. "No one can get the computers to work right," the guy had explained. Apparently, the projectionist was resting peacefully on the rink.

The IMAX was relatively soundproof, and it was huge. The place also had speakers. Surely a computer genius such as he could get at least the audio portion of the system running. And it had lights on dimmers—*party lighting scheme, check*. The only issue was getting people in there unnoticed.

The IMAX, unlike the bowling alley, would require people to cross a fire stairwell, not run from one side of the main hallway to the other. This meant he had to find a way to bust open one of the magnetic doors permanently, or he had to station himself at the door and let people through all night, which, given his decision to make himself scarce at the actual event, was not an option. Which was why he was eating his lunch in front of the first-floor fire exit door near the bathrooms.

"You know, there are tables in the courtyard."

Marco glanced over his shoulder and spotted the senator's kid approaching. *Were we supposed to meet?* He had to play things cool.

He cleared his throat, pulled something witty from the creative void. "But out there, you don't have the luscious aroma of the johns to accompany the delicious stink of the meal."

She smiled. It was weird, having a girl flirt with him.

Lexi looked around where he was sitting, perhaps thinking he was hiding something. "You're all alone?" she asked. "No girlfriend?"

Marco was confused until he recalled having told her about his having a girl who was a friend. "Just needed to think," he said.

"I get that," she said, sitting next to him.

Clearly she did not get it if she was sitting with him. "I'm kind of in the middle of something," he said. He had twenty minutes to figure out how to bust the door lock, find Ryan for the names of the rejected guys, and locate Mike and Drew to ensure they never found out about the party.

She fidgeted with her sneaker. "Maybe I could help?"

Marco did not want to drive the girl away permanently, so there was no sarcasm bomb dropping allowed. He decided to take her up on the offer. He pointed to the door. "I was wondering if it was possible to permanently unlock one of these doors," he said. "In case I lose my card and we have a date."

He had not fully understood the phrase *Her face lit up* until he watched the change that came over Lexi's as he spoke.

"Oh, yeah," she mumbled, blush visible even on her dark cheeks. "I mean, sure, I think I could try, I mean, it's a mag lock." She stood and trotted to the door, poked at the mechanism between the door and the frame, then pushed the door open. "Just unscrew this," she said, pointing to a metal panel on the door. "Assuming you can open the door, which deactivates the lock, you'll have like thirty seconds or something to unscrew the panel from the door before the alarm sounds. Once the panel is off, you place it so it touches the magnet, which is this box attached to the door frame. That will engage the lock, trick the system into thinking the door is sealed, and the alarm won't sound. Meanwhile, the door will swing free." She let the door close. "The screws are on the face of the panel. It shouldn't be hard to get it off the door if you use a screw gun."

It was so simple, it was genius. He wanted to kiss her. Literally. He had an image in his head of actually touching his lips to hers. It was bizarre. It was unnerving. He began sweating in unfortunate places.

"Thanks," he managed.

Lexi hugged her arms over her chest. "If that solves your problem, do you want to finish your lunch with me?" She fidgeted with her sleeve, shrugged slightly.

Marco couldn't come up with a reason why not. Lexi ran to grab her plate from where she'd left it, then they found seats at a small, plastic table.

"I had hoped survival rations would be less depressing," Marco said, running his spoon through the stuff.

"They're not called enjoyment rations," Lexi said, swallowing a mouthful. "It's the bare minimum—eat only what you need to survive."

"*Spaceballs*?"

Lexi smiled warmly. "A fellow dork?"

"Was I hiding it that well?" Marco was actually surprised his dorkiness was news.

She took another bite. "You seemed pretty cool to me."

Marco was utterly speechless. This girl thought he was cool.

"I mean, until now," she said. "Now the dork is just coming off you in waves."

"Alas, I'm only Bruce Wayne without my suit of cool."

"Bruce Wayne is still pretty good."

Marco wasn't sure if they were flirting or talking about Batman.

"How are things in the boys' dorm?" Lexi continued. "The JCPenney is a sorority nightmare. Last night, the bathroom on my floor was mobbed by six girls in the middle of a who's-got-the-better-boobs competition."

"It's Lord and Taylor of the Flies over there," he said.

"Someone nailed a pig's head to the wall?"

"If there were a pig," Marco replied, "I'm sure some guy would decapitate it."

They were chatting, talking, like people did on television. Marco was even enjoying himself. It wasn't until ten minutes later that he happened to notice the time and realized he had a mere five minutes left to complete two necessary tasks. He shoveled the last bites of his meal into his mouth.

"I have to go," he said.

"Oh," Lexi said, dropping her spoon. The smile evaporated.

"I mean, I don't want to go, but I have to do something." He was now observing the polar opposite of a face lighting up—a face shutting down. "Tonight. I'll see you tonight, right? In your office?"

"Oh, okay," she said, face brightening. "Right, the lock."

"Exactly," he said. "So I'll see you then."

"Yeah," she said. "Great."

"Good." He grabbed his plate and walked away to shut off the verbal diarrhea erupting from his lips.

It had taken all morning, but Ryan had managed to scrounge some Pepto tablets from a drawer under the checkout counter of Victoria's Secret. He'd run into the store to avoid a patrol of guards, but once inside, he'd taken a moment for himself. All the sexy stuff was gone, but there were still pictures all over the walls of half-naked chicks. He wasn't a pervert or anything, but still, seeing a picture like that, all air-brushed and whatever, got a guy going. He wondered if it was too early to visit Shay. He wondered if she wore stuff like these models had on—not here obviously, but like at home.

He had to focus.

There was still a line of people waiting for the showers when he got to the pavilion, but they were all women this time, and there was now an old lady handing out the towels and soap. It would look weird if he loped down the stairs now—the only reason a normal mall person had to go to the garage was to shower. So crap. How to get to Jack?

He stood near a crowd of guys loitering around the central fountain and tried to think of a plan. In that moment, Ryan wished that he were more like Marco—though he'd be damned if he'd ever admit that fact out loud. Marco was a thinker. He planned things.

"Dude, you hear about the party last night?"

Ryan turned his attention to the guy standing behind his right shoulder.

"Some guys got a hold of a keg and ran a party in the bowling alley."

"You think it's on again tonight?"

"Hell if I'm not checking it out."

Mike and Drew would have to move back to the parking garage—no way they'd stay anywhere people were going to start haunting on a regular basis. So now he had to figure out a way to get to Jack, then get back up to the third floor, then get Mike and Drew back to the garage, all without stupid Marco, who seemed to drift in and out of existence.

"What the hell are you doing here?"

Speak of the devil . . . Marco appeared in front of him, brow knit like he actually gave a crap if Ryan got caught.

"I had to get some medicine," Ryan replied coolly, not letting Marco's asshole tone get him riled. "For my kids."

"That entire thing you have going is a mistake."

"Like your party idea was so stellar."

Marco smirked. "About that," he said. "You kicked some people out? Can you tell me who they were? Maybe pick them out in the lunch crowd?"

The guy had to be smoking something. Like Ryan remembered— "Him." No joke, the tool who'd picked a fight with Drew was hitting on a hot girl by the soda machine.

Marco's smirk became a scowl—it was like his face could only express varying degrees of pissed off. "Awesome. Thank you." He began to walk away.

"Wait!" Ryan said. He had the planning expert right in front of him! "I have to get to the basement, then up to the bowling alley to tell Mike and Drew to clear out. Those guys by the fountain said they were planning on checking it out tonight. They think there'll be another party." From the strange look that flashed across Marco's face, Ryan sensed the guy had not stopped whatever weird projects he was running behind Mike's back. "Is there going to be another party?"

Marco waved Ryan away like he was a bug. "No, whatever, I'll talk to Mike. And if it will get you off my back, I'll let you into the service halls." He walked toward a hallway, then disappeared down it. Ryan followed.

Taco slid his card through the reader and pushed open the door. "First right, through the door, down the stairs."

"Thanks," Ryan said.

Marco didn't respond, just grunted and speed-walked back toward the central fountain.

What was the guy's deal? He *was* helpful—or, really, his card was helpful. But still. Something was off with him. He was running some kind of play behind Mike's back. And Ryan would find out what the hell it was.

Lexi could not have felt better if John Lasseter himself had called and told her he was using one of her CG shorts at the beginning of the next Pixar film. She'd actually had the balls to talk to Marco in public. And he'd responded! And then had lunch with her! That was totally another date. They were dating! And he was meeting her later that night!

When she returned to the table she'd started at, where Maddie and Ginger sat gawking at her like hungry dogs, Maddie had grabbed her wrists and said, "Details."

"He's nice."

Maddie faux fainted, dropping onto the bench of the picnic table.

"*Nice* is not going to cut it," Ginger said.

So Lexi told them. Every word. Every facial expression. About their rendezvous for later that night. She wanted them to know because then they could tell her if she was reading things right. "So that was a date, right?" she asked when she got to the end.

"That was lunch in the cafeteria, not a date," Maddie said with authority. "A date involves the potential for *badness*."

"Badness?"

"She means hooking up," Ginger clarified.

This took Lexi back a few lines of code. Did Marco expect her to "hook up" in the office later that night? She was in way over her head.

"I think I need help," Lexi mumbled.

"Well, sister, you have come to the right place." Maddie clapped her hands like she'd been waiting all day for this moment.

"I think we ask to be assigned to clothing for the afternoon?" Ginger was consulting with Maddie like Lexi was not even there.

"You take Miss Thang to clothing," Maddie said, slinking her hands through both Ginger's and Lexi's arms, "and I will check out what's available in the lingerie department."

T
W
O
P.M.

Marco had found it less awkward than he'd expected to talk to the pale, lanky, goateed *pendejo* identified by Ryan as the guy he'd thrown out, who was also assumedly the perpetrator of the assault on Jessica McClintock. It was bizarre how easily he'd transitioned from silent and pissed-off outcast to mouthy assholio. All Marco did was turn up the volume, so to speak. He said all the crap that went through his mind every day: Every snarky remark, every insult, he just let them fly. Okay, not every insult, but for a guy who'd maybe said three words total to anyone his own age in years, his current facility with conversation was astounding.

However, the real surprise was that no one had kicked his ass yet. Being an assholio opened you up to certain dangers of retaliation. Call a guy a douche, and he is likely to respond, either verbally or with his fist. Maybe it was just that he'd grown taller in the last year. Maybe it was harder to kick around a skinny kid when he had four inches on most guys.

Or maybe it was simply that Marco had approached the guy with the offer of his own private party in an IMAX theater. "All you have to do is spread the word and show up," he'd concluded.

The guy had looked at him like he was selling magic beans. "Are you for real?"

"Completely real."

His friends had started fist bumping and slapping shoulders, so Marco assumed they were in agreement with his plan. He explained that he'd leave a trail of glow-in-the-dark stickers from the Lord & Taylor to the place.

"What's in it for you?" the *pendejo* asked, still wary.

Marco aligned his frame into his best Mike Richter–esque posture. "The pleasure of sharing the wealth with my friends."

The guy raised an eyebrow, then shrugged. "Why the hell not?"

There was power in that posture, in copping an attitude. You didn't necessarily have to feel confident to act like you were. What an awesome revelation. Sparks crackled along Marco's veins.

During a bathroom break, he found Mike and Drew in the bowling alley storage room. "I spoke to Ryan," he said by way of a greeting. "He's heard a rumor that people are going to crash this place tonight, searching for another party, so you should clear out before Lights Out."

"Not happening," Mike said.

Marco had already turned to leave, not expecting a debate. "You actually want to deal with a bunch of randoms?"

"No, Big T," Drew said, hopping off his perch on a pile of machinery. "We want to host another party. Last night was fricking awesome."

"How'd you know about the party?" Mike was eyeing Marco like a hawk targeting his prey. "You know who got the keg?"

Crapcrapcrapcrap . . .

"I just heard about it in the dorm from this guy."

"Then why was Ryan under the impression you were running the party?" Mike leaned closer.

CRAP.

"I don't know," Marco said, covering, his armor of confidence rattling at the seams. "Maybe because I told him about it? Who cares? The fact is I have no idea where the keg came from."

"Then I think it's time we went back to the Grease'n'Suck and relieve it of some of its liquor."

Marco had to haul ass if he was going to make it back to work without anyone complaining. Luckily, Mike and Drew were eager to get their hands on the stuff and hauled ass right alongside him. It was easy enough getting into the Grill'n'Shake; the only problem was that once there, they were faced with an empty liquor cabinet.

Mike checked the door twice before slamming it shut. "Why the hell would they move the booze?"

Marco was as clueless as Mike. "Beats the crap out of me." The entire bar was emptied out, and even the fridge had been busted open and relieved of its remaining kegs.

Drew punched the wall, then kicked a chair for extra measure. "This place freaking sucks!"

Mike grabbed Marco's arm. "You have the magic key,

you find us the drinks. They had to have moved the liquor somewhere."

Marco agreed, more because his bathroom break had now stretched into the double digits than anything else, and rushed the two back to the bowling alley.

"Vodka," Mike said, "and beer if you can carry it."

"I'm not promising anything," Marco said.

The look on Drew's face suggested that the failure to procure booze for their shindig might result in the revocation of his get-out-of-a-beat-down-free card.

Marco had little time to ponder Drew's scowl. He bolted back to the HomeMart and checked in with one of the supervisors. "Sorry," he said, clutching his stomach by way of further explanation.

"I hear ya, kid," the guy said, and pointed him to the plumbing section. "Johns on two near the food court need unclogging."

With the amount of crap he was dealing with, both in the literal and figurative sense, Marco wondered if letting Mike and Drew kill him was really the worst-case scenario.

Ruthie was not nearly as grateful as Ryan thought she should have been. She took the Pepto tablets and asked, "Then what?"

"Then Jack will feel better."

"But what if he doesn't?"

"Then I try to get something else to help him."

"But what if there is nothing else?" Tears sparkled along the edge of her eyes. Ryan couldn't deal with girls crying.

"Don't think about that. Just give him the Pepto and I'll come back when I can and figure out what to do then."

"Why do you have to keep leaving?"

Ryan imagined spending the rest of the day with them in the SUV. *Absolutely not.* It's not that he didn't want to care for the two kids, but he had other stuff he had to do. Like see Shay. He promised to visit her after lunch. It was after lunch.

"I just do," he said. He rumpled her hair the way he remembered his brother doing to him. Only Ruthie didn't smile. It had always made Ryan smile to have Thad rumple his hair. She just didn't get how much he was doing for them.

"Why can't we come with you?" she asked. "It smells down here."

The Dumpsters were lined up on the outer wall of the parking garage nearest the SUV, and after all these days trapped in the mall, they were more than overflowing. New garbage was simply being piled on top of the nearest cars.

"I'll try to find you guys a new place," he said. "Keep the door closed." He pressed it into place, Ruthie staring at him through the smoky glass.

As he rode the escalator up to the second floor, he had this crap feeling in his stomach like he'd failed Ruthie and Jack when he'd really been like a freaking superhero to them. Why didn't Ruthie see that? Why did she constantly ask for more?

Ryan tried to push those thoughts out of his head. He had to get into a Shay headspace. The images from Victoria's Secret popped into his mind, only now, all the girls were Shay. And she looked good. Very good.

This was not the way to walk into a meeting with your

would-be girlfriend who was also maybe the girlfriend of your sort-of friend. Then he remembered—*her book*. He hoped it was still in the Abercrombie.

He collected the book, which thank god was still on the shelf where he'd left it, and began tackling the other problem he faced: What the hell was going on between Shay and Marco? He decided he should just address the whole Marco thing up front, get that out of the way, and then try to get back to where he and Shay had left off. So when she hopped over the counter of the Magic Wok, Ryan was prepared to simply hit her with "Are you dating Marco?" only she looked kind of sad. So instead, he led off with "Are you okay?"

Shay shrugged. "Are any of us really okay?"

She was not usually sarcastic with him. Maybe she *was* dating Taco.

Ryan tried to smile. "I'm okay," he said. "You look okay." She raised her eyebrows. He pushed the mask off her face; she let him tug it loose from her hair. He corrected himself: "I mean, better than okay. You look great."

Shay glanced down at her shirt. It was splattered with paint, as were her sweatpants, and her hair hung in strands around her face. "I think *great* is an overstatement." She plucked at a splotch of green paint and half smiled.

"Maybe this will make you feel better," he said, and held out the book of Tagore poetry she'd given him when they met.

Her face melted, and Ryan worried he'd screwed things up. She reached a hand out as if afraid to touch it, then, holding the book, looked up at him, a real smile lighting her face.

They were leaning toward each other and somehow, the distance just disappeared and his lips were on hers. The touch was electric. She kissed him back, opened her mouth to let him kiss her deeper. He felt something blaze inside him. This kiss had gone from zero to sixty in two seconds.

He pulled back to catch his breath.

Shay's eyes were wide. She bit her lip. "Holy crap," she said.

Ryan shifted to hide a direct consequence of their kiss. "Just to be clear, you're not dating Marco, right?"

She pushed her lips against his instead of answering. It was better than answering.

This was nothing like kissing other girls. With them, Ryan had used the kiss as a way to achieve other goals—cop a feel, feel some more, encourage her feeling. Not so with Shay. With Shay, the kiss was an end in itself.

She leaned into his chest, was almost straddling him. The intensity went through the roof. Her fingers snarled in his hair and his arms pressed her body to him. They broke apart for a second, both heaving breath.

They stared at each other in silence. Ryan was afraid to say anything.

"Shay?" The guy Shay taught with poked his head over the edge of the counter. He glanced at them both, then pointed to the mask on the floor. "Miss Dixit? I hate to interrupt," he said, grinning like he knew what was up, "but I could use your help. Kaylee got a wad of Play-Doh stuck in her hair."

Ryan's and Shay's eyes remained locked, his breath matching hers.

Seconds, minutes, days later, she broke eye contact and fumbled for the mask. "Yeah, sure, okay," she muttered, pulling the strap over her head.

Ryan gained the courage to speak. "I'll see you?" *When?* He needed her every freaking second of the day.

"Tomorrow?" she asked. "Same time, same place?"

"Tomorrow," Ryan said, the word feeling like a punch in the gut.

Shay grabbed the poetry book before sliding over the countertop. "Tomorrow."

Ryan slumped to the floor like he'd just run a 10K. It took him several minutes to regain the ability to stand. Why did that jerk Marco have the magic card key that let him go anywhere anytime he wanted? If Ryan had the key, he could sneak into Shay's dorm tonight, he could take her anywhere, hide with her until the morning, until forever.

But Ryan did not have the key, so tomorrow it was. He pushed himself to standing, tried to catch Shay's attention, hoping to at least see her smile again, but he couldn't find her in the crowds, so he slunk back through the Magic Wok kitchen and made his way up to the bowling alley to find Mike.

Marco cut straight to it with the senator. "I found the vandals for you and got them on board with the whole party thing."

"Wonderful." She wasn't even paying attention. Windows clicked across the screen in front of her.

"But I need more alcohol." It was his one shot.

"What?" She glanced at him. "For what?"

"Last night they ran out. I confirmed it with the vandals. So we need more than just the keg." He tried to recall Drew's order. "Maybe some vodka? A six-pack?"

"I'm not having glass bottles at a party full of unsupervised teenagers." She scratched some notes on a scrap of paper. "I'll have security dig up a plastic thing of vodka. But don't expect a fully stocked bar. This isn't an all-inclusive resort. It's a stop-gap, that's all."

Marco threw up his hands. "I don't even drink."

The senator snorted like she thought he was full of it, but truly, the one throat-full of beer he'd had confirmed the rightness of his decision to remain dry.

She turned back to her screen as if to dismiss him.

"I saw something you might want to know about." Marco got comfortable with the lie before speaking it. "While I was fixing toilets on the third floor, I happened to pass by the Grill'n'Shake and I swear I saw people in there."

The senator returned her attention to him. "Food collection team?"

"It didn't look like it," he said. "The security gates were down."

The senator considered his words for a moment. "I'll check into it." She twisted back to the computer screen.

Marco stood to leave. He'd done all he could to solve the mystery of the missing bar.

"Marco," the senator said as he reached the door.

He looked back at her.

"Thank you." She was smiling like a real person, not her usual lizard-y smile. "I'm sorry if it feels like I'm dumping on you," she continued. "You've been a huge help."

"Okay." He was not sure where this was going.

"I just wanted you to know you're appreciated." She smiled again, then turned back to her screen.

As Marco walked down the hall, he felt like crap. He wasn't helping the senator. He was helping himself. And even though that was how it had to be, that this was a live-or-die situation and he'd be damned if he let this crap mall kill him, he let himself feel bad for the time it took him to reach the outer door. He wished he could be the kid she thought he was, a helpful guy, a guy who was on the right side of something. But when you choose a side, there's always a chance you choose wrong and end up a loser. So Marco would keep playing all the angles. He was not a loser. He survived.

Shocks sparked from Shay's body for a whole hour after that kiss. She felt alive, buzzed. The energy must have been radiating off her, because the kids asked her to help them—her, not Kris.

"You're not mean anymore," one little girl said as Shay helped her with a cookie cutter.

The words fizzled away the dregs of Shay's energy. The kids had thought her sadness was mean?

"Thanks," she managed.

She could not survive until tomorrow, wait that long to feel good again. She couldn't make it through to dinner without another kiss.

But how could she find Ryan? She couldn't. He was off the grid, nowhere. Lost to her.

"You're rolling it too thin," the girl said, pulling the Play-Doh from her hands.

"Sorry," Shay muttered.

After cleaning up the Play-Doh, Kris asked her to fill the cups for the kids' snack. She took the stack of plastic cups to the sink in the Magic Wok, hoping that maybe some of the energy was still locked in the space, that maybe she could feel even the echo of it just being in there. But there was nothing. Just the faint odor of greasy Chinese food.

She pulled out her book, hoping maybe Tagore would bring her some shred of comfort, but the words were meaningless, her own notes, incomprehensible. The emptiness felt so complete, she worried she'd crumble apart.

Kris strode into the small kitchen. "Your ass is dragging," he said, noticing the still empty cups. "What happened with that guy? Ten minutes ago you were smoking and now you're a lump of coal." He nudged her, like this was a funny joke, then lifted his mask to splash water on his face.

His lips were nice. Full, smooth.

Shay ripped off her mask and pressed her lips to his. They did not respond. Kris pushed her back gently, hands gripping her shoulders like she was a little girl, a look of shock on his face like she'd bit him.

"Whoa," he said.

Shay felt tears crowding behind her eyes.

"I'm flattered," he said, "but I'm like a million years older than you, and—"

Shay did not want to hear anything else. She felt like she was going to puke. She struggled from his grip and ran out the back of the kitchen.

"Shaila, wait!"

She ignored his call. The last thing she wanted to see

was that pitying look again. There was no fire in his lips, no life. What had she been thinking? And now she'd made a giant fool of herself. How could she ever see him again?

Blind with tears, she stumbled into the nearest empty storefront and hid behind the closest shelf. She was shaking, cold one second, hot the next. She curled her arms around her knees and dropped her head onto the bones. Where were the tears now? Nothing came. She was empty, wholly empty.

Just before dinner, Lexi got the inevitable call from her mother to return to the mall offices. "Now what?" she mumbled.

"I think it's nice," Ginger said, dropping a pile of T-shirts on the cart for transport to the registration area. "I wish my mom could call me."

"Yeah, but your mom wouldn't be calling to force you into doing her a favor."

"I wish I could do her a favor." Ginger had her back to Lexi, but Lexi could hear the hiccup in her voice.

She wasn't sure what to say, so she said nothing. What would make the fact of being trapped in this place without anyone better? Not that Ginger was alone; she had Maddie. But Lexi got that there was something different about a mom. After the riots, when her mom dragged her out from under the wreckage, when Dotty had held her like she hadn't in years, Lexi had been so grateful to have her mother there. She wished the Senator were always so easy to love.

"What about this?" Lexi said, changing topics. They

were still working on the perfect outfit for her date with Marco. She held up a purple hoodie with a silhouette of a skull on the back.

Ginger dropped her head back. "Have we taught you nothing?"

That was the Ginger Lexi was hoping for. "I'm just kidding," she said, though in truth, the hoodie was awesome.

Ginger rifled through a pile near her feet. "I was saving this, but I guess I can show you since you have to go." She unearthed a coral pink strapless dress with a black belt. She held it up to herself, her face glowing like she couldn't help how proud she was of the find. "Go on," she said. "How awesome is it?"

Lexi thought it was nice. She just couldn't picture herself in it.

"You don't like it?" Ginger visibly deflated.

"No," Lexi said with a pinched smile. "I love it." What did she know about fashion? If Ginger was this stoked about a dress, it had to be good. *Right?*

"Let's sneak back to the hoard and try it on." Ginger was practically hopping up and down.

"I have to meet my mom," Lexi said, shrugging like she had no choice.

Ginger sighed. "Fine, we'll try it after dinner."

"Great," Lexi said, walking toward the exit. Maybe her mom's project would keep her until Lights Out and she could avoid the whole makeover thing entirely.

Up in the mall offices, things were hitting the fan. Security guards murmured in groups, examining papers or watching something on iPads. The people her dad had trained on the computer system were helping him with some major database analysis, all of them crowded into the small room, the four workers at their stations, Dad using a laptop on the floor.

Lexi knocked on her mother's door. "You rang?"

Her mother waved for her to enter. "Look at this," she said, turning her computer screen so Lexi could see. On it was what looked like footage from a security camera in the main mall hallway, the one outside the Grill'n'Shake from the look of things, but it was clearly after Lights Out, so it was hard to tell. Two figures wearing brimmed hats appeared on screen, one carrying what looked like the pruning shears her mom used on her rosebushes. The two—men, from the size of them—walked up to the security fence enclosing the Grill'n'Shake, cut the lock, and then disappeared inside.

Mom paused the video. "They don't come out, which means they went out through the service hallways."

"Why would they break into the Grill'n'Shake? I thought you had teams remove all the edible food from the restaurants."

"I had them take out the food, but not the alcohol."

"People are that desperate for a drink?"

"You wouldn't believe," Dotty said, swiping her hand over her hair. The woman sounded like she'd kill for one herself.

"So what can I do?" Lexi asked.

"I have security teams scanning the rest of the footage outside all the restaurants and bars to see if they've hit any other stores and if so, if any of the cameras got a better look at them. Meanwhile, I need eyes in the service hallways, at least outside the doors of the restaurants.

Dad thought you might be able to hook up some wireless cameras?"

"I can try," Lexi said, still wondering why the place seemed to be in such an uproar over some alcohol thieves. "Where are the cameras?"

"Hank can show you." Her mother returned to her videos.

Lexi did not like the head of security. He lurked in the doorway, having materialized there silently as if from nothing.

"I had my teams collect all the wireless systems in the mall." He led her down the hall to one of the rooms with bunks for the guards. On the floor were ten or so boxes. "Will that be enough?"

He sounded like he was overly interested in the answer. "Sure," Lexi said, not knowing at all.

"Good," he said unconvincingly. "I have a team set up to help you install them."

Something told Lexi that she did not want their help. "I'm cool," she said. "No need for a team."

"You sure?" Hank said. He tightened the knot of his arms across his chest.

"Totally." She bent down and began examining the boxes, not bothering to give the jerkwad so much as a good-bye.

Marco had stolen the wrong size bit for the screw gun. He kept jamming the one he had into the screw on the lock plate on the door and it was too big for the holes. *Typical. Just fraking typical.* Which meant he had to go down to the HomeMart, sneak in the back, find the tools, all of which had been commandeered and stowed in one of the offices, then find the drill bits, then find one that would fit the damn screw. Like he had time for this crap.

Forget that he had not one but two parties to set up. Forget that only one of these parties was sanctioned. Forget that if the senator found out about Mike's party, his ass was grass. Forget that if Mike found out about the other party, he'd probably kill him before the senator got her opportunity. All around, life sucked. Was this really better than just being a regular guy in the dorms?

The second screwdriver worked and, even more

astounding, by refitting the plate over the box attached to the door frame, the lock engaged but the door swung free. Lexi had come through in the clutch. He owed her big-time.

Route to the main party established, now it was time to move the additional alcohol swindled from the senator to Mike.

Marco followed his own trail of glow-in-the-dark stars back to the door across from the bowling alley. He'd left the old markers indicating the route to Mike's party on the walls, and added green glowing lizards to mark the route to the IMAX theater. He figured, people could choose their own party path—either they end up with Mike and two handles of "Igor" vodka, or in the IMAX theater with a keg and decent sound system.

Crap. He hadn't hooked up the sound system. *Okay, first deliver alcohol to Mike, then the sound system, then meet up with Lexi and let whatever happens happens, on all fronts.*

Ryan waited for Marco in the shadows near the bowling lanes. He'd never been much good at bowling. It was something his family had done when he was a kid, on the good days when Dad hadn't drank so much and Mom wasn't in a mood. Thad was good at bowling; he was good at everything. Ryan, well, if he was good at anything it was only because he'd worked his ass off.

He wondered if Ruthie and Jack would like to play a game. Maybe he could sneak them out before Lights On. Jack seemed to be doing a little better when he'd checked on them earlier. He'd eaten a roll and two orange slices, according to Ruthie. Still, it wasn't doing them any good to stay in the car. The inside of the car was beginning to smell as bad as the outside. Maybe Marco could help him find them a new place to hide?

On the subject of Marco, where was the guy? Mike had said he'd be coming back with alcohol and Ryan had stationed himself here to make sure he did not deliver. Marco had no idea what Mike and Drew were capable of, party-wise. They needed to be deprived, brought back down to boring stuck-alone-in-a-closet, for their own good. Security knew there was a party in the bowling alley last night, would probably be looking for one here tonight. The party will be busted for sure, and once in custody, Mike would probably do something supremely stupid and get himself killed.

Finally, Marco slunk into the bowling alley.

"Dude, we need to talk," Ryan said, striding toward him.

"I'm a little busy at the moment," Marco said, brushing past.

"You can't give Mike that vodka," Ryan said, grabbing Marco's arm.

Marco shrugged off Ryan's grasp. "He basically threatened to kill me if I don't, so either make some threats of your own or get the hell out of my way."

Ryan was surprised. He'd thought Marco had gained most-favored-lackey status. He had a nickname!

"Whatever he said," Ryan whispered, trying to show Marco that they were on the same side, "Mike does not want to get caught. Security knows people partied here before. Tonight's party is sure to get busted."

"Not a problem," Marco said.

Ryan was surprised by the guy's confidence. "How do you know?"

He sighed like Ryan was wasting his precious time. "I heard a rumor that the party's been moved. So no one's even going to come to this shindig. It'll just be you three getting hammered by yourselves."

"Which will piss Mike off even more." Ryan did not think this guy was quite getting his message. "Mike is serious about his parties. He's kind of insane about them. Maybe just give them the booze and say security's barred the doors to the service halls or something."

Marco adjusted his grip on the bottles and gave Ryan the once-over. "Okay," he said. "I'll try it. But you have my back with this?"

Ryan could hug the bastard. "I've got you covered."

Lexi finished hiding the last camera behind a pipe outside the Pancake Palace. She'd put the worst model down here—there was nothing worth stealing in the Palace and surely these thieves knew that. She hoisted the bag with all the receivers and made her way to the hallway and up to the mall offices.

"Job complete," she said, dropping the bag and her mother's borrowed access card on the desk.

Dotty looked stunned. "I thought you'd finished hours ago."

"Sorry," Lexi said, not really in the mood to fight.

Her mother frowned. "I don't mean it like that, Lex," she said, standing. "I'm sorry you've been busting your butt all night. Did you get dinner?"

Lexi allowed Dotty to pretend to be a mom. She got another Lean Cuisine from the fridge in her office and heated it in the microwave, got Lexi a soda from the cooler in the hall. It was nice to be pampered for the moment. It was nice to pretend.

Dotty laid the tray on the table and immediately got back to work on her computer.

"Don't you ever take a break?" Lexi asked, shoveling the chicken and dumplings down.

"I haven't taken a break in about four years." Her voice sounded a million years old.

"When we get out of here, we should take a vacation. Like go to Mexico or something."

Her mother looked at her like she'd started speaking in HTML, then burst out laughing. Tears rolled down her cheeks. Lexi was not sure what was so funny.

When she regained control of herself, her mother wiped her face on her sleeve. "Yes, baby," she said. "When we get out of here, we are *definitely* taking a vacation."

After eating, Lexi explained how to view the feed from the new cameras. "Just plug this receiver into the USB port on the computer and a screen should show up." She pointed to the right input, just in case her mom didn't know what a USB was. "But don't show Hank," she added.

"Why not?" Her mother examined one of the receivers like it might zap her.

"I don't trust him."

Her mother gave her one of those aren't-you-cute looks. "Honey, if I can't trust Hank, I might as well throw in the towel on everything."

Lexi didn't say anything more—what could she say? She had no evidence that Hank was anything but kind of a jerkwad, and that wasn't exactly a crime. Whatever, she didn't like him. She would watch him. Just in case.

■ ■ ■

Shay had skipped dinner. She wasn't hungry. And she didn't want to see Kris. The embarrassment was almost worse than the emptiness. Her brain kept running the scene over and over, like she needed to be reminded of how much of an idiot she'd made of herself.

Maybe she would hide in this store all night, tomorrow too. There were some decorative pillows on a shelf near the back. They were probably as comfortable as her cot. Maybe she would stay here until she died from the flu or the government let them all out, whichever. Did it even matter?

"Lights Out is in a half hour." Something nudged Shay in the rear.

She glanced back and saw a black boot, the end of a stun baton dangling beside a leg. The fantasy was over. *Time to reenter the hell of my life.*

Preeti was waiting on her cot. She was all folded up like a trap; she sprang to life upon seeing Shay approach.

"You left me!" she yelled. A few women looked their way. Preeti did not notice or apparently care. "You abandoned me at the school! You swore you'd be there! You swore you wouldn't leave me again!"

Shay put on a sad face peppered with a hint of apologetic. "I'm sorry," she said. "I had a headache and went to lie down."

"You didn't tell anyone where you went," Preeti said, somewhat quieter. "Kris was even a little freaked out."

His name made Shay want to puke. "I'll say something to him tomorrow. I'm okay now."

Preeti glared at her for a moment longer, then threw her

arms around her. "Don't leave me again," she whispered.

Shay made herself hug Preeti back, forced her hand to stroke her long hair. "I promise," she said. "Let's put this rat's nest in a braid. It's a mess."

Preeti nodded and let Shay sit her on the cot. Once settled, Preeti rambled on about her day, the hurt of being abandoned blinked out of existence. Shay ran her fingers through the long black hair, twisted the strands into a fishtail, that most complicated of braids. And though she looked calm and *mm-hmm*-ed along with Preeti's stories, the words of Preeti's hurt echoed around inside her like bats in a cave. *You abandoned me. You left me. You promised.*

LIGHTS OUT

Maddie and Ginger dragged Lexi into the stock-room office.

"Let's get you gorgeous," Ginger said, her smiling face unhindered by the mask—they were breaking all the rules tonight.

First, it was makeup. They must have stolen it from the abandoned stockpiles on the first floor. There were three sets of everything.

"Are you going somewhere?" Lexi asked, holding the three mascaras in a fan.

Maddie snatched them from her hands. "Don't fondle the merch," she said. "And maybe you aren't the only one with a date tonight."

"This girl we know who works on the food prep team said she heard there's a party." Ginger was trying to comb Lexi's hair into something other than its usual lank bob.

This did not sound like a Mom-sanctioned event. How much was going on behind her mother's back? How many rules could be broken before the whole structure fell apart?

Maddie took off her shirt to reveal a trio of colorful lace bras running up her torso. "One for each," she said, beginning to unhook one.

Lexi held up her hands. "No way," she said, pointing at her chest. "These are not meant for stringy things like that."

"Oh, ye of little faith." Maddie sighed, handing a strapless blue bra to her. "Like I don't know you have huge tits. Just try it."

As she had asked for Maddie and Ginger's help with this whole date fiasco—and really, could this be anything other than a fiasco?—she decided to play along. Worst case, after they left, she could put back on her own stuff.

Miracle of miracles, the bra fit. Lexi had to admit, it was a hell of a lot nicer than the plain underwires she bought with her mom at the old-lady lingerie store.

"Our ugly duckling will be a swan yet!" Maddie chirped, slipping a hot pink demi over her normal-sized chest. She reached into the pocket of her shorts. "Undies to match."

Did they actually think Marco was going to see her underwear? WAIT. *Does MARCO think he is going to see my underwear?* It was everything Lexi could do to keep from hyperventilating.

She gave herself over to their ministrations. Eyebrows were plucked (*PAINFUL!*), eyelids were painted, cheeks were blushed. Comb was raked across scalp and decorative flower jammed in over right ear.

"Is all this really necessary for a date in a windowless office?" Lexi whimpered.

"A date is a date is a date," Maddie said. "Now pucker." She smashed lipstick on Lexi's mouth.

Ginger pulled the coral strapless dress from a drawer. "Hid this away before dinner," she said.

"The lengths we have gone to make this date a success!" Maddie cried, hand to chest in mock distress.

Lexi unzipped the thing and stepped into the pink sleeve of fabric. It felt silky. It looked expensive. The label was handmade and had a funky-sounding name on it. Definitely designer. This was probably the nicest item of clothing she'd ever touched.

Ginger and Maddie had their makeup on in what seemed like seconds, their clothes on in less. They were done with their whole look by the time Lexi had zipped the dress and fastened the belt.

"Whoa." Ginger's black-lined eyes bugged.

"Now that's what I'm talking about," Maddie said, a smile curling her shimmering lips.

"What?" Lexi said, fidgeting with the hemline on her bust. "Can you see the bra?"

"Get a mirror," Maddie said, nodding her head toward the door. Ginger bolted out of the room.

"Here," Maddie said, pulling a pair of black heels from another drawer.

Lexi would break her legs if she fell in those, which was more likely than not. Still, she was entranced. Did she look *that* good? At all like Maddie and Ginger? Like a real girl?

The shoes changed her view of the world. Four inches did that to you.

Maddie sucked her teeth and nodded. "I knew you had it in you."

Ginger shoved through the door dragging a standing mirror. "A little help," she groaned.

Maddie helped her pull it into the room and turned it toward Lexi. In the glass was a tall girl—no, a hottie, with streamlined hair and an actual waist and long legs that curved like in the magazines. Lexi was afraid to move and discover the mirror was showing someone else, though she knew that was crazy.

"Well?" Maddie asked, hand displaying the mirror as if Lexi weren't staring.

"You win," Lexi said.

Ginger and Maddie fist bumped.

"Our work here is done," Ginger said. They pulled on their own stiletto shoes and left Lexi alone with the girl in the mirror. They couldn't take their eyes off each other.

Ryan was surprised when the first person knocked on the storage room door. Mike and Drew, however, were not.

"Let's get this party started!" Drew whooped, cracking the vodka.

Mike had found some mixers in the freezer they'd busted earlier, but they were not your standard high school party fare, which were generally soda or pink lemonade. To-night, people had the choice of vodka and pineapple juice or vodka and olives. This party was going to get messy fast.

Marco had not listened to him at all. The asshole would learn soon enough. Ryan gave it an hour before security showed up, with the way people were streaming into the room. Mike would do something stupid and get himself Tasered five minutes after that. Then it was all over.

Ryan decided to throw in the towel on worrying. If his world was coming to an end that night, so freaking be it. He grabbed a glass and poured himself a straight vodka. If he was getting hammered, he was doing it right.

It didn't matter if Shay closed her eyes or left them open. Her brain scurried from one horrible thought to the next: Ba worrying alone in the house, Nani's dead face, the hand grabbing her in the dark of the hallway, Preeti screaming for her. Why even bother trying to sleep? She wondered if anyone would care if she took to jogging around the corridors.

Standing, she felt dizzy. Was it the dark? Was it not eating? She sat back down.

So there would be no running.

She lay back on the cot. Her brain began its race against itself. She had to find a way out. *The kiss.* Ryan's lips on hers. The fire burning her from the inside out. Her fingers tangled in his hair, his hands on her skin, running under her shirt.

She caught her breath. She'd found the perfect escape from her terrible thoughts. She could kiss him without him even being there. She closed her eyes and dreamed.

■　■　■

It was after Lights Out when Marco finally got the damn IMAX sound system to work. He plugged an iPod into the audio input and heard a chorus of cries from below. Had people already arrived at the theater?

He stood and looked down from the projection booth. He wished he hadn't. The place was crowded and it was only ten thirty. How had so many people made it there? How was he supposed to leave without being seen?

No, this was good. Lots of people, no one would notice him. Everything was still fine.

He left the booth and crept down the stairs.

"There you are." The *pendejo* Ryan had pointed out, the guy for whom this whole party was planned, had him cornered. "We tapped the keg, but where are the cups?"

AGAIN! Cups were his freaking Achilles' heel.

"I'll find some."

"And food," the guy said. "Find some chips or something."

Was this guy insane? What, did he think Marco was running a freaking 7-Eleven? Why not request a Slurpee? Why not a steak dinner?

Marco found some cups in a nearby restaurant, but no food. He handed the stack of paper cups to the dirtbag, and the guy grabbed his shirt.

"This song sucks," he said. "Put on some better music."

"It's music," Marco said, tugging his shirt free. "Just deal."

The guy took a step toward Marco. "I'm not going to just deal." He placed the toe of his boot on Marco's sneaker.

"You can either change the music," he said, pinching Marco's toes, "or I rearrange your teeth."

This was going down as his worst idea ever. Idea, day, everything.

Ryan had no idea how much time had passed, but he was seeing three of everything, so it had to be a while. He tried to walk to a chair, but was suddenly on the floor, so he decided to crawl. A girl fell over him and started laughing even though she'd smashed her head on the concrete. Some guy stepped on his hand. He just had to get to the chair. The chair would fix everything.

The chair did not fix anything. The room began to spin. The music was really loud. Then it was off.

"Where's Taco?" Mike's voice. Somewhere over there. Right? Which was right?

"How can there be no more vodka?" Drew bellowed like a wounded dog.

A couple of girls next to Ryan were still dancing, singing their own song to move with. A guy to Ryan's left—the opposite side that Mike was on—threw his cup down.

"This sucks," he said. "I'm heading to the other party."

Mike snapped his head. "What other party?"

"There'snother party?" Drew asked, words slurring together.

Mike grabbed the guy's arm. "I asked you a question."

The guy shoved Mike off. "This place sucks anyway."

Even in this state, Ryan understood that things were about to get bad.

Mike punched the guy. People screamed. Began pushing and shoving. Someone knocked Ryan off his chair.

"Mike!" he cried, feet kicking his body. The floor felt like it was made of Jell-O. "MIKE!"

Someone pulled him upright. "Shrimp?" It was Mike.

"I don't feel good," Ryan mumbled, then threw up all over Mike.

"Drew!" Mike shoved a shoulder under Ryan and dragged him over to a pile of something.

Drew swam into Ryan's field of vision. "Whoa," he said. "Shrimp's done."

"Get some water." Mike pulled his shirt off.

"You going to leave me here?" Ryan felt like he might cry if Mike said yes.

"Never leave a man behind," Mike said, fake punching Ryan's arm.

"Ow," Ryan said, rubbing his head.

"I punched your arm."

"Which one?"

Drew came back with the water. "People cleared out."

Ryan was so relieved to hear it, he might have actually started crying.

"Whatever," Mike said. "I'll have a word with Taco in the morning."

Ryan let the black swim up over his eyes. He was with Mike and Drew. Mike and Drew would take care of him. They always took care of him.

"Drink some water, J.S."

He curled into the black, then felt water stream over his skin like a baptism.

■   ■   ■

Lexi had kicked off the shoes first. A half hour later, she now dug the comb from her head, letting her hair spring back into its usual snarl. How much longer should she wait? Wasn't an hour long enough to convince herself that he wasn't coming? She unzipped the dress and took off the lingerie. If she was going to wallow in disappointment, she could do it in her own clothes.

Checking that the coast was clear, she snuck to the bathroom and washed the makeup from her face. There. The usual Lexi stared back at her in the dirty mirror. She wasn't pretty, but at least she recognized the face.

As she walked toward her cot, she passed the permanent shelving in what used to be the pillow department. Was it still there? She snuck between two cots, bent down past the snoring heads, and patted around under the bottom shelf. Amazingly enough, her hand wrapped around the CB she'd left there what seemed like years ago.

She tucked the thing under her shirt and crept back to her office. The radio was still tuned to Darren's channel. Was there any possibility he was out there?

Lexi flicked the machine on. "DMaster?" she asked.

"You're alive!" Darren answered, way too loudly. Lexi wound down the volume.

"Duh, I called *you*," she said, smiling, giddy. "I heard you got busted."

"Some dudes in suits asked me about my online activities." He sounded bored. "They had nothing, not even the CB channel we used—obviously. I switched the dial right after we talked just in case. They searched my computer, but it's not like they cared about my torrent files."

"Piracy wasn't their first order of business?"

"I think they took one look at my room and reasoned any self-respecting terrorist would have fewer posters featuring screen shots from video games."

If relief could be measured, Lexi had just buried the needle. "At least now I know you're not rotting in some skank jail cell because of me."

"I should be so lucky," Darren said. "I'm still just trapped in sucktown, attending crap school with a bunch of losers."

"At least you can go outside." Had he forgotten she was the one in the real sucktown?

"Oh, yeah," he said. "So are people, like, dying in there? The news keeps saying that you're all dead."

News. Lexi hadn't even thought about news. "Obviously, I'm calling you from the Great Beyond. What else is the news saying?"

Darren gave her a quick rundown—there'd been lots of coverage of the mall after the government lockdown, but this morning some guy had shot his whole family before killing himself and now that plus some celebrity divorce were the main stories.

"We've been upstaged by a celebrity divorce?"

"I blame the twenty-four-hour news cycle."

"I guess I shouldn't be surprised."

"What's a couple thousand people trapped in a mall to a divorce worth potentially millions of dollars?"

"Plus, there's a kid."

"Two kids."

"Whoa, now it's all making sense." Lexi hadn't felt so comfortable in days. Why hadn't she thought to call Darren earlier?

"I miss you," he said. His voice was different, like he was closer to the mic. "I mean, talking to you. And gaming. This is the longest we've gone without a game in forever."

She would have said she missed him too, but she wasn't sure she could get the words out without crying. "I haven't played in forever. Probably end up dead in the first five minutes."

"Yeah." He sounded disappointed.

There was a noise outside. A door rattling. Had Marco finally decided to show up? "Crap, D, I have to go."

"Oh, sure," he said. "Can you call again?"

"Yeah," she said, feeling a little weird. Darren was sounding more earnest than usual. It was unnerving. "Sure."

"Well," he said. "Until then, I guess."

"Yeah," she said. "Later."

"Later."

She turned the CB off, tossed it in a drawer, and ran out of the room. Marco hadn't forgotten! The banging was coming from the stockroom door. So he hadn't gotten around to unscrewing the door panel. That was why he was late. "Shut up before a guard comes!" she whispered through the door.

She pushed the handle and not Marco, but Maddie and Ginger fell into her.

"You're a life saver!" Ginger gasped.

"Security busted the party just as we were about to walk in," Maddie said, brushing herself off. "What happened to you?"

Lexi tried not to cry. "Marco never showed."

"Oh, crap." Maddie gave her a squeeze on the shoulder.

"Maybe he got busted at the party?" Ginger, always trying to be helpful.

"Yeah," she said. "You'd better get changed before security busts you in here."

"No joke," Maddie said, and pushed past her into the office.

Lexi didn't bother joining them. She slunk back to her cot, hugged her arms around her body, and tried not to feel the loneliness that crushed down on her.

DAY
TEN

LIGHTS ON

Marco was shaken from sleep by fists gripping his arms. He cracked open his eyes and saw the end of a long black stun baton. "Let me guess," he slurred.

"The senator," said the guard.

Marco nodded and crawled out of his cot.

It felt like he'd just crawled into it. The *pendejo* in the IMAX hadn't let him leave—every time he tried to get away, the guy threatened some breed of violence. Broken limb, broken nose, broken fingers. Marco nearly kissed the security team when they busted the place.

It had been the same as the night before: Everyone was lined up, temperatures were checked, any fever cases were weeded out and the rest returned to their dorms. Marco appreciated the regularity of the business. It was nice when things worked out exactly as you expected. Even this being shaken awake felt like business as usual. And at least the senator wouldn't break his arm.

Marco had to reevaluate this last notion upon being thrust by the guard into her office.

"It was you," she said, seething. "You and your two beefcake buddies."

Marco sat in his usual chair and folded his arms across his chest for protection. Had she found out about Mike's party, that Marco was running it under her nose? Better not assume anything, play dumb. "It was me *what*? You asked me to throw another party, I threw it."

The senator scowled, one eyebrow arched. "It was you who stole the alcohol from the Grill'n'Shake, and elsewhere. Though I'm confused as to why you thought there would be alcohol in Johnny Rockets."

That cleared things up for him. Someone must have seen him stealing the cups. "I didn't go into Johnny Rockets to get beer. I went there to get *cups*. You keep leaving me kegs with no cups."

"Bull." Her face was still twisted in a scowl. "Your two buddies are good, keeping their faces away from all the security cameras. But I know it's you, has to be. You're the only one with a card key." She held out her hand. "I'll be taking it back, by the way."

Now he started sweating. "No way," he said, clutching his pants pocket like that would save his card, his freedom. "I swear, I didn't steal any alcohol. Anything I've touched has been stuff you've given me. And Mike and Drew, they only had what I gave them." Her face remained frozen. "I'm telling you the truth!"

She considered him for a moment longer, then relaxed. "Fine," she said. "If you can prove to me in twelve hours that you did not steal the alcohol, I will apologize for the accusation and let you keep the card. If not, you're done."

"How can I prove that I didn't do something? You know where I was all night, you know that I was setting the thing up all day or working your stupid job like you told me to. What more can I tell you?"

"You can tell me who *did* steal my alcohol."

Marco stumbled from the mall offices, thinking how fraking tired he was of this crap. He was tired of running secret errands for the senator. He was sick of hosting parties he didn't even want to go to. He was sick of every goddamned thing about this mall. Not that anyone cared about his problems. Not that he had a lot of other options.

The first order of business was to confirm that Mike and Drew were not in fact stealing alcohol without his knowledge. He turned toward the bowling alley and began the investigation.

Drew was stumbling down the hall toward him as he entered the staff area of the bowling alley. "Taco," he slurred, sounding like he was still drunk, "Mike is pissed."

Get in line, dickhead. "Great," Marco said. "I just need to know one thing—did you two steal any alcohol from anywhere last night?"

"Hells no," Drew said, pulling open the door to the janitor's closet and pissing in the sink. *Classy.* "And we have to talk about that. Party frickin' kicked like ten minutes after it started. There must be more handles. And a frickin' keg, Taco, a goddamned *keg.*"

Well, that was enough evidence for him. "Okay. Noted. Fantastic." He turned to leave.

"Dude, Mike wanted to see you!" Drew bellowed.

"Later," Marco yelled, not even turning. "I will be back *later*."

The last thing he wanted to deal with at the moment was a pissed-off Mike Richter. *One pissed-off person at a time.*

At least now he knew that neither he nor Mike nor Drew were responsible for the alcohol thefts, so the senator was dead wrong on that front. And surely Ryan the mega-douche was not capable of running such an operation on his own. So now it was just the four thousand or so other people in the mall he had to investigate. *No problem whatsoever.*

But first, breakfast.

The peace of Shay's dream life was broken by the flash of Lights On. Her eyes cracked open—she'd forgotten to take out her contacts. In the bathroom, after cleaning and replacing the lenses, she splashed water on her face and stood in front of the hand dryer. The blast of air fanned her hair behind her.

"There are other people in this place, kid," some lady grumbled.

Shay hit the button again.

When she came out, Preeti was waiting by her cot. "You coming to breakfast?" she said accusatorially, as if Shay had already abandoned her for a second time.

"I'm starved," Shay said.

It was hard to be out in the crowds. People were talking too loud. It felt like they were screaming right in her ear. She had to keep a look out for Kris—she did not want to deal with him at that moment. And the food. God, how she missed things that crunched. But she forced herself to eat when she noticed Preeti staring at her untouched plate.

If only she could make her own Home Store in some corner, live off the grid. Eat Pringles and dried cranberries. Anything to keep from having to move through these days like they meant anything. Like they were not all just treading water.

Ryan. He said he was hiding out, that Marco had found him someplace. What if Shay could hide with him? She would no longer need to dream—she could spend all day with him, with his lips. There could not be a more perfect solution to all her problems.

How to make it happen? She needed to find Ryan. She'd see him later in the afternoon—but waiting would mean seeing Kris first. *Unacceptable.* Like an answered prayer, she saw Marco speed-walking down the side hallway.

"Marco!" she cried, jumping up from the table. She bolted toward him. The end was near! "Marco, wait!"

He glanced over his shoulder to see who called and spotted her. His face brightened. He held out his arms. "Shay."

Understanding he wanted a hug, and figuring she could give him at least that, she flung herself into his waiting arms. He pressed his cheek to her head. "I've missed you," he said.

His embrace was stifling. She pushed slightly on his chest, and he disengaged.

"Sorry," he said. "Is it your head?"

"Yeah," she lied. "I'm so glad I found you," she chirruped, plastering as huge a smile as possible on her face so he could see it beyond the edges of her mask. "Have you found me and Preeti a hiding place yet?"

"Hiding place?" His eyebrows tweaked. "You don't want a hiding place. Stay in the dorms. You're safe in the dorms."

Shay did not like his patronizing tone. "I know what I want and I want a separate place to hide." She pulled her spine straighter. "With Ryan, preferably."

Now she had his attention. "So you've been hanging out with Ryan?" He leaned away from her. "I don't think you want to be slumming it with him and his pals in a storage room. Last I saw them, one was pissing in a sink and the place smelled like the floor of a movie theater."

"So Ryan and I will go someplace else."

"Are you sure Ryan wants to live with you? Don't you think he would have asked you?"

Shay tried to remember if he had. Hadn't he? It was like chasing hamsters, trying to grab a single thought.

"Before you start planning your life with Ryan Murphy, you might want to consider whether he actually has anything to offer. If you remember, I'm the one who's saved your ass every time it needed saving."

Marco had it all wrong. Ryan had *exactly* what she needed. And she didn't want to be saved. She wanted to be kissed. Entirely different.

"Well, thanks for all your efforts on my behalf," she snarled. "Feel free to leave me the hell alone from here on out."

His face clouded over. "With pleasure." And with that, he turned and stomped away.

Tears threatened to fall. Her chin trembled. Why?

Marco was being a self-important jerk! *Screw him.* She would hide out in the Magic Wok and wait for Ryan. Perfect! Then they would run away together. Find their own non-smelly, urinating-friend-free environment.

She returned to the table, where Preeti sat polishing off her breakfast.

"I figured you were done," she mumbled, mouth full.

Shay slumped into her seat. "I wasn't that hungry."

"That was the guy from the Grill'n'Shake. Is he, like, your new boyfriend or something?"

Shay sneered at the thought. "He's not my anything."

Preeti shrugged. "He seemed happy to see you."

"Yeah, well, he seemed happy to see me go too."

"You still have me," Preeti said, a smile crinkling the skin around her eyes.

Shay reached across the table and gave her sister's forehead a shove. "Just what I needed."

Maddie looked up from her slop. "Well, if it isn't the ghost of dates past."

Lexi followed her gaze and saw Marco slinking along the outer hallway. "Should I go talk to him?" she asked.

"No way," Ginger said. "He ditched you. He's the one who has to come to you to apologize."

Maddie shrugged. "Depends on how bad you want him."

Lexi weighed both approaches. She did want him pretty badly. She pushed herself to standing. Then saw another girl rushing toward him. That girl was gorgeous. She had a mane of black hair that whipped behind her like a cape. Marco held his arms out to that girl and she threw herself into them.

It all came back to her. The girl who was a friend, who let him into the JCPenney that first night. How much of an idiot was she? A girl who's a friend. A girlfriend.

Lexi sat back down.

"Oh, crap," Maddie said, eyes widening.

"He sucks." Ginger folded her arms across her chest. "Kevin Reamer totally did that to me two years ago. He was dating Becky Lu—you remember, Mad?"

"Oh, I remember," she drawled, rolling her eyes.

"And then, at David Silver's bar mitzvah, he totally was all over me, asking me to dance, trying to kiss me, and I was like, aren't you dating Becky, and he was all, not anymore, but then at school Monday, they were totally still together."

"Ging, you have *got* to let that go."

"I'm empathizing!"

"You're complaining about something that happened in seventh grade!"

"It doesn't matter when it happened," Ginger snapped. "Kevin sucks. And that guy sucks. What's his name, Lex?"

Lexi drove her spoon in circles through her mush. "Marco."

"Marco. He sucks too."

Maddie clasped Lexi's arm. "Look now."

Lexi glanced back at where the two had been all over each other. Now they stood apart. Marco looked pissed.

Maddie waggled her eyebrows. "All's not well in Eden."

Lexi couldn't stop herself from smiling. "Maybe he did get busted at that party?"

Maddie shrugged.

Ginger poked at her food. "Well, Kevin still sucks."

■ ■ ■

A kick to the rear rocked Ryan awake. He dragged open his eyelids and immediately regretted it. "I'm gonna puke," he mumbled.

"Jesus, J. Shrimp," Mike said, obviously the kicker. "You have the tolerance of a ten-year-old girl."

Ryan wondered what alcoholic ten-year-olds Mike partied with. "Just get me some water."

Mike kicked him again. "Get it yourself." He walked across the room. "Shrimp's alive," he yelled.

Ryan grabbed his head. Noise was bad. Very bad.

Drew stomped into the room, a bag under one arm, crunching something like a cow. "Barely."

"This explains where all the vodka went."

"Jeez, Shrimp," Drew said, standing over him and raining crumbs. "Could have saved some for the rest of us."

Crawling out of the room, Ryan found the janitor's closet/bathroom and ran the faucet. He cupped some water into his mouth, then puked.

"Cleanup in aisle two!" Drew yelled from inside the storage room.

Ryan felt a bit better after puking. He would never drink again. Though this was the promise he swore every time he yacked. This time, though. This time he would follow the rule: Beer good, vodka badski.

He rinsed out the sink, peed, then doused the whole thing with bleach from a bottle on the shelf. Now that the thing was purified, he ran the faucet once more and took several long drinks. *Much better.* Though his head pounded, he at least could stand without the floor moving.

Mike had the police radio out and was scanning the

channels. "Today, we start running our own lives," he said as Ryan entered the room. "Taco is clearly not dealing straight with us, a fact which will be remedied upon his showing his skinny ass in this room. Until that time, we need to start doing some recon of our own. I want to know who threw this other party. I want to know if security busted it the way they busted us the other night. I want to know just what the hell is going on in this place."

Ryan wanted a glass of OJ and an ibuprofen.

Drew crunched the last fistful of whatever had been in the bag, then crumpled the bag and lobbed it at the over-flowing trash can. "I just want to know if that other party had a friggin' keg."

"Whatever the hell is going on, Taco's in the middle of it."

Ryan wondered if he should tell Mike about his own suspicions. But then Marco might try to retaliate, and tell Mike about Ruthie and Jack.

Crap. Ryan had completely forgotten to check on them before the party. He'd left them alone since the afternoon. Ruthie was going to give him that look.

"I'm going to try to find some Sportade," Ryan said, shuffling for the door. He figured it was the next best thing to OJ.

"Steal enough for all of us," Mike said.

Ryan stumbled his way down to the first floor, then to the courtyard. Breakfast was over, so only those on the janitorial crew were around, swabbing the floors or spong-ing off tables with disinfectant. He was lucky to have got-ten a mask at the med center. It was like the token he needed to pass through the common areas of the mall. He wondered if this whole sterilization plan was working. Was the stack of bodies he'd seen in the med center an improvement over what had been there on other days?

Guys were on line for the shower as luck would have it, so Ryan joined the group and got his second shower in as many days. He was almost feeling human by the time he reached the SUV. He gave the special knock. No response.

"Ruthie?" He knocked again.

Nothing.

He tugged the handle and opened the door. No Ruthie. Jack lay on the backseat, his breathing shallow.

Ryan scrambled into the back of the truck. "Jack? Buddy?" He dug around the junk on the floor for water and came up only with empty bottles.

"Ruthie?" Jack moaned.

"Jack!" Ryan could have cried at hearing his voice. "Where's Ruthie?"

Jack struggled to open his eyes. "Did you find the water?" he mumbled, incoherent.

Ruthie must have gone to get water and gotten snatched. Ryan punched the seatback.

"Ruthie?"

Ryan stroked Jack's head. He'd really screwed things up now. Ruthie was bagged and taken somewhere. Jack was obviously not doing well. He couldn't take him to the med center. Not after what he'd seen. He would not let Jack become another body in the pile.

Jack needed water, so Ryan took two empty bottles, shoved them into his waistband, and got back on line for the showers. Lucky for Ryan, the old guy handing out towels was not entirely with it and didn't notice that he was going in for seconds. Ryan filled the bottles from the shower head—which was a hose with a spray nozzle—and ran back to the car.

"Here, buddy," he said, handing Jack a bottle. The little guy needed Ryan to help him sit up to drink it.

Ryan doused a shirt he found on the floor with water and sponged Jack's head. The kid felt like he was burning up.

"Hold this on your head," he said to Jack, though he doubted Jack was really able to understand a word he said.

He had to get Ruthie back. Jack needed her. Then Ryan would move them somewhere where he could care for them better. It would mean telling Mike about them, but if he was cool throwing parties, he would have to be cool with hiding some freaked-out little kids.

Ryan squeezed Jack's arm, like that was any comfort, really, then climbed back over the seat and headed out to save Ruthie.

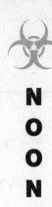

**N
O
O
N**

Shay had done everything short of climbing one of the potted trees in the food court to keep from having to face Kris. Every cell in her body was like RUN AWAY WHY ARE YOU HERE THIS IS HOR-RIBLE, but Preeti was basically holding her hand every second to ensure Shay did not disappear again, so stay in the food court she must.

Alison had all the kids working together on a giant LEGO project—City of the Future. Preeti and her two friends, without a shred of irony, were building a mall. Shay wondered, if she bent down close enough, would she see a tiny copy of herself staring back out.

"You're avoiding me." Kris's breath tickled her hair against her neck.

Shay did not turn around. "I'm here," she said. "Just helping Preeti."

"Our class has started on lunch, you know, if you want

to actually do your job instead of lurking behind trash cans to keep away from me."

She was getting a little sick of boys talking to her like she was an idiot. "What would you like me to say? I'm sorry for trying to kiss you? There, I said it."

Kris rolled his eyes. "You don't have to be sorry." He play punched her arm. "I was worried when you ran off."

Something in the kind tone of his voice made it hard for Shay to keep up her façade of competence. "I'm having a hard time." *Why is that so hard to admit?*

"With what?"

"Life?"

Kris swept his hands out. "Are you trying to tell me that spending over a week in a mall is getting to you? What's *wrong* with you? What, do you normally like go outside or something?"

Shay smiled in spite of herself. "Wait, are you saying the food court *isn't* outside?"

"Crap," he said. "Now I've blown it. Everyone, we're still in the mall! Sorry to have misled you with the trees."

"The giant pots did kind of give things away."

"Well, we were on a budget." Kris grabbed his plate and sat down outside the circle of their little five-year-olds.

Shay took her plate from the trolley. "We're down one."

"Better than yesterday," he said.

"Focusing on the bright side?"

"Always." He held his spork up as if toasting the concept.

Shay raised hers and tried, really tried, to pretend that one gone instead of five was a good thing.

■　■　■

Marco had allowed himself five minutes in a closet to get over Shay. He'd done everything except cry. He would not cry over her. His hand hurt from where he'd punched the wall.

But five minutes was all the time he gave over to feeling. He had a crapload of real estate to search and only eight hours left to do it in. So far, he'd patrolled the service halls and stockrooms of one quarter of the first floor of the mall. He even searched the first-floor stockroom of the med center. No alcohol.

It was not easy, scrambling through all the junk that the cleaning crews had discarded that first day to clear the way for civilization. He expected that the alcohol would be boxed, though if the thieves were any good, they would have hidden it in boxes from the store they were hiding it in, to try to make the stuff blend in.

Sometimes he wondered if he was giving these thieves too much credit. They were probably just alcoholics who couldn't go fifteen minutes let alone a week without a drink. These were not the master-planning types. Marco suspected that at some point he'd stumble on the two of them passed out with a pile of empties in front of them, red-faced and red-handed. Of course, they could be anywhere in the million and a half square feet of retail space afforded by the Shops at Stonecliff.

As he crouched under a giant shelf structure in the back of the BathWorks, Marco's stomach gave off an ugly growl. He'd skipped breakfast—something about his conversation with Shay had turned him off food. *Screw it.* If he didn't eat, he'd pass out, and that wouldn't help him to find the drunk *cabrons* any faster.

He walked out the front of the BathWorks and joined the line for slop. He glanced around him, trying to calculate how much longer the search would take. His figures were not adding up to anything good. Another day and maybe he could cover every stockroom, but eight hours?

"You the guy with the parties?"

Marco needed this like he needed another foot in his ass. "No."

The guy grabbed Marco and forcibly turned him around. "Guy over there says you are."

The dude looked like he was twenty-five and could bench press Marco's weight ten times over. He was one of those short, muscular guys whose shoulders sort of melded into his skull. And behind him were two gentlemen of a similar build. In other words, Marco had little choice but to talk to the man.

"I'm having a bit of a supply problem," Marco said. "All parties are off."

The guy smirked. "Supply problem?"

"Look, I don't piss beer. I get it from somewhere. And I can't get it anymore. So no parties."

"How about this?" The guy glanced at his two compatriots like they offered anything more than ballast to the conversation. "You fix your supply problem or we make life more difficult for you than it has to be."

"I could scream and security would be on you like—"

"Not if I punch you in the throat and break your larynx."

Marco swallowed. He enjoyed having use of his throat. "Look, I don't know what you want me to say. I don't have any alcohol. I can't help you."

"I think you're going to find life in this place very un-comfortable from here on out if you fail to deliver alcohol to my crew and to the gentlemen over there who intro-duced us." He pointed at the *pendejo* who'd spent last night treating Marco like a goddamned valet, then slapped Marco's arms like they were just good ole pals chatting it up and walked away with his two goons.

"The line moved," some asswipe behind him whined.

"Screw you," Marco managed. He shuffled forward in the line and tried to shake off the feeling that everyone in the mall was sizing him up. He felt like he had way back in elementary school, before he'd mastered the art of self-protection through sarcasm, back when every minute was filled with anxiety, waiting for the next punch to fall.

He had to find the alcohol. *How?* He needed access to the security tapes. If the senator had footage of him going into Johnny Rockets, she had to have other footage from the service halls. Anything would help. *Lexi.* Lexi could get her mother to give her the tapes.

And then he remembered that they were supposed to have gotten together last night.

Marco mentally slapped himself in the face. He would fix things between them. Had to. Anyway, Lexi liked him. She'd believe anything he said. And then she would help him. Now, where the hell was she?

After two hours of searching storefronts and ducking security, Ryan kicked himself for not remembering that all children were at the "school" the senator had set up. Ruthie would not be treated like a criminal—would not be treated the way he and Mike were. A runaway kid was to be pitied, not punished. So as the rest of the mall scurried toward their nice hot lunch and actual tables, Ryan snuck up to the food court and looked for Ruthie.

It was not easy, busting into the backs of the food court kiosks and peering over the counters, scanning for one little girl in a crowd of them. He finally gave up the stealth tactics and just walked around the crowds of kids, weaving between the tables and picnickers on the ground.

"Excuse me," a woman's voice barked behind him. "You're not one of my teachers."

Ryan turned slowly, gave himself a second to think. "My little sister," he said. "I just wanted to see my little sister."

"No unauthorized visits during the day," she said. "You should know that."

"Oh." Ryan scratched at his dirty shorts. Everyone else in the place was wearing clean clothes—mismatched clothes you'd expect to see on a senile old bat, but clean.

"I haven't seen you before," she said. "I've seen everyone in this mall."

"I have one of those forgettable faces," Ryan said. "I guess I'll see my sister later." He shrugged and began shuffling away between two rings of kids eating their lunches.

"Stop," the woman said. "Security! I have an unregistered."

Ryan did not wait to see if there were any guards around paying attention; he hurdled two kids and bolted down the hallway. Taking the escalator stairs down two at a time, he launched himself into the crowds on the first floor, then slowed to a walk, hunched his shoulders, and tried to blend in. While he was blending in, he figured he may as well get a decent meal, so he joined one of the food lines.

After a few minutes and no sign of pursuit, Ryan allowed himself to relax and look around the line, spotting Marco a few people ahead of him. Three guys were talking to him, then the one in front grabbed Marco's arms and gave him the kind of pat Ryan had seen Mike execute on guys he was about to bury. What the hell was Marco involved in?

Ryan shuffled through the other people in line—no one seemed to mind his cutting them, like they weren't that eager to get their meal anyway—and tapped Marco on the shoulder. The guy jumped like Ryan had pushed him.

"Dude, it's me," he said, hands up in surrender.

"What do you want?" Marco said, sounding disgusted.

"Nothing," he said. "I just saw you with those guys and wondered what was up."

Marco's face tightened like something was sucking it from the inside against his skull. "Nothing is *up*. And you shouldn't be here."

"I'm looking for one of my kids," Ryan said. "Security took her last night."

"Why the hell do you bother with them? Call security on them yourself and save yourself the trouble." Marco seemed overly angry about a situation he had nothing to do with.

"I bother with them because they have no one else," Ryan said. He was not interested in having Marco crap all over him. "Do you think security would put her in with the other kids? That's what I was thinking."

"I honestly don't care if they pushed her out an airlock

and set her free in the world." Marco kept glancing over his shoulder like he was looking for someone.

"Do you have a date I'm interrupting?"

Marco sneered. "You'd like it if I had someone, wouldn't you? Make you feel better about stealing Shay?"

So that's what this is about. "I didn't steal Shay," Ryan said, trying to be diplomatic. "She and I were kind of together before, you know, I was, well, forced to the sidelines."

"But you knew that she and I had something after you bailed." Marco glared at him. "You only care about you—what *you* want, *your* problems. Get over yourself."

No one had ever looked at him the way Marco was at that moment: like he hated him, really hated him. No one hated Ryan Murphy. Ryan was the nice guy. Had he really done something wrong? How could his being with Shay be wrong? She chose *him.*

"Do you need help?" Ryan said finally.

"Not from you," Marco said. "Now get out of here before someone notices you. You have to be registered to get any food."

Ryan let the line sweep past him, watched Marco's head slink away. Was Marco right? What the hell was he doing out here in the open where any second some guard could bag his ass and throw him in jail again?

But he couldn't bail on Ruthie, not now. He'd promised to protect them, promised Jack he'd bring her back. They needed him. Mike and Drew didn't need him. If anything, he was a leech on their butts. And Shay was safe in this new mall life with her co-teacher and dorm with clean clothes. Ruthie and Jack were the only people who really needed him, Ryan Murphy, and no one else.

How could he not have thought of it before? Shay—of course! She was a teacher. She could find Ruthie for him and help him sneak her out. He had some time to kill before their meeting time—enough to find some scraps left behind in the stores. God, how he missed real food. A burger—his mouth drooled at the thought. But he had to settle for what was available: some half-eaten plate dumped in the trash? No, he wasn't there yet. He turned toward the PhreshPharm and prayed no one had cleared it of its crap food.

"Jerk alert," Ginger whispered, twitching her head to the right.

Lexi turned and saw Marco coming toward where they stood in the lunch line. "Potential jerk," she said. "There's still hope."

"Aw, *hope*," Maddie said. "How adorable."

Marco was holding his plate and soda (*soda today!*). "I am so sorry about last night," he said. "Can we eat lunch together?"

Lexi nodded, afraid that if she spoke she might start squealing like some girl.

He said, "Great," and sounded like he meant it, then kind of nodded to Ginger and Maddie. "Hi," he said. "I'm Marco."

"Oh, we know." Maddie gave him the once-over. "So where were you?"

"Huh?" Marco was more flustered than usual.

"Last night?" She popped her hip, upping the 'tude quotient. "You were MIA. I want to know why."

"I got held up," he said, flinching like he was being poked. "And then security busted me."

Maddie looked at Lexi, who smiled to confirm that this was good enough for her, then rolled her eyes. "We'll catch you back in the scullery," Maddie said, hoisting her plate.

They had been assigned to a new crew this morning: laundry. On laundry duty, you worked in the parking garage and had to don a full suit of plastic, then duct tape the sleeves to plastic kitchen gloves and the legs to wellies, and finally cover your hair in a shower cap, all so that other people's clothing didn't infect you with their germs. Not that they were washing the clothes of the sick. Only the healthy people's clothes got washed for a second use. But apparently, even a mall the size of Stonecliff had trouble providing fresh clothing for thousands of people for more than four days.

Lexi got her lunch and found Marco at a remote little bistro table hidden behind a giant plant pot. "A little out of the way, but I like it."

"It's quieter here," he said, though with all the echoes, no place in the mall was really quiet.

"Did you get held up by that girl I saw you with?" She couldn't help but ask. "The alleged girl who is a friend?"

"What?" He didn't look like his alert and cunning self; bags ringed his eyes and he was all jittery. He glanced up at every person who passed like he expected them to attack.

"Are you okay?" she asked. She touched his arm, more to bring his focus back to her than anything else, but he stared at her hand like it was a lifeline.

"Do you like me?" he asked.

She was taken aback. Lexi shoveled a bite into her mouth to stall. Boys didn't ask direct things like that. She was sure that all communication between the sexes was supposed to be covert, like furtive glances across the caf.

She swallowed, and, lacking a better plan, decided she would go with the truth. "Yes."

He looked like he might cry. "You wouldn't if you knew me," he said.

"You're funny, and smart. And you're nice." He hiccupped a laugh when she said it. "What?" she continued. "You're nice to me. And we both like movies, and I can tell you're a gamer. Why wouldn't I like you?"

He leaned back in his chair, considering her, arms dangling. "Is it really that simple?" He seemed to honestly be asking.

"Marco, what is going on? You're freaking me out."

His face hardened again. "Don't worry about it," he said. "I can handle it." He shoveled a bite into his mouth.

"Can I help you?"

"I said I can handle it. Let's talk about something else. You're a gamer? You play EVE?"

"EVE is for money-grubbing douchebags."

"I've killed people for lesser offenses than the one you just committed."

"I'm sure you have, EVE-verser."

"So, what, you're into Warcraft?"

"Minecraft when I play online, but mostly Xbox with my friends."

"Lame."

"You're lame." She kicked his shin under the table.

"Under-the-table assault? You'd be perfect for EVE."

She put her fork down. "If I can do anything to help you, I would totally do it."

Marco pushed his tray from him, then explained that he had tried to sneak into the Grill'n'Shake where he used to work to scrounge some decent food and got busted. The Senator accused him of stealing alcohol, which he said was nuts because he didn't even drink, but she wouldn't let him off unless he helped her find the missing stuff.

"She showed me a security tape of two people breaking in the gate," Marco said. "I tried to tell her I got busted alone, but she wouldn't listen. The two guys hid their faces from the cameras in the halls."

"But did she show you the feeds from the hidden cameras?" Lexi asked, sensing her opportunity.

As Lexi had guessed, the Senator had not shown them to him, and so she took it upon herself to sneak into her mom's office and steal the receivers for the hidden cameras. But, honestly, was it even stealing? Marco was trying to help the Senator, and Lexi was helping him, so really, she was helping her mom, which made the whole theft totally legitimate. *Totally.*

It was a lot of footage to fast-forward through. Lexi pushed each receiver into the USB port on the laptop she had "borrowed" for their investigation and then ran through all the footage. When they got to the one for outside the Johnny Rockets, Marco told her to skip it.

"No alcohol," he said.

"But they could be stealing other stuff too," she said, and watched it anyway. It turned out Marco did have a reason for wanting her to skip that receiver: He was a freaking liar. The screen showed Marco himself scanning a card to let him into the back of the Johnny Rockets.

Lexi paused and zoomed in on his face. "You want to tell me something?" She hated that the camera had caught him in a lie. She had so wanted to believe him.

Marco kicked the nearest shelf. "Okay, look, I told you most of the truth." He explained that he really was working for her mom, but it wasn't because he got busted for sneaking into the Grill'n'Shake, but rather because he had stolen a universal access card from a cop during the riots. "The deal is I help your mom with stuff and I get to keep the card."

Lexi so wanted to believe him.

"Okay," she said.

She went back to scanning the receiver footage, clinging to his lie like a life raft.

"Wait," Marco said during their tenth scan. "What's that?"

It was the footage from the crappy camera she'd stuck outside the Pancake Palace. The image was grainy, but clearly showed a guy rolling a keg in the back door. A big guy, like a dad.

"I think we've got your thief," she said, pausing on the best shot of the guy, which was still terrible.

A nasty smile twisted across Marco's face. He grabbed Lexi's face like he was going to kiss her. Her heart pumped violently. But then he let go.

"You're amazing," he said, standing like he was going to leave.

"Should we tell my mom?"

"No," he snapped. "I mean, I'll tell her. It's part of our deal."

"Will I see you tonight?" she asked, her body screaming to have him touch her again.

"What?" He was already gone, she could tell. "Oh, yeah. Tonight. Your office. Be there or be a rhombus." He waved and jogged out of the room like he had an urgent appointment.

Lexi took stock of her lunch. *Crap.* It was one thirty; she was late for afternoon work assignment. And she'd stolen from her mother, but only to help someone who was (maybe, hopefully) working on her behalf. She'd almost been kissed and she sort of had a date for tonight. This was all good. Sort of. Assuming not all of it was complete bull. She put the receivers back in the bag she'd stolen, shut down the laptop, and prayed that his lies were truths.

T
W
O

P.M.

Marco had wanted to tell Lexi everything, but when he tried to put it into words, it sounded stupid. That he'd traded protection for use of his escape services with a bunch of assholes, that her mother had blackmailed him into helping her run after-hours parties, that he was the target of every douche with a jones for a beer, that he didn't even know what decision was the safest bet for himself, that every choice seemed to plunge him deeper into a pile of crap that he had no idea how to dig himself out of. To tell her all that was to admit that he was lost, and he didn't want her to see him that way. He wanted to be the semi-cool person she—was she deluded? Insane?—thought he was.

He was almost depressed that his lies had fooled her. But not enough to tell her the truth, which was that he feared the gangs in the mall more than her mother. That he was going to negotiate with this old guy alcohol thief for enough booze to keep his skin on his back—at most recent calculation, that would be whatever was required for three parties: Mike & Co., the *pendejos*, and the no-necks. He would then tell the senator she could find her booze with the *pendejos* and the no-necks, blame them for stealing the alcohol. And tomorrow, with any luck, he'd be back to managing one set of douches, his douches. He could handle them.

He was about to let himself into the back of the Pan-cake Palace, but thought better of revealing his possession of the all-access card. Though he was prepared to confront an old guy or two, drunk off their asses, he couldn't be sure of being able to fight them off if they tried to steal his card. So he knocked. The door didn't open. He heard voices inside. Never one to be deterred by a locked door, he let himself into the stockroom of the PaperClips, and then walked through the plastic-covered hole in the wall into the Pancake Palace.

Instead of two lonely drunks and a pile of booze, he faced what looked like a functioning bar for off-hours cops. Silver-haired men smoked cigars at the counter and swilled plastic glasses of liquor.

"Who the hell are you?" the one behind the bar asked.

"What the hell is this?" Marco retorted.

The guy stepped out from behind the bar and ap-proached where Marco stood frozen by the wall. "*This* is none of your business, kid. I suggest you turn your butt around and forget you ever saw us." He was tall, taller than Marco. And outweighed him by a good fifty pounds.

"I don't want to make any trouble," Marco said, attempting some semblance of control. He was good at talking to adults. He could work this. "I just have a couple of college guys riding me for alcohol. I got word that you had some." He waved his hand at the bar. "Which is obviously the case and I want to negotiate your giving me a keg or three."

The silver-haired guy huffed a laugh. "Well, aren't you a pisser? Negotiate? What the hell do you have to negotiate with?"

"What do you need?" This guy had no idea how resourceful Marco could be.

"Snacks," a guy bellowed from the bar. He was in a security uniform. Marco wondered whether he was here officially or on the down low.

"I can do food," Marco said. "How about I trade you some food for the three kegs?"

The old guy rubbed his stubble. The man had the look of a used car salesman. If Marco were not facing three separate death threats at the moment, he would have bolted.

The guy held out a hand. "You produce some decent grub, and I'll give you your kegs."

It was good enough for Marco. He took the hand, shook it, and got the hell out of there before the guy changed his mind.

Ryan arrived early at the Magic Wok, so he paced in the kitchen until it was closer to his and Shay's meeting time. Shay arrived early, skidding over the counter and whispering his name as if knowing he was there.

"Shay," he said, stepping out to meet her.

She didn't say a word, merely fell into his arms and pressed her lips to his. He almost gave in to her, to the mesmerizing power of her body, but managed to struggle out of her arms.

"I need your help," he said.

She looked at him like he was speaking Greek. Then she seemed to come back to herself. "Is something wrong? Is it Marco?"

"No," Ryan said, grabbing her hand and pulling her into the kitchen in the back, in case that drill sergeant teacher who'd busted him earlier was on the prowl. "It's a little girl I was helping. Her name is Ruthie and she was taken by security last night. Could you see if she's here?"

Shay again had that puzzled look on her face. "You came here to ask me to look for a kid?"

"Is that okay? I just need help to get her back to her brother." Ryan was not sure why this was a problem.

Shay backed away from him until she hit the wall. One hand fidgeted with the sleeve on the other. "Yeah, sure," she mumbled. "Definitely. I'll go check."

"Great," he said, approaching her. He squeezed her hand. "Thank you."

She winced a small smile, then ducked back into the front and over the counter. Why was she acting so weird?

Shay nearly fell to the floor as she slid off the edge of the counter. She'd been pushing herself to survive until this moment, until she could kiss Ryan again, propose their running away together. And he thwarted her. No kissing. Not even a conversation. Just a favor. Like she was a friend, anyone, no one at all. What the hell was going on with him?

She needed to find this Ruthie. Maybe once he knew she was here and was okay, they could pick up from where they'd left off yesterday. Sneak off to his secret lair and just hole up until the end of this nightmare. Yes, all she needed was to solve this Ruthie problem.

"Kris?" She tapped him on the shoulder. She put on her best I'm-normal-and-happy face.

"You're back early." He continued his futile attempt to wipe the glitter glue from his hands.

"Do you know if a new girl named Ruthie was registered this morning?"

"I think Ethel Wisse has a Ruthie."

Shay found Ethel and confirmed that in fact she did have a new student named Ruthie. "She's a little odd," Ethel said, pointing to a skinny girl who looked desperately in need of a bath. "We asked her to help with our section of the LEGO city, but she refuses to leave that corner."

Shay knelt in front of the little girl. "Hi, I'm Shay." The little girl looked away. Shay smiled wide enough that her face hurt—she knew the wrinkles of her smile showed above the mask when her face hurt. "I'm Ryan's friend."

The girl whipped her face around to meet Shay's eyes. "He's not my friend anymore."

She seemed really angry, but little kids were always throwing fits, as Shay had learned after three days of working with them. "He's here and he's really worried about you. He wants to bring you back to your brother."

"Where is he?"

Shay was not sure what all the hostility was about, but she led Ruthie to the front of the Magic Wok and pointed. "He's in there."

"You abandoned us!" Ruthie was a loud one. "You left us and I got caught and now Jack's sick!"

People stared. Kris looked at her like she should do something. Shay panicked. What was she supposed to do with a screaming kid?

"Stop yelling," Shay begged, grabbing Ruthie by the shoulders.

The girl's face was set in a pout. "He left us," was all she would say.

A security guard came over. "Who's the kid screaming at?" he asked, peering into the Magic Wok.

Shay's pulse shot through the roof. The guard couldn't find Ryan, she couldn't lose him now, they were going to escape together!

"No one," Shay answered, then, reconsidering, "Me."

The guard, dubious, asked Ruthie, who said, "A bad boy." She wriggled free of Shay's hands. "My brother is down in the parking garage in a tan SUV. You have to go find him and rescue him."

The security guy looked around like he wasn't sure what to do with the information. "Okay," he said. "Can you show me which one exactly?"

"Yes," Ruthie said. "A boy was trying to keep us down there, but I escaped. It was scary down there. And smelled. And we didn't have any food." She followed the guard toward the elevator.

Shay couldn't believe that the girl was talking about Ryan. He kept them down there?

Once the kid was gone with the guard, Shay snuck back into the Magic Wok's kitchen. Ryan was sitting on the stainless-steel counter, gripping the edge like he might fall off. "Why would she say that?" he muttered.

"She seemed really angry," Shay offered. "Maybe something happened?"

Ryan glanced at her. "I wasn't keeping them down there," he said. "They begged me to help them stay down there. They were scared to leave their car." He sounded angry, very unlike the Ryan she knew and needed.

"I believe you." Shay took a step toward him, tried to take his hand. She would bring him back to himself.

He pulled it away from her. "I've gotta go," he said, sliding off the counter.

"Please stay," she said, trying to control the desperation in her voice.

He didn't stop or respond, just left through the back door.

She'd failed him. Had to have. If she'd done things right, he would have stayed. This was her fault.

No. That was crazy. It was the little girl's fault. It was Ryan's fault. It was this mall's fault.

Shay slid to the floor. She was suddenly deathly tired. She crawled under the counter, tucked her knees to her chest, and wrapped her arms around herself so her body wouldn't crack apart.

Lexi dropped the bag of receivers and laptop in the chair opposite her mother's desk. "Just a return," she said.

Her mother looked up from the iPad on her desk. "Why'd you take the receivers?"

"I was helping a mutual friend," Lexi said. "You never told me you were using teens in the mall as spies."

The Senator seemed to be trying to grasp exactly what Lexi was saying.

"Marco?" Lexi offered. "He's helping you?"

Dotty turned off the iPad. "Promise me you won't go to one of his parties," she said.

Parties? His *parties?* "Wait, you know about the parties?" She had figured that anything Maddie Flynn wanted to be a part of was not legal.

Dotty seemed flustered. "Wait, is that not what you're talking about?"

"How do you know about the parties? And if you know about them, why are they happening at all?"

Mom straightened her lapels. She'd somehow managed to get herself a clean suit every day. "It was a compromise I struck with our mutual friend, Marco. He throws parties for me in designated locations to keep the teens from running wild all over the mall, and security busts them at a designated time. We weed out the sick, and return the rest to their dorms. It's been working out great."

Now it was Lexi's turn to be flustered. "You mean you're breaking your own rules? People have to wear masks and wash their hands fifty times a day, but after Lights Out you can do whatever you want?"

Her mother shrugged. "Everything in life involves compromise."

"But only for the teens?" Lexi asked. "Everyone else has to obey the rules?"

"The teens seem to be the only ones who want to break the rules," Dotty said. "Look, Lex, the plan is working."

She held up the iPad. "Dr. Chen said new admissions are down for a second day in a row, and he's seeing more people survive the flu. I think we're finally beating this disease. If we can just keep things going for a few more days, we might be looking at the end of the quarantine."

Why didn't this make her feel any better? This plan seemed to just write off her friends. If they wanted to kill themselves, then whatever, let them—that seemed to be her mother's view.

The Senator took Lexi's hand. "Just promise me you won't go to one of those parties," she said. "From what Hank told me, they're pretty rough."

Lexi nodded, not agreeing, but just wanting to get away, to process this information, try to figure out how her mother's story fit with Marco's. Why hadn't he mentioned anything about the parties?

The Senator's walkie-talkie squealed. "Ross, we have a situation in Shep's." Shep's had been set up as a gym for people to use before breakfast and in the evenings after dinner.

"What kind of situation?" the Senator said, all business. Lexi remained amazed at her mother's ability to switch modes like a computer.

"You'd better get down here" was the only reply.

Dotty buttoned her jacket. "Excuse me, love, but duty calls."

"I'm coming with you," Lexi said. She would not be kept in the dark about what the heck was really going on in this mall for another nanosecond.

"Might as well combine business with pleasure," Dotty said, wrapping an arm around Lexi's shoulders.

It was a short walk down to Shep's, too short. In less than a minute, they arrived at the wide entrance to the store, which offered a clear line of sight through to the back, which sported a rock climbing wall, where five people dangled like punching bags from the ropes. Blue tongues bulged from mouths. One body twitched, her bare feet dancing. Dotty covered Lexi's eyes, but the one glance had already been too much.

The Senator seemed to swallow her shock in an instant. "Lexi, get back to the JCPenney. Hank, I want a screen set up around this place."

"Already on it. FEMA warned us about the likelihood of crap like this in quarantine situations."

"Get the bodies down, then reopen the gym. As far as the rest of the mall is concerned, nothing happened."

"My thoughts exactly."

Lexi couldn't pull her eyes away.

Her mother grabbed her shoulders. "Please," she said, shaking Lexi to get her attention. "Go back to the JCPenney."

Lexi nodded, mute. She stumbled away, not stopping until she found Maddie and Ginger in the garage. She pulled on their plastic-cased limbs. "They're dead," she said. "They killed themselves."

Maddie shook the water from her gloves. "Slow down," she said. "What the hell are you talking about?"

Lexi told them about the dangling bodies, the dancing feet.

"Well," Maddie said, sliding off her cap. "I guess we should expect stuff like this."

"Expect suicide?" Lexi asked.

"We're basically waiting to die in here anyway," Maddie said, replacing her hat. "You've got to expect some people to take matters into their own hands."

Ginger sat and leaned against her laundry tub. "It's a sin, Mad," she said. "Suicide's pretty major."

"Being quarantined in a mall with a deadly flu is pretty major too," Maddie said, stirring her load.

Lexi slumped next to Ginger, who slung an arm around her.

"It sucks that you had to see that," Ginger said, her mask brushing Lexi's forehead. "Were they really just hanging?"

Lexi did not want to remember, but every time she closed her eyes, there they were. "Just hanging," she said.

"God," Ginger said, and squeezed her tighter.

**F
I
V
E**

P.M.

Mike and Drew were on the pinsetter's catwalk,
not in the storage room where Ryan had first
looked. Only after having a minor freak-out over
them not being anywhere in the bowling alley did Ryan
recall the existence of the catwalk and look there. Mike
and Drew were huddled near the far wall, knees bent,
walkie-talkie on the ground between them. The entire
space just inside the door was crowded with what looked
like all the remaining food from the fridge.

"We had to consolidate," Mike said, waving for him
to come toward them. "Heard over the walkie-talkie that
crews were coming for our fridge, so we cleaned it out
and took cover."

Ryan sat opposite the two of them.

"Where you been all day?" Drew asked.

They were both staring at him, suspicious. "I had this

stupid side thing going," Ryan began, and told them about
Jack and Ruthie. About finding them that first day in the
car, how they were terrified and how he'd helped them,
how in the end nothing he'd done had been enough.
"Jack's sick, flu I think, and Ruthie hates me."

Drew shook his head. "Kids are such assholes."

Mike tossed Ryan a can of tomato juice. "You should
have told us."

"I figured you didn't need another person to take care
of," he said, cracking it open and chugging.

"How am I supposed to watch your ass if you hide crap
like this from me? I could have helped you find food for
them. We could have moved them someplace together. It's
this sneaking behind my back crap that pisses me off."

"Like Marco?"

Mike pointed at Ryan's heart. "Exactly."

Ryan told them what he knew about Marco—that
he had planned that first party on some level, and that steroid-
pumped guys were threatening him. "I have no idea what
he's thinking. The guido guys looked like they wanted to
kill him."

"I know the feeling," Drew grumbled.

"Marco has been a team player," Mike said, cutting
Drew off. "But he's definitely running some scam on the
side and he'd better be able to explain it to my satisfac-
tion." He stood, cracked his neck, and walked toward the
door. "First, we put together another crap dinner."

"If I eat another refried bean, I'm going to frickin' puke."

Ryan practically sprinted for the food. He hadn't eaten
all day and that tomato juice had only made him hungrier.

He'd eat beans of any kind, maraschino cherries, whatever could be scrounged from the fridge of a bowling alley's bar.

Marco let himself into the service halls and tracked his way toward the Sam's Club as soon as he saw decent lines for dinner on the first floor. He knew from his work on construction that all the food in the mall was being consolidated there. He wasn't sure why—maybe just to keep people from living off Jujubes instead of the freeze-dried camp food. Sam's was a good place—fairly isolated from the rest of the mall, it had only one main entrance and exit point, which was gated off. But there were four exits into the service hallways, so he used one of those.

Marco had guessed right that the doors would not be patrolled during dinner—he'd seen guards in the service hallway during the "work day," but none now blocked his path. He slid his card through the reader and pulled open a door.

The Sam's Club was huge, like the HomeMart, only all white. The shelves had been rearranged, and any non-food items cleared and replaced with what could be scrounged from the rest of the mall. Refrigerators and freezers that had been rolled in from somewhere lined one wall. Their thrum filled the cavernous treasure trove.

Marco wanted to be in and out of there as quickly as possible. Not only because the place was like a tomb, but he still had three kegs to move, and a third party location to find, after which he had to get his butt out of everyone's way so he didn't end up serving as party bitch for another consecutive night.

He ran down the few steps and began scanning the

aisles for bags of chips, anything that one might count as bar food. Just as he spotted giant bags of popcorn mere feet away, he heard a voice behind him.

"We have an intruder," the voice said.

And then a lightning bolt struck him. Marco lost control of his muscles and hit the linoleum.

He regained his senses in a dark stockroom. He could not tell for what store. A lone light shone on him like this was some Nazi interrogation. "Where the hell am I?" he said, his voice sounding scratchy.

A large man with a gut sat in the chair opposite. "I believe we've had the pleasure, Mr. Carvajal. I'm Hank Goldman, head of security, and you've been a pain in my ass since day one."

Marco vaguely recalled this man from one of his meetings with the senator; however, the guy seemed to have intimate knowledge of Marco.

He continued, "Rescue of prime targets Richter and Bonner, as well as an assault with fire extinguishers on my guards to rescue the kid on the wire, Murphy. Theft of a police access card key, and suspicion of having assaulted that officer to get it. Numerous absences from your work crew. Detainment every single evening after curfew."

The guy looked up from the paper he was reading. "Quite an impressive list." He shifted on his seat and leaned toward Marco. "What I want to know is why Ross's little pet criminal is sneaking through the food storage center when I have received no clearance for your being there."

Marco could see several shadows outside the aura of blinding light. This was some Gestapo bullcrap. He had freaking rights. "I want to see the senator. I can explain what I was doing."

"Then you can explain it to me." Goldman did not budge.

"I found the alcohol, just like she wanted. But the guy who's holding it said I couldn't have it unless I brought him food, so I was getting him some chips. I was trying to fix this whole party situation and the alcohol problem in one shot." It was almost the truth. It was close enough to save his ass.

"Party situation," Goldman said snidely. "I told the woman this was a mistake. You put criminals in jails, you don't throw them friggin' parties."

"Look, I can explain everything to the senator."

"I don't want you to explain diddly crap to that woman." Goldman stood and flipped off the light. "I'm glad we found you, Carvajal. You are going to be a useful member of our team. See, we needed someone to act as the fall guy to steal us some decent food. Now that the woman has secret cameras hidden everywhere in the service halls, we can't remove merchandise without alerting her to our operations. But you," he said, grabbing Marco's arm. "You can do all that for us."

Gooseflesh prickled from where Goldman held his arm and spread over Marco's entire body. What the hell was going on in this mall? The head of security was running some scam behind the senator's back? This was too much.

"So here's the plan," Goldman continued. "You finish your little shopping trip, roll your pallet of grub back to the Pancake Palace, and then be a good boy and wait for us to pick you up again and bring you to the senator."

"No," Marco whispered. "I won't do it. Screw this, I'm out. Let the assholes find their own liquor."

Goldman twisted Marco's skin. "Buddy, you're so far in, they'd need a friggin' scalpel to get you out."

"Screw you."

Goldman let go. "Kinsey, I think our friend needs some more convincing."

A woman stepped from the shadows, pressed a stun baton to Marco's arm, and Marco lost some time to pain. When he came to, they were all still standing there, like they had watched. Had he peed his pants? His face felt numb, his lower lip, heavy. His thigh would not stop twitching.

For the first time in a very long time, Marco was petrified. There was no fighting these people, no running away. He was trapped in a mall with a head of security who endorsed torture for something so lame as stealing popcorn. What would he do for higher stakes? Now that he had Marco on his radar, what was the limit of his madness?

"F-fine," Marco stammered. "Okay."

Goldman slapped Marco's shoulder. "Now, was that so hard?"

They shoved Marco's head into a sack, half dragged him down the halls, and left him around the corner from where he'd started, in the service hall outside the Sam's Club. When they were gone, Marco made a run for it. He was not falling victim to this crap scheme. He would come up with a plan—once he figured out what in the hell was going on in this fraked-up place.

Run, though, was an overstatement. His legs weren't

functioning at top capacity. His face throbbed and his lip felt like the blubbery appendage of a dying cetacean. He needed to regain control of his muscles, use of his face. He thought of the one place on earth he might feel safe and headed there.

LIGHTS OUT

Lexi, Maddie, and Ginger lay awake and watched the lights blink off throughout the mall. Lexi liked having one friend on either side of her, like buoys she could reach out and touch. "Are you going out tonight?" she asked, afraid of the answer. Their alcove now only contained the three of them, the other cots disappearing over the days.

"Go where?" Maddie answered. "Word is there's no party tonight."

"I don't think I could party tonight," Ginger said. "It would be like dancing on a grave."

"Any dancing in here is dancing on a grave," Maddie said.

Lexi did not want to go to her office. What if Marco never showed? What if she had to spend the night alone?

Maddie rolled, rustling her sheet. "Don't you have a date?"

Lexi took a deep breath. "I guess."

"If you don't go, I'm taking your place." She rolled back. "This is the longest dry spell I've had since the family vacation to Grandma's in the Adirondacks."

Lexi waited another minute before rising and slinking along the wall to the stockroom door. As she turned the handle on the door to her office, Marco's voice called out, "Leave the lights off."

He came.

"You become a vampire since lunch?" Lexi tiptoed into the space, trying to remember its layout so she didn't face-plant.

"I had my face rearranged by a stun gun," he said, sounding wasted. "I'd hate for you to remember me like this."

"Who hit you with a stun gun?"

She heard Marco shift; he was on the desk. "Your friendly chief of security."

Lexi was only mildly surprised. "Why did he hit you with a stun gun?"

"Because he's insane. I think he stole the alcohol, or is at least helping the guy who did."

The edge of the desk chair nudged Lexi's leg and she sat in it. She needed to sit. "You have to tell my mom. You can't let this guy push you around."

Marco remained silent. Finally, he spoke. "Which are better, the Burton Batman movies from the nineties, or the new Nolan ones? Let's not even consider the Schumacher catastrophes."

Lexi was confused as to how this was relevant. "Depends on what you're looking for."

"Just pick one, whatever criteria you want."

She sensed that more rode on this question than an assessment of her tastes, so she took a second to consider. Lexi and Darren had watched all the Batman movies, one after the other, from Burton's 1989 *Batman* through to *The Dark Knight*, before heading to the midnight showing of *The Dark Knight Rises*. The Burton films were funny, kind of silly, more comic book than thriller. They featured things like Danny DeVito as a fat, horny penguin running for mayor. She recalled Darren's remark after switching off *The Dark Knight*: "The world sucks."

"Burton," she answered. "I like Michelle Pfeiffer's Cat-woman. And the Nolan films are so dark."

"I thought you would," Marco said. "I wish I could pick Burton."

Lexi rolled the chair toward his voice and hit his knee. "Sorry," she said.

"Don't be," he said. His hand touched her face, fingers running from her brow down her nose to her lips.

Shivers ran over her skin. She crawled onto the desk beside him. "I like the Nolan films," she whispered.

His breath tickled her ear. "I've never kissed anyone before."

"Me neither."

His lips hit her cheek. She angled her face to meet them, merely brushing lips at first, but then, somehow, they both knew what to do, hers to press harder against his, and his to hers. Their mouths opened like clockwork and Lexi finally understood why Maddie and Ginger were so starved for this sustenance.

Lexi's kiss brought life back into Marco's body. Muscles stopped twitching, his head cleared, everything became focused on the heat burning from her lips down through him. He wasn't sure what to do with his hands, so he gripped the desk, afraid to touch her and freak her out. He didn't want anything to interrupt this kissing.

She pulled away first.

"Sorry," he said. He must have screwed something up.

"No, I'm sorry," she said. "My arm hurt."

"Did I do something?"

"No, no." She moved and they bumped heads.

"We're screwing this up," he said, rubbing his skull.

"How could we not?" She was farther away. "Total amateurs."

He wondered how he could get her to start kissing again. Was there something you were supposed to say? What would Ryan do? He hated himself for even thinking that.

The room was beginning to feel wrong. He slid off the desk and flipped on the light. They both winced in the glare. That had been a mistake. The light ruined whatever shreds of mood had remained between them. He quickly flipped it off.

"I guess I should go," he said, not wanting to at all.

"Oh, okay," Lexi said.

"So, yeah," he said. "I'll see you tomorrow?"

"Sure, yeah."

Not sure what else to do, he slunk out the door. He was no Casanova, but that was it: his first kiss. He'd been kissed. It was the only bright point in the day.

The service hallways echoed with shouts and screams. It was like that first night all over again. He'd failed to deliver on the parties and the freaks were running wild. He had to find cover. And he knew now exactly where he needed to go.

His time in the dark that afternoon had yielded some

glimmer of understanding of the craphole he was stuck in. Goldman was clearly in with the guy in the Pancake Palace; Marco had no idea if they had started on the same side, or whether Goldman saw him stealing booze and decided to assist in his operations, but it was clear that they were working together now. The senator, therefore, was a total dupe. Her whole hippy-dippy, we're-all-going-to-get-through-this-together government was a corrupt joke. How he'd ever gotten sucked into believing otherwise was a critical failure of judgment—the world sucked; how had he forgotten that?

So Marco had to find his own protection. Luckily, he had his own ready-made team of thugs and he was betting that Mike Richter was even more of a psychopath than Goldman. Mike was a career sicko; this Goldman, he was new to the work.

Marco took the shortest route to the bowling alley. The douches were not out in the open, but rather huddled in the back of the pinsetters' catwalk. Ryan, the closest, stood and stared him down.

"Where have you been?" Ryan appeared to have wormed his way back into the fold after his days of wandering.

"I've been unearthing a craphole of epic proportions." Marco laid out for them everything that had been going on: his deal with the senator—though he gave it the spin that he'd been playing her the whole time—the bodies on the ice-skating rink, the attacks by the other gangs, the discovery of the guy in the Pancake Palace.

"Wait." Mike stood. "What did he look like *exactly*?"

"Silver-gray hair, kind of leathery, brownish skin. The guy looked like he had money outside the mall, something about his condescending, I-rule-the-world smug bastard face."

"Reynolds?" Drew asked, looking up at Mike.

"I will frickin' kill him." Mike gripped the handrail like he was gripping a throat.

"Whoever he is, he's working with security. The chief, this huge guy Goldman, took liberties with a stun gun to convince me to help them steal food."

"Really?" Mike said, as if gaining a new appreciation for Marco.

"And so, in conclusion, I propose we take these assholes down." Marco leaned against the handrail and prayed his pitch had worked.

It took Ryan a minute to catch up with the conversation. Marco had essentially ripped the world of the mall apart—it had seemed so safe, so perfect. Kids went to school, there were showers. The head of security was stun-gunning a kid to force him to steal supplies? There were more than a thousand bodies on the ice-skating rink? The number sounded unreal, like a million dollars or fifty years old.

He was the first to speak. "How has no one noticed a thousand people just disappearing?"

Marco shrugged. "People see what they want to see. And it's a big mall."

Mike hoisted himself between the handrails and swung to sit on one, raised up as if on a throne. "My point exactly, Taco. This is a big mall, and what you've said convinces me that my original idea was the best one going. We hide and let this whole crapstorm play itself out."

"I am *not* going into that basement again." Drew folded his arms across his chest as if this alone settled the point.

"Screw the basement." Mike pointed to Marco. "You need to find us a place that is isolated and has few exits for easy defensibility. And it needs to be big enough to store supplies in—we're going to wait out this thing in the comfort of our own bunker."

"Got just the place," Marco said. "The IMAX theater is soundproof, isolated, and has only two exits—one in the front, and one out into a fire stairwell."

"Go, Taco Supreme!" Drew barked, punctuating his approval with a round of applause.

Ryan thought of Ruthie and Jack, of Shay. How could he leave them in the mall if the place was really the mess Marco said it was? "Shouldn't we tell someone?" he said. "I mean, we can't just leave everyone in the mall to die."

"They've left us to die," Marco said. "The senator was willing to write off anyone who went to these parties."

"But what about Shay?" Ryan thought at least she would mean something to Marco.

"What about her?" he said, voice flat like he couldn't give a crap.

Ryan wondered why he was surprised at this change in Marco. "If we're holing up, she's coming with us. And Ruthie and Jack."

Mike landed on the catwalk, rattling the thing like a gong. "We can discuss recruits after we secure our supplies. Marco, you head to the IMAX and clear out any squatters. Drew, you go with him. Shrimp, you're with me."

Ryan did not like where this was going. "With you where?"

Mike grinned. "I think it's time we pay our old pal Mr. Reynolds a friendly visit."

Shay liked the tight confines of the cabinet. She had crawled into it when Kris came looking for her—she heard him calling and scuttled into the empty stainless-steel space, the door of which had hung open, probably ravaged of food during the riots. Kris passed her by like she didn't even exist. That had been hours ago. She had remained curled like a shell in the dark until the lights disappeared and the black was complete. She felt safe, like she was locked in a vault. Nothing could hurt her in here. Even her mind had quieted to a static drone of random, disconnected thoughts.

Voices invaded the black silence. "Damn if this place isn't cleaned out too." It was a boy.

"Check everywhere," said another voice. "I'm freakin' starved."

Shay's heart quivered in her chest. *I am safe in my vault.*

The door ripped open. "What the?" The speaker knelt down; the dim glow from the other guy's lighter bounced off the shiny surfaces, throwing him into silhouette.

Shay closed her eyes like that would hide her. He grabbed her arm and dragged her out. "She's not food, but she looks pretty damn good to me."

Nothing would happen to her. Someone would come. Security. *Security!*

The guy slapped his arms around her. She did not want this to happen. This couldn't happen. Her brain froze. Some animal part inside her took over, pushed against his chest. He pressed his lips to hers. His tongue wriggled against her sealed lips. The animal part of her would not let this happen.

She bit his tongue. His lips retreated.

"She bit me!" he screamed. He slapped her face.

Shay thrust her knee into his groin. He bent forward with the blow, releasing her arms, and she pulled herself onto the countertop.

The guy's friend grabbed her leg. "Get back here!"

Shay grabbed the nearest thing—a metal container—and smashed it into his head. He fell back. She kicked him in the face and he went all the way down. Scrambling to the other side of the counter, she was clear to run through the doors leading to the front of the Magic Wok. She slid over the counter and ran, kept running, would never stop running.

A baton smashed into her leg. She crumpled to the floor, so fast, she couldn't protect any part of her save her head.

"Got another runner!" a man's voice said. He grabbed her arms, wrenched them behind her back, and tied her wrists together with something.

Her voice was broken, she couldn't catch her breath. He had the wrong idea. She had to get away from them. She struggled, kicked her feet.

"Lie still," the voice said.

The animal part of her would not listen. She rolled, tried to bite the guy's leg, and then she was hit with a jolt that knocked her flat.

Shay was still conscious, just couldn't move. The guy dragged her limp body to a chair and left her slumped in it. He lifted a walkie-talkie to his lips—he was a solid shadow of black against the nighttime light streaming through the glass walls and ceiling of the food court. "One bagged in the food court."

"More coming your way."

As if on cue, more shadows came running. The guy yelled for them to stop. They kept running, straight for the glass. They had something with them. A hammer? A big one. Several big hammers. They ran at the glass wall. *Smash.* They'd broken through! They were free!

Gunshots. From outside. Screaming. Blue flashes in the dark. Thuds of bodies. Shay's brain had trouble processing the information: Had someone escaped? Had someone been shot?

DAY
ELEVEN

MIDNIGHT

Ryan was still several steps behind on the logic of their plan. "Why are we attacking Reynolds? If you want to hide out, let's take what we have here and hide out."

Mike checked his handgun, then tucked it into the waistband at his lower back like some gangster. "We are attacking Reynolds because he took things that belonged to us, to everyone. Plus, you can never have too many supplies."

"He's guarded by security, they have Tasers," Ryan pleaded. "This is like walking into a trap on purpose."

"Listen," Mike said, shoving the squawking police radio at Ryan. "Those people Marco owed a party? They're freaking out, busting windows and basically acting like assholes. Security is a little busy pretending to actually give a crap about the people in this mall. No one is going to be watching Reynolds and his stash." He hefted a metal bar and thrust it at Ryan. "Now stop being a pussy and get ready."

Mike collected a few more traditional weapons—a length of chain, a handful of heavy screws in a sock, some more metal bars, which he strapped to his back like ninja swords. Ryan glanced at Marco and Drew, who were conferring while gathering their own arsenal. It was like everyone had been waiting for an invitation to join a guerilla force. This seemed insane to Ryan, but what choice did he have? He grabbed another metal bar and jammed a wrench into his waistband.

Mike clapped his hands, then held one out. "Taco, we need your card."

Marco slinked back a step. "I'll let you through."

"You said the doors to the IMAX were broken, so you don't need a card. We do." Mike curled his fingers. "You on the team or not?"

Marco seemed to consider this question for a moment, and then pulled the card from his pocket. "You'll give it back?"

"I'll give it back," Mike said, closing his fingers around the thing like it was treasure. He glanced at Ryan. "Let's go."

Ryan hesitated for a moment.

"Do I have to ask *you* if you're on the team?" Mike raised an eyebrow.

"Of course not." Ryan followed him out into the service hallway.

They crossed to the other side of the mall through the parking garage, Mike's thinking being that few guards would be searching down there. Still, they moved along the shadows to the correct fire stairwell. Once on the first floor, they took the nearest door into the service hallway system.

"Taco said there were hidden cameras," Mike whispered. "Let's take them out." He held a hand out to Ryan, then hoisted him onto his shoulders.

Ryan used the light of Mike's phone as a flashlight and quickly located a lone camera—a bulky thing, not even that stealthily hidden—jammed into a bundle of wiring. He unstuck it from the pipe it was attached to, then passed it down to Mike. He helped Ryan off his back, then laid the camera on the ground, iris side down, and smashed it with his heel.

"Camera is off."

The service door into the Pancake Palace was unguarded on the hallway side, but Mike figured it would be covered from the inside. To avoid getting hit, they would pull the door open, but stay against the walls, Ryan behind the door, and then wait to see what came at them. After any shots from inside, Mike would fire a round into the doorway to drive off any attacker. "Let's assume I'm the only one with a gun."

Ryan's heart was pumping so hard, he felt like he'd run laps. *Wait to see what came at them?* He slammed his back against the wall and said a silent prayer that this was all just a big joke and no one would be inside, no shots would fire.

Mike nodded, then ran the card. Ryan pulled open the door.

"Goldman?" a voice inside asked.

Mike apparently considered that a shot. He blasted a round through the door, filling the dark hall with a blaze of light, then ran in screaming. Ryan crossed himself and followed.

He flicked on the light switch, thinking he'd like to see his killer, and was instantly sorry. The room was filled with dad-aged guys, some of whom looked like bruisers. They crouched behind stacks of kegs and boxes, leered at Mike and Ryan like they didn't think much of them as opponents.

"Mr. Richter," Reynolds said from behind the counter. "I should have expected you'd come knocking."

"We've come to relieve you of your stash," Mike said, not flinching.

"How many bullets do you have left? Seven? How's your aim?"

Mike was not a patient person. He leveled the gun at the bottom keg in the stack and fired. Beer spewed from the hole, driving the keg back and toppling the pile. The guys behind it ran, beer raining down over everyone. Mike used the distraction to start swinging his metal poles like a coked-up cheerleader. Ryan dug his poles out and followed suit, whipping them wildly. He knew he hit a couple of things—people?—from the shudder of impact he felt in his hand.

The beer fountain stopped flowing and Mike dove for a table, toppling it in front of himself like a shield. Ryan scrambled to get behind it, dragging another table with him to cover their rears. The old guys were not unprepared for a fight. Three arrows fired from various points in the room and lodged in the tabletops. A pressurized gun like Dad used in construction fired a nail that stuck in the floor mere inches from Ryan's foot.

Mike was undeterred. "There's a box over there marked EVERCLEAR. I want you next to it, throwing bottles on the ground."

"We're trying to literally slip them up?"

Mike looked at him like he was a moron. "Just throw the frickin' bottles."

Ryan waited for the next round of projectiles to hit the tabletop, then dove behind a stack of boxes and crawled army-style to the one marked EVERCLEAR. He jammed the wrench from his belt into the side of the box, splitting the cardboard, and pulled free a bottle. He lobbed it over the stack and kept going until the box was empty.

Mike skidded out from behind the tables, grabbed a candle that sat on the main counter, and dropped it on the floor. Blue flames flashed across the tiles. Guys ran screaming from their cover and Mike smashed every single one of them flat. One guy grabbed him from behind. Ryan vaulted the boxes he'd hidden behind and hit the guy with the wrench. The attacker dropped like a tackling bag.

The blue flames flickered to nothing. The room was silent. Mike hopped over the counter and found Reynolds cowering on the floor.

"Hey there, old buddy," Mike said. A trickle of blood snaked from Mike's hairline down his cheek.

Ryan tried to catch his breath, surveyed the room. He counted eight bodies. Someone whimpered. The pant leg of one was on fire. What had they done?

Reynolds pushed himself to sitting. "Take what you want," he said.

Mike laughed. "Oh, I'll take everything." He pulled out his handgun.

Ryan grabbed Mike's shoulder. "What the hell are you doing? Let's take the stuff and go."

"And let our friend here live to plot his revenge?"

"Mike, let's get out of here before security decides to bust us."

"Turn off the lights."

"Mike. Stop screwing around."

"Turn. Off. The. Lights."

"I will not be a part of this." It was like begging a hurricane not to tear apart his house.

Mike glared at him. His eyes were cracked with red. "You don't have to be." He pulled the trigger.

Ryan ran for the nearest door, like he could outrun the sound of the gun firing.

Shay must have blacked out for some time, because she woke while being half walked, half dragged toward a fully lit store. She was hauled to the changing rooms, shoved into a stall, and the door was slammed behind her. She sat on the stool and tried to calm her breathing. Her heart beat like it was trying to escape her chest.

Voices outside. "Yep, one dead—shot in the head, half outside the building. What the hell were they thinking? There's like a forty-foot drop to the ground out those windows."

"Who said they were thinking? Kids are idiots."

Footsteps. Shay was alone with how many thugs in the changing rooms?

She caught a glimpse of herself in the mirror—her face was bruised, her arms scratched. This was a bad night. Like that first night in the service hallway. She had to get out of there. She would not be caught again.

Hunching her back, she wriggled her bound wrists under her butt and slid her legs through the circle of her arms. Her wrists bled around the thin plastic of the band holding them.

She needed something to cut the plastic. There was a hook in the wall. Shay hung on the hook until it split from the plaster, revealing a nice, sharp nail. She drove the nail through the plastic, pulled and tugged until the thin band snapped. The nail sliced the skin of her wrist. The pain added flames to the fire within.

The door was locked from the outside somehow, barred by something heavy. She bent to crawl under the door. Whatever was holding it closed blocked too much of the space between the door and the floor. Shay kicked it—whatever held her in was too heavy. And the space between the top of the door and the ceiling was too small.

Ceiling. It was a drop ceiling. What was above a drop ceiling? Shay climbed onto the stool and jumped, popping one of the tiles loose. Two more jumps and she caught a handhold on the ceiling's frame. She wriggled and pulled until she had her head, shoulders, torso through the hole, then bent over and rolled to lie flat on the frame's metal grid, spreading her weight so she wouldn't fall back through.

As she'd hoped, the walls did not extend all the way to the actual ceiling of the mall. She crawled, sandwiched between the wires and ducts, and the frame of the drop ceiling and the solid ceiling of the mall. She squeezed over the wall of her changing room, then the next, and the next until there were no more walls. She had to be over the sales floor of the store. In the dim light that seeped through the crevices of the ceiling's grid, she saw that there was a solid wall about fifteen feet ahead of her. That had to be the front of the store. *The exit.*

Shay reached the wall, then slid the nearest tile out of the frame. It was a long way down. She peeked her head through the hole, saw two guards by the changing rooms. When their backs were turned, she slipped her body through and dropped to the floor.

"Hey!" a voice screamed.

Shay didn't wait to hear more. She raced toward the escalators, ran like the freaking wind. Her heart screamed in her chest. She vaulted down the steps, using her arms to swing herself down five at a time. When her feet hit the tiles of the first-floor courtyard, she was off again, running, flying.

She slammed into another body and immediately began to claw it, she had to get free, she would never stop running.

"Shay?" the person screamed.

It took her a few seconds to register the voice. "Ryan?"

He hugged her.

She pushed free. "We have to run," she said, tugging his arm. "Security."

"Parking garage." He started running for the central fountain.

They scrambled down the broad staircase between the escalators in the central pavilion, then shoved out the glass doors and into the dark of the garage.

"This way," Ryan said.

Shay matched his strides as they bolted between the cars toward a far wall, a deeper darkness. Voices echoed behind them: Security had followed. Flashlight beams cut through the black.

"We're trapped," Shay whispered, fear clawing its way up her limbs, freezing her from the inside out.

"Wait here," Ryan said. He fled into the dark. Then, far off to her right, a car alarm went off. Then another. A blinking, bleeping trail led back toward the pavilion.

"She's doubling back!" a voice screamed.

Shay watched the flashlights turn away, back toward the central pavilion, disappear up the stairs. And then Ryan was beside her, heaving breath.

"I can't believe they fell for it," he said, panting.

Shay's legs betrayed her, losing strength and dropping her against the side of a sedan. As she slid down, a lock sprang inside her and the sadness burst through like a flood. Tears choked her. She couldn't catch her breath.

Ryan didn't ask any questions. He tucked his one arm under her shoulders, scooped her legs up with the other, and carried her through the dark. Her head flopped on his shoulder. She was unable to control the crying and soaked his shirt.

"I'm so gross," she sobbed, picking at the fabric.

"If you knew where that shirt's been, you wouldn't feel so bad."

He took her to a room in the garage; she guessed this was where he'd been hiding out. He laid her on a sleeping bag and propped her head with a duffel. He flipped on the light. She asked him to leave it off. He switched them back into darkness and crawled to sit beside her.

Shay had never felt so safe as she did there in the dark, leaning against Ryan, his arms around her. He didn't say anything, just let her unravel. After a while, there were no more tears, just a rupture inside.

"This must be the least sexy thing that's ever happened to you with a girl."

He leaned his head on hers. "No girl's ever been real with me except you. Real is pretty sexy."

"Even when real is just ugly crying face?"

"Well, the light's off, so that helps." He nudged her.

She nudged him back.

"I wish Nani had gotten to meet you," Shay said after a few minutes. "She would have liked you."

Ryan was quiet, then asked, "What do you think she'd like?"

"She just knew about people."

Would she see Ryan now or the Ryan of a half hour ago? The Ryan he wanted to be or the thug that he was?

He felt wrong touching her and shuffled slightly away. "Then it's probably good she didn't meet me."

Shay's hand reached for him, pulled her body back against his. "Why were you in the hall tonight?"

He had a choice: to keep pretending he was some

great guy, the all-American, football-playing, everybody's-favorite hero or to show her the person who had no idea who the hell he was, who was scared and made crap decisions and who'd beaten a bunch of old guys to a pulp in a gutted pancake joint. It wasn't even a choice. He didn't want to pretend with Shay.

So he made the case against himself. From the car crash, to the cop he hit with the radio, to tonight. He told Shay he'd had a girlfriend when he came to the mall. That he hadn't even thought of Emma once after he met her.

Shay sat beside him the whole time. Didn't flinch at anything he said.

"Think she's waiting for you?" she said finally.

"I tell you that I basically kicked an old guy's ass and that's what you focus on?"

She nuzzled her head against him. "How could I judge you? I got my grandmother killed and my sister sick."

"That was the flu," he said.

"I wish I could believe that," she said, her voice catching.

His arms were all he had to offer. He held her until she stopped shaking.

"This mall is just bad," he said.

"The worst," she said, a smile coloring her voice. "So about this Emma?"

"She's kind of an attention hog," he said. "She would make a big deal about knowing someone on the inside, assuming anyone still cares about us. Who knows, though? We've been gone over a week. Everyone might have forgotten about us by now."

"I keep forgetting it's only been a week."

He slumped back onto his hands, and her body relaxed into him. "I came here to buy a Halloween costume," he said.

"I came here to feel normal."

"Too bad the bomb had to go off. That was definitely not normal."

She lifted her face and he felt her breath against his cheek. "This feels normal."

He turned his cheek to meet her. "This feels anything but normal to me."

And the kiss? Definitely not normal.

Marco buzzed with nervous energy. What had he unleashed on this mall? The sheer enormity of it was dazzling—Mike would blow apart the security chief's plans, freeing Marco of all the crap that'd been slung on him. He had shed his problems like a snakeskin. He was reborn.

And so when Drew pushed open the IMAX theater's service door revealing the lanky, goateed *pendejo* who'd ordered Marco around the night before, Marco felt his grip on the metal shaft he held tighten.

The *pendejo* pointed at Marco. "Where's the new keg?" he said, like he had any authority. "This one is skunked." He drained the last sip from his cup.

Drew twirled his pole. "You boys better clear out."

Goatee stepped forward. "Or what?"

"Hey, aren't you the dickweed who tried to mess with us two nights ago?" another asked.

"Where's your pal with the gun?" said the third.

Drew did not reply, simply began smacking heads with

his pole. The *pendejos* dropped, began to crawl along the floor.

"What the hell?" one cried.

"We'll go!" another screamed. "Stop with the poles!"

Drew stepped on one guy's chest. "You know what, I just don't think I'm done kicking your sorry ass." He dropped a knee, then punched the guy in the face.

Marco felt freed from his fear—something about being with someone like Drew, of having these assholes crawling before him made Marco feel invincible. He dropped a pole between the legs of the goatee guy.

"You want to apologize for being such a dick last night?"

"Screw you, dork," the guy answered.

Marco jammed the pole into the asshat's groin. The guy squealed like a girl. One of his pals scrambled to his feet and fled for the doors out into the mall. Marco climbed onto Goatee's chest.

Tears slid down his face, but still the *pendejo* copped an attitude. "You're so dead, loser."

Marco let all the years of crap fill his fists and just unloaded on the guy's face. Every insult, every shove, every time some asshole pissed on his life, from elementary school to the present, he unleashed them all onto this guy, his arms slinging over and over, hitting bone, then not.

Drew grabbed his shoulder. "Holy crap," was all he said, pulling Marco from the guy's bloodied body. Wet breaths bubbled from the wreckage of his face.

Marco wanted to feel guilty, feel bad, but all he felt was powerful. Blood ran in rivulets down his arms.

■ ■ ■

Shay pulled Ryan down onto the sleeping bag. She wanted to kiss him deeper, longer, and her wrist had begun to hurt. Funny, how she'd never thought of wrists when she'd dreamed of kissing.

She'd had a lot of ideas about kissing, from books, from movies. She'd even kissed boys, but not like she kissed Ryan now. They'd even kissed before, but that had been more like an escape. Now, this kissing—this was more like sharing. She explored his body as if it were her own, wanted his hands on her. In the darkness, she felt so close to him, there was nothing separating them but skin.

Mike appeared in the doorway and surveyed the scene. Marco dropped his hands, thinking it was probably inappropriate to keep admiring his blood-red gloves.

Drew lifted the *pendejo* he'd dropped and hauled him across his shoulders. "We ran into some resistance."

"He alive?"

"He's breathing."

"Bring them down to the pancake place," Mike said, unfazed. "We have to move the supplies up before security finds us."

"Where's Shrimp?" Drew said, hefting his unconscious baggage out the door.

"He needed a moment."

Marco took the arms of his fallen enemy and dragged him across the floor toward the door. As he passed, Mike grabbed his shoulder. He held out the universal card key.

"Nice work," he said.

Marco dropped one of the guy's arms and took the card, slid it back into his pocket. "Thanks."

Ryan couldn't believe he'd ruined everything. "Oh, god," he said, trembling, pulling away from her. It was middle school all over again.

"It's okay," she said, her voice thick.

He fumbled on the floor for a T-shirt, anything to clean her skin off.

"Hey," Shay said, her fingers finding his arm. "It's okay."

Ryan wasn't sure whose clothes were whose. He just needed something. He couldn't believe how he'd screwed this up. Everything up. What *hadn't* he ruined tonight?

"Ryan," Shay said, stopping his floundering.

"I wanted this to be perfect," he said. He would *not* cry.

She placed her hand on his chest, wrapped her body around him. "This is perfect."

He felt cold all of a sudden, not from his nakedness. She rested her head against his shoulder like he could hold her up.

"I'm not good enough for you," he said, the words feeling like rocks in his mouth. "I've hurt people," he managed. He couldn't control the trembles that shook them both.

Shay held him tighter. "It's this place," she whispered. "Remember? This mall is just bad."

And still, she held him.

LIGHTS ON

Lexi awoke to a changed mall. Not in the sense that she was now a Girl Who Had Been Kissed, which in itself felt revolutionary, but like, literally, the mall had changed. Whereas every other morning, she walked out into the blinding light of the first-floor courtyard, sunshine streaming down from the skylights in the ceiling four stories up, this morning, there was only the dull glow of the fluorescents lighting the space. Looking up, the explanation for the change presented itself. The windows were blacked out, covered by something from the outside.

"What the . . . ?" Maddie said, mouth agape. If even Maddie was shocked by this development, Lexi knew that her astonishment was legit.

Ginger's face melted. "No sunlight? How I am I supposed to live without sunlight?"

"What are you, a ficus?" Maddie said, recovering her

caustic self. "So the place has gotten slightly crappier. Why are we surprised?" She marched over to the food line.

Lexi could tell that this slight increase in crappiness was not going over well with anyone. Everywhere she looked, people were staring up at the ceiling like it threatened to drop on their heads. If morale had been in the toilet before, it was now sluicing down the sewer.

The mall speakers squeaked—word from the Senator was coming to soothe the fears of the masses. Lexi prayed her mother could pull another miracle out of her butt.

"Good morning," the Senator's voice boomed. "As you have undoubtedly noticed, the government has deemed it necessary to seal over all of the windows. This is due to an ill-thought-out escape attempt by some deviants last night after Lights Out. Might I remind everyone that escape is not an option. All windows and doors are now sealed over, and every air vent out of the building is hooked up to a massive micro-particle filtering machine that would crush you alive. Even if you could get out, this facility is surrounded and cordoned off by an impenetrable electric fence topped with razor wire. So please, for your own safety, refrain from making the mistake of trying to escape. You must be patient.

"I ask you to be patient because there is good news. Over the last three days, since the implementation of the hygiene protocols, we have seen a decrease in the number of new flu-related intakes at the medical center. I and Dr. Stephen Chen, head of the medical center, have been in contact with the CDC and believe that if we maintain our vigilance with wearing our masks and keeping surfaces clean, the quarantine might be ended within a week.

"So please, remain calm. Stick with the hygiene protocols. And cease all deviant behavior. Curfew will be
enforced through whatever means the security teams
deem necessary. Any resident found outside his Home
Store after curfew will be detained and his threat to the
community assessed before being released back into his
Home Store. Thank you for your cooperation."

Lexi instantly thought of Marco. Had he been snagged
by security after he left her office? If Goldman already had
it in for Marco, he would be sure to never let him out of
captivity again. Lexi did not want Marco thrown in some
solitary confinement just because she had asked him on
a date.

"I need to go see my mom," she said, refitting her mask.

"Tell her that the deviant community is considering her
request." Maddie shoveled another bite into her mouth.

"Let us know if you find anything else out?" Ginger
begged, eyes wide in panic.

The mall offices were like a hallway at school just before the bell for first period: People everywhere, pushing,
yelling, and all trying to get someplace else. Lexi fought
her way past a woman barking numbers to a man at a
computer terminal, guards suiting up for what looked like
duty in a maximum security prison, and an old lady with
actual paper on a clipboard waiting outside the Senator's
office.

Inside the office was Goldman. "There was only one
body in the Pancake Palace, but there were several injured
men," he was saying.

"And the alcohol?" Her mother alternated her attention

between reading her computer screen and an iPad while he spoke.

"There were some broken bottles and some empties, but the place was cleaned out. One of the injured said they were attacked by two young men, one of whom had a handgun."

"Great," her mother said, smoothing her hair as if the gesture could soothe her brain. "So now I have gangs taking each other out?"

"I warned you that these types had to be dealt with." Goldman folded his arms across his chest. "And the dead guy? He was the one the Spider-Man kid saved."

"You think that kid and his friends did this?"

"Could be," Goldman said, shrugging. "From what the injured guy said, Reynolds spoke to the kid before the guy shot him."

"Bring Marco in," her mother said. Lexi froze up hearing his name before remembering Marco said he'd been working with her. Had Marco told her yet about Goldman?

"I have reason to believe that your pal Marco is involved with these vigilantes."

"No!" Lexi shouted, bursting in from the hall.

Both Goldman and her mother glared at her.

Dotty spoke first. "Lex, I am very busy at the moment."

Lexi pointed at Goldman. "He's lying," she said. "Marco told me that *he* was involved with those alcohol guys."

Goldman didn't even flinch. "Ma'am, I know you trust your daughter, but I should also tell you that the hidden camera outside the Pancake Palace was removed and destroyed. Only you and your daughter knew the placement of those cameras."

Lexi's throat closed up. She'd told Marco about the cameras, but would he have told anyone else? Was he with whoever killed that guy? No. Marco wasn't a killer. But he'd been so weird, asking about Batman movies. *No.* No way.

Lexi swallowed, regained use of her voice. "That camera was bulky," she said. "Maybe they just saw it."

Were this one of her movies, Lexi would have drawn fumes rising from her mother's skull based on the look on her face. "But how would they know there were any cameras to *look* for?"

"I told Marco about the cameras," Lexi blurted. "But he said he was working for you, helping you find the stolen alcohol. I was helping you!" She could not keep her voice from cracking, nor dry up the tears that bulged in her eyes.

Her mother smoothed her hands across the surface of the desk, sucked in a deep breath, then drummed her fingertips on its edges. "Lexi, I appreciate your trying to help, but I'm going to need you to run all information you receive from Marco from here on out by me."

"He was coming to tell you about Goldman," Lexi pleaded. "He told me he would."

"Lexi, Marco did not check in with his Home Store last night, nor did he get dinner. He has not checked in this morning. In other words, he has left my employ. I'm assuming that he's involved with these vigilantes now, based on what you tell me about him having knowledge of the secret cameras and the obvious discovery of the cameras."

"Goldman knew about the cameras," Lexi said, getting

desperate. "He could have destroyed the one outside the Pancake Palace!"

"Good god," Goldman said, slapping his arms on the armrests and standing. "Why the hell are we listening to this, Dotty?"

Her mother's shoulders slumped. "Sweetheart, I know you like Marco, but really."

Lexi felt like maybe she was having a heart attack. She hadn't seen Marco's face. Could he have been lying about Goldman zapping him? Could Marco have lied to her about everything? No. She wouldn't believe it. She kissed him. She *knew* him.

Her mother continued her meeting with Goldman as if Lexi had evaporated. "Last I heard from Marco, the Spider-Men were hiding out somewhere in the garage. If they're not there, I'm going to need your teams to start reviewing the hidden camera footage, see if we can't find them. Then we need to discuss plans for tonight."

"I've already located two sites for use as holding cells for deviants."

"Then do whatever you feel necessary to prevent their going anywhere else."

Goldman left. Her mother called in the next appointment, the woman with the clipboard. They started talking about quantities of beans and rice. About shrinking rations to survival levels.

"Should the girl be in here?" the clipboard lady asked.

"I think she's learned her lesson about whom to trust."

The implication was clear to Lexi: Trust family, no one else. But wasn't her mother breaking that rule, taking Goldman's word over hers? Of course, Lexi herself was relying on Marco's word over Goldman's. But Marco wasn't a liar. *Was he?*

She left the room without having to be asked. Across the hall, she saw that her father was still in bed.

"Dad?"

He didn't respond.

"Daddy!"

Guards pushed past Lexi, held her back away from her father. One stuck a handheld thermometer in his ear, then her father and his cot were lifted and a path cleared down the hall and out of the office space. Lexi watched as if viewing a movie, someone else's life. Her mother joined her in the hall, took her hand.

"We're okay, baby," she said. "We're going to be okay."

They followed her father down to the medical center.

Shay awoke. That alone surprised her. She'd actually slept. Her body wasn't exhausted. She felt somewhat alert. And she wasn't alone anymore. Ryan was curled next to her, breathing softly in deep sleep. Faint outlines of shapes were visible; the lights had been turned on in the parking garage, and white shone through the seams of the door to their closet. It wasn't much, but it was enough for now.

Having some use of her mind, Shay pulled out her notebook and its lighted pen and tried to get a hold of her situation. She would not leave Ryan. She knew that much. The only question was whether she should take Preeti out of the regular mall system to hide out with them. Apart from the obvious need for privacy, there was the issue of Preeti herself.

Preeti was doing well in the school, and the Home

Store was a safe place for her. Shay had watched Preeti hanging out with her friends in front of a Wii game miming dance steps. It would be a major battle to get her to leave all that and hide out in the basement. And what had Shay really done to protect her sister, anyway? Kris was the one who was watching out for her.

Was she rationalizing? Was this just her finding an excuse to leave Preeti so she could be alone with Ryan? Oh god, who was she to know? Rationalization though it may be, her thinking made sense. The last time she'd talked to Preeti, all they'd done was scream at each other. And she could sneak out every once in a while to check on her. She would leave Preeti in the mall; she and Ryan would live here, together. This was a good plan.

A door slammed nearby. No one had come near their corner of the parking garage in all the time they'd been there. Was it Ryan's hulking compatriots? Or, worse, Marco?

Shay grabbed whatever clothing she could and began covering herself. Footsteps tapped outside the door.

"Ryan!" she whispered, shaking him.

He mumbled something.

She shook him harder. "Someone's coming!" she hissed through her teeth.

Ryan pushed himself up and dragged on a pair of shorts. He peeked out the door and instantly pressed it shut. "Security."

An animal panic seized Shay. They'd found her. They'd drag her back to jail.

Ryan knelt by her, took her hand. "They must be here looking for Mike."

"They found me," Shay mumbled. "They're here for me."

Ryan squeezed her hand. "They think you went back into the real mall. But Marco may have told security that we lived here when he was working for the senator."

"Marco was working for the senator?" All the clarity Shay'd felt evaporated.

"Yes," Ryan said hurriedly. "Just hide. They'll see me and won't even look for you."

"I'm not leaving you."

"We don't have a choice," he said. He kissed her, then pushed her toward a corner where a bunch of sandwich boards announcing "Lot Full" were piled.

"I don't want to hide."

"I don't want them to take you. Go back to the Home Store. I'll find you."

Security banged on the door. "Michael Richter, we know you are inside and have you surrounded. Place your firearm on the ground and come out with your hands where we can see them."

Ryan turned back to her. "Please!"

Shay was so scared, she just did as he said. She lifted the pile of signs and arranged them over her. Ryan tossed a few pieces of clothing on the pile, then walked to the door.

"Mike isn't here," he shouted.

The door burst open, knocking Ryan back. The lights flared on and guards flooded into the tiny space. Two grabbed Ryan's arms. Shay's heart was in her throat.

"Where's Richter?" one guard asked.

"I don't know," Ryan said. "I left him last night."

"Only one sleeping bag is unrolled, the other two are over here."

"Could be a fake-out," the lead guard said. "Let's see what Goldman can get from him."

The guards dragged Ryan out of the room. Shay remained hidden under the signs for a while longer, trying to calm her animal brain back into rational thought.

She would not leave Ryan to whoever this Goldman character was. She would rescue him. But she needed help. No, she needed the card key she and Marco had stolen. She could search for Ryan herself, door by door through the whole mall. But where to find Marco?

If he was working with Ryan's friends, maybe they were where Ryan last saw them: the Pancake Palace. She would start there.

The door to the Pancake Palace was closed, but unlocked. Shay pulled it open and found a mess. A telling mess. Two tables were overturned in the corner, their tops bristling with arrows. Black scorch marks marred the walls in several places. Broken glass sparkled on the tile floor. But worse, much worse, were the brownish stains on the floor. Blood.

She remembered what Ryan had said about what he'd done, that he'd hurt people. For some reason, when he'd said it, she hadn't pictured anything, just saw her Ryan, the guy who held her when she needed holding. But seeing this . . . She'd never hurt anyone, had never been involved with violence until she was run over by a rioting mob. Had Ryan caused another person to feel the way she'd felt? The thought made her sick.

Something about this room and sickness triggered her

brain. *Nani.* She glanced at the opposite wall; there was a hole cut into it. This was where Nani had died.

Shay ran from the room, just making it into the hall before collapsing on a bench. How many horrible things could happen in one place?

N O O N

Ryan stood when he saw the shadows of feet outside the door. He'd been locked in a closet in the
back of some store for hours now and his legs
were tight and creaky. The door opened. A largish guy
with a smug face and the nose of an old drunk stood in
front of him.

"Jimmy Murphy's kid," he said. "I thought I told you
to keep out of trouble."

His father's name did not inspire the same feeling of
terror it once had. His father did not exist in this world.
Ryan stared the guy down. "I'm not sure what trouble you
think I've been involved in."

The guy held out a hand like he was escorting Ryan to
a table at a fancy restaurant. "Why don't you join me in
my office?"

The man was referring to a chair under a light in the
stockroom. The chair was for Ryan. The light was blinding.

The man pulled a chair in front of Ryan and sat his fat butt in it. "Young Mr. Murphy," he began, "I feel that you have fallen under the influence of some rather unfortunate friends."

Ryan kept quiet. He had no idea how much this guy knew.

"They've led you to try to bust out the garage with your friend's Beamer, bust out the ceiling, and now you've busted in on some thieves and killed a man."

So the guy knew a lot. Ryan remained silent.

"Now, all I want to know is where the fellows you've been hanging out with are right now. If you give them up to me, I might be inclined to forget you were ever involved with them. Might just let you join the rest of the law-abiding folks in the mall."

It was all Ryan had ever argued for since the quarantine: to just be a regular person in the mall. Not some stupid outlaw living off crackers and defrosted chicken strips in a closet. All he had to do was sell out Mike and he could be with Shay, no scheming, no scrounging for scraps, but really with her in the regular mall world.

"I told your guys, I left Mike last night. I haven't seen him since."

Whatever the offer, he would not sell out his teammates.

The man frowned, folded his arms across his chest. Ryan was used to men who got off on being bullies. He'd lived with one all his life.

"I'm disappointed in that answer, son," the man said.

Ryan braced himself for whatever came next.

In his experience, it usually involved bloodshed.

■ ■ ■

Marco had yet to wash his hands. There was something magical about looking down at them. Every time he felt weak or scared, he glanced at his fingernails, still rimmed in blood, and remembered the power he'd felt beating the crap out of that asshole. He was not weak. He would never be scared again.

Mike surveyed the theater from his perch on a seat at the back. Drew was stacking the alcohol by type down near the screen and Marco was counting the weaponry they'd recovered from the Pancake Palace. Goldman must have been planning some sort of coup with this stockpile. There were weapons or weapon-like objects looted from the sporting goods place—obvious things like compound bows and arrows, hunting knives, baseball bats, but also weird stuff like fishing hooks and line and fencing foils—and crap from elsewhere that could serve as weapons; like cast-iron pans, nail guns, welding torches, and battery-operated curling irons. There was defensive gear too, like catcher's pads and football helmets. It was quite the spread.

Mike hopped down from his perch and began loping down the aisle. "We need more men," he said.

Marco stuck the pen in the spiral of his notebook. "Absolutely not."

"More men?" Drew asked. "They bringing their own beer? Because I count only enough kegs to last me, myself, and I through this apocalypse."

Mike ignored Drew. "We need to clear out all these seats. Make this space open so that if there's an attack from either door, we have a direct line of escape." He knelt in front of the first row of seats. "They're all screwed to the floor. It's a two-day job, at least, for the three of us, but with more, we could get it done tonight."

"If we get attacked," Marco said, "they are probably going to try both doors. Our best plan is to fortify the two doors so they can't get in."

"Even if we fortify the doors, the three of us are going to be wiped out in a freaking minute."

"Four," Drew interrupted. "Remember, Shrimp."

"If he's not here by now, he's not coming." Mike sounded the slightest bit heartbroken. It was the only crack Marco had detected in the impenetrable emotional fortress around Mike. There was some comfort in knowing every tough guy had a weak spot.

Marco did not disagree with Mike's assessment of their odds. This was an operation that succeeded mostly on the fact that no one knew where they were, a fact that could not be relied upon for long. The mall was, after all, only so big.

"Do you have someone in mind or are we just going to post a sign: *Wanted, couple of badasses to hold down a fort*?"

"I have a couple guys in mind," Mike said. "We just need to—"

All conversation ceased at the sound of someone knocking on the theater's door. Mike held a hand out to silence the room, pulled his gun from his waistband, and walked slowly up to the door. Marco stared at the pile of weapons, trying to decide between the hunting knife and baseball bat.

"It's a girl," Mike yelled down. "Ryan's girl."

He opened the door and let Shay into the theater. Marco hated how happy he was to see her. He'd thought it impossible, but somehow, she'd become even more beautiful. But she'd made her choice. He could live with it.

Shay walked right up to him. "I need our card," she said without so much as a hello.

"How did you find us?" he said, trying to keep the feeling of power from cracking off him like a shell.

"Ryan said something about the IMAX," she said. "I checked the pancake place first." She looked at his hands. He was suddenly ashamed of them, then pissed at himself for feeling ashamed. Shay glanced back at his face. "Were you responsible for some of that?"

Marco decided to avoid this line of questioning entirely. "Why do you need the card?"

Shay raised an eyebrow. She looked meaner than he remembered. Her eyes were cold and she wasn't smiling. "We stole it together, so it's both of ours. Just give it to me."

"Where's Ryan?" Mike asked, joining them.

Shay kept glaring at Marco. Why was she so angry with him? She spoke evenly. "He was taken by security and I need the card to find him and get him back."

Mike snickered. "You know where he is or you planning to search every goddamned store in this mall?"

Shay turned to him like a cannon on a target. "I'll do whatever I have to."

"Knew I liked you," Mike said, cocking his head. He pulled the police walkie-talkie Marco had given him from his back pocket and flipped it on, began scanning channels.

"*Non-essential store lockdown on second floor west completed . . .*"

"*Suspected flu case in HomeMart removed to med center for evaluation . . .*"

"*Deviants found hiding in BathWorks engaged in inappropriate contact. Transfer to lockup?*"

Mike turned the volume up. The walkie-talkie bleeped, then the answer came:

"*Shoe Hut lockup full. Transfer to Stuff-A-Pal Workshop.*"

It took a sick bastard like Goldman to turn a stuffed animal factory into a jail.

Mike turned off the radio. "So he's either in the shoe outlet or the stuffed toy place."

Drew hefted a bat. "I'm ready to stuff some pals."

"No," Mike said. "You go talk to the Tarrytown guys. They should all be on the first floor catching lunch. See if you can't convince them to join our cause."

"How convincing should I be?" Drew said, swinging the bat.

Mike grabbed the bat. "We want them to help us, not join the guys trying to kill us."

Drew seemed deflated at having to leave his bat in the pile.

"I don't think I want your help," Shay said. She was like a different person, all in-your-face and shut-the-hell-up.

Mike slid the radio back into his cargo shorts. "I don't think you have a choice."

"I saw what you did in the Pancake Palace," she said. "Ryan told me you hurt people."

"And you think that's all me, right?" Mike said. "Did Ryan tell you what *he* did?"

Shay seemed to back down a little at that. "I don't care what he did," she said, not entirely convincingly. "I just want to get him out. I don't want to hurt anyone." She held her hand out to Marco. "Just give me the card."

Mike spat a nasty laugh. "You think you can just walk into what these guys are calling a lockup and take Ryan without hurting anybody?" He pointed to Marco. "Tell her what they did to you," he said.

Marco straightened his spine. "Shay, let us go get Ryan. You wait here."

Shay pointed at Marco's hands. "Did *they* do that to you?" she asked. "Whose blood is that, Marco?"

Marco did not like her self-righteous tone. "No one *did* that to me," he said calmly. "The head of security used a stun gun on me several times in an effort to convince me to join his plot to overthrow the mall government."

"I don't believe you," she said, though from how quickly the blood drained from her face, Marco knew she did.

Mike picked up Drew's bat. "You don't have to believe us," he said. "Just wait here and we'll get Ryan."

Marco placed a hand on her shoulder, and she shrugged out from under his touch.

So that's how it was now between them? *Fine.* "Don't touch anything while we're gone," he said.

Shay pulled a thick leather floor-length jacket from Goldman's stash over her shoulders and began buttoning it up. "Don't think I'm not coming with you."

"Wait here," Marco ordered.

Mike rolled his eyes. "She wants to come, let her," he said, then glared at Shay. "But I'm not guaranteeing your personal safety."

"Who asked you to?" she growled back.

As Marco watched them exit into the fire stairwell, he allowed himself a brief moment to catalog how much had changed between when he and Shay had met outside the Grill'n'Shake, when they were on the same team, and now. How then, she'd let him kiss her and now she flinched at his touch. *Screw her.* He grabbed a hockey stick, tucked a hunting knife into his belt, and ran after them.

Shay watched Mike smash a person's chest like a baseball as Marco checked another guy in the face. She'd made a decision outside the Pancake Palace to do whatever it took to get Ryan free, but now she was less sure of her choice. Not about Ryan, but about accepting this. The one guard hit the floor like a doll, head lolling. The other bent over clutching his side and called out for help. What had she done?

They were in the back of the Stuff-A-Pal store. Around her were boxes of pelts, the unstuffed carcasses of what would have been toys for children. Shay closed her eyes and tried to stay focused on her goal: to find Ryan and free him. That was all that mattered.

She ran past the terrible pair of Mike and Marco and pulled on the first door she found. It was locked. They would need keys. She crouched low around the edge of the fight. Two more guards had come to answer the other's call.

Her hands shook as she patted the body of the fallen guy.

Something hit her jacket. Shay examined her sleeve and saw a small pronged object lodged in the leather of her coat. The object was attached by wires to a gun-like thing in the hands of a large man who stood in the doorway.

"Piece of crap," he said, dropping the gun, then stepped forward and punched Shay in the face.

Lexi's butt was falling asleep. They'd been sitting outside the medical center all morning waiting for the inevitable bad news about her dad. Finally, she saw Dr. Chen coming toward them and knew that news was here.

"Steve?" her mother said, standing.

Dr. Chen seemed uncomfortable. "It's the flu. He's showing symptoms, the usual symptoms."

Dotty, in a rare break from protocol, allowed her lip to tremble. She grabbed Lexi's hand like it was she who needed support.

Dr. Chen cleared his throat. He looked ready to bolt. "I'd say his prognosis is the same as any man in his age group, though he does have the disadvantage of sustaining previous injuries, which may have somewhat weakened his immune response."

Now Lexi tightened her hand around her mother's. *Previous injuries.* Was this guy saying that because Dad had come to rescue her, because he'd been shot, fallen down stairs, and been crushed and broken in the riots—all because of Lexi—that he was going to die?

Dr. Chen kept his eyes on his iPad, kept sliding his

finger over the screen. "That is the best information I can give you at this moment. I will be sure to update you personally if there is any change in his condition."

Was that it? Her father would be just another body on the ice?

"Thank you, Steve," her mother said. Dr. Chen nodded his head and fled back to whatever closet he'd crawled out of.

Dotty stared after him for a moment, then took a deep breath in and straightened her lapels. She turned to Lexi, smoothed Lexi's hair over her scalp. "I think we should both try to get back to our regular lives."

"Like get out of the mall? Yes, please." Lexi watched the hallway into the med center like any second Dad would come running down it, the whole thing being some misunderstanding, a bad joke.

Her mother smiled weakly. "We can't do anything for him here."

Lexi couldn't do anything for him anywhere. "Can I stay with you?" She didn't want to deal with the mall.

"I'm not sure my office is a good place to be, for you or me, only I don't have a choice." Her mother smiled like this was funny, but didn't she have a choice? Who told her to take over running the mall anyway?

"Why didn't you run?" Lexi asked. "When you first saw the bomb, you could have just grabbed me and Dad and left and none of this would have happened."

Dotty didn't yell, which was in itself a surprise. "You're right," she said. "I could have run, we could have escaped. But what if one of us was infected? What if we brought this flu out into the world? This is the deadliest flu virus anyone's documented. Millions—and I'm not exaggerating, millions of people in the tri-state area alone would have died. Around the world, who knows? Billions? So I made a sacrifice. I made a very hard choice to choose the whole planet over the individual needs of myself and my family. I hope you can understand that, if not right now, then someday."

Lexi hugged her mother. If the choice had been up to her, she would have run. Lexi wasn't a martyr. A part of her was glad that her mother had some hero streak, that she chose to save the millions. But the rest of her stared down the hallway into the med center, her mind's eye seeing straight through to the ice-skating rink above it on the third floor, her father's body added to those anonymous piles, and hated her mother for choosing them over her family.

"I'll check in with you around dinner?" Lexi said, releasing her arms.

Her mother nodded. "If I hear anything before, I'll have a guard let you know."

People were still settling down with their lunch trays as Lexi approached the center of the first floor. She heard some grumbling about portion size, that there was less slop than normal on their plates.

"You hated the slop, and now you want more of it?" she heard one guy quip.

This was the mall for you: complaint after complaint after complaint.

She passed a group of guys around her age heading for a store full of crap. She noticed that the crap had been moved around, like these guys had decorated. The only problem was a lone guard who was trying to figure out how to lower the security gate over the store's entrance.

"Dude," the lead guy said to the guard. "This is our place."

The guard kept tugging on the chain like that would get the gate moving. "I have orders to close down all non-essential stores."

"This store is essential. It's where we eat."

Another guy chipped in. "Who cares if this one store stays open?"

The guard gave the chain a final yank and the gate came crashing down. "Look, I was told to lock up all the unused stores. You got a problem, then talk to the people upstairs."

"I'm talking to you," the guy said, passing his tray to a friend. "Open that gate."

The guard pulled out his stun baton. "Back off before we have a problem."

People at nearby tables were staring. The guard kept glancing around like he knew he was the center of attention.

The kid did not seem at all deterred by the stun baton. "You open the gate and we won't have a problem."

The guard lunged. The kid dodged and grabbed the baton above the pronged end, jerking it down. The guard lost his hold on it. For a moment, they both stared at the long, black stick dangling in the kid's hand. Then the guard made the poor choice to grab for the handle. The kid whipped it back. His friends laughed.

The guard sensed the bad way this was going. "Gimme that back."

"Open the gate," the kid said.

The guard went for the walkie-talkie on his belt. The kid stunned him and the guard fell to the ground. The group of them stood over the guard like they couldn't believe what had just happened. Then someone at a lunch table screamed. Then another. The kids dropped the stun baton and ran. Security guards swarmed.

The mall speakers crackled to life with an announcement—Goldman's voice, this time. "All residents, return to your Home Stores until further notice. I repeat, return to your Home Stores immediately."

People did not react well, it seemed, to interruptions in their routine. They looked around—there was still another twenty minutes before the end of lunch. And what about afternoon work duty? Lexi heard one woman worry that she'd left a load of laundry soaking and would the colors run if she didn't get back to it in time. It took the nearby patrols of security guards yelling and brandishing their stun sticks and Tasers to get people moving, hurriedly, some with their lunch trays, back toward their home stores. Every face Lexi saw looked completely freaked out.

T W O

P.M.

Marco was caught behind a toppled stack of boxes with the unconscious Shay at his feet. Mike had some insane plan to flank the guards, but Marco was not sure what two guys and an unconscious girl could muster against the seven or so armed guards who'd arrived to subdue them in the stockroom. Mike had toppled the nearest stacks of boxes to distract them from his flanking move, but now Marco was left to hurl the few hard accessories he could find for the Stuff-A-Pals. Why couldn't they have put the lockup in a kitchen store?

He was not fool enough to think his puny assault was doing much other than distract or, at the very best, annoy the guards. The only thing keeping them back was the fear of Mike and his gun. He'd fired a single shot at them and that was enough to hold them off. Of course, once they realized Mike was not behind the boxes, Marco was screwed.

And then he heard them. Screams erupted in the front of the store and then the bodies flooded in. Mike had freed the prisoners. The guy was a freaking genius. Why hadn't Marco thought of it first?

Not wasting any time, he hauled Shay's body onto his back and began to kick the different doors in the stockroom. "Ryan!" He wasn't sure that any amount of screaming would be heard over the noise the prisoners were making on their way over the guards and out into the service hallway.

Finally, he received a kick in response to his own on a door. He held his ear to the wood and yelled for Ryan. He answered back, "Taco?"

How much did he hate this kid?

"We don't have a key, so we're going to have to bust the door," Marco yelled.

"I'll stand back."

No really, stand right in front of the door, please . . .

Marco propped Shay in a nook out of the way of the fleeing felons, then lined himself up with the door. He kicked as hard as he could, then slammed his shoulder against the wood.

That hurt. A lot.

Mike grabbed his arm. "Nice attack, but the frame's metal. No luck with a ramming tactic."

"So what do you suggest?" Marco asked, rubbing his shoulder to regain sensation.

"This," Mike said, pulling a fire ax from the wall.

The ax demolished the door to splinters.

Ryan was crouched in a corner with his hands over his head. "You could have warned me there would be an ax!" he yelled when Mike pulled him up by the arm.

"No, 'thank you'? No, 'I can't believe you found me'?"

Ryan tugged Mike's arm and the two embraced. Marco couldn't help but be jealous of what they had. What Ryan had with everyone. What was so great about freaking Ryan?

Releasing Mike, Ryan saw Shay slumped against the wall. He immediately dropped next to her, cupped her face like that was going to help anything. "What happened?" he whimpered, looking only at Shay.

"She asked us for help," Marco said. "Goldman punched her, but she's okay."

"This is okay?" Ryan tucked a piece of hair behind her ear.

"I told her to stay behind," Mike said.

Ryan pulled her to him, lifted her like she was light as air. "Let's go," he said. Marco could have sworn there were actual tears in his eyes. *Pussy.*

Back at the IMAX, Drew was screwing around with a couple of guys who, from the looks of them, represented the meatiest members of the Tarrytown football team. They held plastic cups of beer and were tossing around what turned out to be a dead rat Drew had found behind the curtain under the screen. Sitting in the seats facing them were a couple of what could only be described as blond, airhead groupies.

"You dirty rat!" one guy said in this fake scratchy voice, then threw the thing at another. Marco doubted they even knew what film or actor they were misquoting (Jimmy Cagney, *Blonde Crazy*).

"That's disgusting," Mike said.

"The hero returns!" Drew shouted, arms akimbo, beer

sloshing from his cup. The girls in the audience turned to see what fresh meathead had arrived.

"I see you wasted no time." Mike waved a hand at the tapped keg.

"Advance payment for services to be rendered," one of the Tarrytown guys slurred.

"About those services," Mike said. He began listing the various chores he had in mind to fortify the IMAX. Both guys and girls sulked.

Ryan snuck up a side staircase with Shay, laying her on the floor in the back. Marco followed at a distance, not wanting to admit what was obvious: He was not needed or wanted. He wanted to be wanted by Shay. Taking off his sweatshirt, he offered it to Ryan and said, "It's kind of a pillow."

Ryan glanced up at him. "Thanks." He took the thing, rolled it, and gently placed it beneath Shay's head.

"Do you think she needs anything?"

"I've got it." Ryan didn't look up at him again.

Fine. If Ryan wanted him gone, he'd go. Screw Ryan. Screw Shay. Screw everyone. There was plenty he needed to do. Mike was handing out tasks? Marco would be his go-to guy.

"What can I do?" he asked, approaching Mike.

Mike surveyed Drew and the four Tarrytown guys as they attempted to lift a row of seats. They strained, veins popping from their skin, but the things wouldn't budge. "We're going to need some screw guns."

"On it," Marco said. He was the only one with an access card. He was the only one who could do jobs like this. He was needed.

■ ■ ■

Lexi lay on her cot blinking closed one eye, then the other: *camera right, camera left, camera right, camera left . . .* Her view of the ceiling tiles and track lighting shifted ever so slightly with each blink.

This was how bored they all were.

Maddie threw the copy of *Us Weekly* at the wall. "I've memorized the fine print of the Botox ads, I've read this thing so many times."

Ginger was biting her nails. "Why would they lock us in here over some kids taking a stun gun from a guard?" She tugged on a hangnail and winced. "Something worse is going on, I know it."

Maddie tossed her a copy of *Seventeen*. "Read the article on page twenty about the cuticle damage you're inflicting on yourself."

Lexi sat up and surveyed the room. All the women seemed as nervous as Ginger, huddled together in groups, glancing out the gate into the mall like they expected a horde of zombies to rattle the links at any minute. This was a situation primed for Bad Things to Happen.

Ginger's cuticle crisis gave Lexi an idea. "Where did you get that makeup from the other night?" she asked.

Maddie shrugged. "I found it in a pile of stuff from the cosmetics counters shoved in the stockrooms," she said. "Makeup was not a 'priority item,' I guess."

"Let's see what else is in that pile," Lexi said.

The cosmetics supplies were piled in a dark corner near the farthest wall. Ginger commandeered three of the carts they'd used sorting clothes and the three of them piled all the bottles of nail polish, plus the makeup and perfume, creams, cleansers, and tonics, onto the carts. They then each took one cart and rolled it out into the store.

"Anyone want to try some NARS eye shadow?" Maddie called, hoisting a black box.

"I have Sephora nail polish!" Ginger chirped, waving a few bottles on the other side of the room.

"Face cream!" Lexi hawked. "Get your ridiculously overpriced face cream right here!"

It worked like a charm. Women surrounded each cart and began sampling the various wares. Count on people to meet stereotypes. But even Lexi had to admit that it was fun to get a pedicure from Ginger after they'd handed out all the supplies on the two floors. And the mood in the Home Store? One hundred thousand times better.

LIGHTS OUT

The best Ryan could do in place of ice was cold, wet cloths. Shay would have a nasty black eye, that was for sure. Why didn't she listen to him? She could have gone back to life in the mall and been fine. Now she was tattooed, but in a different way than when he'd met her. This was the gift he'd given her: violence.

At least their faces would match. Ryan had enjoyed the hospitality of Goldman's fist himself. There seemed to be no check on the guy's sense of self-importance. Didn't he report to that woman on the loudspeaker? Didn't she give a crap that he was beating kids up in a back room?

Shay kept groaning, starting in her sleep. Ryan wished the crew down in the front would shut up for five minutes, but there seemed to be a heated debate over some bull. Everything was always the biggest deal. When would things go back to the boring crap they usually were? Certainly not before they were out of this hellhole.

There was a knock at the door to the fire stairwell.

"See?" Drew barked. "There are people who want to join us."

"There are people who want to drink our beer," Mike growled, eyeing the bimbos. Why Drew had thought it wise to take not only the Tarrytown players, but their female companions, Ryan had no idea. Maybe Drew figured Mike would forgive him his insatiable libido, the way he always did.

"We don't have enough food to last us more than three days," Marco said. He sat apart from the rest, knees scrunched up, back against the wall like some outcast.

Another knock on the door. A muffled voice from outside.

"So we get more food," Drew said.

"We nearly got killed busting into a makeshift jail," Mike said. "How do you suppose security will react to our charging the food stores in Sam's?"

Drew frowned. "Taco will figure something out."

Marco chuckled in his corner. "I appreciate the vote of confidence, but I am at a loss regarding the Sam's Club. I tried to bust in there, remember, and ended up a guest of our friendly security forces."

Banging now, whistles. Ryan thought it sounded like girls at the door.

"Dude," Drew said. "That's totally a chick. Girls don't even eat. I'm letting her in."

"Do not touch the door," Mike snarled. He honestly sounded pissed off at Drew.

"We had a vote and the vote was for more chicks."

"Do *not* touch the door."

Ryan trotted down the stairs. "Guys! Let's all chill a second."

Drew began removing the barricade made of stacked rows of seats from the door. It was like Ryan hadn't even spoken.

Mike pulled out his gun and fired. The sound was deafening. Everyone froze.

Mike tucked his gun back in his waistband. "I'm not sure when you all thought this became a democracy, but let me clear this one thing up: I am in charge until someone else saves everyone's collective ass. As I am the one who planned our little commune, I have final say on who the hell gets in on it."

Drew glared at Mike, then threw down the row of seats and went to the keg to get another beer.

Ryan approached Mike. "What the hell?" he said. "Are you just going to fire the gun every time someone disagrees with you?"

"Maybe." Mike was glaring at Drew's back.

"He's your best friend," Ryan said. "Remember?"

Mike flicked his eyes at him. "And what are you?" he asked. "My friend or that chick's boyfriend? Just remember who's saved your ass time and again." Mike stalked toward the back of the theater, past Shay, and disappeared. The lights flicked on in the projection room. Ryan waited to see Mike look down, give some signal through the little window, but none came.

"Guess you're not the golden boy anymore, *Shrimp*." Marco slipped by like a fart in the wind and joined Mike in his skybox.

■   ■   ■

Lexi sat alone in the dark of her office. She held little hope of Marco actually showing, but she couldn't make herself leave. A small part of her would not let go of the hope that everything he'd said had been true, that there had been no lies between them.

How much of an idiot was she? She'd morphed into one of those girls she'd sworn never to become: hanging on a guy who was a total jerk. But then a voice inside her got all offended, *He's not a total jerk. He helped you investigate the ice-skating rink. He liked you. He kissed you.* Like this amounted to anything other than a desperate rationalization for having fallen for the wrong guy.

God, but what if he wasn't the wrong guy?

This place had messed with her brain waves. She used to be so in control. Feelings: All over them. Boys: No problem. Now she was this weepy mess wringing her hands over whether some guy "really liked her." Who *was* she?

She desperately needed a reality check. Digging in the bottom desk drawer, she found the CB radio and called Darren.

"Darren?" she whispered.

She waited a few minutes.

"DMaster?"

No response.

He'd said he'd leave his radio on. He'd said he'd wait for her.

She threw the radio in its drawer and kicked it closed. She would not cry. This was baby crap. This was not who she was.

But her dad was sick. And she'd been screwed over by

the first guy she'd kissed. And her best friend had bailed. Maybe this was an okay time to cry.

The door creaked. Lexi froze—security was on freaking paranoia steroids. Would they have the audacity to haul her into jail for hiding here?

"Lex?" It was Maddie.

Lexi wiped her face with her shirt. "Yeah, hey."

"Bastard didn't show?"

"I feel like an ass."

Maddie flipped on the light and joined Lexi on the desk. "Boys suck." She put an arm around her.

Lexi dropped her head onto Maddie's shoulder. Maybe all her friends hadn't abandoned her.

The IMAX was dark when Shay awoke. She knew Ryan was beside her—even after only a day of being together, she could sense his body as a discrete element in the universe. Some people snored at the front. She recalled a party of some sort earlier. It must have already kicked.

She tried to piece together the events of the last few hours and only came away with scraps. She remembered finding Marco and his new friends, Ryan's friends. She remembered their ridiculously ill-thought-out plan to invade the Stuff-A-Pal stockroom, and she remembered being punched in the face by a large man with a Taser. Shay touched her eye and winced. Beams of light shone from the projection room, so someone else was awake, but for the most part, things were quiet. Quiet enough for Shay to actually think.

Fumbling in the dim light, she found her bag against the rear wall near the rumpled sweatshirt she'd been using as a pillow—it was just like Ryan to think of things like pillows even when sleeping on the floor of a movie theater. Shay pulled out the journal and light pen and began to make a list.

Reasons to Go:

Preeti

Safer in the mall (She put a question mark next to that.)

Less chance of getting punched in the face (She put a question mark next to that too.)

Better food, beds, bathrooms, etc.

The list of reasons to stay was singular: *Ryan.*

It was selfish, to want Ryan. She liked being with him. She felt better with him by her side. But he didn't need her. He had his friends. They'd survived all this time together. Ryan and his little clan were good at surviving.

Preeti, on the other hand, was not. Shay had failed as a sister for days now. She prayed that Kris had taken care of her while Shay was out of commission. Not that it was fair to leave that task to him. Shay owed him an apology, Preeti an apology, her parents—they must be completely freaking out. But she had to start somewhere, and that somewhere had to be Preeti. She would make things up to Preeti. She would go back and take care of her, protect her. The fierce animal thing that had awoken in Shay was still there—it would help them both. Especially now that things in the mall were so terrible. Whatever it took, she would help Preeti survive.

Shay closed the book, clicked off the pen, and laid her head on Ryan's shoulder. She would miss this. She could actually sleep with his arms around her. She kissed his shirtsleeve and nuzzled in for one last night together.

DAY
TWELVE

T
W
O
A.M.

Marco and Mike sat in the projection booth for a while in silence, Mike staring at the wall from his office chair, and Marco first standing, then sitting against the wall nearest the door in case he needed to run. After an uncomfortably long period of time, Mike pulled a cardboard box from beneath the computer station that operated the IMAX projector. The box contained several bottles of what the label proclaimed to be thirty-year-old scotch.

"Private stock?" Marco asked.

"No need to waste quality time on those people," he said, jerking his head toward the theater. He swiveled around to face Marco and held out a plastic cup. "First sip tastes like ass, but then you can't taste anything."

Marco took the cup. He was unsure whether this was a request or an order. He decided the gentlemanly thing to do was to share a drink with his coworker. He downed the stuff in one swallow and tried not to vomit.

Mike sniggered. "Now that's what I call a sip."

Marco tendered the cup back to Mike.

Mike poured himself another. "This is what my dad drinks," he said, swirling the stuff around. He then downed it in a single shot. "No wonder he's such a dick."

Marco did not feel so great.

"You look like you need another," Mike said.

Marco took the cup. If Mike thought he was man enough to drink it, Marco would be that man.

He drank this one in sips and what do you know, the stuff did taste better the more you drank. Mike rambled on about his dad. The guy had major daddy issues, to put it lightly. Marco thought of his own dad. He wondered if he was working right then. He wondered if his parents had been able to get any time off from work to join the vigil beyond the mall fence. Marco had seen the tiny lights of candles beyond the gates, like people were already mourning the loss of them all.

He suddenly felt bad for not having called his parents on the CBs. He should have taken time out of his insane hamster wheel of administrative bullcrap to let them know he was still alive. He hoped his parents hadn't done something crazy like quit their jobs to wait for him. Then again, he kind of wished they did. How much would they have to love him to give up a job for him?

Time began to ooze out and contract like water. It seemed they'd been talking—well, that Mike had been talking for eons, but also only for like five seconds before he looked at his phone and said, "It's two."

There was no noise from below—the party had died out at some point. Mike's face was distorted. Marco would look at his eyes, and his mouth would seem far away, but then not. He looked down and saw his cup was full. He didn't remember filling it. The bottle of scotch was nearly empty. How much had they drank—drunk? *Drunken?*

"I have a plan," Mike said. His words didn't slur at all.

Marco focused on the computer screen to keep the room from sliding. "Plan?"

"For food," Mike said. "You saw Reynolds cut through the security gate on the security tapes? That's what we should do. Those assholes will never expect us to cut through the gate."

"Cut?" Marco was having trouble with basic concepts.

"The bolt cutters." Mike slapped Marco's face. "They were in the haul from the pancake place."

The pain helped to focus Marco. "Bolt cutters. Yes." When he'd busted into the Sam's Club, he'd gone through the doors, and security had been watching. But maybe Mike was right. The gate was locked. Why watch it?

Mike pulled two bottles of Sportade from his box of wonders and tossed one at Marco. "Pound it," he ordered. "I need you sober."

Marco opened the plastic top. He was not sure one bottle of Sportade was going to cut it, but hell if Mike looked like any issue was open for discussion. Marco guzzled the red liquid, which felt like a balm, then stumbled down the stairs after Mike. "Are we getting the troops together?" he asked.

"No troops," Mike said, stepping over Ryan's and Shay's sleeping bodies and continuing down the empty terraces of the theater toward the weapons stockpile. "This is a stealth mission."

Marco paused at the sleepers. Shay was curled against Ryan, and he had his arm slung over her. How dare they look so calm, so happy.

Mike pulled out the bolt cutters, a machete, which he slung over his shoulder, and a duffel bag. He handed another duffel to Marco. "Small weapons," he cautioned. "We need to be able to run."

Marco donned Shay's leather coat—it worked against Tasers, which was good enough for him—and took a bat. They had several. Worst case, he could throw it and run. He put the empty duffel on like a backpack and followed Mike toward the door to the fire stairs.

The IMAX was situated almost exactly next to the Sam's Club, only two floors up, so Marco led them to a door into the regular mall that was a little ways away from the main entrance into the service passages in case security had installed additional hidden cameras to monitor the halls surrounding Sam's. Mike had the walkie-talkie on him and they listened to the full range of bandwidths before deciding this portion of the first floor was free of guards.

The hallway was pitch-dark—security had extinguished the few safety lights that used to be left on after Lights Out. But it was more than that. Marco looked up and saw no ambient light from the outside world, no stars. Then he remembered some announcement about the skylights being covered over. It was like the government was trying to make life in the mall as craptastic as possible.

Marco felt in his pocket and found a glow-in-the-dark

sticker—a leftover from his party-planning days. He stuck it on the floor outside the service door to mark their escape.

They felt their way along the hallway, crouched low to the floor to keep from tripping. Dim light glinted from a hole in the wall about fifty feet away, which Marco correctly guessed indicated the gated entrance to the Sam's Club. Security had left a few lights on inside the store, most likely so guards or hidden cameras could pick up any movement. He and Mike would have to knock out the lights once inside, or just grab whatever food was in reach and leave before anyone noticed they were there.

Mike took the bolt cutter and positioned its jaws around the thin bars of the gate. The metal snipped apart like string. Mike smiled like even he hadn't thought it would be this easy. He made quick work of the gate, cutting a hole they could both easily sneak through.

Marco pointed to the lights. "We grab whatever we can and get out before they even know we were here."

Mike nodded like this was obviously the plan. He hopped down the steps and began shoving fistfuls of whatever was in front of him into the duffel. Marco took the next aisle over. He didn't get three handfuls into the bag before all the lights flashed on in a blinding white glare.

Marco didn't wait; he strapped the duffel on his back and ran for the gate. He saw Mike was already there, squeezing through the hole.

"Stop! We will fire!" Footsteps echoed on the tiles. It was as if security had hoped for an assault on Sam's to try out a new battle plan.

Marco slammed against the gate, then shoved himself through the hole. Something hit the links of the fence above him and then a noxious cloud descended, choking him. Mike grabbed Marco by the jacket and tugged him away from the gate. Marco was blind, dependent on Mike to drag him back down the dark hallway. He heard gunfire. Was Mike shooting? No, the noise was too far away. Security was shooting. Shards of broken wall tile peppered Marco's face. Security was shooting live rounds.

Mike dragged him back a step. "The card!"

Marco fumbled in his pocket. Thank god the hall was so dark. Even if security was following, they couldn't see anything. Cracking open his eyelids to see the reader, Marco noticed flashlight beams slice across the floor. Finally, he dug out the card and opened the door. Mike shoved him through it and followed behind, shutting the door silently behind them. A flash of white illuminated the outline of the door. Security had turned on the hall lights. Had Marco been a second slower with the card, they would have been screwed.

Marco led them back through the halls, both he and Mike jogging, not wanting to stop until they were safely behind the barricade in the IMAX. It began to seep through Marco's alcohol-slogged brain that he could have died. That security was no longer threatening to kill him, but actively engaged in the pursuit. It was almost funny, that a loser like him was now considered such a threat to order and stability. It was almost sad. It was almost a compliment.

■   ■   ■

The lights woke Ryan. He quickly shielded his eyes, then thought to shield Shay's with his body. Why the hell were the lights on? Was it morning already? He tented his shirt over Shay's face so that she could keep sleeping, then turned his half-awake attention to the floor of the theater.

Mike and Marco stood over two half-empty duffels. They were both out of breath and Marco's face was bright red. The barricade across the stairwell door had been moved, though the door itself was closed.

Ryan loped down the aisle toward them. "Did security attack?"

"Not here," Mike answered.

Drew sat up on his elbows, checked a phone. "What the hell?" he said, yawning. "It's the goddamn middle of the night."

"Sorry for waking you," Mike snapped. "We just thought you might want to be prepared in case security attacks." He explained his and Marco's failed attempt to steal food from the Sam's Club. "I swear, it was like they were waiting for us. Like they knew we were going to come in through that gate."

"It's logical," Marco said, voice sounding choked. "They know the food's a target. They would concentrate resources there. I imagine it will only get worse from here on out."

"Why would you leave without telling anyone?" Ryan felt like this was an obvious question. "We could have all gone in, maybe gotten more food."

"You would have left your precious girlfriend to help the team?" Mike glared at him like this was his fault.

Ryan felt that any direct response would just bring on the fight Mike was looking for. "You should have told someone," he said. "What if you'd gotten caught?"

"Who are you, my mother?" Mike said. "We need to set up stations at the two doors, watch for anything in case they followed us."

Drew flopped back on the floor. "Screw that," he said. "Turn the lights off. They'll never know we're here."

Mike looked ready to shoot Drew. Ryan grabbed Mike's arm; he smelled like a dive bar: alcohol and sweat. He smelled like Dad. "It's late," Ryan said, holding Mike back. "You're drunk. Calm the hell down and leave it until the morning."

Mike wrenched his shoulder, throwing Ryan off. "Don't tell me what to do."

Still, he listened, slunk back to his skybox and turned off its light. Maybe he'd sleep it off. Maybe things would be better in the morning. *Then again, maybe not.* Maybe it would be better if he and Shay weren't here when Mike woke up.

Marco was using beer from the keg to wash his face. How much had they had to drink? Ryan grabbed a water bottle from the stack near the wall and tapped Marco on the shoulder.

He didn't turn. "What do you want?" The thick leather duster Shay had worn lay in a pile at his feet.

"You get hit with something?" Ryan asked, holding out the water.

"Tear gas." Marco took the water and poured it over his face.

"Mike's not some superhero," Ryan said. "He thinks he's invincible, but he's just a regular guy."

Marco glanced at Ryan like he was a moron. "You think I followed Mike on this little adventure like some drooling sycophant?"

Ryan had no idea what that word meant, but assumed it was not good. "I think you think Mike has some clue about what he's doing and I just want you to know he's as screwed as the rest of us."

Marco wiped his face clean with his shirt. His eyes were red and his face splotchy. "Funny you should say that, because he's dragged your ass back from the abyss how many times? For a clueless douchebag, he seems to be doing pretty well."

"I'm just trying to give you some friendly advice," Ryan said.

Marco handed him the empty water bottle. "And let me give you some in return," he said. "You think Shay is all truth and love? Well, she cozied up to me when she needed something and dropped me like a bag of dirt when I couldn't help her anymore. So just watch *your* back, loverboy. You might find a knife in it."

Marco slunk to the corner nearest the weapons pile and curled up like a dog against the wall. Ryan returned to where Shay slept. Her hair fanned out from underneath the shirt he'd left covering her face, and her one hand crossed over the other arm, which was tucked under her head. Her body curved around where he'd been sleeping, like they were two pieces of a single whole. Ryan felt sorry for Marco. It was tough liking a girl who didn't like you back.

The lights blinked out—Mike must have some master switch up in the projection room. Ryan laid his body down beside Shay and put his arms around her, and she nuzzled into his chest, and he knew that even if she put a knife in his back, this—her and him together—would still be the best thing that had ever happened to him.

LIGHTS ON

Lexi heard the mall announcement that morning: Resume your normal schedule. It sounded a lot like "Pretend yesterday never happened," or "Just kidding about the whole lockdown thing." But she guessed people were plain happy to get out of their Home Stores, because everyone seemed one notch below giddy at breakfast. Even Maddie, queen of the downers, said something nice about the food.

"I think this is, like, *real* powdered egg," she said, poking another forkful.

To Lexi, that merely meant more bad news. She recalled the woman in her mother's office mentioning something about survival rations and using food from the Sam's Club. If they were serving "real" powdered eggs, that was only because they'd run out of the government-issued freeze-dried food. The downside to more people surviving was that they were consuming resources at a faster rate than had been anticipated by the fleeing government troops, Lexi guessed.

At the end of breakfast, some names were read out over the loudspeaker to come to the mall offices for reassignment. Lexi assumed this only meant more bad news—what new jobs were needed at this late stage in the game? The mystery was solved when the guard who surveyed their work in the laundry was replaced with a regular mall person bearing a stun baton.

"Are you serious?" Maddie said, staring at the newcomer.

Ginger paled to an even whiter shade. "Do you think he got any training on how to not kill people with that thing?"

"My mom wouldn't let people out in the mall without some sort of lesson," Lexi said, trying to convince herself as she spoke. "She's all about proper usage of power tools."

Maddie turned back to her pool-cleaner-turned-laundry stirrer. "Let's just say I wouldn't want to be the one to test his skills."

Ginger was folding dry clothes from the lines that webbed the ceiling of the parking garage. "I think I might need some cheering up." This was code for wanting to take a trip to their closet full of designer goodies.

"I could use a break," Maddie said, pulling off her shower cap.

Lexi had no interest in donning clothes that would make her feel even worse than she did already. "I think I'll check in on my dad instead."

The three of them informed the plainclothes guard that they were taking a bathroom break.

"You have fifteen," he said, sounding way too aware of the power his new stick implied. "Don't make me come looking for you."

As they rode the escalator to the first floor, Maddie held her hands up and made a face like, *Oooh, I'm scared.* Lexi wasn't sure that they shouldn't be, given the swagger that guy was sporting.

Lexi checked in with the woman at the front of the med center. "Sorry, honey," she said. "No news."

"Can I see him?" she begged.

"Flu patients are off limits," the woman said.

Lexi sat in the waiting area anyway. Maybe Dr. Chen would walk by and she could wheedle him for more or better information. Was her father still running a fever? Was he coughing up blood? Was there any hope at all?

Finally, without seeing a single other person and not wanting to risk giving the guard at the Laundry a reason to try out his stun gun, Lexi left to return to work. Thinking Ging and Mad needed an outside influence to pry them away from their treasure, she first stopped in at the JCPenney.

Residents were allowed access to their Home Store during the day, so there was no problem checking in with the guard. It was only when Lexi tried to enter the stockroom that she ran into trouble.

"No entry," a voice said.

"I just need to get something," Lexi whined, pushing on the door.

The door swept open and a guard in full riot gear stood in front of her. "Are we going to have a problem, miss?" he asked.

Lexi saw behind him two other guards who each held Maddie and Ginger, their hands bound behind them, their heads lolling on what looked like broken necks.

"Those are my friends!" Lexi screamed.

"Your friends are in a heap of trouble," the guard growled. "I suggest you find some new ones."

Lexi's heart was in her throat. They couldn't take Maddie and Ginger from her. She'd have no one without them. *The Senator*. Her mother could stop this.

Lexi ran from the guard, bolted out of the JCPenney, took the stairs two at a time to the third floor, and banged on the glass. The guard on duty buzzed her in.

"Mom!" she yelled.

Her mother was in a meeting with the food woman and some other guy. "What is it?" her mother said, looking concerned.

"Security!" Lexi said, heaving breath. "They took— Maddie and—Ginger."

The Senator frowned. "I'm sorry, honey, but they are out of my hands."

"You're in charge of the mall," Lexi said. "How can they be out of your hands?"

"I handed complete control of security matters to Mr. Goldman," she said. "You can speak with him on your friends' behalf, but if they have been detained, they must have been doing something."

"They kept some clothes that should have been thrown out," Lexi said. "It wasn't a big deal. And what about innocent until proven guilty?"

Her mother looked like she was sad for Lexi and her simple ideas about justice. "Baby, this is not a courtroom.

This is a crisis. I'll mention it to Goldman when I see him. Anyway, I hear the lockups are nearing capacity. Your friends will probably be questioned and released."

Questioned and released? This was supposed to be a comfort? How was she supposed to survive by herself until their release? And where were they being questioned? In some jail with a bunch of crazy deviants? Maddie would be fine, but Ginger?

Lexi couldn't catch her breath. She stumbled down the hall and out the door, then stopped against the railing. If her mother couldn't or wouldn't help, then Lexi would have to find someone else who would. And she only knew of one person with the ability to unlock locked doors: *Marco*.

Shay awoke and guessed it was some time around Lights On. She was used to waking up at this time by now; it didn't matter that she was currently in a dark theater outside the rules of the rest of the mall. Gathering her things was easy—all she had was her bag. She put on Ryan's sweatshirt, the one she'd been using as a pillow. It wasn't cold, but she wanted something of his near her.

Using her penlight, she picked her way down the terraced steps of the theater to where she'd seen Marco earlier, curled near the weapons pile. He was still there, alone, apart. Shay couldn't blame him for being wary of his new friends. After all, she was.

She knelt beside him and whispered his name. He stirred, then pushed himself up onto his elbows. "What do you want?" he said snidely.

"I need a favor," she said.

"Why would I do you a favor?"

"Not me," she said. "Preeti. I need to see her, make sure she's okay."

He looked at her body. It was unnerving, but something about her shirt softened his face. "What can I do to help you with that?"

"I want some guarantee that we can escape if we need to," Shay said. "I want to borrow your card key."

She knew she was asking a lot. Marco clearly depended on the card for more than its ability to open doors. It was his one claim to power within the gang. And she was asking him to give it away to help her. It was a long shot. A very long shot.

Marco touched her shirt. Shay was afraid he would ask her for a kiss and she would have to say no. There was no more pretending on that front. But instead he said, "Is Ryan going with you?"

"He'd get caught the second we stepped out into the mall," she said. "I can't ask him to risk that."

Marco dug his hand into his pocket and pulled out the card. He pressed it into her palm. "You should let him decide if he wants to take the risk."

He rolled over, away from her, toward the wall. Their conversation was over. Still, she crouched there over him for a moment longer.

"Thanks," she whispered.

He didn't respond.

Shay wondered if he was right. If she were Ryan, would she have wanted him to give her the choice? The answer was obvious. She crawled back up to where he slept and kissed his cheek.

He started awake, then relaxed seeing her face in the dim penlight. "You okay?" he asked.

She knew then that she'd made the right choice. Of course he agreed to go with her. He grabbed what few things he had and got up immediately.

"It's a big risk," she whispered. "That guy's probably looking for you."

"So we stay under the radar," Ryan said. "Blend in." He laughed, ran his finger lightly over her black eye. "Maybe we need to find some Halloween makeup."

They pushed aside the barricade at the fire stairwell door and snuck out into the fluorescent light together.

N
O
O
N

Lexi took her tray to a large, empty picnic table. She wanted to make sure there was room for Maddie and Ginger when they showed. She even took her plate off its tray to keep her footprint to a minimum on the tabletop. Her eyes scanned the crowds. Where were they? Why hadn't they been released yet?

As she scraped spoonfuls into her mouth, one after the other, it became harder to pretend Maddie and Ginger were ever going to join her, which meant she needed Marco. She'd had no luck finding him earlier, and ended up in trouble with her geriatric supervisor for being late back from break. The old bat put her on extra laundry duty for the afternoon. This meant lunch was her only time to find Marco until dinner, but alas, she didn't see him in the crowd.

The perimeter of the first-floor courtyard was surrounded by guards in full riot gear. Lexi wondered where the armed civilians were stationed. And why were they all on high alert? Something must have happened. The "deviants" must have done something to piss Goldman off.

Lexi found she was no longer hungry. What if something happened? What if there was another riot? What then? She was alone—her father was maybe dead, her mother was locked away with her job, and her friends had been taken from her. She felt the weight of that dead body crushing her spine. Heard the screams of those trapped around her. She couldn't breathe.

"Miss, are you all right?" A man placed his tray on the table, then held Lexi's shoulder.

Lexi couldn't control her breathing. Her throat felt like it was collapsing, the room began to spin. Her heart beat in her ears.

"I think I need some help here!" the man cried.

Lexi felt herself lifted up and laid on a gurney. She watched the black of the skylights pass above her before everything went black.

Marco was shaken awake by Mike. The lights in the ceiling, though dim by mall standards, still probed his brain like ice picks. He had a hangover of epic proportions. "If you keep shaking me, I will puke," he mumbled.

Mike dropped his shoulder. "You seen Shrimp? He and the girl aren't here."

So she did ask him. . . . It had been a bit of a test: Was she wearing his shirt because she was leaving Ryan or because she was cold and the shirt had been there? Did she even know it was Marco's? Apparently, she had put the shirt on for reasons having nothing to do with him. She had gone back for Ryan, asked him to join her, and clearly he had.

Marco eased himself up to sit against the wall. He needed its support for his throbbing brain. "They left," he said. "Shay wants to rescue her sister."

Mike looked confused. "Are they coming back?"

"I would bet not."

Now Mike looked angry. He gritted his teeth, then spit on the floor. "Screw him. Fine." He turned to the rest of the sleepers. "Everybody up! We have crap to get done!"

It took a while to get everyone up and moving. Mike acted like this was the army, but this was more like a sleepover. The girls were annoyed at not having a bathroom. The guys were happy to piss down the stairwell. The bathroom situation was one in need of solving, so of course Mike looked to Marco.

"Take them somewhere," he said, like Marco was a counselor at his camp.

"I gave Shay my card," Marco said, feeling oddly free.

"What?" Mike looked ready to tear him a new asshole.

"It was half hers anyway," Marco said, a dizzy lightness mixing with the nausea and pounding headache.

"How the hell could you have given it away?" Mike said, sounding less angry than exasperated. "How the hell are we supposed to survive without it?"

"We were in need of a more permanent solution anyway," Marco said. "I have some ideas."

He hefted a crowbar from the pile of weapons. Marco walked past the stunned crowd and slammed the hooked edge of the thing into the wall above the door. After a few slams, he was able to wrench apart the drywall exposing the wires of the magnetic door lock system.

"Perfect," Marco said, pointing to the hole.

"This solves nothing," Mike growled.

"It solves everything," Marco said, suddenly needing the support of the wall again. "See," he said, closing his eyes and pressing his temples for a moment. "If you rip those wires out, you cut the power to the lock. It'll be open season for everyone, card or no."

Drew was the first fan of this tactic. "We'll have free run of the place," he said.

Mike was less thrilled. "Won't security notice that their doors are off line?"

"Security has a lot of things to worry about," Marco said, still trying to stem the throbbing in his skull. "Broken doors will be merely one in a list of hundreds of things they have to manage."

Drew took the lead with the defense of the plan. "If we all head out in different directions, busting doors and stuff, they'll have no idea where to strike first. It's brilliant, Taco." He held up his hand for a fist bump. Marco missed on his first try, hit weakly on the second.

Mike was still frowning. "It slows us down. But you've left us with no other options." He perched himself on top of a stack of boxes. "And it doesn't change my plans."

Mike proposed that they recruit more people to their cause. "We're going to need more food at some point and we need our own private army if we're going to get into the Sam's Club."

"I think I smell a party coming on," Drew said, throwing an arm around Mike.

"Party, recruitment, whatever, I just need people. You guys get them here, then we organize our move on the Sam's Club."

Drew and the Tarrytown guys high-fived like they had this covered. Mike, however, turned to the girls. "More guys will come if they think there will be girls, so you're in charge of recruitment. You guys work on this door situation with Marco."

Drew seemed crestfallen. "And you? What are you doing?"

"Coming up with a way to get us into the Sam's Club."

Marco grabbed a water bottle from the dwindling pile and joined Mike as he stalked up the steps toward the stairwell to his "office." "You need help?" he asked, swigging the water like it was life itself.

"You're lucky I don't plant your ass through the wall," Mike growled.

"Busting the doors will be better in the long run," Marco said, unfazed. "This way, we can split into groups. Less chance of getting caught all in one fell swoop."

"You should have talked to me about it."

"You want me to talk to you about things, then you let me in on planning."

Mike paused at the door to the projection booth stairs.

"Fine," he said. "You babysit Drew and make sure he doesn't do anything stupid, then I'll let you in on my plans."

Marco nodded. It was a good enough start.

Ryan had no idea what he was doing, but he knew that the alternative—letting Shay go—was not possible. Where he would live, how he would eat once she returned to the real mall, he had no idea. But they were together, and somehow Shay had gotten hold of Marco's magic card, and for now, that was all he needed.

They wound their way down service halls, trying to use store names as a guide through the crisscrossing passages, until they found Target, then crossed to the opposite side of the mall through its abandoned and heavily picked over stockroom, and began their twisting way back toward the center of the mall and down a level to the food court. Shay's plan was to find Preeti there and try to talk to her, patch things up. She kept muttering her apology as they walked down the halls.

"Is she really going to be that pissed?" Ryan had never felt so entitled as to be angry with his older brother. Thad had abandoned him plenty of times, sometimes on the bad nights when Dad was rampaging. Ryan had hid in his closet and waited things out. When Thad resurfaced, Ryan would be grateful, not angry.

"I promised I wouldn't leave her," Shay said. "Then I did."

Ryan still found the idea ludicrous. If he had yelled at Thad, it would have driven Thad away, not made him guilty enough to risk arrest to patch things up. Still, this was Shay, not Thad. Ryan recognized that there was a world of difference between the two.

When they reached a door leading out into the food court, Shay told Ryan to wait in the service halls. "You don't need to get caught our first hour out in the mall," she said.

He agreed, but then snuck out after her, hiding in their usual spot in the abandoned Magic Wok. He would not let her out of his sight.

Shay wandered out into the crowds of kids and adults, peering into each. Then a tall guy approached her. Ryan remembered him—the one who'd constantly interrupted their meetings. *What was his name?* Kris? That felt right. Ryan was usually good with names.

Kris did not look happy. He seemed to be yelling at Shay. He pointed to her face. The bruised eye would not be helpful if Shay's goal was to prove that she'd been fine while she was away. Then Shay got a word in, turned and began searching for Preeti again. Kris grabbed her arm. Shay jerked her arm back.

This did not look good. Ryan crept closer to hear what was being said.

"You just up and left her," Kris shouted. "She had kind of a breakdown."

"A *breakdown*?" Shay asked snidely. "She's ten. You just don't want me to see her."

"I want you to see her, I just want to know what the hell happened to you and what the hell you think you're doing falling off the face of the earth and then showing up like nothing's happened, meanwhile you're covered in bruises and look like hell."

Shay glared at him. "What happened? What happened was that I had my own breakdown. I tried it your way—pretended to be happy, but I can't pretend that much for that long. Preeti will understand."

"She told me she doesn't want to see you." Kris sounded like some know-it-all jerkwad.

"I'm her sister," Shay growled. "You have no right to hide her from me."

"You asked me to take care of her," he said calmly. "I'm taking care of her."

Ryan couldn't take this asshole for another second. He strode out from behind the trash can where he'd been hiding and grabbed Shay's shoulders. "Where did you hide Preeti?"

Both Shay and Kris looked at him.

"You're with him?" Kris asked. "You left your sister for some guy?"

"Ryan, I told you to wait."

"He's being an ass," Ryan said.

"Buddy, you're the ass," Kris said. "I see you're sporting some bruises too. What the hell have you two gotten yourselves into?"

Ryan felt the anger rising inside him. "Just take us to her sister."

"Are you going to try to drag her off into some backroom hideout?" Kris asked, eyeing the two of them. "She's safer here than with you."

Shay smacked Kris. "I trusted you."

Kris glared at her. "Preeti trusted *you*."

People were staring. Ryan noticed a guy with a stun stick moving toward them.

"We have to go," he said, pulling Shay's arm.

Shay let him pull her away. Ryan ducked between the nearest food kiosks and then dragged Shay at a run to the door.

"The card," he said. "Scan it."

Shay kept looking over her shoulder, back at the food court. Her lip trembled. She looked ready to fall apart.

Ryan grabbed her shoulders. "We're fine." He saw the guard peek between the kiosks. "So long as you open the door now. We will find Preeti."

Shay nodded, pulled the card from her pocket and unlocked the door. Ryan opened it and shoved her through. The guy with the gun was trotting toward them, yelling for them to stop. Ryan prayed the guy didn't have a similar card and slammed the door shut behind him.

"We have to get away from here!" Ryan yelled.

Shay couldn't piece a thought together. Preeti had a nervous breakdown? Was she that mad at her? Or was Kris just being a dick? He seemed angry with her for getting herself hurt more than for abandoning Preeti.

She let Ryan drag her through another door, down a hall, her feet slapping the cement obediently.

Ryan was right. They would find Preeti themselves. Tonight. They would sneak into the JCPenney and talk to her.

They turned another corner and Ryan stopped abruptly. Shay ran into his shoulder. Several older-looking kids hefting long metal sticks with hooked ends had them surrounded.

"You're trespassing," a guy who appeared to be their leader hissed. "And we don't like trespassers."

The two other members moved swiftly, throwing heavy bags over both Shay's and Ryan's heads, tugging the thick material down over their shoulders and arms, and then pushing them over some sort of short wall and into a bin, which then began to roll.

F I V E

P.M.

Marco and Drew, along with the Tarrytown guys, had broken most of the doors between the Lord & Taylor and the JCPenney, plus most doors leading to the fire staircase next to the IMAX. Marco tried to keep tabs on each of them as they moved from door to door in case someone got electrocuted and needed to be shoved off the current, but so far, they'd all destroyed the door locks without destroying themselves in the process. It was getting late, though his iPod had died and so he had no idea what the actual time was. From the increase in noise, he guessed it was around dinner.

"We should get everyone together," he said to Drew, who was tugging on a stuck hammerhead. "If it's dinner, which I think it is, security has more manpower at its disposal to address our door busting."

"Just one more to go," Drew said, freeing the hammer.

He reached into the wall with the plastic coat hanger they'd stolen and tugged all the wiring loose.

"Why are we busting into the pet store?" Marco asked, noticing the label on the door.

Drew kicked it open. "Dinner," he said.

The pet store was on the second floor, so there was little chance of being spotted barring a rogue guard patrol. Still, Marco didn't want to see a bunch of dead pets in their cages. He was surprised when Drew was greeted with a chorus of barks.

"Crap!" Drew shouted, running to the cages like that would quiet the dogs.

The front wall of the room was lined with cages, each cage containing a puppy. Someone had obviously been assigned pet care duty, from the relatively healthy condition of the dogs. Drew tried to stick a finger into each cage to calm them.

Marco crossed his arms. "There is absolutely no way I'm eating a dog," he said. There were limits to what he would eat, even half starved as he was.

Drew looked at him like he'd suggested they eat each other. "Of course we're not eating Fido here. Go see if any of the fish in the tanks are big enough."

Marco was not thrilled to be given the job requiring exposure to the outside. But the thought of a fish—even a small fish—was tantalizing. He'd seen *A Fish Called Wanda*. He knew you could eat the little suckers.

Careful to duck behind the low shelves lining the sales floor, Marco took one of the bags from the stack near the tanks and scooped up some water, then collected what looked to be the meatiest fish in the joint. They were not bluefin tuna, but hey, they were better than another night of soup crackers and beer.

Just as a test, he reached into the tank filled with goldfish. It took three tries, but he finally got one. It wriggled in his hand, its little mouth gasping, its pathetic life beating to its end. He tossed the fish back into the water. There was no way he could eat it alive. At least not while sober. He tied off the bag he'd filled and snuck back into the stockroom.

Drew stood triumphantly in the middle of the floor with a large birdcage. In the cage was a rather fancy-looking duck with a white swoop over its eye and a frill of orange feathers on its wings.

"Found him in a back office," Drew said, a goofy smile on his face.

"That bird is not legal," Marco said, pointing to the handwritten note taped to the cage. "There are no other birds in the place."

"Who gives a rat's ass?" Drew said, poking the bird through the cage. The thing gave off a honk. "This looks like some fine drumstick action to me."

"How the hell do you expect to cook it?"

"There was a blowtorch or something in the haul from Reynolds's stash." Drew waggled his eyebrows. "We're going to torch this mother."

Marco shrugged—if Drew wanted to torch a bird, so be it. *Bird torchers.* This was the class of people he'd aligned himself with. "Try to keep it from squawking. We want to make it back to the IMAX without alerting every guard in the mall."

"Aye, aye, Cap'n," Drew said.

■   ■   ■

Lexi found her mother waiting for her when she was finally released from the medical center.

"Are you feeling okay?" Dotty asked, her face stricken, expecting the worst.

"They said it was a panic attack," Lexi said, embarrassed to have caused so much trouble over something so ridiculous.

"But are you okay?" Dotty seemed to be way overreacting.

"They gave me some oxygen and an anti-anxiety pill." Lexi held the tiny blue oval up.

"We should be passing those out like candy," her mother said. "I'll ask Chen about adding it to the water."

Lexi leaned against her mother. It was nice that she took the time to check on her. "Anything falling apart while you're here with me?"

"What's not falling apart?" her mother joked, though neither of them laughed.

"Did they tell you anything about Dad?"

"No change," her mother said. She stroked Lexi's head, then kissed it and released the hug. "You should get dinner before it's gone."

"Is there a chance of that?"

Her mother smiled. "I hope not."

"Do you know if Maddie and Ginger are out?"

"Oh, god, honey," her mother said. "I'm sorry. I haven't had time to check."

Lexi shrugged. "I guess I'll find out soon enough."

"I'll look into it tonight, okay?"

Dotty looked like she meant it, even though Lexi knew that her mother would forget, that something much more pressing than the illegal imprisonment of two minor thieves would come up. Lexi nodded, blew her mother a kiss, and walked alone toward the central courtyard.

Not surprisingly, Maddie and Ginger were nowhere to be found. Lexi got her ration of dinner, which seemed awfully small on the plate, and ate it standing next to the garbage. She knew what she had to do: Locate Maddie and Ginger herself and rescue them using Marco's access card. But just waiting for him to show up had not proved successful, so she had to become proactive.

If Marco was with the vigilantes as her mother and Goldman suspected, maybe all of them would be at these alleged parties Maddie and Ginger kept trying to attend, if there even was a party tonight. Lexi glanced around for a person who looked like they partied, meaning a person who looked like Maddie and Ginger. *Someone with plucked eyebrows.*

Two pretty, skinny blond girls sat at a table chatting up some beefy-looking guys. Lexi steeled herself, then stepped up to the edge of the table. "Hey, you guys hear about a party tonight?"

The conversation stopped. One of the girls gave her the once-over. "I dunno," she said.

One of the guys ran a hand over Lexi's ass. "She can come with me."

Lexi nearly vomited up her measly dinner. "Where should I meet you?" she said, trying to sound as much like Maddie pretending to be Sexy Maddie as possible.

The other blonde rolled her eyes. "Fine," she said. She curled a finger indicating Lexi should lean in. "IMAX," she whispered. "Invite only."

Lexi nodded and batted her eyes like she totally understood that this was an exclusive gig. The letch pinched her ass and sucked his teeth as if he were inspecting her haunch for later consumption. Lexi giggled and swished her hips as she walked away, then hid behind a column and tried not to cry.

She just had to get to the IMAX, then she'd find Marco and everything would be fine. The only question was, how to get there. Guards monitored all movement after Lights Out. She would have to go through the service halls like a regular deviant. She prayed she didn't get too lost.

Shay had been encased in the stifling bag for long enough that the rough fabric had chafed a welt on her skin. Every time she moved or tried to wriggle out of the bag, she was hit with something, likely the metal sticks. Shay could hear their captors whispering around her. When first captured, she and Ryan had yelled threats at them, but soon they realized this was not achieving anything and shut up.

After an interminable period, Shay felt hands grab her bag and she was pulled upright. The top of the bag was cut open and the bag dragged down until her head was free.

She was in a bright, open stockroom. There were about ten people she could see, some sitting on the heavy-duty shelving that lined the walls. From the picture of the president and the various USPS stickers all over, Shay realized she was in the back of the mall's post office.

"How long have you been here?" she asked. There were sleeping bags stretched on the shelves like bunks and bags of trash peeked out from a distant corner. A few of the people had laptops and from the uniformity of the screen images, seemed to be reading the same thing.

"A while," the lead guy said. He had a row of what looked like silver claws lined against his knuckles like rings.

"What are you doing with the laptops?" she said, nodding toward the people on the shelves. "Did you get the Internet back?"

The guy smiled proudly. "We hacked the mall's intranet. We know who's where, how many have died, how much food is left and where it is." He swung down from his perch and flicked the stick at her. "Now, I have a question. How'd you get through our door?" He pointed at the nearest stockroom door. "Only way in requires a card key."

"How did *you* get through?" Shay tried to get a bearing on her surroundings—she was next to a mail sorting bin, in which was a large bag with Ryan's legs sticking out the bottom.

The guy with the stick twirled it. "We have our ways," he said.

As if to demonstrate, someone slammed in through the door. Shay caught a glimpse of something on the magnetic lock panel.

"Sydney," the leader groaned. "Way to give secrets away." He pointed at the door. "We traded some stuff rescued from the mail with a guard in return for his opening a few doors for us. Once open, we covered the lock's contact plate with a couple of layers of aluminum foil. The magnet reads as locked, but it's way less powerful and you can just shove it open." The stick pointed back at her. "Now you. How do you get through doors? You didn't slam into the door, so I know you didn't know our little trick."

Shay was not about to tell him they had an access card. "Ryan's strong," she said. "We saw the edge of the foil and he just pushed it."

"I think you might have the rumored magic key." He pointed to the girl, Sydney, who'd busted into the room. "Search her."

Shay yelled for Ryan, who yelled back, but Sydney was fast. Her hands felt up Shay's legs like she worked for the TSA. Shay would not lose the card to these people. She made the only move she could and dropped to the floor. She rolled into the cart and kicked it hard. Ryan somehow intuited her plan: He rolled with the jolt from her kick and toppled the thing over.

Sydney collapsed onto her and resumed her molestation. Shay wriggled every which way, but really, there's little you can do trapped in a mail bag with a person sitting on your legs.

"I've got it!" Sydney yelled.

"Screw that!" Ryan said, tackling her.

And then the whole mess of postal people piled on. Shay took the opportunity to escape her bag, then began tugging at random articles of clothing to uncover Ryan. It was a testament to his skills as a football player that he emerged from the edge of the pile, one arm tucked to his chest, and yelled to Shay, "GO!"

Shay bolted for the door Sydney had come in through

and tore it open. Ryan ran out. Shay jumped up, grabbed the tin foil sheet from the lock, and slammed the door closed. They ran to the next door. Ryan opened it with the card, and Shay again removed the tin foil and slammed it shut.

"I think we've locked them in," she said, trying to catch her breath.

"Let's not wait and find out," Ryan said, grabbing her hand.

Adrenaline rushed through her body and she felt an undeniable need to kiss him and so she did. He kissed her back, but then pulled away.

"Come on," he said. "There's plenty of time for that when we're not in a hallway facing a mob of angry postal workers."

They made their way to the nearest fire stairwell and ran to the parking garage, thinking they could hide out and regroup there. Alas, the parking level was crawling with people. Ryan held a finger to his lips and led her down the aisles of cars. Skulking behind him, Shay saw that his ankle was covered in blood and his shoe ripped. She recalled the postal leader's fist of claws.

"You're bleeding," she said, touching his ruined shoe.

"I'll live," he whispered, and kept going until they reached a brownish SUV.

"Yours?" she whispered.

"Sort of."

He pulled open the door and was greeted by a plastic bag full of something to the head.

"Get out!" a young girl's voice screamed.

Shay was about to oblige when Ryan said, "Ruthie?"

It was the little girl Shay had tried to save for him, the little girl who had nearly outed him to security. Shay felt this was a prime moment to run.

"Ryan?" the girl said, sounding much friendlier than she had in the food court. She appeared from behind the second row of seats. Seeing him, a waterfall of tears burst from her eyes. "Jack's dead!" She flung herself over the seatback and wrapped her arms around Ryan.

He hugged her like they were family. "Crap," he whispered. "I'm so sorry."

Shay felt like she should leave them alone, but there was nowhere to go.

Ryan glanced up at her. "We have to stay," he said.

Shay nodded. Of course they had to stay.

LIGHTS OUT

When the lights blinked out along the parking level, Ryan lifted Ruthie's sleeping head from his lap and crawled into the middle row of seats with Shay. She was writing in a notebook with a lighted pen.

"Any deep thoughts?" he asked.

Shay closed the book, but left the pen on for light. "Just trying to pull together a single thought. My head's taken quite the beating."

"Can I do something?"

"Have any spare heads?"

"I'd give you mine, but that would be a little weird. I'd have to kiss myself, which is wrong."

"You're not bad-looking," Shay said. "I mean, *I* would kiss you."

"Really?" he said, leaning in.

Shay stopped him. "The ankle," she said. "Have you cleaned it?"

"I told you," he said, leaning closer, "it's fine."

He kissed her—though she stopped things before he really got going.

"We need a plan," she said. "I have to get Preeti and we need to find somewhere to live that isn't this car." She looked down at the floor like it might ooze up over her feet, it was so covered in garbage.

"We should bring Ruthie back to the mall people," Ryan said. "She might be upset, but it's not their fault Jack died."

"It's not *not* their fault." Shay's voice was cold. He'd forgotten that they'd let her grandmother die.

"Still, she's safer with them."

"I guess," Shay said, looking back at Ruthie.

"We could all go live with Mike?"

Shay looked at him like he'd suggested they live in a snake pit. "We are not living with Mike."

Even though he totally got why she didn't want to live with Mike—he'd gotten a little scary over the last few days—it still hurt. Mike was a good guy underneath it all. At least, he was good to Ryan.

"I could go up there," he suggested, "just to get us some food. I haven't eaten all day."

Shay looked around, like maybe she was willing to eat the floor garbage rather than accept any handouts from Mike. "Fine," she said. "But just go and come back. Don't leave me all night."

He kissed her. "Never."

Ryan took a fire stairwell up to the third floor, then exited. He was surprised to find that his card key did not work on the first door he tried—the reader flashed red. He pulled on the door and it opened. Looking up, he saw that the mechanism for the lock system had been ripped from the wall. So this was Mike's solution to losing the universal card key. It wasn't neat, but it worked—classic Mike.

It wasn't hard to find the IMAX. Ryan simply followed the busted doors, and then the thump of a bass line. He opened the door to the theater and found the place dark, crowded with people, and smelling of that strangely appealing combination of alcohol and sweat. Ryan pushed his way through the dancing bodies. He hoped that the food was still kept near the front—he wanted to get in, steal something, and get out without being noticed.

The music cut out. Ryan ducked behind a tall guy. Drums started up—just people slapping their thighs, but the effect was drummish. Then he swore he heard a bird honk.

Ryan peeked out from behind the giant to get a look at what was going on. Drew—shirtless and wearing the feathered headdress from a kid's Indian chief Halloween costume—held a birdcage between two tiki torches. Drew opened the cage. The bird shuffled away from his hands, but didn't put up much of a fight once he got his fingers around its wings.

"I need some meew-sik," Drew slurred. He was obviously completely wasted off his ass.

Heath, one of the Tarrytown guys, was on air guitar and Leon, another, began to beat his chest and legs. Both of their faces were striped with war paint. After a few seconds of howling, Heath began squealing out something that might have been an attempt at a song. People in the audience joined in, the song blooming into AC/DC's "Highway to Hell." Drew, nodding his head, held the duck like it was a feathered football, in one hand, feet out, displaying it for the crowd. The bird didn't seem too upset. What was wrong with this bird?

Everyone started shouting the chorus: "I'm on a highway to hell!" Then Drew screamed—not screamed, but growled. Ryan had no idea what was happening. Drew shoved the duck's head in his mouth and twisted the body. Ryan lurched behind the giant to avoid seeing any more. Was Drew *ripping the bird's head off with his teeth?!*

The backup musicians gave up on their song and just started screaming and howling.

"Dude, it's just like that heavy metal guy with the chicken!"

"That's a lot more blood than I thought there'd be in a bird."

Ryan tried to keep from throwing up. When he'd regained control of his gag reflex, he dared to look. Drew was coated in blood and in his hand was the head of the duck, which he pumped toward the ceiling like a pompon. Everyone was screaming and clapping.

What the hell had happened to his friends? He'd seen them party hard—had seen people get messed up beyond recognition. One dude, while drunk, had decided to bust empties over the back of his head and ended up tearing his freaking eye out. But this? Eating live animals? This was beyond messed up.

He had to get Mike to put an end to this party.

No. He'd made his choice. He had to think of Ruthie, of Shay. If Mike and Drew wanted to behead animals and dress like lunatics, then that was their business. He just had to get the food and get the hell out.

The speakers began to blare "Pour Some Sugar on Me," which was Drew's personal theme song. Everyone was shouting along with the music, writhing with each other. Ryan saw the bird's head on top of a tall pole, which began to make rounds through the crowd. A girl sloshed half a cup of a sugary beverage on his shirt. Ryan was so hungry, he was tempted to suck the fabric.

The food had been moved. The front of the theater beside the screen contained three large barrels, each a different color. People were dipping cups in and pouring the stuff down their gullets.

Ryan forced himself not to drink any—the last thing he needed to be right now was wasted. He turned around and began to make his way between the partiers toward the back of the theater. Surrounding the dancers were the two sets of non-dancers—those hooking up and those who thought they were too cool to dance. Ryan would have been in the latter category. It took a lot of beer to get him shaking his butt.

The back of the room was calmer, filled with observers, non-drinkers, or the already-passed-out. Ryan kept out of view of Mike's skybox. Even with the place packed like this, he had the odd feeling that Mike would be able to single him out, swoop down, and beat his ass. Finally, in the back corner near the barricaded doors leading to the mall, Ryan found an area blocked off by rows of seats. Inside the makeshift wall were all the weapons on one side and on the other, all the food. In between sat Marco, a bottle between his knees.

"The prodigal son returns," Marco said, though he was barely audible over the pulsing rhythm of the drums. "Have my card?"

"I just want some food," he yelled, then added, "For me and Shay."

Marco smirked, then leaned forward to speak directly into Ryan's ear. "Then get it yourself." He pushed Ryan's shoulder as a means of excusing him.

Ryan clenched his fists. Marco raised his eyebrows, then hooked his thumb toward the skybox as if threatening to unleash Mike if Ryan didn't clear out.

He was not afraid of Marco, but Mike . . .

"You weren't always such an asshole," Ryan said.

"Yeah, but now I'm badass." Marco waggled his eyebrows and brandished what looked like a two-foot-long knife.

Ryan wound his way back down the terrace of the theater, avoiding the area right beneath the screen where Drew pantomimed some weird tribal dance while guzzling beer through a funnel. The bird body was on a sort of spit between the two tiki torches and Heath was setting its feathers on fire with what appeared to be a welding torch.

He had made his choice. He shouldn't have come back here. He finally made it to the door and escaped into the relative silence of the service halls.

The music was loud even in the stairwell, which was a blessing because Lexi had spent the better part of the evening lost in the service halls and the thumping bass had provided a sort of beacon. Most of the security doors were broken, the actual circuits to the doors ripped out through the drywall, but the doors on the stairwell were disabled using the method she had taught Marco: plate unscrewed and laid on top of the magnet to fool the lock. Yet another piece of evidence that she had been duped. Not that it mattered anymore. She just needed him to help her free Maddie and Ginger. Not even him, just his card.

She pulled open the door to the IMAX and was greeted by a wall of noise and cloud of smells that caused her to stumble back and nearly twist an ankle. The music hurt her brain; the bass seemed to be literally hammering her skull. And there were so many people—masses of bodies. The first thing that popped into her head: the ice-skating rink full of corpses. But all these people were drunk— or at least that was how Lexi explained the crowds of kids laughing and falling over and grinding against one another, plastic cups of colored liquid spilling over their arms and necks and clothing. She'd never really been to a party before.

Lexi figured that Marco would be like her—somewhere off to the side, nowhere near these crazy dancing people. Keeping glued to the wall, she shuffled up, up, and away from the movie screen, each level containing fewer and fewer dancers. At the back wall, Lexi began scanning the non-dancers for Marco, though she guessed that he would be against the back wall like her, as far from the insanity as possible.

As Lexi had expected, Marco was in the darkest corner farthest from the dancing. Her first reaction at seeing him? Joy, excitement, giddiness, thoughts of kissing him. But

then she remembered that he was a liar and maybe a killer
and that he'd used her to help his psycho party friends.

Even so, her brain froze when she stepped up to where
he was sitting behind what appeared to be a dislodged
row of movie theater seats.

"Lexi?" he said, standing. She couldn't tell if he was
happy or simply shocked. It didn't matter. She was here
for one thing only.

"I need to borrow your card key," she yelled. "I need
to rescue my friends."

Marco's face withered into a scowl. "Everybody needs
something."

She didn't deserve that look, not from him. "You lied
to me! Goldman told me all about what you and your pals
did!"

"Goldman," Marco said, smirking. "I'm sure he told
you a lot."

Lexi was not about to engage him in an argument. First
of all, she could barely hear herself think. Second, he
wasn't denying that he lied to her. And here he was, surrounded by people partying with the stolen alcohol and
guarding what looked like an arsenal for a guerilla front.
What *could* he say to counter Goldman's accusations?

"Are you going to help me or not?"

"Wish I could." He sat back down, forcing her to lean
awkwardly over the barrier of chairs to hear him. "But I
recently lost possession of the card. I'm of no use to you."
He said it like all of this—his being held behind the wall
of seats, his involvement with murderers, his lies—were
somehow her fault.

She was not going to allow him his self-pity. "No," she

yelled, "I guess you're not." She turned her back on him and walked away.

Alas, the grand dramatic exit she was hoping for was impossible in this sea of people. She pushed and shoved her way through the crowds, letting all the anger and frustration channel into jostling every body that was in her way. She felt like crying, so she cried. It wasn't like anyone would notice, or even if they did, remember her tear-streaked face.

A guy fell against the wall near her. "You're h*ooooooot*," he said.

The guy stunk of stale beer and sweat. Lexi tried to push past him.

"I have a kiss with your name on it." He grabbed her arm.

Lexi elbowed him in the chest, knocking him loose, and shoved forward into the crowd of dancers. It was harder to keep her footing once away from the wall. She was reminded of the riot, of being lifted by the crowd and carried along as if caught in a river, and that brought her heart rate up into the panic attack zone. She would not black out here.

She pushed off the nearest body and launched herself backward through the dancers, finding herself at the center of a small circle. A huge guy in a feather headdress whose body looked slick with blood and sweat hoisted the charred body of a chicken over his head.

Strangely, Lexi's first thought was, *Where'd he get a real chicken?*

He looked down at her, his eyes bloodshot and face red with drink. "You want a piece of me or the chicken?" He slung an arm around her back and pulled her to him. "Or maybe both?"

He pressed his lips to her face, smearing grease and blood on her cheeks. Lexi felt bile burn the back of her throat. Finally, he released her and howled to the crowd like a dog. Lexi dropped to the floor, ready to vomit. Sensing she was free, she crawled along the sticky rug between the stomping legs, tears nearly blinding her. What a horrible second kiss. What a horrible first party.

After several kicks to her chest, Lexi found herself again near a wall. She stood, tried to catch her breath, and then slunk along the wall to the door and out into the darkness.

Marco would not cry, and so he drank. There was something purifying about scotch. It burned out your insides and left you clean. So what if Lexi hated him? Who the hell was she anyway? She didn't matter. Survival was what mattered. Sneak, steal, lie, attack, defend—all that mattered was that he was still alive. All. That. Mattered.

He took another swig of the scotch. It was like French kissing a shot gun, but it left him clearheaded in a way he'd never been clear before. He would survive this. He and Mike. They would do what they had to do. They weren't afraid to admit they were survivors.

As if summoned from the air itself, Mike appeared in front of him. "A security detail is investigating noise coming from the stairwell," he barked.

"Then let's welcome them." Marco grabbed his bat and a nail gun and tucked the machete into its holster on his belt, covering it all with Shay's jacket.

Mike selected a crossbow and lacrosse stick, then strapped on a helmet.

The dancers moved out of their way, perhaps sensing their power. They were freaking monsters, he and Mike. They would breathe fire.

They met the five security guards on the stairwell, Marco going out first to catch the Taser cartridges in Shay's invincible coat. Then Marco fired off the nail gun, driving the first guard back and down the stairs. Mike hit one in the shoulder with an arrow, flipping him over the railing. The bat took care of two more. The lacrosse stick broke over the last guy's neck. Only one was left conscious, and as he reached for his radio, Mike kicked him in the face.

"Easy peasy," he said.

Marco held a fist up and Mike bumped it.

They were a team.

Returning to the party, Marco felt the need to dance. He left the coat and weapons under the curtain beneath the screen and began moshing with Drew, who looked like some primordial demon. They screamed in each other's faces. They drank whatever was handed to them. Someone dangled a wriggling fish in front of Marco's face and goddamned if the thing didn't wriggle all the way down his gullet.

DAY
THIRTEEN

T
W
O
A.M.

Shay waited until Ryan fell asleep to attempt what even she was willing to admit was a relatively crazy plan to contact Preeti. She wanted to talk to Ryan about it, had even tried when he came back from failing to secure food from Mike. He'd seemed rattled. When she asked him what had happened, he said, "Things are getting bad out there." When she said she was going to try to contact Preeti in her Home Store, Ryan had said, "Not tonight."

It was okay for him to be afraid, and for him to be afraid for her, but if things were that bad in the mall, then Shay had even more of a reason to find Preeti. She had to make sure her sister was okay. Preeti didn't have to join her in the underworld. Shay just needed to say she was sorry and see that Preeti was safe.

She put these thoughts in a note and tore it from her journal, then she slipped the card from Ryan's pocket, careful not to wake him, replaced it with the note, and snuck out of the SUV. Shay walked swiftly across the dark parking lot, using her penlight to keep from running into any cars. She guessed which fire stairwell was closest to the JCPenney, and once on the first floor, used the store names on the doors along the service halls to guide her back to her old home. At every turn, she held her body against the wall and checked for any lights—she did not want to run into another living soul.

The door to the JCPenney stockroom was unguarded on the outside and the card reader seemed broken. It blinked red over and over and wouldn't read her card. Shay checked around the door and saw why: There was a hole in the wall along the top of the door frame, out of which sprang a snarl of frayed wires.

She opened the door and found a guard asleep beside it. Creeping around his legs, Shay entered the stockroom and then the sales floor. She dropped to all fours and crawled between the sleepers to avoid being spotted should a guard be on his hourly night patrol.

Preeti's bed had been located beneath the edge of a large crystal chandelier. When Shay reached the spot, she found a space. She looked around. The neighboring beds were 652 and 654. Preeti had been 653.

Shay's heart pounded in her chest. Had Preeti been taken to the med center? Was she sick? Dead? Is that why Kris had hid her? He didn't want to tell her the truth?

She looked in each of the neighboring beds. Not Preeti. She began crawling back toward the wall. She needed something solid to hold on to. She needed to think.

As she crawled, she passed where her own cot should

have been. It too was gone. Maybe Preeti was only missing? Shay herself was not in the med center. Maybe Preeti, like her, was simply off the grid.

That was worse. At least if she were in the med center, Shay could find her, save her.

How could she find out the truth? The answer came to her instantly. *The crazy postal people.* They had access to the intranet. They could at least tell her if Preeti had been admitted to the med center. If Shay tried to investigate that maze on her own, she faced a high risk of being caught and she needed to be sure Preeti was there before taking that risk.

The postal people would want something in return for helping her. A group of thugs willing to assault and jail anyone who ventured near their compound, they did not seem like charitable types interested in helping a girl find her lost sister. And she only had one thing to trade.

Shay crawled along the wall and back into the stockroom. Luckily, the guard was still asleep. She stood and reached for the door handle.

The door slammed open and two drunk girls tumbled in, laughing and shrieking. They both fell onto Shay, which set them into even more hysterics. Shay pushed them off, eyeing the guard constantly, waiting for him to wake and zap them all.

Freeing herself from the tangle of their limbs, she ran into the dark hall. The guard began to shout behind her, the girls began to scream. Shay ran and ran, slamming through broken doors, there were so many broken doors!

She reached a stairwell and fled down it. Bursting into the parking garage, she finally stopped and caught her breath. Shay fell back against the wall and tried to slow her heart. She hadn't intended to return here, to see Ryan again—she didn't want to have to argue with him or explain anything—but now she needed him. She needed to feel safe.

Shay stumbled back to the SUV, opened the door, and crawled next to him. He groaned, then shifted his arms to wrap them around her. She closed her eyes and snuggled into him and tried to forget that she had to leave him in the morning.

Marco swallowed the last gulp from his cup while Drew relieved his bladder against the nearest wall. The party had died down—Mike had cut off the music, and most partiers had either passed out on the floor or stumbled back to their Home Stores. Some, though, had stayed around to see what happened next. Marco eyed these potential recruits, but found the alcohol had made critical thinking rather difficult.

Drew staggered back to their perch on the first riser up from the screen. "Dude, I don't feel so good."

"You ate a raw duck." Marco tossed his glass into the general mass of garbage on the floor.

"What duck?" Drew asked, looking genuinely interested.

Marco decided to leave the details out. "Nothing," he said. "But you might want to dig up some Tums or Pepto or something just in case."

"Taco, Drewski," Mike barked from above. He stalked down the terrace in long strides. Arriving in front of Marco and Drew, he tossed two bottles of Sportade at their heads. "We need to pull out."

"Yeah," Drew said. "It smells in here."

"Perhaps we should stop pissing on the walls." Marco guzzled the Sportade as if it were the nectar of the gods.

Mike continued, ignoring them, "Security's bound to notice our little scuffle with their recon team. We have to gather the most valuable players and regroup with them in a new location."

"Bowling alley?" Marco suggested.

Mike shrugged. "As good as anywhere else at this point."

"Dude," Drew whined. "You mean I have to haul all this crap across the goddamned mall again?"

"You'd rather face Goldman?" Mike did not need to say more. Drew was up and staggering toward the nearest Tarrytown player.

"What are you looking for in an army?" Marco said, trying to focus on the face of the nearest guy. His head kept floating around like a bubble.

"More of you," Mike said. "But sober."

Marco could not help but feel a sense of pride in Mike's compliment. He downed the remainder of the bottle, tossed it aside, and dragged his semi-conscious ass toward the nearest sitting body.

Lexi was lost. It was dark, dark, dark and she was all turned around. She stumbled down the halls, stumbled into and through doors.

Someone must have slipped her a drug. Lexi knew herself well enough to know that something was way off inside of her. She hadn't drank anything, so it had to be something she touched. Or someone who touched her. *The gross guy.* The one who'd kissed her. He must have slipped something into her mouth.

Her head hurt. She heard footsteps and turned to meet them, but they were everywhere. Then a body slammed into her, laughing, ran past her. Lexi reeled back and slid down the wall.

She had to get out of these hallways. The floor felt uneven against her legs. The black spun around her—how was that even possible? But there was definitely spinning. She clung to the wall. Closed her eyes. That didn't stop the spinning.

Where was her mother? Maddie? Ginger? *Anyone?* Even that asshole Goldman would be a welcome sight.

Lexi crawled along the wall, hoping to meet a guard. If they carted her off to jail, at least she'd be with Maddie and Ginger. At least she wouldn't be in the dark. At least she wouldn't be alone. *Again.*

More footsteps. A person. Lexi lay flat against the wall. Feet slapped by her, voices echoed.

"Help!" she cried.

Nothing. Feet farther away. Echoes quieter, quieter.

Pushing up to try to crawl again, Lexi's arms gave out. She felt so weak and cold. Her fingers, numb. What had he given her?

She kicked off her shoes, drove herself forward with her toes, friction. Her hands patted the walls, searching for a door. She had to get off of the hallway. Had to find a quiet place to rest, stop spinning.

Fingers dropped in from the wall. *A door.* Lexi pressed herself against the metal, struck up with her arm searching for the handle. Turned. The door opened and she fell into more black. Quiet. She pushed herself forward. Spinning, spinning, spinning.

Lexi laid her head on the floor, kicked the door closed with her toe.

"Help," she whispered.

LIGHTS ON

The lights glaring through the SUV's windows woke Ryan to the happy sight of Shay curled in his arms. He carefully extracted himself from their embrace without waking her, exited the car to pee near the Dumpsters, and then filled two empty water bottles from the shower heads before anyone came down to begin the daily cycle.

As he walked back to the car, he discovered a folded paper in his pocket on which was scribbled a note of apology from Shay. She had apparently abandoned him last night and then, at some point, reconsidered. What the hell? Did she not believe him about the extreme danger level? Did she have a freaking death wish?

She was up when he got back to the car. He opened the door and waved for her to join him outside of it.

"Are you insane?" he asked, holding up her note.

"I forgot to take that back," she said, grabbing for it.

She did not seem at all sorry. "Why didn't you wake me up at least?" he said. "I could have gone with you. What if you had met some crazy security nut job? Do you not see my face? These assholes are serious!"

Shay touched his cheek. "I see your face," she said.

He was caught between wanting to kiss her and lock her in the car. "I can't lose you," he managed.

She leaned into him and wrapped her arms around his chest. "Losing you is not my goal."

Ryan held her, embarrassed to need her so badly. This was weak, girly crap, this feeling so desperate. He kissed her head. He had no choice in the matter. Girly crap or not, he was desperate for Shay.

He heard voices from the pavilion and shuffled with Shay to the back of the car, which hid them from view. "So now what?" he asked.

"Preeti wasn't in the JCPenney," Shay said. "Her cot was gone." Her voice broke then and she wiped her face with her shirt. "I have to find her. And there's only one place to go."

Ryan was confused—was Shay proposing she try to get security to tell her? "I don't think security is going to help you out. You busted out of their jail, remember?"

"Not security." She pulled out Marco's magic card. "The postal people."

Shay had clearly lost her mind. "No," Ryan said. "They will kick your ass and take the card from you. They've already tried! What the hell do you think has changed in a day?"

"They're my only chance," Shay said. "They can check the intranet, see where Preeti last checked in."

"But we need that card!" He had to stop her.

"Not as much as I need to find my sister."

She had already made up her mind. Ryan could tell from the set of her jaw, the tone of her voice. "Then I'm going with you."

Shay smiled, then cocked her head at the car. "And Ruthie? You'll just leave her alone in this tomb of a truck to see what happens?"

Ryan was ready to tear himself in two to keep from leaving Shay. Of course she was right—he would not leave Ruthie. Not after everything. But leave Shay as a result? Impossible. He couldn't.

"They'll hurt you," he said. It was lame, but true, and he couldn't stand to think of her getting hurt.

Shay held a finger up, ducked back into the SUV, and returned wielding a tire iron. "I saw this on the floor," she said, assuming a karate stance she must have seen in a movie. "Pretty threatening, right?"

She looked about as threatening as a puppy with a stick. "Very."

Shay broke her stance and shrugged. "Our options suck," she said, "but I'm not abandoning my sister and you're not allowed to abandon Ruthie for me." She tucked the tire iron into her waistband, which dragged her pants to the floor.

They both burst out laughing. Shay tugged up her waist-band, hiding those legs, then slung the tire iron through the strap of her bag like it was a bandolier.

"Now I look fierce," she said, showing off her getup.

"They'll pass out with fear."

The smile left her mouth and she pulled herself against

him. "I will meet you back here before dinner," she said into his shirt.

"Dinner," he said, controlling his voice so she couldn't hear how scared he was. Would this be the last time he saw her? *No.* No matter what happened, he would find her, save her. If he had to kill every one of those postal people—would he? He would. For Shay, he would.

They kissed one last time, and then she walked away, using the cars to hide her from the line of showering people. She waved when she reached the wall. Ryan smiled, waved back, then shut himself in the SUV to keep from running after her. He would see her again. No matter what.

Ruthie groaned in the back row of seats.

Ryan leaned over the seatback and pulled the shirt she used as a blanket over her. "You're safe," he whispered.

He hoped he could protect at least one person in this hellhole.

Marco sat on the pinsetters' catwalk in the bowling alley and scanned the police channels on the walkie-talkie. The security guys he and Mike had shut down had been found. One was in critical condition, the others would recover. He searched himself for some guilt or regret, but found none. This was a survival of the fittest situation. They had tried to kill him; he'd survived. If they died, it was because they were not fit.

Drew shoved his way through the door, arms laden with hockey and lacrosse sticks, duffels of smaller weapons, and other treasures recovered from the Pancake Palace. "A little help, please," he grunted.

Marco waved the radio. "I was put on recon," he said, grinning.

Drew dropped his haul by the door, then leaned his head on the wall. "I feel like ass."

"More Sportade?" Marco said, waving his head toward where Mike had left his private stash. Surely Mike would share anything with Drew.

"It's not a hangover," Drew groaned. "Hangovers I know. This is, like, bad."

Marco scowled, flipped to another channel. A guard was at the med center.

"Just dropped off another kid from the jail, one of the partiers from last night's catch. Lady at the desk said this was the tenth flu intake who was a kid this morning."

"Roger that. Will relay to the Bitch." Goldman's voice, and Marco assumed that he was referring to the senator. So things were not going well between them.

He looked at Drew, who had taken another Sportade and was drinking it so fast, red liquid cascaded from the corners of his mouth. Was this the effect of the raw duck, or was Drew a victim of the flu? Someone must have brought it with them to the party last night. Mike had been wrong to think they needed an army. They could have gotten food without risking exposure. What else could Mike be wrong about?

Mike and the Tarrytown guys busted in with the remains of the haul from the IMAX. Behind them was the handful of people from the party whom they'd recruited to their cause. It was tough squeezing them all onto the catwalk, but it was the safest place either Mike or Marco could think of.

Marco pressed himself against the far wall and listened to the radio chatter while Mike brought the n00bs up to speed on the situation. Everyone seemed pumped for a battle with security. Clearly, some of the new recruits had been residents of Goldman's jails and were interested in getting some payback.

The radio provided nothing of interest, mostly just movements of people, more teens at the med center. And then things changed.

"New orders." It was Goldman again. *"Bitch says to evac all healthy adults and children to the HomeMart. Chen confirms new strain affecting teens."*

Marco nearly choked on his own spit. New strain? What new strain? How could there be a new flu strain? *Unless.* Unless this was some sort of weapon. Had the senator concocted some mutant flu with Dr. Chen in the med center to take care of her teenager problem now that the party thing was off the table? No. She couldn't. Impossible. She *wouldn't* do anything like that, even if she could.

Then again, her security force was Tasering people at will and stun gunning guys in the nuts to gain information. What was really outside her moral code at this point?

He decided to run the concept by Mike.

"You have got to be screwing with me," Mike said.

Marco turned on the radio and let Mike hear the chatter for himself. The HomeMart was being reorganized to accept more residents. The number of teenaged flu victims was up fifty percent.

Mike handed Marco back the radio. "Should I be surprised? They shot at us. This is just a new weapon. These people are sick bastards." He ran his hands over his face.

"Fine. Great. So the gloves are off. Perfect." He then kicked the handrail with such force, Marco was surprised that the thing did not explode off its hinges. After a few breaths, Mike again looked at Marco. "If they're moving to the HomeMart, they've got to take food with them."

"Which means they've got to move the food either through the service halls or across the main hallway." Marco sensed where Mike was going.

"They'll take the main hallway," Mike said. "It's faster, and they sound like they've got a deadline."

The term struck an odd chord in Marco. *Dead*line.

Mike stood and clapped his hands. "New plan, people," he said. "We hit the food convoy. Ready yourselves for a showdown."

It took all Shay's willpower to keep from running back to Ryan. Screw Ruthie. The kid could fend for herself. Shay needed Ryan. The only important thing was getting to Preeti.

But she did not turn around. She would do this herself. She gripped her tire iron and made the last turn in the service halls before entering the dominion of the post office.

"Hello?" she screamed. "Crazy postal people?"

Her voice echoed around her. Maybe they had a less insulting name for themselves.

"I've come to trade for what you wanted!"

The door in the wall down the hall slammed open.

"It *is* her," said the girl who propped open the door. The same girl Shay had attacked. *Sydney.* She had a nasty scratch on her cheek.

Shay took the tire iron from its holster. "I am willing to give you the card if you give me some information."

A flood of people poured out in front of the girl.

"Oh, you'll be willing," she said.

The gang ran toward Shay. She did not move. When they came within range, she swung the tire iron. The first guy dodged her swing and grabbed the metal, wrenching it from Shay's grasp. Hands grabbed her arms and legs and lifted Shay up, carrying her toward Sydney.

Sydney patted Shay down while they held her.

"Where is it?" she asked after having completed a disturbingly thorough search of Shay's person.

"You think I'm stupid enough to have it on me?"

The gang dropped Shay to the floor.

"So you wised up since yesterday," Sydney said.

Shay rubbed her butt—a nasty bruise was forming. "You tell me what I want to know, and I will tell you where the card is."

Sydney held out a hand. "Deal."

Shay pushed herself up. "Let's see if you can help me first."

Sydney led Shay through their system of slightly sealed doorways to the mailroom, where the claw-fisted leader sat perched on his mail sorter.

"What the hell is she doing back here?" he snarled. He sported a black eye. *A gift from Ryan,* Shay guessed, smiling.

Sydney explained Shay's offer.

"Information?" he asked, turning back to Shay.

"I need to know where my sister last checked in."

The leader glanced over at one of his cronies with a laptop. "You give me a name, and Giles over there can find her for you."

"Preeti Dixit."

Giles typed, then nodded.

The leader cocked his head. "Where's the card?"

Shay had to decide whether to trust him. Screw it. She didn't trust him, but what other choice did she have?

"Behind the fire alarm, around the corner from where I met your girlfriend over there." Shay nodded toward Sydney.

The leader pointed at Sydney, who was out the door and back in less than a minute. As she walked back in through the door, she waved the card above her head and grinned like she'd discovered the thing all on her own.

The leader then pointed to Giles.

"She last checked in at the JCPenney," Giles said, immediately returning to whatever his job was on the laptop.

"That can't be right," Shay said, confused. "I looked for her in the JCPenney last night. She wasn't there."

The leader shrugged. "You asked me to tell you where she last checked in, not where she was."

"But your guy is wrong."

"Girlfriend," the leader said, "my guy is just reading what the mall people have in their system, and if their system is good at anything, it's tracking the people who want to be tracked. If your sister wasn't in the JCPenney, that's because she went off the grid, like yourself." The leader pointed at Giles again. "Where is this little lady supposed to be at this moment?"

Giles typed, then said, "I have two Dixits, one Preeti

in the JCPenney, and one Shaila who was last checked in as 'Jail.'"

The leader raised his eyebrows. "You're a real rebel, aren't you?"

Shay felt like the wind had been knocked out of her. Preeti in the JCPenney? But where? She began walking toward the door.

"What, no thank-you?" the leader yelled.

Shay pushed past Sydney and made her way toward the nearest exit. All the security doors on the JCPenney side of the mall were busted, so getting back into the service halls was not an issue. She would sneak in the back and search every square inch of the JCPenney until she found Preeti. And if she wasn't there? *No.* She would be there. She had to be there.

NOON

There was nothing more frustrating than trying to deal with a stubborn six-year-old, it turned out. Ryan had had an easier time suffering through tackle drills during preseason two-a-days than waiting out Ruthie's moods. She was currently hunched over her knee, making a friendship bracelet.

"You can take as long as you want, Ruthie," he said, breaking the stuffy silence. "But you know I'm right that you have to go back into the mall." He'd spent the entire morning trying to convince her of the craziness of staying in this SUV. He and Shay trying to scrape together some survival strategy? Insane, but possible. He and Shay and the six-year-old Tahoe Tyrant? Just totally insane.

He shifted on the seat so he was at least somewhat in her field of vision. "We haven't eaten all day," he said. "The only food is either held by gangs or doled out by the mall people. I can't risk stealing food from the gangs when

I might get hurt or caught and leave you starving in this truck waiting for me."

Ruthie snapped a knot into place. "They let Jack die." The bracelet was an inch thick and wrapped in a complicated pattern like a snake.

Ryan put his hand over the bracelet, drawing her eyes away from it and to his face. "Whatever else the mall people are doing," he said, "they're not trying to kill anyone."

He wanted to believe that was true. Even after the chief of security beat him. It was just like after any time his dad hit Thad or his mom or him. Something told Ryan that there was caring behind the fist. Maybe it was just the fact that his dad never actually killed any of them. That little bit he held back—wasn't that a type of care?

Ruthie continued her bracelet, tied each knot with a fierce tug. Tears trickled down her cheeks. Ryan wondered if this was a good sign. He dug around in the disaster on the floor for a tissue of some sort and, finding one, held it out to her.

"I will try to keep you safe here for as long as I can, but I can't promise—"

"I'll go." Ruthie took the tissue and wiped her face dry. She tucked the bracelet into her pocket and climbed over to Ryan.

She sounded angry. Did she think Ryan was just trying to get rid of her? *Am I?* He placed his hand on her shoulder. "I'm sorry," he said. "About everything."

Ruthie smiled, then dug the bracelet out and held it in her open palm. "Take it," she said. "So you remember me."

Ryan closed her fingers around it. "Finish it," he said. "Give it to me when we get out of here."

Ruthie tried to hold on to her smile, even as she started to cry. "When we get out." She nodded her head like that made it so.

She collected what few things she wanted from the SUV into a plastic bag, and then they walked toward the central pavilion. Ryan noticed that the showers were all off and no line waited to use them. He tried not to take that as a bad sign. But then they arrived in the empty first-floor courtyard. Shouts echoed around the vacant hallways, and Ryan heard the rattling of a gate, but saw no one.

"Where is everyone?" Ruthie pressed against his leg.

Ryan was clueless, as usual. "Let's check the school."

But the food court was empty. He led Ruthie by the hand up to the third floor, less to make sure she didn't run away than because he needed the reassurance that he wasn't alone. It was completely freaky not being sur-rounded by strangers after all this time.

Baxter's was empty. Whole rows of books had been removed from the shelves. Taken by people. But where?

Ryan heard a noise in the back. He dragged Ruthie toward it. No gang of teenagers would be sneaking around Baxter's. And he was right—it was Shay's old buddy Kris the asswipe. He was packing books into a hiking backpack.

Ryan cleared his throat. "Is this all that's left of the school?"

Kris was so startled, he dropped the books and fell back against an empty shelf. "You scared the crap out of me," he said when he saw it was Ryan.

"Where is everyone?"

Kris scowled. "Where're Shay and Preeti? Have you gotten them into trouble?"

This guy seemed desperate to get punched in the face. "Shay is looking for Preeti, seeing as you were so helpful in letting her see her sister."

Kris pushed himself up. "I was trying to cover for the fact that Preeti's been MIA for days. I just wanted Shay to come back. I want to keep her safe."

"So do I."

Kris shook his head. "Running around in the service halls playing bandit is not safe."

Ryan took a deep breath and recalled that his mission here was to get Ruthie into the mall's protection, not kick the crap out of losers with attitude. Ruthie was hiding behind the shelf. Ryan dragged her out. "Don't worry," he said. "This guy is a teacher."

Kris's attitude changed upon noticing Ruthie. "Why is she still out here?"

"Out where?"

"Everyone who's not you or me, meaning between the ages of thirteen and thirty, has been evacuated to the HomeMart."

"Evacuated?" Were some people being allowed to leave?

"There's some new flu strain," Kris said. "It only affects people our age, they think. So the senator ordered that everyone who isn't a teenager or college-aged person be protected from this new disease by segregating them in the HomeMart. The rest of us are being rounded up to die."

This smelled like a lie to Ryan. The senator just didn't

want to deal with the likes of Mike anymore. She was cutting them out of her little society. Well, fine. No problem. Like Ryan had gotten anything from them but a black eye. But Ruthie. She could be protected.

Ryan pushed Ruthie toward Kris. "Take her with you," he said. "Please."

"*With* me?" Kris asked, laughing cruelly. "Were you not paying attention? I am persona non grata in the Home-Mart, so bully for us." He swung his arm like this was a joke.

"Then take her to the HomeMart when you take these books there," Ryan said. "You are packing them for the HomeMart?"

Kris looked at Ruthie, who was scanning the Baxter's as if she expected the books to attack her. He nodded.

Ryan helped Kris pack the rest of his stash of books, CDs, and DVDs, then they hoisted the boxes and began the trek down to the HomeMart with Ruthie hanging from Ryan's shirt like a tag. Everything was empty until they reached the first floor. As they exited the elevator near the HomeMart, Ryan noticed a pallet of food leaving the Sam's Club, guarded by five security guards. It rolled toward them. Then he heard a scream. Screams.

Kids came pouring out of the service halls. Ryan didn't have to see Mike or Marco to know that this was their gig. He dropped his books, hoisted Ruthie like a fumbled ball, and ran for the HomeMart.

As he reached the half-shuttered entrance to the gigantic hardware store, a wall of security formed to halt his advance. They leveled Tasers and stun batons at him, raised riot shields.

"Get back, punk!" one shouted.

Ryan held up Ruthie. "I'm just dropping her off!"

Ruthie screamed and writhed in his arms. "I don't want to go!"

A woman poked her head between the riot shields, then shoved the guards apart. "Give her to me!"

Kris, who'd finally caught up, took Ruthie. "That's Alison," he said. "She will take care of you."

Ruthie, maybe simply because she was scared out of her mind, stopped crying. Kris walked her to the line of security while Ryan remained where he was, hands up before the firing squad.

When Kris passed her to the woman, Ruthie began screaming again. "RYAN!"

He did not move except to wave to her and smile, like this was totally normal, him standing arms raised before a line of men in riot gear. Then the gunshots echoed around the space. It took Ryan a second to realize he had not been shot, or even shot at.

Kris grabbed his arm. "We have to get out of here!"

Ryan looked around for where the shots had been fired. "Is someone shooting?"

"A gang is trying to loot the food caravan."

Turning, Ryan saw more pallets of food rolling out of the Sam's Club. At the center of each pallet was a guard with a gun, and he was firing on the crowd of people running toward the line. A crowd of people that included Mike and Drew—even wearing ski masks, they were recognizable to Ryan.

Ryan jerked his arm free of Kris's hold and drilled into the nearest guard, took his stun baton, and zapped the gunner. Ryan then rolled away from the convoy and behind the protection of an escalator's handrail, then began scanning the mess of people for Mike or Drew. There were four other pallets, each with a gunner, but they weren't firing blindly. They probably had a limited amount of ammo, and had been warned about blowing it all in the first minute.

The teens had taken cover behind the giant pots and benches, scaffold columns and garbage cans. Ryan peered over the handrail and caught sight of Drew. He was leaning on a column. He clutched his chest. Had he been hit? He coughed and blood dribbled from his mouth. Drew looked at the red sputum on his hand like he was confused.

Ryan bolted out from behind the handrail to where Drew stood. "Where are you hit?" he yelled.

Drew held out his hand. "Why am I coughing blood?"

Ryan searched his body for the entrance wound. There was nothing. Drew stumbled forward, grabbed the column for support, then dropped to his knees.

"Drew!" Ryan screamed. "Did they shoot you?" He grabbed Drew's face. His skin was hot and dry.

"Shrimp?" Drew asked, as if seeing him through a fog. "Where've you been?"

Ryan tried to drag Drew to his feet. He had to get him out of there. "Get up, dude!" he yelled, leaning back against Drew's weight. "You need help."

Drew's eyes rolled back into his head. He began to convulse, jerking himself free of Ryan's grasp and dropping onto the tiles. Bloody, foamy spit bubbled over his lips.

"Drew!" Ryan screamed, stepping back. What the hell was happening?

Mike was suddenly beside him, then kneeling next to Drew. "Drewski!" he screamed, shaking Drew's shoulders. He slapped his friend in the face. "Drew, you ass, get the hell up!" Drew's head flopped on his neck.

A bullet blew out the neon sign on the scaffold above Ryan's head. "Mike, we've got to get out of here!"

Mike shook Drew again. "Drew!" Blood was now running out of his nose and mouth.

A crowd of riot-gear-clad security guards came flooding out of the HomeMart. Ryan knelt, shoved an arm under Mike's chest, and lifted him. "Get up, you idiot!" Ryan drove Mike away from the nightmare like a tackling bag down the practice field.

Mike clung to Drew's shirt until it ripped. He stumbled backward, letting Ryan push him toward the wall, then into the service hall and into the dark. The screams from the main courtyard followed them until the door slammed shut and left them in silence.

Marco's team exploded onto the scene from the empty store across from the Sam's Club. He had unlocked the gate from the inside and at the precise moment of his command, one of his team had cut the chain, causing the thing to roll up like a snapped shade. He had waited until the caravan was mere feet from the gate, and his team was able to completely overwhelm the first pallet's guards and clean the whole thing of its food.

How disappointing, amidst this triumph, to look over and see Mike backpedaling away from the battle ground with that defector Ryan. It was almost as if it didn't matter that Marco had stuck by Mike through everything. That

Marco had made Mike's very survival in the mall possible.

Well, frak him right in the ass.

"Leon, take team two and hit the next pallet from the other side of the escalator!"

Leon nodded and raced from the store, nail gun sending out a spray of cover fire to clear a path for his team. Marco waved for his team to attack from this side, pinning the second pallet between two screaming hordes of starving, mildly hungover, and incredibly pissed-off people wielding bats and other assorted weaponry. It almost wasn't fair.

The reinforcements Goldman had sent out were afraid to come too close, thanks to the guy and girl Marco had armed with bows on the second floor. A near constant, if not necessarily on target, rain of arrows held them back. Then there were the four girls Marco had given hairspray and lighters to: instant flamethrowers. It was truly an impressive display. If he weren't defending his pile of Cheerios boxes with his trusty hockey stick, he would have patted himself on the back.

"Fall back to base!" he screamed, seeing that most of the second pallet had been cleared.

Even Mike's teams signaled their agreement and everyone began to flee for their assigned service exits. Marco had plotted varying routes through the service halls for each team to take back to the bowling alley such that if one got caught, it would not be immediately apparent where they were headed. Yet another stroke of genius. Stroke after stroke after stroke. If Mike wanted to turn tail with Shay's douche-y boyfriend, then who the hell needed him? Marco could run this operation solo.

■ ■ ■

After searching the stockroom on the first floor of the JCPenney, Shay moved on to the second-floor stockroom. She had to find Preeti. Because if she wasn't in the JCPenney, then she was lost somewhere in the maze of the mall and all hope was lost.

Near the back corner, beyond a clutter of nearly impenetrable toppled racks, Shay noticed a large stack of cardboard boxes. They were conspicuous in that they were the only such pile in the room. She had to remove the racks one at a time, dragging them back across the floor—it amazed her that no guard had come to arrest her, given the ruckus she was making crashing around. Finally, she pulled the first box from the pile and struck gold.

Preeti stared at her with bloodshot eyes from within the cave of boxes. On the ground next to her lay two young girls. Shay had seen them before at the school.

Preeti screamed, but then realized that it was Shay and not a guard. She dissolved into tears and flung her arms around Shay's neck. "I'm so sorry!" she cried.

It was the exact thing Shay had wanted to tell her sister. What did Preeti have to be sorry for?

Preeti wailed about how her friends had gotten sick two nights ago. They were all scared, and Preeti didn't want them to go to the med center and leave her all alone, so she convinced them to hide with her in the stockroom. Only they had gotten worse and worse and were now asleep, she thought, and burning hot. "I just didn't want them to die like Nani," she whimpered. "I couldn't lose anyone else."

Shay hugged her sister. Hidden beneath these words

was her own betrayal. Preeti would never have had to worry about being alone if Shay had held it together for her sister's sake. She clung to Preeti as tightly as she could and whispered into her hair that it would be okay now, that everything would be okay.

When Preeti had calmed down enough, Shay let her go and sat her outside the cave. Then she took a look at the two other girls. Both of them had terrible fevers. They groaned when Shay touched their foreheads, as if her warm hand were a cooling cloth.

Shay took off her sweatshirt and tore it to pieces, then told Preeti to wet them in the bathrooms. She dug Nani's children's Tylenol bottle out of her bag and dribbled what was left in it between the girls' cracked lips. When Preeti returned, she handed Shay the dripping cloths.

"I screwed up," she said. "I killed them."

Shay heard her own fears from her sister's mouth. She placed the cloths on the girls' heads, then took Preeti's hands. "You couldn't do anything to help them." Shay led her out of the cave and fished in her bag for her hand sanitizer, then rubbed it on Preeti's skin. "Even the people in the med center can't help people with the flu. You tried to save them the best you could. Now it's time we take them to the professionals and get you somewhere safe."

Preeti nodded, seemed happy to leave the decisions to Shay.

Just then, the mall speakers squealed. "Residents of Stonecliff. The mall is now on lockdown. Remain where you are until further notice. Any individual found in any of the open hallways or in the service hallways will be deemed hostile and dealt with in the appropriate manner. This is your only warning."

Preeti's eyes were wide with fear. Her lip trembled. Shay wanted to scream and run—what had happened to cause this new terror? How would she get back to Ryan? But she had Preeti now; she had what she'd searched for. She would do right by her sister, the way she should have since the beginning.

Shay took Preeti by the shoulders. "We are going to be fine," she said. "Let's look for cups or bottles or something and get some water, and then we'll search for some food."

"What's going on?" Preeti whined.

"I'm here now," Shay said. "Everything is going to be okay."

Preeti nodded her head like Shay's very words could alter reality. Shay smiled as if the world were already coming up roses. Preeti wiped her hand under her nose and began hunting for bottles. Shay allowed herself five seconds of terror, then got up and followed her own advice.

F I V E
P.M.

Ginger had never been in trouble before, and so even though she and Maddie were only in a fake jail in a Stuff-A-Pal Workshop in a quarantined mall, she was still completely freaked out. Insane thoughts like *Will this end up on my permanent record?* and *Will Princeton know I stole designer clothes?* burbled through the general fog of anxiety that was her brain.

For Maddie, this was nothing special. But Maddie was a rebel. Maddie once had to be picked up by her mom at the police station after getting nabbed running out the back door of a party at some senior's house.

"God, will these people ever shut up?" Maddie groaned, shifting her position against the wall. The other inmates were banging on the security gate and hollering at the air. Ginger was too terrified of them to say anything, but Maddie? She would pick a fight at this point just to end her boredom.

"I feel like screaming too," Ginger said. "Those gun-shots this morning? What is going on?"

Maddie shrugged like gunshots were so blah. "It's the beginning of the end, dearest. Bend over and kiss your tight little ballet butt good-bye."

Maddie could be absolutely infuriating with her end-of-the-world, bummer sarcasm. Like it helped anything to give up. Ginger never quit anything. First of all, it looked bad to quit. There were sayings—Quitters suck and some such. Maddie never cared about how things looked, but Ginger did. And through her caring she'd saved Maddie's rear end on more than one occasion. Call her a tight-ass or whatever, but sometimes being a tight-ass made all the difference.

"The next time the guard comes by, I am asking him to call Lexi's mom again."

"Your senator in shining armor is not going to swoop in and save our collective butt. You've had him call her, what? Five times now?"

"She's busy." Ginger was not a quitter. Even after five calls. Had she not gotten a date with Geoff Renner through persistent calling?

Maddie rolled her eyes. "Not like there's anything bet-ter to do anyway."

They'd been in jail for over twenty-four hours. Bottles of water had been thrown in along with granola bars twice now, as if they were animals at the zoo. Ginger felt like they should have been given a phone call or seen a law-yer or something. That was what happened on TV. Of course, not only were they not on TV, but not even in the real world. Rule of law was a foreign concept. Her father would not be happy to hear about that when they got out. Ginger was always careful to say *when* and never *if,* even when only thinking it to herself.

She spotted a guard coming. *Probably coming to feed the tigers once again . . .* But the guy was empty-handed. Maybe food was a luxury hardened criminals were no longer allowed.

She pressed herself against the security gate and waved her arms for his attention. "Hey!" she yelled. "Has the senator sent a message for me yet?"

The guard looked at a scrap of paper in his hand. "You Ginger Franklin or Madeline Flynn?"

Ginger's heart leaped. "I'm Ginger!"

The guard told her to take Maddie and go to the back of the sales floor, to the farthest door on the right. When it opened, there were two guards in riot gear with tall, clear plastic shields.

"Ginger Franklin?" one asked.

Ginger raised her hand, prompting a groan from Maddie. "This is not homeroom."

Flashing Maddie a smirk, Ginger shuffled between the shields, then waited in the blissful emptiness of the stockroom for Maddie to be let through. The guard led them down a series of back hallways and staircases up to the third floor. A lot of the doors looked like they'd been attacked—holes marred the door frames above the locks, and ripped wires hung loose like stiff hairs.

"Is there something going on?" Ginger asked. Between the gunshots, the lockdown, the busted door locks, and the makeshift jails, things did not seem to be running quite as smoothly as earlier in the week.

The guard laughed. "Something?" He pushed open a service door leading back into the mall proper. "Kid, the crap has hit the fan."

Maddie raised her eyebrows, as if to say *See?*

The guard let them into a collection of offices off the hall near the skating rink. He pointed to the far wall and said, "Last door on the left." They walked inside and he slammed the door to the mall behind them.

"The hospitality here is first rate," Maddie said as they walked. "And the décor? *Fab-oo!*" She waved her hand to indicate a stack of cots like the ones they'd slept on in the JCPenney, next to which lay piles of dirty clothing.

The senator was talking on a cell phone—*CELL PHONE!* How did she have a cell phone?

"Look, Commander, I am not making this up to spoil your grand endgame plans. Yes, I am happy to know that this new development puts on hold your final solution, but I am also in the unfortunate position of informing you that the virus has in fact mutated."

Ginger was afraid to breathe for fear of alerting the woman to their presence. Maddie too stood uncharacteristically still and quiet.

The senator continued, "Dr. Chen told me he suspects it might be another H5N1 strain, or something very similar. No, I have no idea why he suspects this. You want answers, you'll have to talk to him. Well, he's a little busy right now actually doing the research you want information about."

She wheeled in her chair and noticed them lurking in her doorway. "Commander, I will call you back." She touched the phone's screen and placed it on the desk.

"Girls," she said, smiling. "I'm sorry it's taken so long to get you out of that jail."

Lexi's mom indicated that they should sit, and so they did. Maddie's jaw hung open slightly. Ginger took that as her cue to answer for them both.

"No problem," she said, smiling. *Mutated flu?*

"I hate to admit that I was only able to get you released for a single purpose."

"Anything," Ginger said, hands squeezed between her jiggling legs. *Final Solution?* Wasn't that what they called the Holocaust? Was there a holocaust in the plans for the mall?

"I seem to have lost my daughter." She slid an iPad across the desktop. On it was displayed Lexi's check-in record. "Lex seems to have checked in to the JCPenney yesterday and has not been seen since."

"It's not like we did anything," Maddie said, suddenly recovering the power of speech. "We were in jail the whole time."

The senator nodded. "I'm not saying you did anything. I'm asking for your help. I can't leave this office without a four-man security detail. But you two, you can look for her without attracting so much attention."

"Why not send your security goons to look for her?" Maddie said. Ginger did not think the senator was a woman who took kindly to attitude from any corner.

But Lexi's mom did not rise to Maddie's taunt. "Security is rather busy at the moment controlling a small riot of unruly teenagers. I have been informed that they will commence searching for Lexi at their earliest oppor-

tunity. I would like to begin the search earlier than that."
Ginger noted the bitter tone in the senator's voice. There
was clearly a problem between the senator and her security team.

Ginger was fine helping look for Lexi, but she recalled
the earlier announcement of a lockdown. "Excuse me,
Senator, but didn't you announce that anyone caught in
the halls would be shot or something?"

"She doesn't care if we get shot," Maddie snapped.

The senator frowned. "I would care very much if you
got shot. If there was any other way, I would do it, but
you're my only hope. Here." She pulled a card out of her
pocket. "Take my access card. It will let you through any
door in the mall. Once you find Lexi, bring her to the
HomeMart. We're segregating the adult and child population from the teens and college-aged kids. It seems this
new variant of the flu only affects you guys, but Dr. Chen
said we shouldn't take any chances. However, I will protect you three. I've designated a special room for you in
the HomeMart."

A special room? Was this supposed to be a comfort?

Maddie snatched the card from the table. "We'll look
for her," she said. "But not for you."

The senator smiled. "Thank you," she said. "If you get
in trouble, call on this." She slid a walkie-talkie across the
table. Maddie snatched that up as well.

"You'll protect us?" Ginger finally blurted.

"Just bring Lexi to the HomeMart," the senator said.

"Let's go," Maddie said, grabbing Ginger's arm. She
didn't so much as nod good-bye to the senator.

"Bye," Ginger said. Politeness was a reflex; it felt wrong to be rude.

Maddie practically dragged her down the hallway. "I can't believe it," she muttered. "I can't freaking believe it."

Ginger staggered to walk straight. "What can't you believe? That Lexi's lost?"

Maddie gave her that I'm-sorry-you're-that-slow look she often flashed. "Lexi disappearing I can believe. She went after Marco, obviously. What I can't believe is that I was right. From the beginning, I was like, they're just going to blow the mall up with us inside it, and I was totally right!" She laughed. What she said was not remotely funny.

"No." Ginger shook her head for emphasis. "That was not what she meant."

Maddie turned the look up a notch. "What do *you* think she meant?"

Ginger kept shaking her head as if that could change things. "Not that. My dad wouldn't let them blow me up."

That really got Maddie laughing. "You're dad's a pretty scary asshole, but he's not Superman. If the army or government or whoever wants to blow you up, he can't do diddly crap about it."

"You're wrong," Ginger said, though she wasn't entirely clear on what she thought Maddie was wrong about. Her dad hadn't been able to get her out of the mall. And the senator did say "final solution." What was more final than ending the flu where it started by nuking the place?

Maddie opened the service door and led them into the back hallways. Ginger was uncomfortable in the blank, tomblike service halls. Maddie, on the other hand, moved through them like she worked there. Maddie had an excellent sense of direction. Or perhaps it was just that all their time in the Shops at Stonecliff had finally produced a practical benefit.

Many of the doors were broken, so Maddie only used the card to let them into stockrooms when they heard someone coming. They agreed that running into anyone was worse than missing Lexi. First off, if she was running through the halls, she would probably be caught and end up in jail, and the senator would find her without their help. They agreed that the senator could not be counted on to get them released from jail a second time, seeing as she only got them out to save her daughter.

Second, Lexi was not the kind of person who would run blindly through the halls. Lexi thought stuff through. She would know that stumbling around the halls after a lockdown was utter idiocy. She would hide out. So exploring the stockrooms was both a defensive maneuver and part of the overall plan.

They reached a fire stairwell, on the other side of which was the door to the IMAX, which was the last known location of the party Maddie and Ginger had consistently failed to get into. Maddie figured this was the first place to look.

"Lexi said something about Marco being at the party," Maddie said. "It seems a logical place to start."

"Assuming she went looking for him." Lexi had been pissy with Ginger ever since the whole Abercrombie thing. Why did Lexi blame her for running away? She was protecting herself! Even Maddie had forgiven her.

"Trust me," Maddie said, pulling open the door. Of course, Maddie was snarkier than normal. Maybe "forgiven" was too strong a term.

The IMAX was relatively empty, but Ginger could tell from the stench of stale beer and sickly sweet fruitiness emanating from the carpet that there had been a party of major proportions in the place.

Maddie peered into a giant plastic bin near the wall. "Looks like we missed quite the event."

Some kids stood around a keg trying to squeeze the last drops of skunked beer from the bottom. Others simply loitered on the terraced floor and chatted like this was the high school's courtyard during free period. They must have decided it was safer to stay in a forbidden location than wander the halls during the lockdown.

"I don't see Marco," Maddie said, scanning the room, hand shielding her eyes.

"I don't see Lexi either."

"So I guess we start combing the million or so square feet of the rest of the mall?" Maddie smirked. This was an impossible task, and they both knew it.

Just then, the back doors to the theater exploded open and the unhinged rows of seating stacked in front of them were launched into the room. The closest ex-partiers screamed and crawled away from the debris. Then two muffled gunshots echoed around the walls. Columns of smoke hissed up from the floor. A girl near the canister grabbed her face and screamed, "My eyes!"

Maddie pushed Ginger toward the door to the fire stairwell. "Go!"

Ginger watched another canister fly through the air toward the lit tiki torches beneath the movie screen. One passed too close to the flame and exploded like a firecracker, lighting the nearby curtain on fire. Security guards streamed into the room. People shrieked, ran toward her. Then the sprinklers popped on and a stream of water woke her from the stupor of fear.

Ginger bolted toward the fire door. Maddie was on the other side waiting for her.

"I can't see," Maddie yelled. "Some of the smoke got in my eyes." She coughed. "Throat too." She held out the senator's card.

Was she asking Ginger to take over planning?

"Let's go!" she wheezed.

Maddie had asthma. Even a little tear gas would hurt her. Ginger snapped out of it, grabbed the card, and took Maddie's hand.

She ran through doors, knowing only that they needed to get away from the IMAX. Security was concentrated there. Which meant they would not be in other places. She saw a door marked ACTION ARCADE and slid her card through its reader.

The back of the arcade was dark and cluttered with old game systems and spare parts. Ginger led Maddie deeper into the darkness, finally stopping when she noticed her friend holding her throat.

Ginger dropped Maddie on a chair, then ran to find a sink and a glass. Luckily, there was a bar in the arcade and both were available. She brought Maddie the water, which she slurped, then coughed up.

"We're safe," Ginger said, feeling the need to offer a word of comfort. Were they safe? She had no idea what the word even meant anymore.

Maddie took another sip of water. "I can't breathe."

Ginger remembered Maddie's inhaler. "Your inhaler?"

"Cot," she said.

Ginger nodded. One floor down. She scurried back through the dark storage area, swallowed, then opened the door and ran down the service hall away from the IMAX. She hit a stairwell and went down it. She was next to the Lord & Taylor. The JCPenney was just down the hall. She ran toward it, burst into the back stockroom, then crept through the dim light to the door and onto the sales floor.

Luckily, there was no one in the sales floor area—where was everyone? Who cared? This was a good thing. She crawled to where Lexi, Maddie, and she had slept. Thank goodness, their stuff was still there. She grabbed her and Maddie's purses, found the inhaler, and crawled back to the stockroom. She thought she heard voices, but decided she did not have any interest in sticking her nose in anyone else's business and let herself back into the maze of the service halls.

By some miracle, she made it back to the arcade without first off, getting lost, or second, running into hostile forces. Maddie was lying back against the wall clutching her chest. Ginger handed her the inhaler, which she sucked on several times before breathing normally. Ginger could cry to see her take a deep breath.

Maddie dropped her head back. "And I had given you up as a coward."

Ginger wiped her eyes. "It's incredibly motivating to see someone choking to death."

"But not coughing up a lung?"

What could she say to make up for the past? "I freaked, I admit it. I don't want to die. But I should have stayed. I should have helped."

Maddie kicked her gently. "At least you admit it."

"I'm sorry." Ginger knelt beside Maddie and dropped her head on her shoulder.

"I know," she said, and kissed Ginger's hair.

"Should we go out again?" Ginger did not want to go out again.

"I think we deserve a small rest," Maddie said, taking another pull on her inhaler.

"Lexi will be okay?"

"None of us will be okay," Maddie said. "But she'll live. Or not. With or without our help. Might as well wait until we're at least not being actively chased by the cops to begin our needle-in-a-haystack search."

Ginger nodded. Maddie was back in charge. That was a good thing. Ginger was not good at being in charge. Not in crisis situations. She snuggled against Maddie and felt her arm hug her closer. At least they had each other.

Marco sat against the back wall of the pinsetters' catwalk counting and recounting his army. What had originally numbered somewhere near thirty was down to ten. Only his teams had returned. Mike's were lost somewhere in the mall. Captured? *Probably*.

Scanning the police radio for information, Marco

got nothing but vague chatter. Everything was coded—numbers were rarely given, names never, locations not at all. Goldman must suspect that he and Mike had a radio. Marco switched the thing off and chucked it against the wall.

They had hauled in a ridiculous amount of food. The recruits were busy tallying the stash so that Marco could work out rations. Heath and Leon—all that was left from Tarrytown, from the football contingent entirely—were in charge of considering what remained of their weapons store.

They could survive with what they had now, that much was obvious. But Marco was concerned that without Mike, the troops would disband with their share of the stash rather than stay together. And then where would Marco be? Alone, defending his pile of food like some rat in a hole?

So be it. If that was how it had to be, then that was freaking fine with him. He'd been alone all his life. He could be alone again.

Heath approached with a smirk on his face. "We lost a crap ton of weaponry, dude."

"We'll survive." Marco didn't need Heath or weapons. Didn't need Mike or any of them.

"Dude," Heath said, slapping Marco's shoulder, "I have zero doubts about your ability to survive. The way you went nuts on that guy with the hockey stick? That was completely off the hook."

Marco tried not to flinch from Heath's touch. Was this the olive branch of friendship? "I'm a big hockey fan," Marco ventured.

"Dude." Heath held up a fist. "That was some beyond fan stuff."

Marco bumped the fist. Heath left him alone like solitude was his due. Like he was their leader.

Could it be? Marco scanned the faces of his remaining army. When they looked at him, they smiled. The hairspray girls waved their lighters at him.

As insane as it seemed, as impossible, as unlikely, as completely illogical, Marco sensed that it was true. He was their leader.

A sense of calm washed over him. His shoulders melted from where they'd crept up against his neck. These people would protect him. Looked to him to protect them. These people—dared he think it?—respected him. *Of all the wonderful accidents* . . .

Marco flipped back on the police radio. He would break the codes. He would figure everything out. He would bring the stragglers of his army back from the brinks of capture or rescue them from whatever jails Goldman had devised for them. He would conquer this new flu weapon. He would conquer all.

Ryan felt odd, bringing Mike to Ruthie's SUV, but in the fog of escaping the chaos of the raid on the food convoy, he'd had to make a quick decision and it was the only thing that popped into his brain.

"You own a car I don't know about?" Mike asked when Ryan opened the door.

"It's a friend's" was all Ryan said about it. Mike's Beamer had been "impounded" after their escape attempt—keys taken, wheels booted in place.

They'd spent the afternoon running through the service halls and stockrooms, hiding where they could and creeping through the shadows when they couldn't. Security was on the hunt: Every guard was in full riot gear, Tasers and stun batons ready to jolt any unaccounted-for teenager into submission. At one point, Ryan even swore he saw some gas hiss into the air around them.

Mike must have expected something like this. The broken service doors did more than lead to the IMAX, they allowed anyone to move from one end of the mall to the other, and then down into the parking garage. But more than that, Mike repeatedly proved his chops as a protector, shoving Ryan out of the line of sight, or forcing back any advancing guards with a random gunshot.

They hid in the truck's belly for several hours, silent, the only noise their breathing. No footsteps echoed around them, no flashlights penetrated the shadows. Security had failed to sniff them out.

Mike apparently felt comfortable enough to take apart his handgun. He snapped the bullets out one by one and stood them like soldiers in a row.

Ryan shifted against the wall of the backseat. "You can stop this," he said.

Mike snapped another bullet from the cartridge. "Didn't start it."

"But you can end it," Ryan said. "If you call off your guys, maybe we could get security to back down. Everything could go back to normal."

Mike looked at Ryan, eyebrows raised like he was barely containing a laugh. "When was anything in here normal?"

The magazine empty, Mike pulled out a small plastic box full of minute tools. He began to clean his gun. "Guns take a lot of care to maintain," he said. "It's almost like having a pet."

Mike sounded nuts, but still, Ryan attempted to reason with him. "The people running this mall aren't evil, Mike. Maybe if we try to talk to that senator lady, tell her about the security chief—maybe we could all just chill out until this whole stupid quarantine thing is over."

Mike exhaled, shook his head. "You really think they're letting any of us out of here alive?" He flashed a look at Ryan. "Just because you don't see the disease doesn't mean you're cured. Your friend the senator has done something to the virus, changed it so the only people it kills are our people." He snapped the barrel of the gun. "Look at what it did to Drew."

So Mike was still convinced of his conspiracy theory. "Mike, Drew died of the flu."

"No," Mike said, slapping the empty magazine back into the handgun. "Marco heard on the radio last night that the doc running the med center had developed a new strain of the flu that only affects teenagers." He took aim at the wall. "Apparently, we've become a bit of a nuisance and they're taking us out to save themselves. How's that for the senator not being evil?" *Snap.* Whatever Mike had in his sights was dead.

Ryan's fingers dug deep into the seat cushion. Mike had to be wrong. There was no way the senator would do that. Why would they sabotage their own society?

"I don't believe that," Ryan whispered.

"Believe whatever you want." Mike began jamming the

bullets back into the magazine, counting each out loud like a prayer.

"When was the last time you slept?" Ryan asked when Mike had finished.

Mike leaned back, ran his hands over his face and through his hair. Then he laughed. "I have no clue." He yawned as if at that instant all that not sleeping had caught up with him.

Ryan placed his hand on the gun. Mike glared at him, a guard dog instinct in his eyes, but then released it.

"I'll take first watch," Ryan said, placing the gun between them on the seat.

Mike stared at the gun a moment longer, then nodded and curled against the door. It seemed like the second he closed his eyes, he was asleep.

Ryan did not touch the gun again. He merely leaned his head against the window glass and prayed that Shay did not return to the car in the night.

It had gotten worse over the last hours. Shay was cold, but not like she needed a sweater, rather like her organs were freezing over. She had a headache, though that was at this point a constant bother. Both of these could have been written off, but just now, when she'd coughed, there'd been blood in her spit. That confirmed the diagnosis. How long before she was choking on the bloody, liquefied remains of her lungs?

Had she gotten the flu from these girls? Did it matter? She now had the flu, which meant that if she didn't find some way to get Preeti out of the JCPenney, the girl would have to watch her sister and her two closest friends die.

Shay dipped the cooling cloths in the clean bowl of water she'd placed on the floor beside the two girls, then laid them back across the girls' foreheads. The lockdown had to end soon. They had to feed people, right? She would wait for the announcement, then convince Preeti to leave.

Preeti returned with two mugs of water. "I could only find two," she said, sitting beside Shay. "I think I heard someone, but they didn't see me." She looked at her friends like she expected them to wake up at any moment, like this was all just a bad dream.

"I came looking for you to apologize," Shay said, sipping the water. She suddenly felt desperately thirsty.

Preeti laid her head in Shay's lap. "I'm glad you found me."

"I'm sorry I ever left."

"Me too."

Just touching her sister's head, knowing that at least she would survive, was all the forgiveness Shay needed.

DAY
FOURTEEN

SHAY

A cough wracked Shay's ribs. She leaned over the clothing rack to avoid hacking lung all over Preeti. A cardboard box caught the spatter; it must have been mostly blood, because Preeti's face crumpled.

"You have the flu?" she asked. "You said it was a cold."

They'd been awake for a little under an hour, Shay guessed, though it was hard to tell. The lights had stayed on all night in the mall, though in the stockroom there was only the one or two usual dim lights glowing, so she had no idea what time it was. Not that it mattered. Whatever the time, Shay had to get Preeti out of the JCPenney.

"I wanted it to be a cold," Shay lied. "But I guess this proves me wrong."

Preeti hugged herself. "You're going to leave me? Again?"

Shay pulled a cooling cloth, now warm, from one of the girls' foreheads and used it to wipe her mouth. "I don't have much of a choice," she said. "So how about this? I'll make you a deal. You go to the HomeMart and stay with the healthy people, and I will stay here and take care of your friends."

Preeti began to chew on her hoodie string. "I don't want to be alone," she said. "Don't make me leave."

"Here," Shay said, pulling the Tagore book from her bag. "He's always kept me company."

Preeti glanced up from the book's cover. "Nana's book? You're giving it to me?" She looked even more miserable.

Shay held Preeti's shoulders and put on her best Scary Parent face, the one Ba always used. "I will only stay and help them"—she glanced at the prone girls—"if *you* go now. The people in the HomeMart will make sure you're safe. You have to stay healthy, okay? One of us has to make it out of this for Ba and Bapuji."

Preeti flung herself into Shay's arms. "I don't want you to die," she whispered.

The room was spinning. Shay wasn't sure how much longer she had before she would pass out. "I'm sorry," she mumbled into Preeti's hair.

"I love you," Preeti said, still clinging to Shay's neck.

Shay felt tears in her eyes. She ran her hand across her lids. She couldn't cry. Crying would only scare her little sister. She needed to put on a good show of health or Preeti would never leave.

"Stop being dramatic," Shay said. "You lived through the flu, right? So will your friends."

"And you?"

"Why not," Shay said, swallowing back the blood of her lungs. "Now go," she commanded. "If a security guard stops you, play dumb and ask directions."

The bitchy-big-sister voice worked like a charm.

"Stop being such a boss," Preeti said, snagging her bag from where she'd left it and shoving Nana's book into it. "I've been doing perfectly well without you telling me what to do."

Shay gave her a playful shove. "So keep on with that."

Preeti gave one last mournful look back, then exited the door. Shay collapsed against a shelf.

She slid to the floor and crawled to the two girls, who were curled like pencil shavings on the floor. Shay shoved the rear end of first one, then the other. "Wake up!" she droned as loudly as possible.

Both girls stirred. Two pairs of red eyes blinked at her.

"Get up and follow me," Shay said. "We are going to the med center."

"But that's where my mom went and she never came back," one of the girls whispered.

"If you stay here, you will die," Shay said in as serious a voice as she could muster. "In the med center, you have a chance." She summoned what strength remained in her and stood. "Now get up!"

The girls, perhaps out of fear that Shay might physically drag them to their feet—an impossibility, though they couldn't know that—pushed themselves to standing.

She held her hands out; they each took one. Then together they stumbled down the escalator and out into the eerie silence of the main hallway.

R Y A N

yan had dozed off; Mike's fist in his shoulder knocked him to waking. Light streaked by the SUV's blackened windows. It was a flashlight beam. Security must have come to flush them out.

Mike pushed one door open slowly, silently, then dropped to his knees on the pavement. He signaled for Ryan to stay, then crept around the side of the SUV.

Ryan crawled forward between the front seats of the truck and peered over the dash. Voices echoed throughout the cement maze of the garage. It was hard to tell where the people were, as opposed to the ghost of a voice.

He could hit the horn, give them away. Get security to take Mike in, stop him from his and Marco's bizarre war. But something kept him from moving: They were teammates. Mike had saved him from the flu, from the cops again and again. How could Ryan throw him to the wolves after all that?

Mike crawled up into the back of the SUV before Ryan could answer the question.

"They've cut us off from the broken door," Mike whispered. He flipped off the gun's safety. "I'll take out two of the closest, then you make a run for the pavilion."

"No," Ryan said, noticing the keys dangling in the ignition. "No more killing."

"Don't be naïve," Mike said. "You think their Tasers are set to tickle?"

"There's another way," Ryan said. He pointed to the keys. "You want to drive?"

Mike's mouth curled into a smirk. "Hell yeah, J. Shrimp."

They got settled into the front seats and buckled their belts before starting the SUV. They had one shot at this— they would drive to the pavilion and make a run for it from there. Mike nodded and turned over the engine.

He slammed the car into gear and hit the gas. The truck squealed out of the space and rammed the car in front of it. Security guys screamed; the nearest guards charged them. Mike dropped the car into reverse, spun the wheel, threw it into first, and drove straight at them. Ryan waved his arms for them to get out of the way. The guards dove for cover. Mike blew past them down the pavement. Ryan gripped the overhead handle as Mike took the turn without braking, nearly flipping the truck.

On the straightaway, Mike floored it for the central pavilion. Guards scattered out of the way, while others rushed to catch up with them from behind. Ryan wondered if they'd actually be able to beat security into the pavilion. Then he saw feet coming down the stairs and escalators.

They would be caught between two different groups. It was over.

How he underestimated Mike.

Mike must have seen the guys on the stairs, because instead of turning and trying some new plan, he sped up.

"You're going to hit the pavilion!" Ryan screamed.

"That's the idea," Mike growled.

The SUV jumped the curb and blew through the glass wall. Shards flashed and flew out; people screamed; security bolted backward up the steps. Mike kept his foot on the pedal. The truck bumped up the wide stairwell between the up and down escalators, the door panels scraping and squealing against the metal walls on either side.

"What the hell are you doing?" Ryan screamed as his head hit the ceiling.

"Escaping," Mike mumbled, sounding far too calm.

The SUV bounced and rumbled up the stairs, then launched out onto the first floor. Mike tried to avoid what tables he could, but he wasn't too careful. The tires must have blown, because the truck shimmied all over the tile and carpet.

Ryan gripped the door frame. "Security's coming up behind us," he shouted, glancing in the fragments of the side-view mirror that remained. "And the car's smoking." Black clouds billowed behind them.

"Then let's get off the road."

Mike turned into the BathWorks, then jerked the wheel and pulled the e-brake, ramming the side of the SUV into a massive wall of shelving. The wood whined, then beams split and the wall fell like a giant domino against its neighbor.

"Ride's over," Mike said, unclipping his seat belt and busting out of the door.

Ryan's hands were shaking and his door was blocked. He undid his belt, kicked what remained of the windshield out of the way, and slid off the hood. Mike bolted toward the back of the store, slammed through the stockroom doors, and raced for the service door. Behind them, Ryan heard sounds of destruction—breaking glass, booming. The walls of shelving must have been toppling, hopefully cutting off any pursuit. Mike had saved his ass once again.

Mike didn't say anything when they reached the service hall. He just raced to a door marked FIRE STAIRWELL, then climbed the stairs like nothing had happened, like he hadn't just taken out most of the first floor of the mall and destroyed an entire store. Ryan's legs felt weak beneath him. He was barely able to make it up the two flights.

The rally point turned out to be the pinsetters' catwalk in the back of the bowling alley; Ryan recalled the door from the stairwell that led right into the hall outside the storage room. It had been busted like the doors near the IMAX. Mike shoved it open and walked right through.

A handful of people lounged around the rickety metal walkway. Security must have taken out most of Mike's team. But not Marco. The instant Mike busted through the door, the kid slunk out of a shadow.

Marco looked terrible. Not that any of them looked particularly good, but the kid was giving off a psycho vibe. He sneered at Ryan. "Rejoined the team?"

Mike threw an arm around Marco. "Leave Shrimp alone," he said. "I'm glad to see you made it, Taco."

Marco's eyes did not leave Ryan's. The hate came off him in waves.

Mike released Marco and clapped his hands. "Let's get this started," he called to the others. "We have a medical center to bust open."

Ryan grabbed Mike's arm. "You're still going through with this?"

Mike patted Ryan's hand. "Of course," he said. "And you're going to be my wingman."

But Ryan had already made this choice.

He pulled his hand from Mike's. "I can't do this."

Mike's eyes narrowed. "I just saved your life," he said. "You owe me."

"I won't hurt people," Ryan said. "I can't survive like this."

"How else do you think you're going to survive?" Mike turned to give Ryan his full attention.

Ryan drew himself up, rolled his shoulders back. "Not this way."

Mike's shoulders drooped for a second. "You sure you want this?"

"I'm sorry, man," Ryan said.

"Me too." Mike snapped to attention, brought the gun up level with Ryan's eyes. "Get out of my sight."

Ryan stared back at Mike. Then nodded and left.

Security was not hard to find. Ryan walked out the front of the bowling alley and looked down over the third-floor railing to see masses of them rallying on the first floor, bunches of black bodies preparing to assault the BathWorks. If they thought Mike was still holed up in there, they did not deserve to find him.

Forget the mall. Let Mike and Marco tear it down. Ryan had to find Shay. She was all that mattered at this point. Ryan took the steps two at a time down the escalators. The instant he hit the second floor, he had guys on him. *Murphy Luck strikes again . . .*

"Hands in the air!" screamed the closest guard. The guy sounded completely freaked. Perhaps the car stunt had unnerved the guards as much as it had Ryan.

He raised his arms. "I'm unarmed!" He did not need a pit stop in jail keeping him from Shay.

The nearest guard grabbed his arms and another shoved something in his ear.

Ryan didn't put up any fight. "I swear, I'm just trying to get to the HomeMart."

"Sure you are," muttered the guard pinning him.

The guy pulled the thing from his ear. "He's clean."

The one holding Ryan's arms pushed him forward. "Move."

Ryan stumbled into a bench. "I'm telling you the truth," he said. "Please, just let me go there." He would figure a way to escape and find Shay once free of these assholes.

The guard didn't even respond. He grabbed Ryan's arm and dragged him toward the Shoe Hut. That was when Ryan began to struggle. The last thing he wanted was another "interrogation session" with Goldman.

"Where are we going?" Ryan asked. "I'm just trying to get to the HomeMart!"

The guard opened a service door with a card key,

dragged Ryan to another door, into the back of the Shoe Hut, then through a third door into the already packed sales floor and slammed it behind him. Inside the room were about twenty other teens, a number of whom hung on the security gate looking out on the mall.

Ryan banged on the door. "You're making a mistake!" he screamed. "Listen to me! I can help you!"

One of the girls told him to stop banging, that he was hurting her head. Another informed him that banging only made them angry. The guard had said that if they didn't keep quiet, they wouldn't get lunch. Apparently, they'd been denied breakfast already.

"You screw up my lunch and I will screw you up," some big kid in a SUNY sweatshirt grumbled from his perch on a display table.

Ryan flung his shoulders against the nearest wall and slid to the floor. He slammed his elbow into the plaster and received a second threat.

It was all over. He had to admit that he'd failed. He'd left Mike to destroy the mall and abandoned Shay inside the destruction. He wished at that moment that he believed in God, in anything. It would have been nice to pray.

GINGER

They'd searched exactly four stockrooms and two kitchens on the third floor and were both beginning to feel hopeless about their search.

"How many stockrooms are there in this godforsaken mall?" Maddie said, opening the door to what looked like a crap shop full of As Seen on TV junk.

Ginger's brain swam in her head. Had she breathed in something in the IMAX? She'd heard of smoke inhalation. Did that screw with your brain? Or was it that she hadn't really eaten anything in—god, when was the last time she ate something?

"Mad," she said. "I don't feel so good."

Maddie instantly turned around and slapped a palm to Ginger's forehead. Then she sighed. "No fever, so it's not the flu. You'll live."

"Do you see any food?" Ginger sat on a large box.

"Does a Magic Dicer count as food?"

"Maybe we should taste it to make sure."

Maddie knelt beside her. "You're a ballet dancer," she said. "I thought you guys didn't eat as a matter of course."

Ginger winced a smile. "Lettuce," she said. "Feed me lettuce."

"All right," Maddie said, standing. "I'm calling off this wild-goose chase. You're wasting away, and I'm breathing on the reserve cylinder in my inhaler. I say we check in with the senator at the HomeMart. Maybe Lexi's already there and we are just wasting our time."

Ginger nodded. Like she had any other choice.

Like two broken dolls, they shuffled through the service halls and out into the mall. They made it to the first floor before they were stopped by a security guard in full riot gear.

"Place your hands on your head and drop flat on the ground!"

Maddie and Ginger looked at each other. Then Maddie reached into her pocket. "I have the senator's card," she began, but the guy hit her in the gut with a stun baton. Maddie doubled over and dropped to her knees.

"Stop!" Ginger screamed. "She has asthma!"

"Get on the ground!"

Ginger tried to help Maddie.

"I said drop before I hit you!"

Ginger folded herself down onto the floor. Every part of her body shook and tears dripped uselessly from her eyes. "Please!" she cried out. "We are working for the senator! Just let us get to the HomeMart!"

"No teens in the HomeMart," the guard said, stepping on Ginger's spine and fastening something around her wrists. He then removed the foot and stepped on Maddie, who groaned and wheezed in response.

"The senator said we were a special case!" Ginger pleaded. "We are helping to find her daughter!"

The guard laughed. "The senator is no longer in charge of the mall, and my orders from Goldman are to bag and tag only."

He shoved a thermometer first in her ear, then Maddie's. He frowned and pulled out his walkie-talkie. "One sick, one clean."

"We're not sick!" Ginger shouted. "She has asthma! Check it again!"

The crazy voice worked. The guy glared at her, then retested Maddie.

"Check that, two clean," he growled into the walkie-talkie. "Where do I take them?"

"*Stuff-A-Pal*," the radio answered. "*New store still being set up. I got one sick to deliver to Harry's.*"

The guy hoisted Maddie onto his back, then pointed a Taser at Ginger. "You going to walk or am I going to have to drag you?"

Ginger crawled to her knees. "I can walk." It was all she could do to keep from shaking to pieces.

He directed her back to the Stuff-A-Pal Workshop, which was now crammed full of people. They banged on the gate as the guard passed, screaming for food, water, freedom. Ginger tried to keep from throwing up. They were locking her in *there*? With *them*? *Again*?

He shoved her and Maddie back through the doors from which they had only recently exited, into the sea of bodies.

"Get off!" a guy screamed, shoving Ginger back like she had landed on him on purpose.

Thanking god for her flexibility, Ginger managed to free her wrists from behind her back, then grabbed Maddie's slumped body and dragged her to the nearest wall. She fumbled in Maddie's bag for her inhaler and gave her a pump.

Maddie coughed, then shook her head. "Don't waste it," she said.

"What should we do?" Ginger asked, knowing how dumb the question was, given their situation.

Maddie looked around at the forest of legs in front of them. "Pray?"

Ginger closed her eyes and wrapped her arms around her friend. "Dear God," she began.

"I was kidding," Maddie said.

But Ginger continued to pray in silence. It was all she had left.

M A R C O

Ryan had long since left the room and yet Mike still held the gun out to where his head had once been. Mike was trembling; his jaw was locked in a snarl.

"He's gone," Marco said, eager to forget Ryan's existence. "Screw him. I'll be your wingman."

Mike remained frozen for a few seconds longer. Then he mimed firing the gun. "Bang." He turned to Marco. Sweat ran in rivulets down his forehead and his eyes were bloodshot. He looked like he hadn't slept in months. He looked like he and Marco were on the same page.

"We're thinking of starting a revolution," Marco said. "I think you could be of some help with that."

"The senator and her security assholes killed Drew," Mike growled. "They've taken everything."

Marco needed Mike, or whatever was left of Mike, to focus. "Sure," he said. "But if you want to beat the senator, we need to take out her eyes and ears. Which means taking out the mall offices."

One of the flamethrower girls joined the pow-wow. "But we just want to stop them spreading this new flu, right?" she said. "Shouldn't we go to the med center?"

"They will stop you dead in your tracks," Marco said, "because they can see you coming. There are cameras covering every inch of the mall. We take out the cameras, we can move without fear of Big Brother."

Mike clapped a hand on Marco's shoulder. "I like it. How do we knock them out?"

Marco figured they could just walk in the front door of the mall offices and take out anyone standing in their way. The hallway was short and narrow enough that they could cover the whole thing from the front door, then neutralize anyone in the adjoining rooms as they moved toward the senator.

"We could snag her as a hostage," Mike said, sounding excited. "Those doctors will have to give us the virus if we have her."

"See how it's all coming together?" Marco replied, hefting Shay's coat. Everything was coming up chaos.

Mike pulled a black ski mask from his pocket and dragged it over his skull. "Let's move."

Marco had determined that a shock-and-awe entrance to the battlefield would best serve their purposes. Thus, Heath hefted a chair through the glass reception window of the mall offices, crawled in, and buzzed open the door. Much to everyone's surprise, the offices were devoid of people.

"What the hell?" a girl observed.

"Interesting," Marco mused. Something strange was going on indeed.

He told Mike to cover him as he broke into the monitoring room for the closed-circuit camera system. There was no one in there either. But from that room, they could see the entire mall. There were few people save security in any of the monitored areas of the mall; teams of security seemed to be moving up the escalators toward the third floor; but the most intriguing activity was at the other end of the mall, at the HomeMart.

"They're done abandoning ship," Marco said, pointing to the relevant screen. On it was pictured the closed-over front of the HomeMart. "They've taken the residents two by two and locked themselves in an ark."

Mike spat at the screen. "If they're not here, then they're not watching. I say we take out the med center."

Marco pointed to a blinking red light. "Remote access. They must have set up a link inside the HomeMart."

"Then unlink it," Mike commanded.

"Why would I know how to do that?" he said.

"So what, then?" Mike was completely relying upon him. It was a delicious feeling.

"We even the playing field." Marco walked out of the room. "If we can't see them, then they shouldn't be able to see us either."

They'd divided into two teams. Marco took Heath and one girl, Kaylee, with him on his mission to the parking level. He handed them little strap-on camping headlamps when they reached the door marked ELECTRICAL.

"Won't there be a light?" Kaylee asked.

"Not for long."

The electrical transformer wasn't in a cage like the HVAC system. It just sat in a room, four fat cubes with little yellow warning signs depicting a hand and a bolt of electricity. Wires came out the top and ran up the wall and across the ceiling.

"What do we do?" Heath asked.

Marco opened the door on one of the cubes, revealing the curved casing of the transformer. "Take the bat off your back and get to it," he said, pointing at the thing. Marco had selected these two in particular because they had wooden bats strapped to their backs.

Heath stared at Marco for a second, a dubious expression on his face, then shrugged and unsheathed his bat.

"This one's for Drew!" he shouted.

The two of them whaled on the thing for a couple of seconds with no result.

"The lights are still on," Kaylee remarked.

Marco flipped up the collar to his coat and took the hockey stick from his back. "Keep hitting it until they no longer are."

The three of them took aim at different parts of the thing, but no amount of abuse led to even a shuddering of the lightbulb. More drastic efforts were needed. Kaylee had a climbing ax hanging from her belt.

"Might I borrow this?" he asked, pointing to the weapon.

She unhooked it and passed it to Marco. There were gloves in the coat's pockets, which Marco slipped on to protect his hands, then he took aim at the center of the nearest cylinder and drove the spike into the transformer's side.

The explosion knocked Marco across the room. Kaylee was thrown into the adjacent transformer. Sparks flashed. She screamed, then didn't—her body fell to the floor. The lights flickered, then blinked out.

A headlamp flashed in Marco's eyes. Marco saw Heath's lips move, heard the word "Marco" all thick like they were under water. Heath grabbed Marco's leg and began dragging him from the room. Marco noticed his arm was on fire. Panicked, he unbuttoned the charred leather coat and let it slip from him. It sunk in that without the coat, he'd have been fried. *Like Kaylee.*

Once in the parking garage, Marco kicked his foot loose from Heath's grasp.

"I can walk," he rasped. He stripped what remained of the leather gloves from his hands.

"Then let's get the hell out of here," Heath said.

As they ran between the cars, headlamp beams bouncing before them, they heard sizzles, saw flashes of light—their lamps bouncing off shattered windshields. But the world was dark now. Marco enjoyed the black.

DR.
C
H
E
N

Doctor Stephen Chen lugged a crate of paper files closer to his worktable in the back of the second-floor stockroom of Harry's department store. Every time he picked anything up, he was reminded of the foolishness that got him, one of the world's experts in influenza epidemics, trapped in an outbreak. *Help carry in a box,* one of the FEMA guys had ordered in those last hours before the lockdown. A single box. One of the godforsaken patients had attacked him as he was leaving the PaperClips and ripped his hazmat suit, exposing him to the virus and thus forcing him to be included in the quarantine. Now he was one of his own statistics. The flu was not without a sense of irony.

He was grateful for the little shrine of candles one particularly religious family had left to honor their dead relation. Because of them, he didn't have to work in the dark.

He was close now, he knew it. He looked over the charts once more. The pattern was in there.

Somewhere outside, a person yowled in pain. It was strange having to deal with real people. He hadn't had a live patient in a decade. As an epidemiologist, he was an expert in computer modeling, calculating the spread of a disease, analyzing how a particular strain of the virus worked to kill a population. Not since residency had he worked with this many actual living, breathing patients.

He was currently examining the charts for those dying or dead from this novel influenza strain. There were some strange anomalies, beyond the obvious only-killing-the-strongest/healthiest/youngest. For example, there were kids who carried dying friends in, kids who'd been completely exposed, and yet they showed no symptoms. What did they have that the others didn't?

His laptop had a few hours worth of battery—if he conserved it, he was sure he could work out what connected them all.

"I found a lantern," Rachel said, appearing in the stockroom. Dr. Rachel Kleinman was the only other doctor in the mall. Statistically, this was improbable. Dr. Chen wrote the anomaly off by assuming that the other doctors had all died. After looking at the vast mounds of corpses on the ice above him, it did not take much of a leap to assume such things.

"We should move anyone with a chance of survival back here," Steve said. "The dark is only going to exacerbate the chaos."

Dr. Kleinman nodded. "I'll get Leslie and Jazmine to

help." They were the remaining two nurses. Ms. Ross had ordered him and all healthy staff to abandon the medical center. Rachel and the two nurses wouldn't leave the patients. Steve himself had stayed to finish his research.

Influenza was a terrible, yet fascinating foe. It was one thing the first time you met it, and something completely different the next. It liked to mutate, was almost designed to do so. Every time it replicated in a cell, there was a slight mutation in the antigens on the surface of the virion. But it was bizarre for the virus to have changed so radically in so short a time. It was almost as if a new strain of the flu had been introduced—from where, though, could it have come?

Steve had become fascinated with the flu early on in his career. He'd been shocked to learn that more people died from the Spanish flu than in all of World War I. In America, whole towns were wiped out; children died in their homes because there was no one alive left to care for them, every adult having been taken by the virus. Carts rolled through the streets of cities collecting corpses piled in the gutters and on the porches of houses. Ordinances were passed forbidding such things as handshaking; and schools, churches, stores, and theaters were closed to try to prevent the spread of the disease. He couldn't believe he'd never been taught about this pandemic before med school. How could this not be in the consciousness of every American?

Jazmine and Leslie rolled in the first two beds.

"Got some kids who just crawled in," Leslie remarked, parking the first gurney. "They're alive at least."

"I'll take a look," Steve said. *When I'm finished.*

The initial strain of what had been termed the Stone-cliff flu appeared to be some hybrid of an avian flu that was extremely infectious. Steve had hypothesized that the terrorists had infected a sick pig with bird flu, and somehow cooked up a disease with the virulence of the H5N1 avian flu and the transmutability of H1N1 swine flu. A potent and deadly combination if there was one.

In those first days, they'd thrown everything but the kitchen sink at those infected. Vaccination didn't work to protect people, and antivirals proved useless, as usual. The CDC had ordered him to abandon the willy-nilly disbursement of the drugs for fear of wasting stores when the nation was on the verge of a pandemic. Somehow the senator had finagled a few crates for them, but Steve hadn't bothered prescribing them. Why throw good medicine after bad?

He flipped through the initial intake forms for everyone in the mall. After Mr. Ross had input all the raw data, he freely parted with the hard copies; for all his work on computers, Steve liked paper. Now that there was no electricity, this peccadillo proved useful.

At some point, everyone had been asked whether they had gotten the flu vaccine. Those who were vaccinated had a *V* marked beside their names. Steve cross-referenced the answers on the paper intake forms with the names of the sick kids. All were unvaccinated. He checked the names of the healthy kids who'd brought in their sick friends. They'd all reported getting a flu shot.

Could it be that, however the flu had mutated, the strain

that was currently making its way through the population was in some critical way similar to one of the strains in this year's flu vaccine? If so, these kids were dying from a very different virus than what had been injected into the air by the bomb. And if that was true, might there be some chance that the antivirals would at least slow the rampage of this incarnation of the disease?

Dr. Chen figured that it might be worth a try. At this point, what was there to lose?

He dug around in the corner where they'd been storing supplies they weren't using and found a crate marked TAMIFLU. He flipped open the plastic top and grabbed a package of the oral suspension dose. The two beds contained girls, one older than the other. Steve recognized the older girl. *Dixit?* Her grandmother had died. She'd fainted in his arms.

He would try her first.

"Miss Dixit?" he said, pulling on gloves.

She groaned.

He took a syringe of the oral suspension with the dose for an adult—she was close enough. He shook her shoulder. "Miss Dixit, I need you to wake up."

The girl rolled her head toward him. She was pale and her breathing was labored. Her skin was burning hot. She coughed, then opened her eyes, which were bloodshot. He hoped he wasn't too late.

"I'm going to give you some medicine."

She blinked. He took that as consent.

He slipped the plastic cylinder into her mouth and pressed the plunger. She swallowed, then drifted back into the haze of her fever. Dr. Chen dosed the other girl, and then each of the other patients as they were rolled into the stockroom.

Rachel pushed in a gurney carrying an older patient. Dr. Chen waved the old man past.

Rachel raised her eyebrows. "We only trying to save the young?"

Steve shrugged. "He has the original flu. If he's going to die, he's going to die. Why waste the medicine?"

Rachel nodded and rolled the man to the corner opposite the kids.

The women went back out to examine more patients. Steve and Rachel had argued early on about his role in the med center, Dr. Chen insisting he was of more use continuing his research. After seeing him attempt to get a case history from a woman, Rachel had agreed and told him to stay in the back. He was only brought out to examine unusual outlier cases or when Dr. Kleinman was busy. He wondered if he should offer to help at this point; he decided he'd wait for Rachel to ask.

Returning to his desk, he bent over his notebook and began to make notes on this new treatment experiment. Just as he was finishing up, he heard a gunshot. Then women screaming.

The chaos had reached the medical center.

Dr. Chen pulled together all of his notes and his laptop and looked for somewhere to hide them. He wasn't sure why he thought anyone in the mall would want his scribblings, but they were his life, his legacy. He wanted at least to keep them from getting ruined in a scuffle.

Marauders would most likely avoid the sick. He crept

over to the gurney containing Miss Dixit and slipped everything under her bedcovers. Her body would guard his work. As he patted the blanket back down over her legs, she fluttered her eyes. He could have sworn they were no longer red.

Before he could examine her more closely, a gentleman bearing a handgun appeared in the doorway, the barrel of his weapon pointed at Jazmine's temple. She was weeping.

"Where's the virus?" the gentleman snarled.

Dr. Chen's first reaction was one of bewilderment. "Virus?"

The boy tightened his grip on Jazmine. "Don't screw with me. You have a new flu weapon and I want it."

The boy's ignorance would have been amusing if not for Jazmine's obvious distress. "I'm sorry," Dr. Chen said, "but there is no new flu weapon."

The kid pointed the gun at Steve. "You think I'm kidding?" He did not give Steve a chance to argue. "I am not screwing around here. Give me the goddamned weapon!"

The boy replaced the gun against Jazmine's temple and shot her.

For all the death he'd seen, Dr. Chen had never seen someone shot. Watched a person just fall away dead, like a sack of meat. "What have you done?" he asked, eyes filling with tears. Jazmine was a good woman. She'd been wonderful with the children.

"I'll find it myself." The kid aimed at Dr. Chen and fired.

The bullet ripped into his gut. Steve slid down the footboard of the gurney to the floor. Pain seared through his insides. For the briefest moment, he viewed the pain with clinical interest—he'd never before had a serious injury.

The kid riffled through the papers on the desk, tossed around some boxes. Dr. Chen thought how wonderfully clever and entirely inadvertent it'd been to hide the antivirals in with the extra bed pads and catheterization kits. The pirate kid rummaged through the first few crates, then gave up.

Another marauder appeared. "Find anything?"

Dr. Chen wondered what had happened to Dr. Kleinman and Leslie. Surely they were dead. They were martyrs; they would have died before letting a patient come to harm.

"Nothing," the pirate kid said, throwing handfuls of plastic catheter bags at the wall. He holstered his gun and loped out of the room.

Steve's last thoughts were of the virus. He saw the spikey orbs bouncing in front of his eyes. How lovely they were. Vicious and lovely.

■ **END OF BOOK TWO** ■

ACKNOWLEDGMENTS

Thank you to my early readers on this one: Anne Cunningham, Jennifer Decker, Mary-Beth Mc-Nulty, and Matthew Weiner. I especially depended on their fresh eyes to see through the morass of verbiage. And to Christine Kaufman, my mom, for doing that final read-through with me.

Thank you to my panel of "experts": Karen Mangold, super-awesome doctor friend, answerer of icky questions, accomplice to all my characters' injuries and deaths; John Kaufman, my dad, whose background in designing key-card access systems made him the perfect coconspirator for busting the heck out of them, and who told me I needed another explosion; Justine Clinch, who helped guide me through the world of fashion; Bill and Sue Ward for brainstorming what might be found in the back of a post office; and finally, for filling me in on the lingo, Cate Williamson, *mi hermana*; Erin Sheridan; Angela LaCour; and the Quattro Quatros—McKenna, Keaton, Hallie-Blair, and Hudson—and their mom, Jamie.

Thank you to my team at Dial Books: Greg Stadnyk, for creating a stunning cover that shines from the shelf; Jason Henry for his subtle, effective interior design; Regina Castillo, my copy editor, who helped me refine the rough patches; and Jessica Shoffel, publicist extraordinaire!

To my exemplary editor, Kathy Dawson, I owe

a great deal of thanks. It was her detailed and un-flinching editorial letter concerning the rather pitiful first draft of this puppy that helped me shape it into the complicated plot-octopus (ploctopus?) that it is today. Everything I write is made better by her keen yet kind eye, and her support and enthusiasm help me keep going through the dark nights of revision.

Thank you to my excellent and extraordinary agent, Faye Bender. I depend on her advice, enthu-siasm, and support. Thank you for holding my hand through everything.

Thank you to Evelyn for putting up with Mommy when she was writing instead of playing. And thank you to Jason Lorentz, who makes my life a love story.

Look for the
breathtaking conclusion:

When the entire mall is thrust into darkness, the Senator provides shelter for the families and adults inside the Home store.

But the teens are left on their own.

Ginger, Maddie, Ryan, Shay, Mike and Marco find themselves making impossible choices and doing things they'd never do in any other circumstance. Fighting to stay alive, and sometimes, fighting to the death.

They don't know where Lexi is.

They don't know about Dr. Chen's discovery.

They don't have any safe place to go.

There might be a way to end the quarantine, but even if they are eventually allowed to leave, how will they ever return to the life they once had?

Read the suspenseful trilogy!